THE *Trust Factor*

BRITTANY WILSON

THE TRUST FACTOR

Copyright © 2024 by Brittany Wilson

This novel is entirely a work of fiction. The names, characters, organizations, businesses, places, events, and incidents portrayed in it are either the work of the author's imagination or used fictitiously. Any resemblance to actual persons, living or dead, events or localities is entirely coincidental.

The Trust Factor **is a steamy college romance with strong language and mature themes. For a full list of content warnings, please visit the author's website.**

Book Cover Design by Sam @inkandlaurel

Editing by Sadie @DotTheIEdit

ISBN-13 (paperback): 979-8-9882216-3-0

ISBN-13 (eBook): 979-8-9882216-2-3

For my brother, Cody.
August 7th, 1998 – June 25th, 2023

You always followed your heart and were never afraid to dream.
24 years young, and you never wasted a second of it.
Here's to hoping that heaven has an abundance of sweet potato fries,
pineapple upside-down cake shots, Corona, and seafood.
Champion, Monopoly, and iced matcha with blueberry.

Until we meet again, I love you.
Brittany

THE TRUST FACTOR is a college romance filled with humor, friendship, and open-door scenes. While it carries tones of lightheartedness and fun, this story also tackles some sensitive topics that I would like to share with you before you read. If you would like to read some information about possible trigger warnings, please continue.

Both main characters in this story have been through difficult experiences. I understand that everyone battling trauma, grief, and anxiety moves through those experiences differently. I also want to note that the viewpoints, scenes, and perspectives portrayed by the characters stem closely from my own experiences and are not meant to represent the following topics as a whole.

Panic attacks, grief, anxiety, and a therapy session will all be included on the page. Conversations about the loss of a sibling and attempted sexual assault will also be included, but the acts WILL NOT be on the page. There are also a few scenes and conversations on the page that include a toxic parent demonstrating emotional and mental abuse.

While some of the topics mentioned in this book might be difficult, my hope is that some readers may see it as a way to process and know they are not alone. If any of the details mentioned above could cause sensitivity, please take this into account before reading. Your mental health and well-being are more important.

With love,

Brittany

I don't know what grief
will look like tomorrow.
But I'll face it.
I'll feel it.
As your memory
washes over me.
One day at a time.
One wave at a time.
For such a love,
grief is the price of admission.
The cost of the human condition.
So, I'll pay it over and over again
until I see you again.
The love was worth it.
-Liz Newman

CHAPTER ONE

Deacon

THIS WAS IT.

My preparation for next year was about to pay off. I was a planner—I planned things. I liked knowing what would happen and when it would happen.

Have I mentioned I was a planner?

Falcon Flames, by definition, were two people who met at and then graduated from Bowling Green State University. Shortly after graduation, there was a wedding ring, and then once the "I Do's" were spoken, the bond was sealed. You became part of a long list of people who found love where they went to college.

While asking my Falcon Flame to room with me next year in an apartment had been on my agenda for months, the whole event was a little ironic. I would've never waited this long to find a place. Most people had their leases signed months ago, and May was cutting it close. Luckily for me, my chemistry partner from last year worked for the landlord's office, so he was able to make sure the property could be off the market for the time being.

Grounds for Thought was the perfect location for me to pop the question. I met Cassie at this bookstore freshman year and couldn't wait to take the next steps with her. I could see it now: I would ask her to marry me right after I moved to Minnesota. Cassie's family lived in Minnesota, and she wanted to return home after graduation. Cassie and I could come back to Grounds for Thought and take engagement photos, and we could even get on the waiting list for Prout Chapel, the iconic location known for marrying Falcon Flames.

I took a deep breath and scanned the rows of books around me. The smell of coffee and spring was in the air, and the shop was buzzing with students excited about the end of the semester and warm weather.

I checked my phone for the fourth time and placed it on the table in front of me. Cassie and I agreed to meet at two, and it was already ten after. Cassie only ran late for something when she was nervous or didn't feel like going. Neither of those options made sense for coffee.

I snatched my phone and clicked on her contact photo. The phone rang three times before she answered.

"Hey, Deacon," she said, sighing.

I smiled at the sound of her voice. "I know we said two, so I was just calling to make sure everything is okay. I was starting to get—"

"Deacon, I'm sorry."

"It's fine, baby. I got our table and your iced coffee and—"

"No, Deacon . . . I'm sorry, but I'm not coming for coffee."

I stared at her drink in front of me, water dripping along the sides of the cup and gathering on the table. The entire time I had been here, I was worried that it would taste too watered down for Cassie. She liked her coffee strong. I even added an extra shot of espresso for her.

"I've been doing some thinking." Cassie took a deep breath, and my heart pounded against my eardrums. "I can't do this anymore."

"You can't do what?" An exasperated laugh left my chest, and I shook my head. "Come for coffee?"

She went quiet for a moment, and I could hear her staggered breathing on the other end. It sounded like she was crying, and my heart fell to the fucking floor.

"Cass?" My throat tightened as her name left my mouth.

"Deacon, I want to break up. So much has happened since we met, and it all feels so fast. I'm going into my senior year of college, and I feel like the reins are being tightened around me."

"Reins?" My eyebrows shot to the top of my forehead. "Cass, I was gonna ask you to move in with me next year, not offer you a promise ring."

I would, however, be lying if I hadn't looked at engagement rings this morning. The browser history on a cell phone was arguably the riskiest feature ever created.

I glanced around the bookstore, and all our engagement pictures rose in flames—not a romantic Falcon Flame, but the flames that took down three-story buildings and ran rampant through a forest. It was suddenly too hot in here to sit. I snagged the iced coffee off the table and headed for the exit.

"I'm sorry, but I have to do this. I don't want this to be something I regret."

"*Stop* saying you're sorry," I begged, coming to a halt in front of Grounds for Thought. In front of the same shop where I met Cassie; the girl I planned my life with. "Cassie, don't do this."

"I'm sorry," she whispered, and the line went dead.

I wasn't sure how much time went by as I stood in the middle of the sidewalk, like a weirdo, with my mouth hanging open, a dripping cup of iced coffee, and my phone still on my call history. My feet felt like someone had bolted them to the ground. My girlfriend of three years just broke up with me—over *the phone*.

How long would she have left me waiting for her if I hadn't called? Had she been late on purpose because she knew I would call?

In my head, I was *fuming,* pissed off that I had to try and sort out Cassie's decision she threw at me via speakerphone. I knew I was on speakerphone. Cassie hated talking on the phone and took almost all her calls that way.

My heart was trying to keep it together as a crack formed right down the middle of it. Shock crept into every cell in my body. I wasn't a crier, so at least I had that going for me. I imagined the sight of a man getting his heart broken in front of a coffee shop wasn't at the top of everyone's end-of-the-year list.

Three years of Cassie. Three years of *me*—gone just like that.

I brought the iced coffee to my mouth and took a sip. Just like I anticipated, it was watered down and lukewarm. The drink lacked flavor, and the almond milk was starting to separate from the coffee. If that wasn't a metaphor for my day, I wasn't sure what was.

I walked across the street to my car, and once I was inside, I cranked the air and sat in silence. Music wasn't appropriate right now since everything I listened to would remind me of Cassie. That's what happened when someone was your everything for so long. They became songs, movies, phrases; anything that seemed like a shrug to someone else consumed your whole being.

I glanced up at the sky, hoping to be handed some clarity. "What the hell just happened, Dom?"

CHAPTER TWO

Lyla

I KNEW I SHOULDN'T have worn these jeans.

Every female owned a pair of standing-only pants—a pair of jeans they loved and looked fabulous in. They hugged every curve because they were tight as hell and could practically be a second skin around the waist. The downfall to these jeans? They were tortuous to sit in.

Yet here I was, completely aware of this phenomenon, sitting at a coffee shop table wearing my standing-only pants. The button of my jeans dug into my skin. I took a deep breath, taking in the scent of old books, freshly ground coffee, and whatever yummy cologne the guy in the red shirt was wearing from a few tables over. This was one of my happy places. Grounds for Thought offered a vibrant crowd, but it was cozy enough that if one wanted to read or study, they could do so without getting distracted.

I leaned back, relieving my stomach from my tight, light-wash jeans. At least I hadn't committed the cardinal sin of pairing the standing-only pants with a crop top. I saved that combination for the bars.

My chai tea latte had to be cool enough by now to sip on. I snagged the cup from the table and stood up. I was meeting my best friend and roommate, Charlie, to discuss and borderline talk shit about our other two roommates, Michelle and Keira. It was nothing personal, but Charlie and

I had to decide if we wanted to take chances with two new roommates next semester. Considering next year was our last year at Bowling Green State University, it was a big decision.

As soon as I turned around to check my phone, Charlie came flying through the entrance of Grounds for Thought. She swiped the stray hairs from her messy bun out of her face and was about to walk past our table when she saw my bag on the chair.

Her eyes narrowed. "Why are you standing?"

I swallowed another small sip of my chai latte and shrugged. "Standing-only pants."

"Ahhh." She nodded, helping herself to the seat across from me. She tore open the wrapper of her straw and stuck it in her smoothie. "Sorry, I'm late. Some hot weirdo was standing right in front of the door. I couldn't figure out a polite way to ask him to move, so I waited until he walked across the street."

"A hot weirdo and *you* didn't know what to say? You *always* have something to say."

"Why don't you have a seat in your standing-only pants," she snapped.

I sucked my teeth. "Hard pass. I'm seeing Jake after this, so I won't be home for like an hour."

"Which one is Jake? Is he the blonde from The Attic?"

"I don't know if we met at The Attic or 149," I pondered. They were both popular bars we frequented, so either choice was a possibility.

Jake was the hot blonde guy I had been sleeping with for the past month. Guys usually had a thirty-day expiration date. It was long enough to figure out what we liked but short enough to keep them out of my personal life.

Charlie answered a text message. "Who was Mr. April?"

"No one was Mr. April. Jake is May, but I'm considering extending his trial period to August because it will save me time when we get back in the fall."

"*Mr.* May," she corrected.

"It would be too much to have a last name change at the beginning of the year," I exaggerated. "Shit would just be confusing. Best to stick with May and August for now."

She squinted like I was speaking a different language. "But half the fun of Opening Weekend is finding you a Mr. August. I *live* for the frat-boy douchebags."

"Technically, we get back at the end of August. So maybe the Opening Weekend guy can be the September guy."

She chuckled, slipping her phone into her purse. "Your schedule sounds exhausting."

I disagreed. *Relationships* sounded exhausting. If one person didn't work out, there was always the next guy. I was picky about the guys I kept around. I once went two months without getting laid because every guy I met in January and February had an agenda for Valentine's Day. No fucking thank you.

"I like to think of it as exciting," I said. "What's exhausting is figuring out if we are staying with Michelle and Keira next year."

"Do you really feel like hunting for a place to live?" Charlie groaned. "You know all of the good apartments will be taken. At least if we renew our lease at Falcon's Pointe, we know what we're getting."

I nodded, weighing the pros and cons in my head. I had no desire to hunt for another apartment. Signing new papers meant I would need to contact my dad again for his banking information, and the thought of speaking to him made my chai latte churn in my stomach.

"I think Falcon's Pointe is our best bet then. Why did we have this meeting?"

"Because in three days, I'm going to have to wait three months to see you again," Charlie murmured.

My bottom lip stuck out in a pout, and we chuckled sadly into our drinks. Charlie and I had been through everything together. We both started our journey at BGSU in the dorms. We weren't roommates, but we lived across the hall from each other. In our sophomore year, we requested to room together, and by junior year, we were living in Falcon's Pointe with Michelle and Keira.

My phone buzzed on the table in front of me. I leaned over to sneak a peek at the screen and picked it up when I saw the name.

Mom

Call me when you get a chance Jean Bean!

I completely forgot to call her back this morning. "Ah fuck," I moaned quietly to avoid disturbing the innocent readers. Grounds for Thought wasn't the type of place you just dropped an F-bomb.

To my surprise, Charlie stood up and gestured toward the door. She had a mouthful of smoothie, but I knew she was signaling that it was time for us to leave. It was her typical move when she spotted someone she didn't feel like talking to. I waited until we were on the street to ask who the culprit was.

"Kyle." Charlie rolled her eyes, and I rewarded her with a few seconds of silence before I gave her shit.

I cackled unattractively. "No Style Kyle was in Grounds?"

Charlie looked away from me so she could pretend like the nickname wasn't funny.

I kept my eyes forward. "Was he still wearing those dad shoes?"

"New Balance has come a long way!"

"Says every dad cutting grass in the '90s!" I exclaimed.

We both burst into hysterics and held onto each other for support. We stopped in front of my car to gather ourselves before going our separate ways.

"I'll see you back at the apartment," she said, still laughing. "Jake lives by Kroger, right?"

I nodded. "Do we need anything from there?"

"She gets serviced and then serves others," Charlie swooned. "Lyla Brooks, you are *so* giving."

"Don't make me drag Kyle out of Grounds by his New Balance shoes."

Once in the car, I turned down the music and sat silently for a full minute before I pulled out my phone. I stared at my mom's contact photo. It was from our trip to Florida last summer, and we had taken it right before my dad called and ruined my mood.

Two weeks before school started last fall, Aaron Brooks thought my schedule had too much time in the mornings for me to sleep around and do nothing. He threatened to withhold his payment for the spring semester if I didn't change my schedule, so I made an appointment with my advisor the next day. It was a shitshow, honestly, having someone who wasn't even part of your life have so much fucking say in it.

A year from now, everything would be worth it. A year from now, I'd be free from him.

Chapter Three

Deacon

It was July 24th. Not that I was marking my calendar with every sunrise, but in three weeks and six days, I'd be moving back to Bowling Green. While I wasn't sure how to feel about returning to the same zip code as Cassie, I was ready to tackle my last year of undergrad classes.

I was also three weeks and six days away from not having to hear another uplifting speech from my parents, grandparents, or grandpa's proud congregation. My family had always supported my positive life choices, but when I mentioned that Cassie and I were no longer together, it brought back memories of the last time people had to try and comfort me with words. People meant well and felt inclined to say something in times of tragedy.

"He always has a plan," Grandma Edna reminded me.

Grandpa Dale used a closing line from one of his popular sermons. "We have to have faith and keep moving forward. You've got a bright future, Deacon."

Ms. Laura said, "You'll find love again."

"Any plans for when you might be ready to move on?" Mom asked, still hoping I would give her a grandchild in the next three years.

"It's part of the college experience," Dad said simply. "Someone else will come along."

"Finally!" my brother Drew exclaimed, a little too enthusiastically for my taste. "Cassie was okay, but now you get to screw around with whoever you want for your senior year!"

Drew's comment didn't exactly fit in the same bucket as the others. However, it was probably the most comforting response I received after the news spread of Cassie and I breaking up. It was the first one that didn't make me feel like the sad and pathetic guy who got broken up with during a phone call.

Drew and I were very different. Drew was incredibly laid back. He barely studied, even though he was going to Penn State for engineering. He always seemed to have everything figured out and under control. Even if his life seemed chaotic to everyone around him, he was never bothered by how things turned out.

It was Sunday, and Grandpa Dale's sermon just ended. Drew and I were standing among the crowds of people outside of the church, and right there on the holy grounds, Drew was trying to convince me that I should just "fuck and move on" to ensure I was over Cassie. Considering what day it was, Drew just wanted to look deep in conversation so no one would approach us.

"I'm just saying, man. Girls come back all horny and pent-up, just waiting for a guy to swoop in and do that damn thing." Drew shrugged, paying no attention to the line of kids weaving through the huddles of adults.

A little girl who couldn't have been older than five caught my eye, and I jammed my hands nervously into the pockets of my dress pants. "Could we table this conversation until we get back to the house?"

"Like look over there!" Drew cocked his head toward the parking lot. "Nina hasn't stopped looking at you since we stepped outside. I bet she gives great blow—"

"Pops!" I exclaimed, shaking Drew's shoulders as the line of kids circled us again. "Let's go find Pop."

My parents stood by the car with a few of their friends while they waited for Grandpa to finish saying his goodbyes. Grandma had already returned to their house to start dinner, set in her routine after being married to a reverend for fifty years. It would be at least another twenty minutes until Grandpa was ready to leave.

"Come visit me at Penn," Drew offered. "I have a list of girls who would be down to sleep with you."

"What is your obsession with getting me laid? It's starting to weird me out."

"That's what I'm here for. To make sure my older brother doesn't have an obnoxious dry spell because he's stuck on—"

"Watch it," I warned, mainly because a group of women dressed in their Sunday best were passing us, but I couldn't hear Drew call Cassie a word that made me cringe.

"Hi, boys!" Mrs. Simms waved as she crossed the tree lawn.

Drew smiled. "Hi, Mrs. Simms. Good message today?"

She smiled back. "As always, Reverend Scott knows what he is talking about." Her face fell when she turned her attention to me. "Deacon, I heard about Cassie. I know it's just awful, but a good-looking guy should have no problem meeting another nice girl."

I shook my head. "Mrs. Simms, I—"

"That is *exactly* what I keep telling him!" Drew patted my shoulders. "Gotta get back out there."

For the next fifteen minutes, Mrs. Simms told me all about her granddaughter in Florida, who was returning to Detroit because she got a teaching job. Drew nodded and kept asking questions—like an asshole—and when she finished writing down her granddaughter's phone number on a piece of paper, I folded it up and put it in my pocket.

Mrs. Simms offered a sympathetic grin. "I won't keep you both, but you're in my prayers."

"I can't keep this up," I murmured as soon as Mrs. Simms pulled out of the parking lot. "If it isn't you bothering me about getting laid, it's someone's grandparents shoving phone numbers and profile pictures in my face. What about me reads, 'I'm going to be single and alone for the rest of my life. Send help.'"

"To start, probably the fact that you avoid females."

I stopped walking. "I don't avoid females."

"Go talk to Nina. Right now," Drew challenged.

I shot him a condescending grin. "I don't have to talk to Nina to prove I'm not avoiding females. Did you ever consider that I don't *want* to get involved with anyone because I'm not sure how long this breakup is even going to last?"

"So Cassie has reached out to you?"

"No."

Drew shrugged. "Until you have proof that Cassie isn't"—he chose his following words carefully—"*exploring* other territories, don't wait around for her, man. I've been watching you wait for two months. You check your phone all the time, look around wherever you're standing like she's just going to show up . . . she broke up with you, Deac."

"It was mutual," I argued.

"You can keep telling everyone else that, but I know it's bullshit," Drew said through a smug smile.

We spent the rest of the afternoon at grandpa and grandma's house. Grandma Edna made a massive meal, and Grandpa Dale blessed the food. Everyone around the table smiled and laughed as multiple conversations were exchanged. I sat back and enjoyed the scene happening around me. For the first time in a while, my name didn't fly across the table. My mom kept asking me if I had enough food. Drew shared a few funny stories from school, and Dad eyed him up the entire time to make sure they were appropriate.

I stacked my plate on Dominic's and took them into the kitchen. I washed the dishes and stared out the window above the sink as staggered clouds rolled over a bright blue sky. Part of me felt guilty for finding happiness when everything was so different. Time was a weird thing. Something that flew by one moment could completely stand still in the next.

It had been two months since I talked to Cassie, and it was finally starting to hit me. When I returned to Bowling Green in three weeks and six days, I'd be single.

Chapter Four

Lyla

I'VE BEEN TOLD THAT getting a bikini wax wasn't as terrible as it sounded. The first time hurt like a motherfucker, but by your fourth or fifth visit, it became more of an inconvenience to schedule the appointment and go. You built a tolerance to the pain, and in the end, you left feeling fabulous and fulfilled.

When did that shit happen with people?

I wasn't sure what was more concerning, that I just compared my father to a bikini wax or that I was bracing myself for the shots he hadn't fired yet. It was our annual end-of-the-summer catch-up lunch. Dad and I got together at whatever luxurious location he flew me out to so we could pretend that what we had was normal. He felt obligated to talk with me because I was his daughter, and I felt compelled to comply with his requests because he was in charge of my trust fund.

It was a small price to pay for the money I needed to build my life after graduation. Some people would frown at the concept of engaging with a parent who was terrible because they had money. Unless those people offered to pay my lease in Chicago and support my business, they could politely sit the hell down. I had no shame. I was too close to getting what I needed to throw it away now.

"I wouldn't expect you to understand, Lyla." Dad sipped his wine and then wiped his mouth with a cloth napkin. "To understand what I just said, you'd have to pass our licensing exam, and we know you couldn't do that. Too many numbers. Too complicated for someone with your logical thinking skills."

I accepted the comment, impressed by his ability to delay the first shot for so long. We were halfway through lunch, and Aaron Brooks hadn't insulted my clothing, hairstyle, or the fact that I was going to school to earn a degree in business and English literature.

I studied him from across the table with his black hair slicked back and perfectly pressed cream-colored suit; other than the green eyes that had somehow slipped through the gene pool, we had nothing in common.

"Did you mean to have your hair uneven like that?" He pointed, and I followed his gaze as if I could see myself by looking up. "You never do leave yourself enough time to do ... well ... anything. Did you rush over here? You did come by yourself, didn't you? Or is some lowlife back at the hotel waiting for you to finish here?"

And just like that, I spoke too soon. Disregard the fact that Aaron Brooks made it halfway through lunch without a single shot. He just decided to deliver them all at once.

I smiled politely and gripped my water glass. "It's the humidity. My hair doesn't do well in Florida, especially in July."

I told you that last year, asshole.

"Your mother's never did either. But she never gave herself time to get ready."

"Lovely," I said, wishing I could turn my ice water into a vodka on the rocks. "Could we discuss the matter of my trust fund? No lowlives on this trip."

Dad raised his eyebrows and took another sip of wine. He had to be thinking of our lunch in Orlando last year. I might have invited my pool friends up to the penthouse suite and ushered one of them out later that night. I had a fabulous time. Dad was furious. His whole reaction was theatrical, drawn out, and boring.

Aaron Brooks would *never* survive Parents Weekend at BG. He would probably sue the school and somehow win whatever bullshit lawsuit he created. That's how it worked for Dad. He always came out on top.

"You actually sound put together when you try and talk business," he said with a smile. It was creepy, and I couldn't tell if he was trying to compliment me or reload his gun.

I prepared for more rapid word fire. "I was going to move back in with Mom for a month after graduation so I could look for a place to lease. I'd like the store to be downtown, but I'm willing to wait and see if—"

"Once I give the okay, I'll release the funds in a few weeks. It's a pretty straightforward distribution. As we discussed, you'll get the money after you graduate."

I nodded, unsure of what to say back. Dad didn't want to hear how someone would waste their money on books and dreams. I came into this lovely reunion needing clarification on the timeline and got my answer.

We ate the rest of our lunch in silence, but I wasn't mad about it. Eventually, one of us had to say something so we could leave. Dad drew me in for an awkward hug, and when we broke apart, he walked outside where his driver was waiting.

Most dads would ask their daughters if they had a ride home. Most dads would offer to drive their daughters back to the hotel so they knew she made it there safely. Most dads would find their daughter's dreams interesting.

Aaron Brooks wasn't like most dads.

Chapter Five

Deacon

Nothing was worse than the smell of an apartment that had been closed up all summer.

This wasn't in my plans for moving back in the fall. I should've been returning to an apartment on the other side of campus. It was a two-bedroom apartment that probably belonged to a set of long-time BFFs or a couple who had successfully moved in together for their senior year.

I wasn't bitter. I was just irritated that I was moving into a three-bedroom apartment on North Enterprise with two guys instead of the cozy set-up on Juniper.

Andre and I shared the same unsatisfied expression and worked quickly to open all the windows. Andre was the first friend I made at BG, and when he said that he and Nathan had a spare bedroom, I jumped at the opportunity. I wasn't technically on the lease, but their third roommate, Greg, was never there. Greg was happily taken and planned to spend most of his time at his girlfriend's place. Maybe they were decorating my apartment on Juniper.

Again, I wasn't bitter.

Andre pointed down the hall. "Greg's room was the last door on the right. All his stuff was out of there when we left in May, so the room should be empty."

I grabbed the rest of the stuff from my car and set up my room. I scheduled a truck to arrive from Detroit with my furniture tomorrow morning, so my mattress sat on the floor. I placed my MacBook on my desk and hung my clothes in the closet. It wasn't my apartment, but I was grateful for the space. It would be home for the rest of the school year.

When I came back into the living room, Andre was testing the cable on the TV and wiggling a cord in the back of the internet modem.

"I don't know why this happens every single time," he said, growing more frustrated with the cord. "These idiots act like it's this crazy process to turn the signal back on."

I chuckled at the sight of him losing to a thin yellow cable.

Just as I was about to offer to help, Nathan walked through the front door with a giant smile. "No signal?"

"Appears that way." I extended my hand. "What's up, man? I'm Deacon. Thanks for letting me crash here."

"No problem. Andre told me what happened. That's rough."

My stomach dipped as the memory reel from Grounds for Thought replayed in my head. Just because I had my plan for the future flipped upside down didn't mean I had to sulk. Cassie certainly wasn't. Her Instagram page told me she was taking trips and meeting new people. I would lose my mind if I read another hashtag that said, "thriving."

"Shit happens," I said casually. The last thing I wanted to be was the roommate everyone tip-toed around. "Do you guys wanna go get some food? Maybe when we come back, we'll have some internet."

We waited for Nathan to unpack and change before heading down the street to Beckett's. If there was one thing I missed about Bowling Green, Ohio, it was Beckett's burgers.

When we rounded the corner of Main, it was clear that a good amount of other students missed the hot spot too.

Beckett's opened at eleven, and since it was only five after, the line outside the restaurant moved quickly.

"So what's the move tonight?" Nathan asked once we were seated.

Andre didn't seem thrown by the question. In fact, he was smiling down at his phone and looked up to see my response.

"What did you guys have planned?" I asked slowly.

"Hit a few bars," Andre said. "It's Opening Weekend, so we usually just let the night plan itself out."

Their unplanned evening was the exact opposite of what I did on campus last year—all the more reason to lean into the changes I needed to adjust to.

"We should hit up a gas station on our way back and get some beer," I suggested.

Nathan smacked my arm and smiled. Andre laughed and went back to texting. My approval was clearly needed to set the tone for the evening.

When the waitress returned with our drinks, we all ordered food. I took a hefty sip of my Corona and relaxed in my chair. I listened to Andre and Nathan go back and forth about class schedules, women they hooked up with over the summer, and people they would invite for pregaming tonight before we all went out. It was amazing and saddening at the same time how the world could just go on when you felt yours was at a standstill. Everyone else was eager for another semester to start. I had a detailed image of what this year would look like, and I needed to give myself a chance to draw it differently.

Maybe space would work in my favor. Cassie would go out, meet new people, and realize how many shithead guys attended this school. College students were a toss-up, and the thought of dating anyone else right now seemed painful.

Maybe Cassie "thriving" as a single woman would bring her back to me. I wanted to see her happy, but I wasn't ready to give up on the idea of us being together.

Just as I was about to answer Andre's question about when I wanted to start pregaming, Cassie walked into Beckett's. She looked beautiful—blonde hair pulled back in one long braid and shorts that cut off just above her ass. I was surprised to see her in such a low-cut tank top, but I understood when I saw the two guys that followed behind her. She was with a small group of people, and I only recognized Clara, her roommate. Since I was seated at a corner table, Cassie didn't notice me. She walked toward the back of the restaurant and would have no idea I was in the same place as her.

My throat went dry. Even after another sip of beer, I couldn't find the words to answer Andre's simple question. So instead, I nodded and continued acting like nothing in the world was wrong; like my gorgeous ex-girlfriend didn't just walk into a restaurant we used to come to every Wednesday with two guys who probably wanted to fuck her.

Okay, maybe they didn't want to fuck her. I wouldn't make assumptions. It was just throwing me off that Cassie and I weren't doing that anymore, that I couldn't just walk across the room and hug her without it being weird. As I mentioned before, I wasn't bitter. My heart was still mending from something that only happened three months ago, while it was clear that Cassie had already moved on.

Chapter Six

Lyla

It was officially Opening Weekend, and while I thoroughly enjoyed another summer with my mom while ignoring my dad through all forms of communication, I was delighted to be back in BG. I even smiled at Michelle and Keira when they asked if I was going to vacuum my room.

Yes. It was good to be back.

To celebrate, the four of us were going out. Charlie had the grand idea at the liquor store of everyone buying a bottle for us to make a new drink. Once everyone poured a good bit of their alcohol into the serving pitcher, it was time to taste test.

"This . . . is . . . wild," I said in between sips.

Michelle drew her mouth from the cup when she got a whiff of the potent aroma. Keira took it like a champ, and I thought Charlie was going to fall over at the sight of them contributing to anything that involved drinking or being social. Maybe we did make the right choice to room with them again this year. Perhaps the senior-year versions of Michelle and Keira were fun.

"That wasn't the worst thing I've ever had." Keira shrugged and chased the taste down with a White Claw.

"Let me taste that." I reached out my hand, and Keira handed me the white can. It tasted like sparkling black cherry. "That could be dangerous."

"I saw them for the first time over the summer!" Keira exclaimed. "Have the rest of it. I bought a bunch of them just in case they weren't in Ohio yet."

Before I knew it, I was four White Claws in, and the girls of Apartment 3C were all singing along to The Chainsmokers. We embraced our last Opening Weekend and welcomed senior year with open arms. In just nine months, I would have everything I needed to start the next chapter of my life. I would graduate, move out of Cleveland, and finally put my business classes to use. The agreement with my dad was simple: once I graduated, I received the money in my trust fund.

Aaron Brooks was many, *many* things, and while father-of-the-year would never be one of them, he did know finances. I guess I would have something to thank him for in his eulogy.

Here lies Aaron Brooks: crap father, and crappier ex-boyfriend, but a fantastic Financial Advisor.

"Lyla?" Charlie asked, pulling me from my eulogy writing. "Will you be ready in ten? It's almost eleven."

I slipped down the hall to do a quick outfit change. Since it was warm, I decided on my yellow sundress that made my green eyes pop and brown wedges. I tugged on my hair tie and fluffed my loose curls so they fell evenly around my face. After some lipstick and a quick swipe of mascara, I did one final kiss to the mirror and was satisfied.

"Finding Mr. September!" Charlie yelled, clapping as I entered the living room. She looked amazing in a tight white crop top and high-waisted jean shorts.

We laughed at our inside joke and cheered as Michelle and Keira came down the hall. To my utter surprise, they both wore cute tops and . . . *standing-only pants*?!

What the hell were they putting in those White Claws?

"One last shot, ladies!" Keira poured the mixture into our empty glasses and held hers up.

We toasted to a fabulous evening and new beginnings. It was my last clear memory of the night, because I was on a new vibe about three hours later.

We were cutting it close to last call, and Charlie wanted one more pineapple upside-down cake shot before we walked back to the apartment. I giggled as she clung to the guy she just met out on the patio. He was cute and seemed normal, the only two essential items for people you just met. The standards weren't impressive when it came to the college lifestyle.

The Attic was known for a few things: a heated patio, pool tables, a stripper pole, and good music to dance to. It was also known for running into someone to go home with at the end of the night. I had no idea what it was about this place that made people come running around at one in the morning. Bowling Green was home to at least a dozen bars, but The Attic was a staple closing-time location.

I leaned against the counter and put my hand on my forehead. I was drunk. *Very* drunk.

"Let's just do one more!" Charlie begged over the music.

The lights behind her danced along with the beat of the song, and I had to blink a few times to focus. I felt someone grab my hand, and I closed my eyes. When I opened them, a row of shots lined the counter.

"Are you good?" Michelle asked and handed me my shot.

I nodded, tasting the pineapple as it slid down my throat. "Yeah!" by Usher boomed through the bar, and screams came from the dance floor. We all ran to the commotion, and I completely forgot about trying to leave only a few moments ago. It was the last thing I remembered before I blacked out.

CHAPTER SEVEN

Deacon

MY ALARM WENT off at precisely nine o'clock. The moving truck I ordered would arrive with my stuff at eleven, and I wanted to get a workout in before it came.

The apartment was quiet, and I was about to learn how Nathan and Andre recovered from a night out at the bars. In my experience, there was nothing a Gatorade, a greasy sandwich, and a workout couldn't fix. I only had a few beers last night, and the last memory I had from The Attic was of a girl having a fantastic time on the stripper pole.

After I saw Cassie at Beckett's, I needed some time before I indulged in the party scene. In the meantime, I could live vicariously through Nathan, who had his arm slung around a girl on our living room couch.

Even though my attempt at putting together my pre-workout was barely audible, Nathan's head lifted slowly off the pillow as he looked around the room. We made eye contact, and I pressed my lips together to avoid laughing. He stared sleepily down at the girl next to him and raised his eyebrows at me, trying to figure out if I knew who the girl was.

I shrugged my shoulders, and he slumped back into the pillow. It was the shortest non-verbal conversation I had in a long time, but it felt monumental for my friendship with Nathan. How people supported each other in the morning-after light said a lot about them, and I was in no position to judge anyone for how they chose to have a good time.

It was a chilly morning, and there was a dampness in the air. The sidewalks were wet, but the sun peeked through a few lines of clouds in the sky. If it rained last night, I had no idea that it did. I passed out as soon as my head hit the pillow.

A hint of fall swept through the street, and a few water droplets from the trees hit me as I passed. It was a sign that summer was officially ending, and when I passed a house with mums and pumpkins that lined the porch, I immediately thought of Cassie.

Everything about this morning brought me back to the first time I kissed her. The weekend after I met her at Grounds for Thought, we went out with friends the following Saturday. It rained that night, so she and I dozed off on my living room couch, looking almost identical to Nathan and his lady friend this morning—only I knew who Cassie was when I woke up.

I walked her to her friend's house, and I remembered wishing she lived further away so I could keep talking to her. She was right in the middle of asking me what I was doing later before I kissed her. Rain from the night before fell from the trees overhead, and we stood on a porch decorated with yellow and red mums.

My jog slowed to a walk, and I ran my hands down my face. What the actual fuck was wrong with me? Guys who had moved on from someone else were waking up all over campus this morning. Why did I have to make everything about this so hard?

I had done everything right. Everything my parents encouraged me to do growing up, I had nailed down the moment I got to Bowling Green.

Get into a major that will provide a good living and make you successful. *Check.*

Have fun, but devote time to your studies. Fun from college doesn't help you once you enter the real world. *Check.*

If you fall for someone, make sure they are there for more than the parties and the social scene. You need a partner who will help you build a life, not someone who expects you to provide for them. *Check.*

Well, I took that last check back. I thought I had that person. I thought I was going to build a life with Cassie. We were both going to work in the medical field. Cassie would be a physical therapist, and I would be a pediatric surgeon. We'd support each other through medical school and seek opportunities. We'd understand the toll our jobs would have on our relationship. I did what I was supposed to. I just didn't plan on losing it all before senior year.

Since my run was no longer taking my mind off things, I walked the next two blocks to the apartment. I took one last look at the sky before heading into my building.

After I showered and got dressed, it was almost ten-thirty. Nathan and his friend were nowhere to be found, and Andre was running out of time before I woke his ass up. He offered to help me unload the moving truck when it arrived, and I had every intention of taking him up on it.

I called it at ten-forty-five. I knocked twice on Andre's door and waited. When there was no answer after my third attempt, I closed my eyes and opened the door. I learned the hard way from my roommates last year to never open a door with eyes wide open. There were some things in life you just *couldn't* unsee.

"Andre?"

When no response came, I opened my eyes and scanned the empty room. I pulled out my phone to call him, and I had a text message.

Andre

> I didn't forget! Call me when you get this.

In his defense, I received this message before ten-thirty. I must've still been in the shower when he sent it.

"I'm at Falcon's Pointe," he murmured into the phone after the third ring. "Apartment 3C."

I tossed my head back and sighed, knowing the answer to the question I was about to ask. "You need a ride?"

Chapter Eight

Lyla

If I kept my eyes closed, my body might think it was just tired. I was confident that I would hurl all over my brand-new, fluffy, white carpet if I got up. My head was pounding, and I was no newbie when it came to mending a horrendous hangover. I needed water, some ibuprofen, and an order of Campus Pollyeyes breadsticks. It had been an entire summer since I had the giant chicken and cheese stuffed breadsticks from the famous local establishment, and I couldn't think of a better time to reunite with one of my favorite BG staples.

I didn't remember returning home last night but was relieved to find my bed empty and the apartment quiet. I didn't want to hear from Michelle or Keira about how I might not be hungover if I had controlled my drinking last night, and I didn't want to usher out a stranger and have the morning-after conversation.

I rolled—literally rolled—out of bed and onto the floor. The cushion from the carpeting softened the blow, and I used my end table to pull myself up. I looked down at my shorts and T-shirt combo. At least last night's version of me could get us down for bed.

It only took two steps for the rumbling in my stomach to start. I darted across the room to the bathroom, and after ten minutes of unattractive and unforgiving dry heaving, I decided I was okay to continue my recovery journey.

"Never . . . again," I mumbled into the toilet bowl. My head was only inches away from where I peed last night. There was no lower point a human could sink to.

I stumbled into the hall and made my way to the living room. Empty bottles and cans from last night littered the counters. I gathered everything up and slid the contents into the trash can. If I caught any whiffs of last night's concoctions, I'd start dry heaving again.

After a few sips of water and three ibuprofen, I leaned against the counter and nursed the rest of my drink. I did a double-take when I noticed the incredibly attractive guy staring at me from the couch. My hand flew to my chest, and I almost dropped my water bottle.

"Have you been here this whole time?" I exclaimed. I rubbed my throbbing temples and watched him survey the rest of the room.

He slowly lowered his phone. "Uhm. Yes?"

The wheels began to turn, and my stomach sank.

Did I bring this guy home last night, and now I'm an asshole because I just asked if he had been here THE WHOLE TIME?!

"Fuck, I'm sorry. Did we?" I gestured to the space between us.

Shame on me if I forgot this man. He was gorgeous. Shame on me for forgetting, but kudos to my drunken judgment for upholding my standards. Not enough credit was given to the behind-the-scenes effort.

He shot me an amused grin. "No, we didn't. I just got here a few minutes ago. My roommate stayed the night here."

I nodded, keeping the movements minimal to give the ibuprofen more time to kick in.

"I'm Deacon."

"Lyla." I raised my hand and dropped it back down to my side. "Which roommate was it? I can go in and wake them up."

"Andre's in the shower now. He shouldn't be much longer." Deacon moved from his seat on the couch and helped himself to the bar stool across from me. "Rough night?"

"Nah. I always look this good in the morning." I drained the rest of my water and tossed the empty bottle in the trash.

Deacon laughed. It was the kind of laugh that drifted from your chest, and you kept it going because it made everything else feel good.

I pressed my lips together to keep from smiling.

"I feel like I've seen you before. Did you live in the dorms last year?"

I shook my head. Deacon's eyes were captivating. I usually favored blue or green eyes, but his were the perfect shade of light brown.

"My girl—I mean, ex-girlfriend lived in the dorms last year. I wasn't sure if maybe I had run into you there."

Deacon sighed and pulled out his phone again. His entire demeanor shifted, and I ignored any further prompting questions that popped into my head. I wasn't in the mood for any heavy conversation. An awkward silence hung in the air, and I decided it was time for my recovery nap.

"Well!" I announced. "It was nice meeting you. Have a good Sunday."

Have a good Sunday? For all that was holy, I was out of practice. It had been a dry summer, and I needed to get back out there pronto.

"Wait! I knew you looked familiar," Deacon exclaimed, his smile returning to full force. He thrust his phone in my face. "You're Stripper Pole Girl." He said the name so confidently that he convinced me I should sign all my legal documents as "Stripper Pole Girl" moving forward.

I could've melted into the floor. I recognized the yellow dress and my drunken dance moves. However, I didn't recognize how full and bare my backside looked moving up and down next to a stripper pole.

"What!" I screeched, putting emphasis on the T. I snatched Deacon's phone and hit replay on the video. There was no denying that it was me putting on a performance to Usher for everyone in The Attic.

"Nooo," I whined, and a low rumble crept out of my chest. I put my hand to my forehead. "No . . . no . . . no . . ."

Deacon backed away slowly in case I turned into a gremlin and attacked him.

"You found this on the *internet*?" I asked as if the internet were some foreign space I didn't understand. I sounded like No Style Kyle in his New Balance shoes.

"I mean, it's Usher. It's not all bad. A friend sent it to me on Instagram last night." His eyes moved to my mouth, and he bit the inside of his cheek. It was clear there was more.

"And?" I prompted.

"And Snapchat." He winced, running a hand through his hair. "I can say something positive if you promise not to take it the wrong way."

I crossed my arms and cocked my head, letting him know it was okay to continue. Even in this highly problematic moment, I wanted to hear *everything* this guy had to say.

"You look good," he admitted. "I don't think you have anything to be ashamed of."

I was intrigued by Deacon. We had met less than ten minutes ago, and even though my ass—as he clearly could see on his phone screen—had been plastered all over the internet the night before, he was still trying to be reassuring.

The sound of my ringtone drifted from my room. I handed Deacon back his phone and made a beeline for my own. When I saw my dad's name on the screen, I closed the door behind me and took a deep breath before I answered.

It was a quick conversation. Aaron Brooks screamed at me, saying he received a video of his daughter dancing on the pole like a hooker from someone on InstaSnap. I didn't bother correcting him. He probably got a message sent to his Instagram account since he had one for work, but that piece of information seemed irrelevant given the topic of conversation.

He yelled. I listened. This wasn't necessarily a new response or routine. Dad only paid attention to items that brought negative attention to his brand, and everything I posted eventually made it to A. Brooks Financial Firm. Of course, none of my top-tier selfies or beach shots ever circulated.

"If you think you're getting *anything* come graduation, you're kidding yourself," Dad seethed.

That sentence got my attention.

"Dad, it's just one video! It's not like I told someone to press record."

"I don't care to know any details, Lyla. I knew twenty-three was too young, and you're clearly not trying to do anything serious with your life. I don't know why I expected anything different. Just because it's your senior year—"

"I'm working to get it taken down," I lied. I needed him to stop talking so I could think. I did a quick rundown of the items that generally pissed Aaron Brooks off. Nothing

I ever did made him happy, so I chose a few things that would make sense in the mini-story I was about to spin. "My boyfriend is working to get it taken down. Called Instagram and everything."

I wasn't even sure if someone could call Instagram, but who was I kidding? I was speaking to the man who thought there was an InstaSnap. He wouldn't question that detail.

"Boyfriend?" His tone dropped a few notches. "What boyfriend?"

"Yeah," I said, my voice taking on an obnoxiously high pitch. He would've heard I was lying if he knew me at all. "We've been dating for a few weeks. He's currently searching for the asshat who recorded it in the first place. I'm sorry about the video, but it really looks worse than it is."

"Your ass is on my phone screen, Lyla," he said, taking another deep breath. "Let me know when it's removed from InstaSnap, and then I can properly thank this new ... *boyfriend* of yours when I come in for Thanksgiving. But if he isn't worth my time, Lyla, don't even bother. You have until graduation to convince me you have your shit together."

My mouth went dry. I wasn't sure who hung up first. My hand dropped to my hip, and I threw my phone on the bed. Yesterday, everything I wanted was only a graduation away. Today, I was nursing a hangover and needed more water so my head would stop spinning.

When I ventured out back into the kitchen, Deacon was still sitting at the counter.

"Everything okay?" he asked while my head was in the fridge.

I spun around and averted my eyes from his mouth. How could someone's lips look that full and inviting by just existing?

"My dad saw the video, and I told him my boyfriend is trying to have it taken down," I said slowly. "He's also trying to find the person who recorded it."

"Your boyfriend sounds like a good guy if he's trying to have it taken down."

"Yeah"—my voice took the high-pitched tone from before—"except I made him up. So, really, as endearing as this boyfriend sounds, he doesn't exist. And now my dad wants to meet my knight in shining armor when he comes for Thanksgiving."

Deacon winced. "That sucks."

I buried my face in my hands and groaned.

"Is there more?"

I heard the playfulness in his voice, and I smiled despite my misery. I was glad *someone* was getting enjoyment from this. Deacon leaned forward on his elbows, and his eyes met mine.

I pulled myself onto the counter and smirked. "I have to convince him that I should still get the money he promised me for graduation."

"Damn. That part *really* sucks."

It went against all of my instincts to provide more details of my personal life to a guy I just met. Guys were predictable and disappointing, and just because Deacon seemed genuine didn't mean he was.

I decided it was best not to come onto him for Deacon's sake. For now, I'd just enjoy how his plain white T-shirt hugged his chest. He had to have some sort of cardio routine.

Charlie's voice drifted from the hall, and I forced myself to stop mentally undressing the man in front of me. Charlie—and who I assumed was Andre—came into the living room. Andre smacked Deacon's hand the way guys do, and Charlie rounded the counter to sit next to me.

"Is he Mr. September?" she asked, bumping my shoulder with hers. "He's cute."

I crossed my arms in front of my chest. "He's *not* September."

Andre and Deacon exchanged a few laughs, and I was jealous of their carefree conversation. I was wrong before when my head was hovering over the toilet. That wasn't the lowest point a human could get to. It was having their ass on the internet and their future in their prick-of-a-father's pocket.

CHAPTER NINE

Deacon

WHEN I RECEIVED VIDEOS of Stripper Pole Girl through all forms of social media last night, I never expected to meet her the next morning. In the video, Lyla wore a yellow dress, and her hair fell in curls around her face. The woman in front of me, wearing an oversized T-shirt and athletic shorts, performed Usher only a few hours ago. Lyla was gorgeous, and now that I knew she had a wild side, I found her even more intriguing.

I needed to take a mental picture of this moment. It was the first time since Cassie that I even looked at another woman as a possible . . . *date*? Option? Rebound? I didn't like *any* of those terms, so I just decided to chalk it up as a win.

"Ready to go?" I asked, and Andre looked at me like I spoke French. "We're moving my stuff in today."

Andre groaned, and the girls laughed from the counter they were sitting on.

"What are y'all up to today?" Andre asked them.

Lyla hopped off the counter. "I'm ordering food and napping before it gets here."

"Second that!" Charlie added.

"What if we buy you food?" Andre gestured to the space between us and motioned for me to go along.

Charlie spun on her heels, and Lyla stopped walking halfway down the hall.

I read Andre's desperate expression and decided it wouldn't hurt to have the extra hands. "Brunch?"

Lyla took a few steps into the living room. "Does it include mimosas?"

I shrugged. "Why not."

The girls shared a silent exchange. Andre started a slow clap of encouragement, and Charlie smiled.

"Fine," Lyla said before she disappeared into her bedroom. She returned with her hair in a bun and her face free of last night's makeup.

On the drive to the apartment, Andre rode shotgun, and the girls made themselves at home in the back seat. I turned up the radio and pulled onto the main road. "Closer" by the Chainsmokers came through the speakers, and I watched Charlie and Lyla sway to the beat.

"This your jam?" Andre chuckled and turned up the volume.

"It was last night's anthem," Charlie yelled before she and Lyla burst into song.

"Chainsmokers and Usher, huh?" I grinned in the rearview and felt a kick to the back of my seat.

Lyla sang to the mirror, and the performance ended as I pulled into our parking lot. The moving truck was already there, and a tall gentleman with red hair leaned against the driver's side door.

"Are you Deacon Scott?" he deadpanned.

"Yeah, sorry I'm running behind—"

He shoved a clipboard into my chest and snapped his gum. "Sign here."

I signed my name, and he led me around to the back. The door slid open, and the remainder of my bedroom sat in front of me.

"Think you can have it out in forty-five minutes? I don't want to have to charge you an extra hour," the driver murmured.

When I peered around the corner of the truck, Andre was laughing with Lyla and Charlie on the hood of my car. Lyla noticed me staring, and she tapped Andre's shoulder.

I gestured toward the truck. "Still want brunch?"

With the extra hands I wasn't expecting to have, we unloaded the truck in half an hour. I put together my bed frame, and Andre helped me lift the mattress. Everything else could be unpacked later today.

"I think I chose the heaviest tote," Lyla whined and set her haul gently at the foot of my bed. "Are all the labels this specific?"

I stopped hanging clothes and turned to see what she was talking about. The tote read "Freshman to Junior Year with C," and my heart sank. When I told my parents to load everything out of my bedroom back home, I forgot to mention that they should leave this one behind.

"Not really, no."

"Hmm." She eyed the label curiously and ran her fingers over the tape. "Who is C?"

I slipped another shirt onto a hanger, and my shoulders fell. When I turned to face her, she had a sly grin on her face.

I cocked my head. "Why are you so nosey?"

"I wouldn't call it *nosey*. I prefer the word observant."

"Okay, then. It's just some old stuff. It'll probably just sit in the back of my closet."

She drummed her fingers on the side of the tote, eyeing me with her bright green gaze. She was waiting to see if I'd offer more information.

Nosey ass.

"Sometimes it's just nice to have parts of people with us," I admitted.

Lyla handed me more hangers and pondered my answer. "I could see that."

"You don't agree?"

She shrugged. "The relationships in my life are pretty linear. If you're in my life, great. If not . . . I don't need any reminders."

I smiled reassuringly. "Reminders don't always have to be a bad thing."

"Noted," she said. "Now come on. You owe me a mimosa."

My eyes lingered on the piece of my past I was desperately trying to get a break from. Freshman to Junior Year with C had burned its way back into my memory; this time, it wasn't even my fault. Sun peeked through the curtains, and I peered up at the sky. I wasn't sure whose sense of humor this day was following, but it definitely wasn't mine. I was putting in the effort. I was trying, and even when I thought I was beyond the point of failing, the universe just kept pushing the past back in my face.

CHAPTER TEN

Lyla

ANDRE CHOSE A SHITTY time to admit to us that there wasn't a single breakfast place in BG that served mimosas. There was a Bob Evan's and a few family-owned restaurants, but none stocked the champagne necessary to make my morning bubbly. Part of this was my fault. I spent three years on campus and should've known this information.

I sighed against the car door and watched the trees blur by on our way down Main. My stomach grumbled, and I glared at Charlie. Her lips made a thin line, and I knew she was trying not to laugh.

"What about coffee?" Deacon's eyes met mine in the rearview. The way the sun hit them was extraordinary. "We promised you food, right?"

I decided his offer was too sweet to pass up. "I can do a chai tea latte from Grounds."

Deacon dropped his shoulders and signaled that we were pulling over. I tried not to act too impressed with how well he parallel parked with an audience. I firmly believed that if parallel parking were the only option, I'd find another place to stop or happily walk myself from a nearby parking lot.

Grounds for Thought was the perfect spot to spend a Sunday recovering. The usual chit-chat buzz and casual coffee house playlist were in the background, but it was a bright and relaxing atmosphere to get back on track. Last night had been a doozy, and this morning followed close behind it.

I had no idea how to fix the hole I dug last night, and because of it, I was losing to Aaron Brooks and his financial upper hand. The stakes I set for myself weren't impossibly high. I needed a knight in shining armor boyfriend who had his shit together. But I came up blank as I scrolled through the list of guys on my phone, reuniting with calendar names I hadn't seen since last year.

I couldn't even get past the labels of some of these contacts. If I slept with them, they were in my phone as the month and their first name, for God's sake. Something told me there was no way I could get May-August Jake to go along with being my boyfriend for a few months. If I didn't sleep with them, I provided a context clue. I had no idea who Penthouse Josh was.

I leaned my face into my hands. Andre and Charlie laughed at something on the other side of the table, and I decided to put my issues on hold until I was more equipped to deal with last night's damage. Deacon called my name from across the shop and waved me over. I met him at the register, and his light brown eyes were laced with sorrow as he delivered the news.

"They're out of chai tea. Anything else you want?"

I forgot he had been there this morning to witness a re-play of my Usher performance and my dad's threat. I stared blankly at the tip jar, and Deacon tapped my shoulder.

"Do you like matcha?"

"Yeah, why?"

Deacon turned his attention to the cashier. "Do you have blueberry syrup?"

The cashier nodded. "We have that."

"Can she have a large iced matcha with blueberry syrup and oat milk, please?"

The cashier looked at me to confirm the order.

I shrugged. "Why not?"

Since Charlie was practically in Andre's lap, I decided to stick around the counter with Deacon to wait for our order. I eyed him suspiciously. It was such a specific order he had on the tip of his tongue that I had to ask. "Matcha, huh?"

Deacon looked down at the ground and smiled. "I took a shot. It's one of my brother's favorite drinks." When he looked up, I did my best to make it look like I wasn't staring at him.

A barista called out our drink orders from behind the counter. "Iced black coffee with caramel and vanilla! Iced matcha with blueberry and oat milk!"

I plucked two straws from the cup near the tip jar and handed one to Deacon. "No creamer or anything?"

"Nah."

I wasn't sure if I should be concerned or impressed with how much this man smiled. The barista placed two more drinks before us, and I grabbed Charlie's staple strawberry banana smoothie.

As I sat there listening to Andre's recap of the night at The Attic, I knew Charlie would see him again after this. She could barely keep her eyes off of him.

"I can't believe that was you on the pole!" Andre exclaimed.

I leaned forward to face Deacon. "You told him?"

"Everyone has kind of seen it already," he said with an apologetic shrug. "I didn't show it to him out of spite! Trust me, it was all positive reviews."

Andre nodded and took a long sip of his drink. I rolled my eyes at the two of them, and Charlie shielded her mouth with her hand so I couldn't see her laughing. Even though I couldn't *see* her response, she had been waiting to laugh about this all morning.

"Is Aaron still freaking out?" she asked.

"I've received a text every twenty minutes since he called me this morning."

"Is Aaron your boyfriend?" Andre prompted eagerly from the seat across from me. "Is he pissed about the video?"

Deacon patted my forearm and smiled into his iced coffee. He enjoyed being in the inside circle of my ongoing saga. I glared at him while Charlie giggled through a response to Andre's question for me.

"Lyla doesn't *date*."

I searched my brain for a conversation change. "Have you scanned the crowd for No Style Kyle? Is he here this time?"

"Don't bring up my shit because—wait a second." Charlie shifted in her seat and pointed to Deacon. "I've seen you before. I knew you looked familiar! I've seen you *here* before."

"Was I with you?" I asked, invested in the epiphany, because if I was in the same room as Deacon, I would have remembered him. He was too pretty to pass up.

"Yes!" Charlie exclaimed. "It was the day we decided to keep our lease at Falcon's Pointe."

"That was what, the end of—"

"Last year." Deacon sighed, drawing the attention of the table.

Andre peered out the window like something got his attention.

Charlie locked eyes with me and shrugged. An entire minute passed, and I couldn't stand the silence anymore.

"Who knew we'd meet up again?" I offered lightheartedly to the group.

Deacon smiled faintly. "Are you guys ready?"

It was a short ride back to Falcon's Pointe. After Charlie and Andre exchanged numbers, we bid our goodbyes and walked up the stairs to the apartment.

"I'm totally seeing that guy again," Charlie said with a massive grin. "His friend is hot, too."

I scoffed at her suggestion. "Not my type, Charlie. He's way too nice. He could never survive thirty days with me."

Chapter Eleven

Deacon

After a week of classes, my mind finally shifted to something other than school or Cassie. Maybe it was my unplanned reunion with Grounds for Thought. Maybe it was because I felt at home in my apartment and enjoyed living with Andre and Nathan. They carried the same energy Drew did when coaxing me to move on, and between the constant prompting and trying to survive my longest dry spell, my mind shifted to sex.

I needed and actually *wanted* to sleep with someone else other than Cassie. I considered this an essential milestone in figuring out what I was doing with my personal life. Heartbreak wasn't a roadblock to getting laid, and wanting to feel wanted wasn't a sin.

I went out with the guys on the first Friday night of the semester with a game plan. Find a girl I thought was cute, make sure she could carry on a conversation, and see where things went. It had been a while since a woman looked at me like she could devour me right on the spot. It was exciting to have the little touches back; running their fingers down my arm, touching my shoulders, smacking at my chest when I said something to get a rise out of them. I was reminded of my first week as a freshman before I met Cassie, and suddenly, I was chasing a high I didn't even know I wanted.

Serena was the first. She was gorgeous—dark brown hair, light brown eyes, and a line of freckles that ran across her cheeks. She made me laugh, and when she invited me back to her place, I didn't hesitate. It was like riding a bike. Only this bike could speak some Italian and had a set of tits that fit perfectly in my hands.

Amber was the second and most surprising encounter. We met at a pregaming party, and before we even left for the bars, I was in her bedroom.

Then, my following weekend consisted of Melissa on Friday and Becca on Saturday. As I said the names aloud to Andre and Nathan over lunch at Mr. Spots, I realized I was in danger of sounding like a Petey Pablo verse. Was this considered a hoe phase? I was confident I had mine in high school, but could a person have more than one?

"Serena, Amber, Melissa, and Becca," Nathan stated proudly. "Who knew you were such a dog, Deac."

"Me?" I exclaimed. "I'm afraid if I sit on our couch, I might catch something. You've had so many girls over that I've lost count."

Nathan grinned. "We aren't talking about me, though."

"For real, that couch needs fumigating," Andre muttered, turning his attention to me. "What's the move tonight, then? First long weekend of the year . . ." He rubbed his hands together like he already had a plan mapped out.

"You gotta keep your streak," Nathan added.

"Streak?"

"It's bad luck to mess up your streak," Nathan explained like I should've already known. "Once you mess up your streak of hot girls, you risk letting an ugly one slip in."

Andre smacked Nathan's shoulder. "Is that why your dumb-ass brings home broads every night?"

"And are any of them ugly?" Nathan challenged, sending Andre and me into a fit of hysterics. He smacked the table, drawing the attention of everyone in the restaurant. "I'm taking you to Shots tonight."

"Shots?" Andre scoffed, looking to me for backup. "You thought the couch was bad."

Our conversation paused when one of the workers announced our order number. Once we had plates full of chicken tenders, fries, and hoagies, we continued with our evening agenda.

"I've never been to Shots," I said with a mouthful of Philly. If I had to determine my last meal on earth, it would be Mr. Spot's Philly with fries and a side of cheese sauce.

"You've *never* been to Shots?" Andre's eyebrows flew to the top of his forehead. He shook his head and took another bite of his sandwich.

"It's a right of passage," Nathan declared. "We'll start there tonight."

I rolled my eyes and listened to Andre and Nathan go back and forth about the upcoming hockey season. I pulled out my phone to check what time the library closed tomorrow since it was a holiday, but the unread text message drew my attention instead.

Serena

Are you going out tonight?

I tucked my phone back into my pocket and forgot about the library. I had all day tomorrow to finish my essay. Right now, I was intrigued to discover a bar called Shots and get Nathan's opinion on what the algorithm said about sleeping with someone twice. I had survived living in our apartment with Nathan's infested couch for almost three weeks. How bad could one bar on campus possibly be?

Shots was everything Andre warned me it would be. As Bubba Sparxxx's "Ms. New Booty" came over the sound system, I watched a group of girls grinding on each other in the middle of the dance floor. Shots allowed anyone over eighteen through the door, meaning some of these girls had just graduated high school. An hour felt like plenty of time to complete my right of passage.

"I feel like I'm committing a crime just standing in here," I yelled to Andre over the music.

"I told you, man!" He laughed, placing his empty cup on the bar. "Let's walk over to Nate & Wally's."

Nate & Wally's was the bar next door that served giant fishbowl drinks that tasted like Kool-Aid. I followed Andre through the crowds of people, careful not to get pulled into any dance circles. When we were only a few steps from the exit, I wasn't sure why I looked toward the bar again. Maybe it was the music changing to another song or the drinks hitting my system.

I should've just followed Andre out the door. Instead, I found myself walking toward Cassie. She stared at me from across the room, and I recognized the tight black dress from a wedding we went to last summer. It was the same dress we didn't even bother taking off when we fucked behind her cousin's lakehouse.

I didn't realize how close I was until her perfume flooded my senses. Her mouth parted slightly, and she tucked a blonde curl behind her ear. She didn't look surprised to see me, and the way her blue eyes scanned my chest assured me she wasn't angry that I was standing in front of her.

She reached behind her for her drink, and when she faced me again, she wore a smile that could've made me do anything she asked. "Hey, Deac."

I exhaled slowly. "Hey, Cass."

She sipped her drink and continued to look me up and down. I crossed my arms and bent down so my eyes were level with hers. This prompted a small giggle from her soft lips, and my heart skipped a beat at the sound of it.

Fuck me. I smiled and forced myself not to reach out and touch her. "What are you staring at, hun?"

Cassie shook her head. "Nothing. You just look different, that's all."

"Different?"

"Yeah." She shrugged, taking another sip of her drink. "I never thought I'd see you here. It's Sunday."

"No classes tomorrow, remember? The guys wanted to start the night here. We're heading over to—"

"Are you here with anyone?" she asked as a guy I recognized from Beckett's put his arm around her shoulder. The same guy had followed her into the restaurant the day I moved into my apartment. He didn't even notice me standing there. "I wasn't sure if you were seeing anyone, you know, since it's already been a few months?"

If there were ever a scene where I could disintegrate into the ground, I would choose this one. Cassie looked at me with a mixture of sympathy and embarrassment. It was a side of her I never got to meet while we were together, and it fed a fire inside me I didn't know I had. This fire apparently refused to see me as a newly wounded single when I ran into my ex-girlfriend for the first time.

"The girl I've been seeing couldn't come out tonight," I lied.

Cassie's eyebrows raised slowly up her forehead. She interlaced her fingers with Beckett Boy and tugged his arm tightly against her chest.

"Pizza and a movie night tomorrow at her place?" Cassie leaned her head into Beckett Boy's chest. "Same old Deacon."

I wasn't sure if she meant to make me feel like I was just kicked in the balls, but my name sounded horrible coming out of her mouth.

Same old Deacon. Seeing Cassie with someone else, standing against him like she had known him for years—I wanted to tell her I slept with someone. I wanted to give her a detailed summary of all four nights. Tell her I was doing okay and that we could have the life we talked about during the late nights when we couldn't sleep or in the mornings when she was too cold to get out of bed.

It was hard, always trying to keep my emotions in check. We seemed to bite our tongues the hardest for the people we loved. I could find girl number five at the next bar. I could sleep with someone tonight if I wanted to and force the feelings of rejection aside until they returned tomorrow morning. As much as I wished I could be that guy, that just wasn't me. I missed waking up next to the person who held a piece of my heart. The last thing I wanted was for sex to become a disposable act while Cassie continued her journey of soul-searching and thriving.

I heard Andre calling me from the exit. He twirled his finger in the air, signaling that they were moving on to the next bar, while Nathan strolled out behind him with his arms around two blonde girls.

"That's my cue," I said, laughing. "I'll see you around?"

"Yeah. I'm sure we'll run into each other again." Her dismissive tone from earlier returned. "I know your schedule, remember?"

I hated how easy this seemed for her; moving on and pretending everything she knew about me was suddenly a turn-off. I was missing something—a piece of the puzzle that would put me one step closer to getting Cassie back. I knew what she was looking for, and when I watched a few girls spinning on the pole in The Attic, I knew a person who might be able to help me out with what I was lacking.

CHAPTER TWELVE

Lyla

"Mom, I am *BEGGING* you to please stop shouting. It's nine in the morning, and I just got to bed like four hours ago." I wasn't exaggerating. The walk home from Jake's place was at least a forty-minute trek.

My mom sighed happily on the other end of the phone. "Late night with the boyfriend?"

"Ew. Jake's not my boyfriend, Mom."

Ah, fuck. I collapsed back onto my pillow and dragged my hands down my face. I threw myself into a relationship only two weeks ago and was already blowing it.

Mom didn't miss a beat. Aaron Brooks was borderline hopeless when picking up anything about my personal life, but Mom? She was pretty good at snagging things before they flew over her head.

"Wait, what?"

"Jake is a friend, Mom," I murmured as exhaustion began to take over my common sense. "People who date are allowed to have friends."

After years of preaching to her that relationships were a waste of time, I knew she questioned my new relationship status. Mom would continue to give me the benefit of the doubt until it personally impacted her everyday life. That was the beauty of our relationship—she did a fair job keeping her distance until she needed to intervene.

"Have you talked to your father?" she asked.

I sat up, unable to find comfort among the mountains of blankets piled on my bed. Just the thought of having to say anything to my dad right now rattled my core.

"What?" I snapped. "Fuck no."

Mom sucked her teeth. "Lyla Jean."

I rolled my eyes at the woman's response to a word she used as a filler in her everyday vocabulary. "Don't *Lyla Jean* me. The man promised me my trust fund—the only reason I still engage with him—and forced me to have this bullshit lunch with him in *Miami*. Mom, who the hell goes to Miami in *July*?"

She sighed again. "He does business there."

I went into the kitchen for some hot green tea. I wasn't falling back asleep anytime soon.

"He also does business in New York, and I heard Central Park is beautiful that time of year," I argued, taking my anger out on the tiny bear-shaped honey bottle. "I'm just tired, Mom." I didn't bother to explain why. The longer I stayed on the phone with her, the more opportunities I had to get caught in the lie I constructed.

There was a knock on our door. I waited to see if any of the roommates crept from the shadows of the hallway and was surprised to be met with silence. It was rare I had the entire place to myself.

"Mom, I gotta go," I said quickly. "I'll call you later."

"Okay, Jean Bean. I love you."

Another knock came from the front door, and I padded across the kitchen, zipping up my sweatshirt jacket. I'm sure whoever was on the other side of the door wasn't ready to see my nipples peeking through my tank top this early on a Monday.

"Yeah?" I yelled, throwing open the door.

Jesus. Mary. Joseph.

The guy from Opening Weekend stood on the other side of the door. The one who coined me as Stripper Pole Girl and witnessed my morning spiral into chaos. The one who took us to Grounds for Thought after we helped him move.

He placed his hands on his hips and peered down at me through thick, dark lashes. His light brown eyes had hints of gold around the iris. Were they like that last time? Was it because he glistened in sweat that I noticed how his T-shirt stretched along his shoulders? His *broad* shoulders. I almost buckled in the doorway when his tongue grazed the center of his bottom lip. He took a deep breath and raised his eyebrows, unsure what to do next since my awkward ass decided to stay silent.

I swallowed to give my voice the time it needed to gain composure. "Darren, what are you doing here?"

His smile grew wider. "Deacon, actually."

"Fuck, yeah, your name is Deacon. I'm sorry." I stepped aside so he could come in. "Your friend isn't here by the—"

"I know he isn't." Deacon leaned his back against the counter. "Charlie is at my place. I talked to her before my run this morning."

I winced at the thought of going any faster than my stroll a few hours ago. "Did you run *here*?"

He shrugged his shoulders. "It's not that far."

"I beg to—"

"She told me you aren't seeing anyone," Deacon interrupted. His voice was gentle, but it didn't lack urgency. "Have you found your fake boyfriend yet?"

An exasperated laugh escaped my chest. "Uhm . . . no, I haven't."

I had forgotten about that little problem. I was too busy picturing how good he'd look with me straddling him on the couch. I averted my eyes from the bulge in his athletic shorts and reprimanded myself for being so childish. It wasn't like I never encountered a gorgeous man in the past. Deacon was no different.

His full lips curved into a proud grin. "I'll do it."

I wasn't sure what I expected him to say, but it sure as hell wasn't that. The morning I met Deacon, I knew I had to cross him off as a potential calendar option. He was too nice.

"Deacon," I said sweetly. "Humor me. Why are you offering?"

He pushed his lower back against the counter and closed the space between us. Even though he was covered in sweat, he smelled incredible—like cedarwood, and was it lavender?

"Because you can help me." He smiled, leaning forward so his eyes were level with mine. "And I can help you."

 Deacon

LYLA WAS EXACTLY HOW I remembered her. She wore shorts that cut off right before her ass, and by the way she kept tugging on her sweatshirt jacket, I assumed she wasn't wearing a bra. Her hair was messy and slept on, and she illuminated the same carefree glow she had the morning we met.

As striking as she was, I remembered her eyes the most. They were a beautiful shade of green, and even though they were skeptical, she was intrigued with what I had to say.

"Hear me out," I said slowly.

She blew out a long breath and ran a hand through her hair. She rubbed her eyes and rounded the kitchen counter, her shorts riding up to reveal a sliver of black lace. I averted my eyes to the steaming cup of tea in her hand and sat on the bar stool across from her. She peered over the rim of the mug and waited for me to continue.

"You need to convince your dad that you're dating a reputable guy. Someone who has his shit together, correct?"

She nodded, taking another sip of her tea.

I smiled. "I can be that guy."

Lyla leaned over the counter until she was inches away from my face.

"Okay," she pondered. "And how is it I'm going to help *you*?"

The words gathered in the base of my throat. If things went south, I could exit the apartment and never have to see this girl again.

"I need to make my ex-girlfriend jealous," I admitted, unashamed of how pathetic it sounded. "If she thinks I'm dating a girl like you, my crazy idea might just work."

Lyla stood up straight and cocked her head. "A girl like me, huh?"

Fuck. That sounded terrible with no context.

"You caught my attention the morning I met you," I said quickly, trying to save my chance before it crumbled onto the counter in front of me. "You're fun and witty and cute and, from what I saw in that video, a decent dancer—"

"So this has *nothing* to do with the fact that you saw my ass on a phone screen?" She crossed her arms in front of her chest and looked down to ensure she was covered. When she looked up, I had to bite my cheek to keep from laughing.

"What?" I exclaimed. "No!"

Lyla started toward the door. "Look, Deacon, this was fun, but—"

"Lyla." I rounded the counter and reached for her hand. She didn't fight my touch, but I could tell she was unsure. I dropped her hand immediately and took a step back. "I'm sorry."

She gestured to the space between us, and a slight smirk crept into the corner of her mouth. "You're witnessing all of this, right? Like, you're here for this? You *actually* believe you could pretend to be in a relationship with me?"

I didn't know at this point if I was winning or losing. I thought Lyla was getting ready to kick me out, but now she looked a little disappointed at the way I tried to stop her. Either way, if there was one thing I knew how to do, it was being in a relationship. I couldn't give up now—not when the perfect girl who checked Cassie's jealousy boxes stood before me.

Lyla was the opposite of the type of girl Cassie would want me to move on with. She was sexy and funny, and she didn't have to try. I had only seen this girl the morning after a night out, and even with her thrown-together appearance and sleepy expressions, I found her adorable.

I needed to persuade her with logic. I turned up the charm and tucked a lock of her hair behind her ears. She kept her eyes locked on mine.

I shook my head slowly and looked her up and down. "I don't have to pretend to be in a relationship, Lyla. When I want something, I work for it, and right now, I want Cassie to want me back. If she wants to explore her options, that's fine. But I want her to know that while she's dealing with little college boys, I'm dating a woman who is everything she wouldn't want me to be with. I *have* my shit together, and I promise I'll be the best fake boyfriend you'll ever have."

Lyla's eyes narrowed as she read my face for any hesitation. She took a deep breath, and from what I could tell, she was going over the last fifteen minutes in her head. She was considering it, and I needed to keep her going.

"You said your dad wants to meet your new boyfriend, right? Parents love me. Cassie will think we're dating, and your dad will get to see you with a—how did you describe it before? A knight in shining armor?"

Lyla chuckled, and before I knew it, she was belly laughing. It was impossible not to smile at the sound of it.

"Cassie, huh?" she said once her laughter died down. "She's not gonna come stakeout my apartment looking for you, is she?"

Cassie would never. That would require her to do an outdoor activity with no photographic evidence. She couldn't be *thriving* if she was peeking in on her ex-boyfriend from a bush.

"So you'll do it?" My question came out as a hopeful statement.

Lyla tugged on her bottom lip with her teeth. My breath caught at the base of my throat, and suddenly, the adorable girl drinking tea a few moments ago was playfully reminding me that we were alone. The most dangerous part about her? She wasn't even *trying* to turn me on.

"Oh, I'll do it," she stated confidently. She gave a dismissive wave of her hand in my direction and shrugged. "I can work with all of this."

I smiled. "What time is your first class tomorrow?"

"Tuesday, Tuesday, Tuesday," she pondered. "Tuesday is Shakespeare, so noon?"

"Noon," I confirmed. "Wait, *noon?*"

Lyla stared at me like I was speaking a different language.

I narrowed my gaze. "You don't get to campus until *noon* on Tuesday?"

"I'm not understanding the issue here."

"That's like right in the middle of the day!"

Lyla sucked her teeth. "And?" She moved around me to return to her mug on the counter.

"Campus is a lot busier in the mornings," I explained. "If we want to get this going before fall break, we need to be seen together by as many people as possible."

"But—"

"Meet me in front of The Union at ten, Lyla." I drummed my fingers on the counter and walked toward the door.

"Ten?" she whined.

I pointed at her from across the room and winked. "Your knight in shining armor will be waiting for you."

I caught a tiny glimpse of her smile before I closed the door behind me. I knew what I needed to do to chip away at Cassie's brand-new exterior. For the first time since the Grounds for Thought breakup, I felt like my plans were finally back on track. Lyla needed a boyfriend, and Relationship Deacon was back.

Chapter Fourteen

Lyla

My only logical explanation for heading to campus this early was that I was still drunk when Deacon showed up on my doorstep.

The universe didn't hand you a solution when you shouted your problems into the void. A gorgeous man didn't appear on your doorstep because you required assistance. That shit only happened in romantic comedies and serial killer documentaries, and I would take Michael Myers any day.

The shuttle from Falcon's Pointe dropped me off near the education building. Deacon was already in front of The Union dressed in a plain white T-shirt, cargo shorts, and black Vans. He looked way too happy to be on campus at ten in the morning.

As I got closer, I gave him a halfhearted smile, and he responded with an adorable grin. Between the sunshine and the brightness of his shirt, his light brown eyes popped against his brown skin.

"Good morning, Lyla." Deacon handed me an iced beverage.

I scanned the Dunkin Donuts label. "Green tea?"

"*Iced* green tea. I figured you didn't want a hot tea since it's almost eighty degrees out. And I didn't want to assume you took matcha before noon."

I nodded slowly before taking a sip. It was perfect.

"So you're sweet, *and* you pay attention," I teased.

Deacon chuckled and motioned for me to walk with him. He seemed unbothered by the silence that hung between us, but I needed something to feed off of. I could only walk around campus for so long before I started to feel awkward.

"So—"

"Why don't we start with our last names?" Deacon offered.

"Brooks." My shoulders relaxed as the word left my mouth. "Yours?"

"Scott."

"So, Deacon Scott and Lyla Brooks. We sound—"

"You think this is crazy, don't you," Deacon said, laughing. "It's okay if you do. I went back and forth like ten times before I came over yesterday. I knew I was taking a chance when I asked you."

I stopped walking, and Deacon followed my lead when I turned to face him. I drummed my fingers along the side of my cup. "Can I ask the obvious question?"

He nodded, a look of concern washing over his gorgeous face.

"I've only spent a few *hours* with you, and you seem . . ."

Deacon rocked on his heels while I struggled to find the word. "Charming?"

"Sure, we can use charming."

"What were you gonna say?"

"I was going to say that you seem downright delightful," I admitted, getting a chuckle out of him. "You show up, drink in hand, and look genuinely happy to see me. You made sure Charlie and I got something for helping you move because you said we would. You give off *zero* creepy vibes. You're actually kind of funny. So I have to ask . . . why did this girl break up with you?"

Deacon sighed, running a hand through his hair. He started walking again, and I followed, giving him a few minutes to compose his answer.

He winced. "Full transparency?"

"We don't lie, Deacon Scott. There's no reason to."

"Full transparency—I plan to *marry* this girl. We met freshman year, and when I planned to ask her to move in with me, she broke up with me. I think she's afraid that she's missing something. We were heading into our senior year together, and I think part of her felt like she was settling by staying with me. She wants to explore her options."

Even though his calm expression didn't shift, I could see the pain behind his lighthearted gaze. That girl broke this man's heart.

"How did she do it?" I prompted gently.

Deacon exhaled through his nose and stared at the ground as we walked. "She called me instead of showing up for our coffee date."

"Your girlfriend of three years broke up with you over *the phone?*" I exclaimed, keeping my voice down so I didn't end up alerting the whole campus. I stared at the cup in my hand and sucked my teeth. "She didn't break up with you at Dunkin, did she?"

To my surprise, Deacon laughed at my comment. "No, not Dunkin. Grounds for Thought. It's where we met, and I thought it would be cute to ask her to move in with me there—you know, since it was the location of the meet-cute."

"Oh my god. When Charlie—wait, the *what* cute?"

"The meet-cute?" He stared at me like I had three heads. "The location where the couple meets in the movies?"

Aaand cue Michael Fucking Myers.

I rolled my eyes and laughed. "Oh boy."

"What about you?" he asked playfully. "You clearly have no interest in actually *finding* a boyfriend."

"So we're just moving on from the tragic story of your break up? Are there any other important details I need to know?"

"Cassie ended things with me over the phone, broke my heart, and I'm ready to get her back," Deacon rambled, shrugging off his crisis. "Your turn."

I sipped my drink to buy me more time. There was no reason to dive into why I didn't want to be in a relationship. That wasn't important to Deacon's role in this plan.

"My parents decided to break up when my dad decided he no longer wanted to be a parent," I explained casually. "Aaron Brooks went off to be this amazing and successful financial advisor, and even though he wasn't around, he insisted on financially supporting my mom and me. He wanted control even though he didn't live with us. Money is power, and my mom struggled by herself."

"I'm sorry," Deacon offered.

"Oh, no, don't be sorry." I forced a laugh, determined to keep the carefree mood between us. "I had a great life growing up with my mom. I couldn't imagine seeing my dad more than four times a year."

Deacon widened his eyes mid-sip. "You're telling me you only see your dad four times a year?"

"I need Aaron Brooks for one thing and one thing only. He set aside a trust fund for me when I was born. Right now, I can access it at twenty-five, but when I saw him two months ago, we agreed the funds would be mine once I graduated. Unfortunately, when my ass made the internet, he threatened to take it away if I didn't get my shit together."

"Hence the responsible boyfriend." Deacon grinned like we were introducing his character on a TV show. "Your dad left but still managed to make you a trust fund baby? That's kind of wild."

"Wild, but true. Once I get that money, I'll be free of him. I can finally start the next chapter of my life; a chapter that doesn't involve Aaron Brooks or anyone else I don't want to bring along."

"So when you get this money after graduation, what are your big plans?"

I smiled at his question. I never got to talk about that part of the plan. People heard I went to school for business and just assumed I wanted black corporate suits and a matching briefcase.

"I want to open a bookstore," I said nervously. I cleared my throat and stood a little taller. "I want to live in Chicago and run a bookstore that encourages indie authors to sell their books there. My entire life, my mom has been a bartender and a writer. She wants to travel the world and publish fantasy novels about women getting swept away into imaginary worlds to find themselves."

On one of our trips to Florida, my mom shared how she'd love to write in an office in the back of a bookstore. For every book she published, she would take a trip and find inspiration for her next story. I couldn't give time back to her, but I could help her move forward into something she loved. It was the least I could do since she got stuck as the default parent.

"Brooks Books," Deacon said.

I retreated from my journey down memory lane. "What?"

"Your bookstore," Deacon explained, throwing his empty cup in the trash. He stopped walking, and I realized we were in front of East Hall.

Deacon turned so he could face me and extended his hand, skimming his thumb over my cheek and down my jawline. My breath caught in my throat.

"Brooks Books could be the name of your bookstore. Genius, I know, and I promise I won't even take credit for it." He studied me with a sly smile, waiting to see how I'd react to a simple touch. A slight smirk crept into the side of his mouth. "I'll see you after class, Lyla Brooks. Go learn some Shakespeare."

The doors of East Hall closed behind me, and I pushed the heavy puff of air from my chest. Fuckin' Brooks Books. The only reason this insanity *might* end up saving me was because Aaron Brooks knew little to nothing about me. He had no idea I would never date a guy as downright delightful as Deacon Scott.

CHAPTER FIFTEEN

Deacon

I SPENT THE NEXT hour and a half in The Union working on a discussion board for class. When it was time to meet Lyla after class, I made it to the doors of East Hall just as she was leaving the building. Her mouth curved into a small smile when she saw me. She'd never say it out loud, but she was happy to see me.

"Still here, huh?" she teased, pulling out her phone. "First things first, I need your number."

"Easy enough." I took her phone, and we exchanged information.

Lyla pulled her hair to the top of her head and secured it in a bun. "Let's do a high-level summary, shall we?"

It tugged on my heartstrings to see a motion Cassie did so often when we did schoolwork together. I loved when she put her hair up. It meant she was thinking about something.

"I'm the fun and witty girlfriend who will make your ex-girlfriend jealous and wish she was with you again. Being with you will convince my dad that the Usher video was a mistake, because I'm a put-together woman who is done playing games and is ready to start her business. We will convince everyone around us that we're a happy couple. Did I leave anything out?"

I nodded approvingly. "That pretty much covers it."

"Cool."

"Cool," I echoed her casual tone.

We walked across the courtyard to the education building. Once we rounded the corner of the steps, a girl who seemed to know Lyla stopped us.

"Hey, Lyla! When you get back to the apartment, can you pull the chicken from the freezer? I want to make those chicken tacos we found on Pinterest last night."

"Yeah, I can. Deacon, this is Keira."

Keira eyed me suspiciously. "Hey."

"Nice to meet you," I said. I waited for Lyla to explain who I was but decided to do it for her when she didn't. "I'm Lyla's—"

"Keira, this is my boyfriend, Deacon," Lyla blurted.

Keira's eyes bounced between the two of us. "Wait, what?"

Lyla opened her mouth to speak, but nothing came.

"We started dating yesterday," I added, hoping to help the dumpster fire scene we were starring in. "We met a few weeks ago when I picked up my roommate from your place."

Keira pursed her lips. "Interesting. Don't forget the chicken."

Once Keira was far enough away, I looked at Lyla and laughed. "Damn."

"What?"

I ran my hand through my hair, unsure how to respond. "Is that how you're going to act whenever we're in front of people? We might as well give this up now."

"I thought that was totally fine for our first encounter!" she exclaimed, whacking me in the arm. "What was so bad about it?"

I crossed my arms and took a step closer to her. "What am I allowed to do in public? In your head, how does a couple act when they're around people?"

Her lip curled in response, and I held back more laughter. "I don't know, cute boyfriend shit." She gestured toward my hip. "Like you can hold my hand."

I raised my hand and pressed my mouth into a hard line. "Cute boyfriend shit, huh? You say the sweetest things to me, baby. Do you even know the basic things of being in a relationship?"

She brushed off my comment. "Ehh, see. You're already breaking rule one."

My eyebrows shot to the top of my head. "There are rules?"

"Yes, we haven't gotten to them because I had to stop myself from throwing up when you called me the B-word."

"Pet names in relationships are normal, Brooks Books."

She took a deep breath and closed her eyes. When she opened them, she wore a confident grin. "That brings me back to rule number one. Remember, this isn't a *real* relationship."

"Okay," I said slowly. "Go on."

"Rule number two is we don't lie. There's no reason to. Not if this is gonna work. Rule number three is you can fuck around with whoever you want. Just keep everything private. We have an image to maintain. And rule number four is no love. You *cannot* fall in love with me, Deacon Scott. You seem like the fall-head-first type, and there is no room for that here."

I processed the well-written rules she thought about during her session on Shakespeare.

"Not a real relationship, no lying, fuck around in private, and no love," I summarized.

"Perfect."

When she turned to leave, I grabbed her hand. If that's all I got, I would take full advantage of the contact. She didn't pull away, and I decided to push my luck for as long as I had it.

"Are you gonna tell me who hurt you now, or . . ."

"Rule number five." She smiled coyly. "Don't ask about each other's past."

We spent the remainder of our walk talking about Lyla's Shakespeare class. Lyla read a lot in her downtime. It was charming to see the softer side of her that came with telling someone a story. Just as she was preparing an argument against the communication in *Romeo and Juliet*, we arrived at the pickup spot for the Falcon's Pointe shuttle.

"I mean, if the play had occurred today, everything would've been solved with a simple text message," she insisted.

"'What's in a name? That which we call a rose, by any other word, would smell as sweet,'" I quoted fondly. "I always liked that line."

She looked at me with a new appreciation for the conversation. "I think that's one of the most intriguing parts. If it wasn't so forbidden, would there have been the attraction in the first place?"

I peered up at the sky and cocked my head. She tugged on my hand when I was taking too long to answer. She kept a tight grip for someone who just laid out multiple terms and conditions.

"I think if you want something bad enough, you find a way to get it," I declared. Even though Cassie and I weren't together, I still had hope. If we didn't work out, it wouldn't be because I didn't try.

The shuttle rounded the parking lot and halted a few feet in front of us. Before Lyla could slip away, I pulled her hand to my mouth and skimmed my lips across her fingers. She eyed me playfully, daring me to try something else while we had a small audience.

"I'll be seeing you, Lyla Brooks." I kissed her hand, giving her one last smile before she got on the shuttle.

Chapter Sixteen

Lyla

Four days into my agreement with Deacon, the word spread like wildfire through our apartment that I was actually dating someone. I thought Charlie was going to break down my bedroom door when Keira asked her if she had met my boyfriend yet.

"What the fuck is this about you having a *boyfriend*?" Charlie demanded. She tossed her bag on the recliner and sat beside me on the couch. Her wide blue eyes told me she wasn't giving up until I offered her an explanation, so I placed my laptop on the coffee table and sank into the cushion.

"It's not a huge deal," I started before I caught myself sounding too casual. I never did anything half-assed, and if I agreed to convince people that I was happy with Deacon to make his ex-girlfriend jealous, then I would play the part as if the role was made for me. "Remember that guy who picked up Andre a few weeks ago? The one who took us to Grounds?"

Charlie gasped and smacked my arm. "The guy you *claimed* wasn't Mr. September? You bitch! You lied to me?"

"I didn't lie!" I exclaimed, holding up my hands before she could get another hit. "He asked for my number, and things just kind of went from there."

"But weren't you just with Jake on Saturday?" Like a true friend, there wasn't a hint of judgment in her question.

"Yes," I admitted as my mouth formed a naughty grin. "But Deacon and I became official on Monday."

Charlie sucked her teeth and stood up. "Lyla Brooks has a *boyfriend*."

I rolled my eyes. "Shut up."

My phone vibrated on the coffee table, and Deacon's name was in the middle of the screen. Charlie's mouth hit the floor. She quickly closed it and retreated to the fridge. I unlocked my phone and read Deacon's message.

Deacon

> I think we should hang out. Does that fit into your rules?

When I looked up, Charlie was staring at me. She stuck out her bottom lip and leaned over the kitchen counter. "Well, that's fucking cute."

My eyes narrowed. "What is?"

"You're smiling at your phone screen. That's some cute shit."

"Don't you have something you could be doing?" I snapped as I texted Deacon back.

Lyla

> I'll allow it. But no rom-com movie marathons. I draw the line at cheesy meet-cutes.

Deacon

> How do you expect to run a bookstore without appreciating a good meet-cute?!

I have to crank out this last paper. I'll be over in an hour or so.

I sent him a thumbs-up emoji and placed my phone next to my laptop.

"I'm heading out tonight for Thirsty Thursday at Ziggy's. So you'll have the apartment to yourself." Charlie winked before disappearing down the hall.

I groaned and sank back into the couch cushions. A week ago, Charlie would've invited me to Ziggy's. We'd spin the shot wheel every half-hour and play darts. Single Girl Lyla would scan the bar for possible prospects, and Charlie would give her feedback. It was Thirsty Thursday, and I was staying in with my fake boyfriend. So far, this whole "having my shit together" nonsense was bullshit.

An hour later, Deacon walked in with a bottle of wine and a giant carryout bag from Campus Pollyeyes. I sat across from him at the counter as he pulled out two boxes of breadsticks and a small salad. It was the second time I appeared empty-handed while Deacon brought contributions.

"Wine glasses?" he asked, surveying the cabinets.

"Solo cups are by the sink." I pointed at the pile of red cups and tried to hide the frustration in my voice. "Deacon, what are you doing?"

He screwed off the top of the wine bottle. "What do you mean?"

I gestured to the items scattered across the counter. "You understand that I've agreed to this, right? You don't have to keep bringing me things whenever we see each other."

He pushed the bottle to the side and handed me my cup. I raised the drink to my mouth as he leaned forward on his elbows. His eyes never left mine as I finished my sip.

"My friend was working at Dunkin yesterday morning, so she gave me a free drink," he explained. "I brought over food tonight because that's what friends *do*, Lyla. They eat food and hang out and watch movies and have small talk to get to know each other."

It was unusual for someone to make me feel like an asshole, but the tone of Deacon's voice was so delicate it suddenly felt like a crime to accuse him of being anything but pleasant.

He helped himself to a breadstick. "I wanna know you, Lyla. I respect your relationship rules, but this whole thing will go much smoother if we actually become friends."

I hadn't been good at friends for a long time. Keeping people at a distance was easier—safer so no one could be disappointed.

I took a deep breath. "Full transparency?"

Deacon shot me a sexy smirk. "We don't lie, Lyla Brooks."

My shoulders relaxed, and I wasn't sure if it was his voice or the wine. "I don't have guy friends, and this whole 'let's hang out' energy you've presented to me is just a little new."

"No guy friends at all? You've never—sorry." He shot me an innocent glance. "No asking about the past."

"One relationship in high school. That's all you get." I plucked a breadstick from the open box and took a bite. There should be a warning label on Campus Pollyeyes breadsticks. They sucked you in and fed parts of your soul you didn't know lacked happiness.

"I'll take that. So one relationship and lots of . . . *fun*."

I smiled at his choice of words. "I am a huge fan of fun."

We spent the next half hour talking about our hometowns and where we came from. Deacon was from Detroit, and his parents still lived in his childhood home. I learned that his younger brother, Drew, went to Penn State and was studying to be an engineer. Deacon was close with his family and hated how everyone looked at him when they found out he and Cassie broke up.

I chose to paint my past carefully when Deacon asked more about my mom and where I grew up. I was popular in high school. I played soccer, went to football games, and attended all of the school dances. I fell for the quarterback and spent weekends hanging out with our friends and going to parties. It was never a conversation whether I would attend college or not. My dad made it clear that I would graduate with a degree from a reputable university. It didn't matter what my dreams were or what I wanted to do.

"Why Bowling Green?" Deacon asked.

"They offered me good scholarships and had a great soccer program. When I graduated, I wasn't sure if I wanted to play soccer in college. I visited the campus with my mom, and something about this place felt like home."

Deacon poured more wine into his cup. "I hear you. I felt the same way when I came for my visit. My first choice was Ohio State. Their medical programs are amazing, but I wasn't sure I wanted a big city feel."

"What are *your* big plans for after graduation?"

"Pediatric surgeon," he said proudly.

I pictured Deacon as a doctor and was pleasantly surprised with the fantasy. He'd fit right in with the cast of *Grey's Anatomy*: a gorgeous male doctor with a knack for squeezing his way into your personal space. There would be seasons of storylines written about him.

"After I graduate, I plan on getting a job and working for a year before returning to school. I figured that would give me enough time to buy a house near Cassie's family in Minnesota."

I wiped the surprised look off my face. Even after this girl broke up with him over the phone, Deacon still considered moving closer to her family after graduation. I waited for him to say more, but the way he stared into his solo cup told me he was thinking about something. I decided to probe. What were friends for, right?

"You'll be a hot addition to Minnesota, Dr. Scott. You and Cassie will be one of those couples painting their master bedroom her favorite color. It's probably pink, isn't it?" I winced at the scene unfolding in my head. "Like a basic bitch pink?"

Deacon chuckled. "I don't know what basic bitch pink is, but I imagine her favorite color is blue or green."

"Wait!" I lowered his cup onto the counter. "You *imagine*? You're going to move across the country for this girl, and you don't even know her favorite color? What the fuck, Deac?"

He opened his mouth to speak but instead shot me a satisfied grin.

"Deac isn't a pet name," I argued. "It's an abbreviation, and that's different."

"Whatever you say, baby." He ignored my death glare from across the counter. "I guess her favorite color just never came up. But I know a lot of other things about her that most people don't know. Do you remember everything about *your* first serious relationship?"

I blamed the third cup of wine for making me comfortable enough to generate an answer. "I thought I knew everything about my first and only boyfriend, and he still proved me wrong. So I guess I'll let you pass with the color thing."

I hopped off the bar stool and motioned for him to follow me into the living room. Even though I was missing a night out, I actually enjoyed Deacon's company. He was easy to talk to, and every question he asked came from a place of genuine curiosity.

Deacon sat beside me on the couch and rested his feet on the coffee table. He moved to rest his body against mine until he realized what he was doing. He tried to pull away before I could notice, but *boy,* did I notice. I'd have to buy this man looser shirts if I was going to stop mentally undressing him every time the fabric pulled at his pecks.

I decided to test my flexibility. Not in the way I *wanted* to with the man sitting next to me, but sharing a couch cushion could be a nice first step. "It's okay, you know. Couples sit together and watch movies, right?"

A nervous laugh escaped his sculpted chest. "I'm sorry. I would say it's just a natural thing for me, but that sounds terrible. I would never want you to feel uncomfortable around me."

I focused on the TV so I wouldn't smile at his sweet gesture. "I'll let you know if that ever happens."

His full lips curved into a small smile. "Good."

STOP STARING AT HIS MOUTH.

I motioned for him to lean against my side, and he shifted so his legs draped over the couch instead of the coffee table. We settled in, and I selected *The Fast and The Furious* from the movie options. Deacon was quiet for the first few minutes until I felt his hefty sigh against my side.

"There's something you're not saying," I suggested playfully.

He took a deep breath and shifted so he could look at me. "We don't lie," I reminded him.

His smile wavered, and he reached back to rest his hand on my knee. It was a delicate touch, but my skin was on fire.

"Not all guys are the same," he said softly. "You said no asking about the past, and I respect that. But whatever happened"—he shook his head and ran his other hand through his hair—"I've only been fake dating you for four days, and I can already tell that you're a pretty awesome person."

I pulled back on my heartstrings and draped my arm across his chest. His skin felt warm through his shirt, keeping my perspective in check. I was mentally taking this shirt off only a few minutes ago. "You're sweet. Are you sure there isn't some dark trait you're hiding that forced this girl to break up with you?"

He chuckled, and his entire body vibrated against mine. "Nah. I like to think I'm pretty normal."

"Says every single guy," I mumbled. "Relationships just seem so . . ."

He looked up again. "What?"

"They just seem like bullshit. Sorry, I know you're looking to get back into one, but they are. You're better off keeping things casual. It's the easiest way not to lose yourself to someone else."

The silence between us hung for a moment, and I wasn't sure if that comment was too blunt for Deacon to handle. I couldn't see why any girl looking for a relationship didn't want to consider Deacon Scott, let alone lose him in the first place.

He sat up on his elbow. "That's an easy way to protect yourself, but it's also an easy way to end up alone."

I narrowed in on his innocent expression. "Watch the movie, sweetheart."

Deacon's laughter filled the room, and he collapsed back into me. Unlike most guys I met in Bowling Green, Deacon listened. He was intelligent, used punctuation correctly in his text messages, and made the room more comfortable just being in it.

Cassie was in for a wild fucking ride if she thought there were an array of options to choose from.

CHAPTER SEVENTEEN

Deacon

IT WAS OUR FOURTH weekend going out to the bars, but everything about this night felt different. I was looking forward to Lyla coming over and *being* out with someone. I understood this relationship was fake, but discovering someone new excited me. I knew what to expect when I went out with Cassie. I knew very little about the bar version of Lyla Brooks.

Lyla and Charlie would be here any minute, and a rowdy pregaming crowd was already out in the living room. I threw on a black V-neck shirt and a pair of jeans. I placed a hat on my head but, at the last minute, decided against it. I was already pushing it with jeans when it came to the heat index in the bars.

Music bumped through the soundbar on the TV, and a game of beer pong was underway in the kitchen. I shook my head at the familiar scene and snagged a beer from the fridge.

Familiar scene? The Deacon from last year wouldn't recognize me. After spending so much time with Lyla this week, I had a good amount of homework I needed to catch up on. Last year I would've stayed in, stressing about due dates and getting shit done.

"Can I get next?" I asked Andre over the music.

He swatted a pong ball as it flew toward the last cup. "Yeah, man. Is your girl comin'?"

It felt like decades since I heard that question. "She should be here soon. Charlie is coming too."

"Fuck, that's right." Andre smiled and took his shot. The ball bounced off the rim and onto the floor. "Charlie's cool."

"Closer" by Ne-Yo filled the apartment just as Lyla and Charlie arrived. I hid my smile behind my drink. My natural reaction to Lyla wearing a black leather jacket and a shirt that showed her stomach was a quick lip bite and a smirk. Then I remembered I didn't have to hide *anything*, so as her crazy-about-her-boyfriend, that's exactly what I did.

Her black jeans hugged her hips as she made a beeline to where I stood. She rolled her eyes in a way that only I would notice, picking up on the energy I was throwing her. There was nothing fake about how sexy she looked standing in front of me. Lyla was cute in the mornings after a night out, but the before image drew the eyes of everyone in the room.

Everyone watched as she pulled a white shirt from the back pocket of her jeans and stood on her toes to kiss me on the cheek.

"You left this at my place," she said with a wink. She patted my chest on her way to the fridge, and my mouth dangled open.

Andre raised his eyebrows, eyeing Lyla as she walked to get a drink. I smacked him on my way to the kitchen, and he burst into hysterics. My fake girlfriend was hot, but just because we weren't actually dating didn't mean that guys could eye-fuck her when she wasn't looking.

Lyla smiled and twisted the top off her beer bottle. "That was good, right? Girlfriend shit?"

Last night, we had composed a list of things we could do in front of people to make this more convincing. We had no idea how long this would play out, but Lyla needed certain obligations from me to uphold my end of the bargain. When her dad came to see her for Thanksgiving, we needed to have this relationship down pat. I looked into her dad's website and watched a few of his interview videos. The man had to read people to help them with their finances for a living. People trusted him with thousands, sometimes hundreds of thousands of dollars. Whether he knew his daughter well or not, he could spot if this was real or fake.

I tucked her hair behind her ear with my free hand. It fell in loose curls around her face and her green eyes popped against her makeup. She really was a gorgeous girl.

"Yeah, Brooks, that's some girlfriend shit. Play the next round of pong with me."

She pulled out her phone and eyed me as she typed. "You should know, Deacon Scott, that I don't lose in beer pong." She ran her hand down my arm as she passed me.

I watched her walk to the table where Andre was standing. He smiled and made room for her to stand beside him while she motioned for me to come over.

"Do we have next?" she asked Andre as I approached the table.

"One second, and you will!" Nathan announced and shot his ball. It landed in the cup right in front of Andre, and the room exploded with excitement.

Lyla cheered along with the rest of the crowd, and I loved how carefree she made everything seem. She didn't waste time trying to find a space to fit in. She made room for herself wherever she went, and I admired the hell out of her for it.

Lyla and I went back and forth with Nathan and Maddie for a while before it started to get interesting. Neither team was hitting, and the more alcohol that flowed around the table, the more intense the game became. Both teams were down to three cups in the same position. No one had reracked, which meant that the first team to clear their side of the table won the game.

"We should do a triangle," I insisted, rolling my ball between my palms.

Lyla pursed her lips. Her eyes showed a slight glaze because of the shots she insisted we take with every cup we made. She bumped my hip with hers. "We got this. They haven't hit a cup in like four rounds."

I laughed as her ball bounced off the rim of the middle cup. "Neither have we, baby."

I tossed my ball and made the cup on the right. People around us cheered and went back to their side conversations. I ran my hand through my hair and took a deep breath. I was officially buzzed and needed to stop drinking until we reached the bars.

The song changed, and I felt a light bump to my hip. Lyla swayed to the music, and her fist shot into the air as the tempo picked up.

"Am I okay to call you that, by the way?" I smiled adoringly at her dance moves. "I realized I never asked."

She tossed her empty beer bottle in the trashcan. "Call me what?"

I cupped her chin so she would take a second to focus on me. Her eyes darkened, and the slight curve of her lip let me know I had her full attention.

"Baby," I said, keeping my voice low. "Am I allowed to call you baby?"

"There's that fucking B-word again." She leaned closer so she could rest her hands on my chest. "It's fine. I told you I would let you know if something bothers me, remember?"

"You did say that."

"Relax, sweetheart. Everything is fine. A pink master bedroom is still in your future."

I chuckled as a ping-pong ball flew between us.

"Two more cups!" Nathan exclaimed, throwing his arm around his partner. Maddie could barely stand with his weight on her shoulders, and they had to grab the table for support. The cup next to Maddie spilled over the side of the table, prompting "boos" and "ahhs" from the crowd around us.

Lyla pointed to the water on the floor. "Party foul!"

I threw my arm around Lyla's shoulders. "We won!"

Nathan tried to talk his way back into the game, but the rules were simple. A party foul equaled immediate disqualification.

Andre's voice came over the crowd a few minutes later. "Last call! We're leaving in fifteen!"

I retreated to the kitchen for water. I was nearing the fine line between buzzed and drunk, and I still wanted to accomplish some things tonight. They all involved Cassie, but the road to recovery needed to start somewhere.

The first item on the list was to find out where Cassie was. That wouldn't be hard since she habitually documented her life on social media nowadays. The second item was making sure she saw me with Lyla, and the third and final item left Cassie with the impression that I was happily *dating* Lyla. It wasn't a complicated plan.

I grabbed another water from the fridge and weaved through the crowd until I found Lyla. I smelled her floral perfume as soon as I came within a few steps of her. When I approached her, she was giggling with Charlie over something on her phone.

"Drink this." I handed her the water, and she took it. When she noticed me staring at her, she rolled her eyes and took a hefty sip. "Atta girl," I murmured.

Her lips curved into a naughty grin. "Deacon Scott. I had no idea."

"What?"

She eyed me suspiciously. "I had no idea there was this side to you."

"There's still a good bit you don't know about me yet."

She nodded slowly, taking my answer as a challenge instead of a statement.

Nathan threw his arm around my shoulders and looked between me and Lyla. "Brathaus?"

I checked Cassie's Snapchat story. From what I could gather, she was at The Attic, which surprised me since it was only eleven-thirty. Most people ended their night at The Attic, and it appeared she was starting hers there.

"Attic?" I suggested, and Nathan grinned. I could've told him I wanted to drive to California, and he would've agreed. The man was hammered.

"Attic!" Nathan yelled, signaling for everyone to drink up.

I held out my hand to Lyla.

"Let me text Jake back really quick," she said.

Yeah, I definitely heard that correctly. "Who's Jake?"

"September," she answered without looking up from her phone.

"September . . . what?"

She gave me her full attention. "Oh, *Mr.* September. He's the guy I've been seeing."

My game plan to make Cassie jealous burst into flames. I scanned the people around us to see if anyone overheard. "Wait, what?"

She continued when she saw we were in the clear. "Rule number three, Deacon. We can see other people as long as we keep it private."

I didn't need a reminder of our terms and conditions, but I decided to entertain her casual approach. "And if we run into Mr. September tonight . . . how are you gonna explain who I am?"

She grinned. "Oh, I'll tell him you're my boyfriend. Not everyone has such a closed mind when it comes to monogamy, Deacon. It *is* twenty-sixteen, after all."

"Lyla—"

Andre threw his arm around Lyla. "You guys coming?" His eyes narrowed when he noticed my slack expression. "What's up, D?"

Lyla smacked his chest. "Oh, I just leave him speechless. That's one of his favorite things about me."

While Andre thought he had just witnessed some type of foreplay, I knew the game that Lyla was trying to play. I was aware of rule number three, but she wanted the best of both worlds. It took one wrong person in the audience to ruin everything we agreed on.

Speechless. Speechless was one way to describe how I felt about tonight, and it hadn't even started yet.

Chapter Eighteen

Lyla

We were about two hours into our evening at The Attic, and I was having *a time*.

Charlie and I had sampled all three Shots of the Month, and I was shocked when Deacon ordered two more rounds of the Fire Green Apple. This offer came from a guy who was practically shoving water in my face back at the apartment, but his boyish grin told me he was having a good time. Our last conversation still lingered between us.

A gorgeous guy I'm not allowed to sleep with had just said "atta girl" while making direct eye contact and wearing that sexy smirk he probably didn't even know he had. At this point, the sex gods were practically dangling a good time in front of me. I had to figure out where Jake was tonight. I needed to get laid to ensure everything between Deacon and me stayed platonic.

I felt like one of those sad and lonely tigers at the zoo that had their food prepared for them. If something *alive* ever wandered in there, eventually, that cat would pounce. For context, I was the tiger, and Deacon was the item I was dying to pounce on. God, if I weren't drunk before the two rounds of shots Deacon bought, I would be soon.

I leaned across the counter and ordered water from the bartender. She quickly placed a plastic cup in front of me, and I took a hefty sip. Deacon motioned for me to follow him, and when I held my arm limply in front of me, he grabbed my hand and led us to the empty pool table in the back of the bar.

"Should I be doing something right now?" I asked once we were alone.

He shook his head, and just when I thought he would drop my hand, he gripped it tighter. "I have a favor to ask you."

I stirred my drink with my straw as Deacon lowered his mouth to my ear. His breath grazed my neck, and I halted my next sip. The last thing I wanted was to spit a mouthful of water onto his already tight shirt.

"Cassie is out on the deck, and—" He drew back and ran his hand through his hair. I raised my eyebrows and gestured for him to continue. He was hesitating, and we were way past the point of beating around the bush.

I cupped his chin. "Spit it out, Deac."

He flashed me a smile that threatened to make my knees buckle. "Can I kiss you?"

I made it look like I was about to say something snarky to his adorable request. My mouth *needed* to be open. Suddenly, I couldn't get enough air into my chest. Could he *kiss* me?

"I was being serious when I said I never want to make you uncomfortable. If Cassie saw me kiss you, then—"

"It's fine!" I exclaimed, placing a hand on his chest. Why was he always so *warm*? I let my fingers linger as I skimmed down to his hip. "I appreciate the heads-up. Couples kiss, right? Boyfriend-girlfriend shit?"

Deacon's gaze lingered on my mouth, and I felt the blood rush to my cheeks. I had never seen someone look so innocent and tempting at the same time. He ran his hand down the arm of my leather jacket and played with the zipper between his fingers. I expected him to lead me to the deck, but instead, he hooked his index finger through the belt loop on my jeans and pulled me closer.

His nose skimmed against mine, and even though my eyes were closed, I knew he was smiling. The music around us faded into a muffled stream of chaos, and the familiar scent of his cologne drifted into all of my remaining articles of common sense. He was waiting to see if I would back off or deflect. He was waiting for me to go the remainder of the way.

I guided his mouth to mine, and when he still didn't budge, I leaned forward just enough to catch his bottom lip between my teeth. He chuckled, and his hand slid over my jawline to cup the nape of my neck. The air hung heavy between us, our mouths close enough to touch if we wanted them to. There was a current I didn't want to turn off—a burst of electricity that allowed us to block out the real reason we were here. For that reason, I caved first. I stood on my tiptoes and kissed him. He leaned into me so I could relax, backing me into the wall I didn't know was behind me.

Kissing Deacon was different than kissing my usual guys of the month. Deacon's lips were soft, and he took his time to let his mouth move against mine instead of shoving his tongue past my teeth. I wasn't mad when he did, and even though this was the first time I had ever kissed this man, it felt like I had been doing it for weeks.

The familiar throbbing between my legs served as an unwanted reminder. My body was under the impression that I could kiss Deacon in the middle of a bar and get the usual after-hours session. My body and my desire were both sadly mistaken.

Deacon pulled away and rested his hands on either side of my head. I tossed the water cup I forgot I was holding in the trash to give myself time to recover. My breathing returned to normal, and I wiped the giddy grin from my face.

"Sorry." Deacon skimmed his thumb along my cheek. "I figured we could practice first. Boyfriend-girlfriend shit?"

I rolled my eyes. "Yeah. Boyfriend-girlfriend shit."

The epic kiss in front of Cassie couldn't have gone more perfect. When Deacon approached Cassie to deliver a casual, "Hi, how are you doing?" I did the usual drunken, "Oh my god, I was looking for you everywhere!" girlfriend squeal that only people in relationships appreciated.

There I was, being that bitch. All because Aaron Brooks had to be an asshole.

I went a little overboard with how loud I was when I ran into Deacon, and we were rewarded with a few cheers from the crowd and even scored a couple of "awws" from a few of the girls under the heaters. It was a quick and flirty hands-all-over-each-other kind of kiss, and from the smile on Deacon's face, it was exactly what he was aiming for.

Cassie rose from where she was sitting and went back inside the bar. A few of the people she was with followed her, and once the coast was clear, Deacon and I clinked our drinks. To the outside world, it was a couple laughing at some super secret inside joke, but to Deacon and I, it was a major step forward in our agreement.

"That was perfect." Deacon drained the rest of his Corona and tossed the bottle in a nearby trashcan. "Thank you."

"No need to thank me." I dragged my hand down his chest and realized the motion was becoming a habit. I traced the outline of his abs through his shirt and forced myself to stay on task. "Girlfriend shit."

"Do you want another beer?" Deacon asked, holding out his hand so Andre could give him a high-five as he passed us.

I handed him my empty. "Sure."

Deacon kissed my temple and followed Andre inside. I cursed myself for smiling at the gesture and pulled out my phone since I didn't know what to do with my hands. Jake's name was on my screen, and the distraction couldn't have arrived at a better time. I told him I was at The Attic and waited for him to respond before tucking my phone into my pocket.

As I regained composure from kissing my fake boyfriend and inviting Mr. September to the bar, Charlie came running toward me. She held onto my shoulder for support and laughed hysterically at something I clearly wasn't there for.

"I need to be on your level," I emphasized before grabbing her hand and dragging us to the bar. I found an empty spot next to Deacon, but the closer I got to the counter, I realized the place on the other side of him was taken. A cute girl with long black hair and perky boobs stood with her hand on her hip and a drink in the other. It was the tell-tale sign of a girl trying to sweet talk her way into a guy's evening, and the way she was batting those baby blues up at Deacon told me she was trying *hard*.

I motioned for the bartender. I ordered six shots of Fireball, and Charlie cheered when she heard my request. I was right on the cusp of getting drunk. Three more shots in my system would do the trick, giving me the boost I needed to have some dull conversation with Jake before we went back to his place. I wasn't trying to stay out much longer. This girlfriend shit could be *tiring*.

Charlie and I raced to see who could take our shots first, and when I slammed my third cup down, Charlie whined in defeat. She knocked her last cup back and pressed her hand to her mouth.

"You good?"

Charlie nodded, letting me know whatever nausea she experienced had passed. A guy in a BG cut-off stopped beside Charlie, smiling when he saw her drunken girl sway. The small suggestion to Charlie sent a wave of heat through my body, making me second-guess my choice to wear a leather jacket.

"I'm good," Charlie said, ignoring the passing guy's disgusting smile. "I'm going to run to the bathroom."

I took the opportunity to get outside as quickly as possible. When I expected a wave of cool air to hit, no refreshment came. I felt like my face was on fire, and I leaned against an empty table to take a few deep breaths. The music and chatter flowed from inside the bar, and my ears began to ring. My temples throbbed, and I became lightheaded to the point where I saw stars.

This was NOT happening right now.

The skin on my chest prickled when I noticed who stepped onto the deck. Jake and his roommates scanned the crowd, and I wasn't surprised when Jake found me right away. His blue eyes lit up, and his smile reached his eyes. He said something to his roommates, and even though he was getting closer, he seemed out of focus. I took in one last breath and threw on a fake smile.

"Hey!" Jake yelled over the music. "Everything okay? You look like you're ready to call it a night!"

His hand skimmed my face, and I leaned away from his touch. He smelled like whiskey and beer and bad decisions.

"Wanna get out of here?" Jake made a hitchhiker's thumb and pointed back inside. He reached for my hand, and his smile wavered when I didn't reach back. I *couldn't* reach back.

Why was this happening? This hadn't happened since June.

Jake took my hesitation as a yes and my silence as consent. His hand wrapped around mine, and he pulled me back inside. Normally, this was an action I didn't mind, especially since I invited him here. Jake knew what I was looking for when I told him where I was. Keep things casual. It was the easiest way not to lose yourself to someone else.

I waited for the nerves to subside, but they weren't going away. The crowd around us faded into blurred images, and I swore I caught a glimpse of Cassie as we rounded the dance floor.

This time felt different. Jake was pulling too hard. We were going too fast. I resisted his grip and retreated backward. His hands loosened immediately, and then I realized he wasn't pulling hard at all. He barely wrapped his fingers around mine.

I needed to find a bathroom—somewhere I could have a moment to get my shit together. It was loud, and the music kept getting louder. The familiar tingles shot down both my arms, and nausea filled my stomach.

I shuffled a few steps, moving further until I hit a wall. Only this wall had arms that wrapped loosely around my hips. There was a warm chest and the calming scent of cedarwood and lavender. I heard his voice, but I couldn't see past the fog. The belt around my ribcage tightened, forcing the air to come in heaves as I fell into his chest.

"Lyla, look at me." Deacon tipped my chin, and his eyes searched mine. His thumb brushed my cheekbone, and I felt his lips on my forehead.

Jake's voice muffled into the background. "Lyla, you coming?"

"Lyla, do you wanna go to another bar?" I heard Charlie ask. "Is she okay?"

"I'll take her back to my place," Deacon said. He lowered his voice and prompted me to look at him. "Can I take you back to my place?"

Unable to speak, I nodded. Deacon's hand fit naturally into mine, and he guided me out of the bar.

Being on the street and in the open air helped. As we approached the apartment, I waited for Deacon to say something . . . anything, given everything he had just witnessed. He probably thought I was one of those girls who didn't know how to handle their alcohol. That I just caused scenes wherever I went.

Deacon unlocked the door of his building and held it open for me to go inside. The silence continued between us as he set out a T-shirt and shorts for me to change into. I was afraid if I stood up again, I'd throw up, so I remained seated against his headboard.

He went into the kitchen and returned with water and some ibuprofen.

I took the bottle from his hand. "Alkaline water?"

"It's better for you," he insisted gently.

I took two ibuprofen and placed the water bottle on the end table. The last thing I remembered before falling asleep was Deacon reaching over me to turn off the light.

Chapter Nineteen

Deacon

It was one of those moments when I knew I was dreaming.

In the dream, my brothers, Drew and Dominic, were being pulled on innertubes from the back of my uncle's boat. We were at our family cabin in Michigan, and it was the last week of July. I was dreaming because when Drew fell off his tube and into the water, I heard a door slam shut instead of my dad's laugh.

I blinked a few times, unable to register anything in front of me because it was still dark outside. I rolled over and checked the time on my phone. It was a little after three.

"Lyla," I murmured, sticking my hand out behind me. I tapped the mattress, reaching further and further, expecting to touch her shoulder. Instead, all I felt were my bedsheets.

"Lyla?" I said, a little more urgent this time. Had she floated out of the room? I was usually a light sleeper.

I hopped out of bed, and when I opened my bedroom door, Lyla was coming out of the bathroom. She squinted as the hallway light popped on above us, and she tried to shield the glow with her arm.

"Jesus, Deacon," she whispered. "What are you doing?"

My shoulders relaxed. "I heard a door, and when you weren't in the bed—"

"I'm fine." She giggled. "I was just leaving."

Lyla crossed the living room and grabbed her purse from the back of the couch. There was no way in hell this girl was walking home at three in the morning.

"Leaving?" I followed close behind her. "What do you mean you're leaving?"

"Deacon, tonight went wonderfully. Cassie saw us as a happy couple. Hell, she even saw us leave together. Let's plan to get together on Tuesday for—"

"Lyla, it's three in the morning," I interrupted gently. "You're not walking home."

She scoffed. "Yes, I am."

I lept toward the door and placed my hand above the handle. Lyla eyed me as I pressed my weight against her only exit. We continued our stare-off for about a minute or two, but I knew when her eyebrows pulled together in the middle of her forehead that she wasn't going to let up.

She didn't have to let up. I could accommodate to fit the situation. I always did.

"Fine," I said, smirking. "Then I'm walking with you."

"*No*, you're not."

I snagged the keys from her hand, speaking over my shoulder as I walked back into my room. "Three paces behind you. You won't even know I'm there."

I threw on a hoodie and grabbed my hat. When I was close to the front door again, I handed Lyla her keys. She assessed my outfit change and let out a hollow laugh. Lyla was in for a rude awakening. I'd never avoid pissing her off because she wanted to do something that wasn't in her best interest. She wasn't walking home by herself at three in the morning. That was prime time for the bars to let out, and all it took was one creep to notice that she was alone.

"You're ridiculous," Lyla snapped. "I'm fine. I just don't want to stay the night here."

I shrugged. "No worries. Five paces back then."

"Deacon!"

I took a few steps toward her, and she took a step back. I pretended not to notice, and she crossed her arms over her chest. She was guarding something, and I worried I might have come on too strong. It looked like she was waiting for me to get angry—like I would blow up and yell back at her.

I took a deep breath and raised my hands in defeat. "If you need to pick a fight with me so you can leave, that's fine. I know you don't know me that well yet, but one thing you *should* know is I'm the type of guy who walks you home in the middle of the night. I'm the guy that makes sure you're okay even when you're pissed at him."

I opened the front door, and she hesitated, giving me one last chance to change my mind. When it was clear I wasn't budging, she rolled her bright green eyes and sighed. "Five paces back?"

I gestured for her to lead the way.

"Fine."

"Atta girl," I murmured, shutting the door at the same time so she wouldn't hear me. Without turning around, she stuck a middle finger in the air. Even with our dramatic exit, she heard me loud and clear.

Bowling Green came to life on the weekends after closing time. The bars let out, and everyone flooded fast food restaurants, local food joints, and nearby gas stations. Taco Bell had crowds circling the building, and Circle K became the hot spot for late-night cigarettes and snacks. The streets were loud and packed, and the way Lyla weaved across Wooster, I had to break into a jog to keep up.

"Could you just—" I grabbed her hand and guided her to the left to avoid a group of guys crossing the street.

We stopped before Manville Avenue, and she pulled her hand from mine. "Five paces back, Scott," she warned without looking at me.

I laughed and let her get a few steps ahead.

Manville was a side street and a straight shot to Falcon's Pointe. Lyla probably *could* walk the rest of the way by herself. We had passed the after-party craziness, and the chances of running into anyone moving forward were slim to none. But I was committed at this point, and the way Lyla was ignoring me was somehow making this fun. Was fun the right word?

The last time I walked a girl home was Cassie after she had too much to drink. She was upset with one of the girls she went out with and called me from the bar. I wasn't out with her and her friends, but I met her before she walked home. I didn't stay, and she didn't ask me to. I wondered if *that* should have been my first clue. Had her feelings started to shift for me back in *April*?

I pulled out my phone. Maybe Cassie updated her story, or maybe—

"What did you say?" Lyla asked over her shoulder.

I looked up, and she was still facing forward. "What?"

Lyla turned around and kept walking backward. She slowed her pace so I could catch up, and whatever anger she had back at the apartment was gone. She wore a mischievous grin when I tucked my phone back into my pocket.

I shook my head. "Nothing. So you're okay with three paces, huh?"

"Three paces is fine. If you do two, I might have to break into a run and try to lose you."

I smirked. "Please. That would require you to actually *run*."

"Believe it or not, I'm pretty fast. I just don't like to run for enjoyment."

"But running from someone on the street, that's a good enough reason?"

"I'm practical, Scott. Running away from a fake boyfriend who followed you home is much more newsworthy than running for personal enjoyment. Shit, that might clear up all of this Aaron Brooks nonsense. Make me some kind of empowered and independent woman instead of Stripper Pole Girl."

"Hey, that Stripper Pole Girl happens to be my girlfriend, remember?" I chuckled at her disgusted expression. Apparently, the G-word was worse than the B-word. "And speaking of Aaron Brooks, what's the next item you need from me?"

Her eyes narrowed. "What do you mean?"

"Tonight was a good move for *me*. Cassie saw us together, and we were happy. You let me kiss you. Now, what do *you* need from *me*?"

"'You *let me* kiss you,'" she echoed through a laugh. "You know you're the first guy who has ever *asked* if you could kiss me?"

Nothing about that surprised me. Lyla told me about her monthly trial periods with guys and how she never let anything go past bedroom benefits and casual conversation. Lyla was the girl who kept it at a good time, and most guys wouldn't budge at the opportunity to be with someone as gorgeous as her. She left no lines blurred.

"What's more boyfriend-girlfriend shit you could do until my dad asks about you again?"

It didn't take me long to think of the one thing I always did for Cassie. I had done it every week since I started dating her. "I could buy you flowers?" I offered.

Her eyebrows shot to the top of her forehead. "Flowers?" She said the word like I had just offered to buy her expired bread.

"Cassie loved flowers," I explained. "I always made sure she had flowers in her bedroom. It might hit a nerve if she sees me buying you flowers."

"Yes, sweet Deacon. You can buy me flowers."

"Don't call me *sweet* Deacon," I objected, even though I loved how it made her smile. "I'm not this helpless little animal you get to tug along."

"You're *literally* following me home. You're also the first guy to do *that*, too."

She spun back around so she was facing forward. I sped up to walk next to her, and she didn't seem to mind that I broke her three-paces rule.

"All those guys you—" I cleared my throat. "Let me rephrase."

She giggled at my attempt to save my next sentence from making me sound like an asshole.

"All of the fun you've had with guys—none of them ever walked you home?"

She scowled. "Please. Most of them don't even notice I leave."

"Not even the next morning?"

"I don't stay until the morning," she said, like I already should've known this information.

The thought of Lyla walking home all those times by herself irked me. Not only was Mr. September interfering with our plan, but he was also an asshole.

"So this wanting to leave tonight didn't have anything to do with—" I caught myself again. Maybe it was the lack of sleep that was causing me to have word vomit. What happened at The Attic wasn't my business. As her fake boyfriend, I should have moved on to a different topic of conversation. But as her *friend*, I decided to pull our line. It was a much safer option and something she couldn't fight me on. It was one of her stupid rules anyway.

"We don't lie, Lyla Brooks," I said softly.

Lyla stopped walking, and I knew she was thinking about what to tell me. Even though everything about this relationship was fake, I didn't see anything made up about our friendship. Lyla didn't have guy friends, but I might be the safest start she'd ever get. She wouldn't have to worry about me getting caught up in feelings that weren't there.

Chapter Twenty

Lyla

We don't lie, Lyla Brooks.

First, Deacon had the audacity to pull another "atta girl" on me, making that two in the same twelve-hour period. Now, he was pulling our line to talk about something I wasn't even sure how to talk about.

Our line. What the actual fuck was happening to me? I gestured for us to keep walking, and another gust of wind rippled through the trees on the street. While Bowling Green's campus was beautiful in the fall, it was also in the middle of nowhere, which meant that when it was windy, it was *windy.*

Suddenly, my leather jacket and jeans weren't cutting it. I picked up the pace, and Deacon followed my lead. All we had to do was cross the street, and we'd be at my apartment.

Deacon was waiting for me to speak. So, to buy some time, I crossed my arms and said, "We don't lie."

He was fighting a smile, and when he stripped off his hoodie and handed it to me, I had to remind myself what the original question was.

So this wanting to leave tonight, it didn't have anything to do with—

Oh, that's right. My episodes that happened every now and then when I was feeling overwhelmed. Maybe overwhelmed wasn't the right word. I hadn't felt overwhelmed when Jake grabbed my hand. It was like someone strapped a belt around my chest and pulled. I couldn't explain it. I just had to escape the scene, and somehow, Deacon knew that.

I stared at his hoodie, and he shook it in front of my chest. "Take it," he said. "You've been pretending you're not cold for about ten houses now."

I rolled my eyes and took his offer. I'm sure my loose curls looked horrible after being laid on and thrown back into the dewy morning air. I pulled the hood over my head. "It happens sometimes."

He nodded. "Okay."

"Okay?" I repeated, surprised to see him so accepting of my simple response.

Deacon threw his arms out in front of him. "What? You told me I'm not allowed to ask about your past. You know these rules sometimes get in the way of each other."

"Touché. I like the new line, by the way." We approached the last road we needed to cross, and Deacon slipped his fingers through mine. He looked both ways and then once more at me. "Atta girl," I said before I dragged him across the street.

He dragged his teeth across his bottom lip, trying to hold back a smile. "I wasn't sure about that one."

"Definitely hot boyfriend shit. Did you talk to Cassie that way?" I was officially intrigued. I was *dying* to get to a level where I could talk about sex with Deacon.

He was hot and undeniably sweet.

He was hot and seemed sure of himself.

He was fucking *hot*, and I just wanted a preview—a snippet of what Deacon Scott was like in the bedroom.

He took too long to answer, so I bumped his elbow with mine. "Is that a yes?"

Deacon let go of my hand and pulled out his phone.

"Do you have *recordings*?" I exclaimed.

He laughed, tucking his phone back into his pocket. "No! I was making sure my brother got in okay. But to answer your question . . . I did sometimes. It just depended on the mood for the night."

"What kinds of moods were there?"

Deacon shrugged, and my cheeks hurt from smiling. "I don't know, Lyla. I guess the mood depended on if Cassie still needed to get off."

Damn. Now, why did that sound incredibly sexy leaving his mouth?

"I had a hunch you were a pleaser." I squeezed his forearm, and when he glanced up at the sky, I knew he agreed with my statement. "Deacon, I have to say. I am *really* struggling to see the reason for the breakup here."

"I always make sure whoever I'm with is taken care of. What's the fun of one-sided sex?"

"You just said a mouthful there, sweetie. Have you *met* half of the guys on this campus? Or any college campus *ever*?"

We approached the staircase leading up to my apartment and slowed our pace. Deacon licked his lips, and a playful light appeared in his eyes. "My turn to ask you a question."

I looked right past his innocent expression.

"All of your fun. All of the guys." He cocked his head while he thought of what to say next. "You can say—with confidence—that your satisfaction rate is . . . let's say eighty percent."

"You lost me at numbers, Scott."

"Just answer the question."

"It's three-thirty in the morning, and I'm discussing percentages with you. I don't really know how to answer that," I argued.

"Pick the last ten guys you've slept with," Deacon urged, holding up ten fingers.

Fortunately, my calendar method made it pretty simple to retrace my history. I crossed my arms and played into his demonstration. "Okay. Done."

"Now, with all of those guys, how many times did you get off?" Deacon ticked his fingers down one by one the longer I took to answer.

I laughed and shoved his hands. "It's sex, okay? It has to be worth it to keep them around."

I turned to head up the stairs, and Deacon reached for my hand. I wasn't sure if the familiar scent of cedarwood and lavender had been in front of me for the last few minutes because I was wearing his hoodie or if I just noticed it because his face was dangerously close to mine.

He tilted my chin with his hand and smiled down at me. "Baby, there's a difference between having sex and being satisfied."

If there was a moment when I thought my stomach could fall out my ass, it was this one. My breath caught in my throat, and suddenly, every witty response I had a moment ago flittered away with the butterflies in my stomach. Alarm bells sounded in my ears. Red flags were waving at such a concerning speed to keep the fucking butterflies out of the picture. My body was betraying me, and it was bullshit.

Deacon's sexy smirk returned. He skimmed his thumb across my cheek, cupping the back of my head through his hoodie and placing his mouth on my forehead. "Goodnight, Lyla Brooks."

He backed away slowly and started walking across the parking lot. I forced my mouth to close before I opened it again to respond. "Wait."

Deacon looked over his shoulder, surprised to see me standing where he left me.

What was I doing? I didn't share beds with guys. Was I really about to offer my fake boyfriend a spot on my *couch*? I couldn't have my roommates walk out to my knight-in-shining-armor boyfriend on the couch. That shit wouldn't fly.

I *did* have the futon in my bedroom. That was always an option.

I gestured to the stairs behind me. "Did you wanna just stay here?"

Deacon didn't ask questions. He didn't comment or shoot me a look that read, "This bitch is crazy."

Instead, he walked back over to me, wearing a soft smile. "Yeah, Lyla. I can just stay here."

Chapter Twenty-One

Deacon

Two weeks passed since that night at The Attic, and I couldn't believe it was almost October. During those two weeks, Lyla and I fell into a routine that seemed to work for both of us.

I met Lyla on campus every morning before her first class. Sometimes, I brought her a drink or a donut from Dunkin. The mornings I was empty-handed, I greeted her with a charming smile and a kiss on the forehead. She never looked completely awake when she arrived and always offered me the same sleepy smile. Regardless of how she appeared, it was adorable, and I was always happy to see her.

Lyla spent Mondays and Wednesdays at my place. Ordering food started getting expensive, so we decided to try cooking together. Lyla's recipes were simple since she could only make chicken and pasta, but she loved that my skills were a little more advanced. I'd tell her what I could make based on what I had in the fridge, and she'd pour over the possibilities. I was a good cook as long as I had the right ingredients, and seeing a girl who wasn't ashamed to eat was incredibly attractive.

After dinner, we'd put on a movie and let it play in the background while we did schoolwork. It was nice just sitting in silence together. It had been a while since I had someone I could just *be* with.

We followed the same agenda at her place on Tuesdays and Thursdays. If I didn't feel like heading back to my place, I crashed on the futon in her room. The sleeping arrangements never bothered me since I had no expectations. I didn't mind sharing a bed with Lyla and always made it clear that she could stay at my place if she wanted to. She never did, and I never prompted her with questions to try and figure out why. I'd do whatever made her comfortable, and this arrangement seemed to fit her rules.

Lyla's mom would call and FaceTime her at least two nights a week. I became a regular guest appearance, and after a few conversations with Jane Nichols, I was pretty sure she liked me. She insisted I call her Jane instead of Ms. Nichols, and she always asked Lyla if I was there with her. We'd talk about her current work in progress and if she had any good book recommendations. She was easy to talk to and always busy doing something in the background during our conversation. I understood why Lyla was so good at multitasking.

Lyla had her mom's smile and smooth, olive skin tone. They had the same laugh and a tiny freckle near the corner of their lip. I had seen pictures of Aaron Brooks a few times, but Lyla's mom could be her twin.

"His eyes," Lyla told me one night during dinner. "Aaron also has green eyes. But other than that, we have nothing in common."

Lyla avoided talking about her dad, and I understood the complicated relationship factor. My instinct to plan things out was starting to invade my headspace, and I felt completely unprepared to meet him in two months. If I had to convince this man that I was dating his daughter, I'd need more to go off of. I just had to wait for Lyla to open up about a topic she tried to forget existed in the first place.

After I spent the last few weeks focused on Lyla's side of the family, I completely forgot my parents were visiting this morning. I made sure I was back at my apartment around eight to be ready for breakfast when they arrived.

When I left Lyla's room this morning, she was still asleep. We hit a few bars last night, and while I took it easy, she insisted on a few fishbowl races at Nate & Wally's. I texted her to let her know I had to leave early but didn't mention it was to meet my parents. I didn't want to cross that bridge until we had to.

Lyla's parents were involved with her side of the plan, but mine weren't. Once we sat down for breakfast, it didn't take long for my mom to ask if I had any new *friends* lately. Telling her I was seeing someone felt pretty damn good, and eliminating the dark cloud that followed me brought light back to the conversation.

"Seeing someone?" Dad placed his glass of orange juice on the table and leaned forward. "What does that mean?"

Mom smacked him playfully on the arm. "Howard, you know what that means."

"I wanna hear him say it!" He shrugged while Mom and I laughed. "Is this a new girl, or is this a . . . I don't know a—"

"Lyla's my girlfriend," I said before I had to hear him go any further. My parents were pretty cool about what I did behind closed doors—but having an actual conversation about sex?

I might as well throw up my French toast and sweet potato fries all over our table.

Mom placed her hand over mine. "Well, we can't wait to meet her."

While Mom was giddy at the thought of me being with someone again, Dad continued prompting me for information. "Why didn't we meet her today?"

"We just started dating like a month ago. I didn't want to rush things, you know?" Geez. Had it only been a month? It felt like Lyla asked about my Freshman to Junior Year with C tote last weekend.

He approved of my answer and dropped the subject. We spent the rest of the morning discussing my schedule and the around-the-house projects they were working on now that it was just them at home. While I loved being back at Bowling Green, I missed our family house in Michigan. As much as the churchgoers continued to express their concern for me being single again, it was weird being somewhere else other than church on a Sunday with my parents. I didn't do well with change. Anything I could do to plan for possible outcomes and situations helped put my mind at ease.

After breakfast, we drove to Kroger so Mom could do a grocery haul for me and the guys. My dad wasn't a massive help since my mom did all of the cooking at home, but he showed support by throwing random cleaning objects into the cart and even insisted on a new set of mixing bowls.

I grabbed a package of Starburst on our way to the register. Dad saw my last-minute addition and eyed me suspiciously. "Since when do you eat candy?"

"Lyla likes them. I'm seeing her later today."

"What's she going to school for?"

I replayed our Brooks Books conversation and smiled. "Business and English literature. She wants to open a bookstore in Chicago."

"Chicago isn't *super* far from Michigan," Mom hinted. Being discreet wasn't her strong suit.

I went to work unloading the cart. Lyla wouldn't need to be close to Michigan because this would all end in a few months. I wasn't sure how my parents would react when I told them I was back with Cassie. They never indicated that they disliked her when we were dating, but it never seemed like they were super impressed with her. Cassie was always friendly to them, but their favorite thing about her was that she made me happy. I guess I thought there would be a bigger spark between my parents and the girl I wanted to spend my life with.

"Did Drew call you yesterday?" Mom asked as we loaded up her car with grocery bags.

"No. Why?"

"He mentioned he was coming to see you for Homecoming Weekend!" She grinned.

"That's *next* weekend."

"Is it?" She shrugged and slid into the passenger seat. "Well, he'll have to tell us what he thinks of Lyla."

"I'm not sure if we want to place our first impression with Drew," Dad murmured.

"Howard!" Mom smacked his arm, and they laughed.

I forced a hearty chuckle as I tried not to panic. The person who wanted me to move on from Cassie more than anything was going to meet Lyla—my fake girlfriend helping me get Cassie back. This wasn't part of my plan. I couldn't ignore Lyla for Homecoming Weekend. It was one of the most popular events on campus. Telling my parents about Lyla was one thing, but introducing her to Drew was another.

Why was it always *something*? I looked up at the sky. Dark clouds began to roll in, and a low rumble of thunder answered my question. Regardless of how it went, at least someone was getting a laugh out of it.

Chapter Twenty-Two

Lyla

IT HAD BEEN EXACTLY one month and four days since I spoke to Aaron Brooks over the phone. When I woke up to an empty futon and a missed call from Daddy Dearest, I tried not to seem too disappointed.

About the phone call, that was. *Not* the empty futon.

I had a text from Deacon that said he had to head out early, and since I took Sunday mornings as an opportunity to wake up around noon, I wasn't bothered by his quiet exit. I didn't mind when Deacon spent the night. It was nice having the company, and it seemed like he was comfortable here. He even talked with Michelle about the different kinds of carpet cleaner she bought for the living room, and he returned the next day. I considered that a win for our relationship status.

Once positioned in my usual Sunday spot on the couch in the living room, I called my dad back.

"Good morning, Lyla. Rough night?"

"What makes you say that?" I said sarcastically. Thank God the man didn't know how to use FaceTime. He wouldn't appreciate my messy bun and no bra combo.

He ignored my question. "I wanted to see if you and your—has that boy broken up with you yet?"

I rolled my eyes and sipped my tea. "No, Dad. I'm still dating Deacon."

"Right. Well, I'd like you guys to come to my corporate Halloween party in Salem. My marketing team went all out this year with a location, and it would be a good opportunity for us to catch up."

It sounded like an opportunity, alright. It sounded like a chance to photograph Aaron Brooks with his daughter in a well-known Halloween location.

Corporate Halloween party? What a fucking snooze fest. I would never give up a Halloween weekend in BG.

"Dad, we can't just fly to Massachusetts for an entire weekend. Midterms are coming up, and Deacon has been studying like crazy—"

"What is he studying?"

The curiosity in his voice caught me off guard. "He wants to be a pediatric surgeon."

"Hmm. Well, Thanksgiving it is, then. I'll figure out a place for us to have dinner."

It wasn't a long conversation, but I'd mark it as successful. We'd talked for five minutes, and he hadn't even insulted me.

I tossed my phone on the couch just as Charlie entered the kitchen. She scanned the living room. "Where's Deacon?"

"He had to run out this morning for something." I closed my eyes and pinched the bridge of my nose. I didn't feel an ounce hungover, and it took one phone call to prompt a rocking headache. I padded across the room and searched the cabinet for ibuprofen. I popped three pills into my mouth and took another sip of tea.

"Is he coming back later? We need to finish that game. If he thinks he's winning because he purchased the entire pink and orange row, he's mistaken."

"I'm sure Deacon will honor his Monopoly commitment," I assured her.

Somehow, the board game responsible for causing family feuds ended up being a weekly activity between Deacon and my roommates. After I lost the first two rounds to Deacon's business strategy, I politely bowed out of the chaos. It wounded my ego to know I was months away from my business venture, and I kept getting my ass kicked by a metallic top hat.

Charlie, however, was one of the most competitive people I knew when it came to games, and she wasn't about to let Deacon win for the third time in a row.

"He said in his text this morning that he would be back"—I leaned forward, checking the time on the stove—"soon, actually."

Charlie grabbed her keys off the hook by the door and hoisted her gym bag over her shoulder. "I'll be back in an hour or so, and Michelle will be back at two. Don't let him leave until we finish our game."

"Michelle is in on this game, too?"

"We needed a third player since you decided to be a buzzkill." She shrugged her shoulders. "He let her talk to him about *cleaning supplies*, Lyla. I'm pretty sure Michelle would bungee jump off of the balcony if Deacon asked her to."

I shook my head and smiled. "Nah. He's too nice. He'd never let her jump."

Charlie laughed on her way out the door, and before it closed, I heard a short exchange in the stairway and a voice that warmed my chest. Or was it the tea? I decided to go with the tea.

Downright Delightful Deacon smiled when he saw me, but his face fell when he looked past me and into the living room. I followed his gaze to the flowers in the middle of the end table. Well, the *remains* of the flowers on the end table.

On the bright side, the vase was still in fantastic condition. The purple glass looked beautiful when the sun hit in the morning.

Every Monday, Deacon showed up to campus with roses, and every Monday, Cassie passed us on her way to the Life Sciences building. It was a tiny gesture, but it was working. Deacon mentioned that Cassie ran into him in The Union one morning and commented on how happy he looked.

"To be fair, you asked if you could *buy* me flowers," I argued. "Nothing was said about me taking care of them."

Deacon shut the door behind him and rolled his eyes. "It's water, Lyla. You have to change the water in the middle of the week, and that's it!"

"Okay, okay." I held out my hand for the bag he was holding. "What did you bring?"

"Some dip my mom made." He leaned his elbows on the counter and watched me rifle through the goodies.

I held up a glass container and read the tape. I shouldn't have been surprised by the label. When I helped Deacon move his things, all of his totes had some sort of description on them.

"Your mom sent you brisket dip?" I pulled out a box of crackers and smiled when I saw the yellow and pink packaging. "And Starburst?"

"The candy is for you, and my mom made the dip like thirty minutes ago."

I popped a cherry Starburst in my mouth and chewed. If his mom made the dip this morning, and his parents were from Michigan, that meant—

"My parents came for breakfast this morning," he said, reading my expression. His mouth curved into an adorable half-smile I was beginning to enjoy, and he helped himself to some candy. "They know about you, though. I told them I've been dating this bombshell named Lyla for a month."

"Holy shit, has it been a month?" I added another Starburst wrapper to the hill forming in front of me on the counter. "I have an Aaron Brooks update for you."

Deacon raised his eyebrows, eager to hear what I had to say next. I rarely mentioned the man responsible for putting me in this position in the first place. It was like announcing the Super Bowl halftime show. What did good ol' Aaron Brooks have to say today?

I prepared myself so I wouldn't laugh through the announcement. "We were invited to his corporate Halloween party in Salem."

Deacon scrunched up his face. "Salem?"

"Don't worry. I politely declined the invitation."

"What a shame," he said sarcastically. "Have you thought about Halloween yet? Are we . . ."

"Deacon Scott, if you are threatening to strip me of my one chance to do a couples costume—"

"No!" he exclaimed. "I just didn't know if you already had some ideas. Cassie always picked our costumes, so I never had to plan them."

I rested my hand on his and gave him a tap of reassurance. "Don't worry, sweetheart. I'll come up with something fun."

He squeezed my hand and reached behind him to grab water from the fridge. "I have an update for you, too, actually." He sounded nervous, which meant I'd have to provide follow-up questions.

"Update about . . . what, exactly?"

Deacon blew out an exaggerated breath and smiled down at the counter. "My brother Drew is coming up next weekend for homecoming. He's gonna wanna meet you, and I wanted to make sure you're cool to hang out with me all weekend?"

His voice went up an octave on the last part of the question. I wasn't sure why he was making this question so difficult to ask.

"That's fine, Deac. We're together most of the weekend anyway. Between going out and pregaming, we really only spend Saturday morning apart."

"I know, but we're both used to having some off-screen time."

I gestured to the empty room around us. "Is this off-screen time?" He sighed, and when he didn't respond right away, I knew there was more. "Is there something else?"

He ran his hand over his jawline, bringing attention to the scruff he forgot to shave last weekend. I didn't mind it. Deacon without scruff was hot, but Deacon *with* scruff was a bonus.

"Drew will think it's weird if I'm walking you home after a night out instead of you just staying over," he said with a nervous grin. "Do you think we could stay at my place next weekend? You don't have to answer right now, and it's okay if you don't want to."

I understood his cautious approach. If I took too long to answer, Deacon would back out of a request that shouldn't be hard to ask for. He stayed here all the time. I was surprised that Nathan or Andre hadn't asked about me staying over before. Unless they had, and Deacon wasn't saying anything to me about it.

I expected to feel a familiar tightening in my chest or the tingling that ran up and down my arms. I waited a few more seconds, but nothing came. I shrugged to convince him that his question was no big deal. "Yeah, that's fine."

He leaned across the counter and held my gaze. "Are you sure? We don't lie."

"I know we don't, and I'm not. It's fine, I promise. Now bring all this stuff to the coffee table because once Charlie gets home, she's coming for you in Monopoly."

Deacon rubbed his hands together before grabbing the dip and crackers. He kissed the top of my head as he passed me, and I turned around just in time to see Keira coming down the hallway.

I had to give it to Deacon. He was on top of shit when it came to being on-screen.

Chapter Twenty-Three

Deacon

When Drew rolled up to my apartment on Friday afternoon, I tried to explain to him that Kroger would be a shitshow. The aisles flooded with locals and students who were doing last-minute shopping. I *hated* including myself in the second category. If we had stuck to my plan, we would've settled for beer and wine from a gas station tonight and brought in the hard liquor tomorrow.

"Should we get two bottles of Jack or three?" Drew scanned the whiskey section and picked up a bottle of Crown Royal. "Or should we get two bottles of this?"

"Jesus, Drew, you really think we'll need that for the whole weekend?" My phone vibrated in the back pocket of my jeans. "Get what you're getting and meet me at the register. Lyla's calling me."

"Lyla's calling me," he teased as I left the liquor section.

Once the door closed behind me, I answered the phone. "Hey, baby."

Nice off-screen moment, Deacon. No one was around, and I was still throwing out pet names.

"Hey, do you have a second?" She was whispering, which meant this call concerned our agreement, and her roommates were home.

"Yeah, what's up?"

"We never talked about what a full weekend together looks like. You're not gonna, like, follow me into the bathroom or anything, are you? Try to sneak a peek while I'm in the shower? Get touchy in your sleep? When I change, are you gonna—"

"Lyla, hold up." I laughed, holding up my hand even though she wasn't in front of me. I didn't take her questions personally. Lyla made it clear she never stayed the night anywhere, and I wanted to make sure she wasn't doing something she didn't want to do. "I've stayed at your place plenty of times. Have I *ever* done any of those things?"

"But you've never stayed the entire weekend! Like, what should I wear to sleep in? When I shower, are you just gonna come in, brush your teeth, and act like you do it all the time? Am I going to have to watch out for you?"

"Watch out for me? Lyla, I'm not a serial killer. Wear whatever you want and pack whatever you want."

She chuckled softly into the phone. "Now that I'm saying this out loud, I realize these are stupid questions. I'm sorry I called. Go back to whatever you were doing."

"First of all, don't ever apologize for calling me. Second, they're not stupid. And third, we don't lie. If you don't want to stay tonight, that's totally fine. All you have to do is tell me."

"No, really, I'm fine." She sounded more like herself. "Honestly, talking with you helped."

I smiled at the last part of her sentence. The bell above the liquor store rang behind me, and Drew strolled out with two giant paper bags.

"Still on the phone, huh?" A mischievous grin spread across his face, and he shouted into the phone, "Hi, Lyla!"

She giggled. "Who was that?"

I shoved Drew out of the way, and he veered off as we passed the chip aisle. "Drew. We're at Kroger getting stuff for this weekend. Did you need anything?"

"Nah. Charlie and I will stop at a gas station on our way over. We should be there around seven."

"Don't forget a suit for tomorrow. And tell the girls they need to have their own pool if they want to get wet."

"There is so much happening with that sentence." She laughed. "*The girls*? Is that who my roommates are to you now?"

I shrugged. "They're the girls!"

"Who all want to get wet, apparently? I don't know when you picked up this talent of making everything sound dirty, but I'm not mad about it. I'll make sure *the girls* remember to bring their pools tomorrow."

I smirked, wishing she was in front of me. "Atta girl."

Lyla and Charlie arrived later that night, and I wanted to get the introductions out of the way. Drew knew Lyla by name but had no idea what she looked like. Part of this was because we didn't have many pictures together, which I needed to bring up to her later. Cassie stalked Instagram like it was her profession, and our lack of photos wasn't necessarily a good look.

Lyla walked in looking amazing like she always did. Her hair was down and curled, and she wore a white top that rested just above her belly button and jeans that hugged her curves. She carried a gray leather jacket, and when she scanned the room looking for me, I made sure she wasn't looking long.

One thing I didn't mind during this whole fake relationship was kissing Lyla Brooks. I missed kissing Cassie, but kissing Lyla sent a spark through my nervous system. It was like taking a shot of espresso right before a road trip. It gave you confidence and made you feel prepared for the long road ahead.

"Can I?" I asked once I got closer.

"Yeah," she said like I didn't even need to. I always would, but she knew exactly what I was talking about.

I cupped her chin and angled her mouth to mine. She smiled right before I kissed her, and when she let my tongue slide past hers, I pressed my free hand against the wall behind her to steady myself. It was slow, and we took our time. It was the kind of kiss new couples had when they went an entire day without seeing each other.

Lyla pressed her lips together in a satisfied smirk. "Top-tier, Deacon Scott."

I smiled. "Top-tier what?"

"Boyfriend-girlfriend shit."

I shook my head, kissing her one last time before standing up straight. I turned to lead Lyla over to Drew, but he had already beaten me to it. He could never wait for anything when we were growing up either.

"Lyla Brooks." Drew smiled, holding his hand out to shake hers. "I'm honored."

Lyla shook his hand. "You must be Drew. I was excited when Deacon said you were coming up!"

She reached behind her, and right before she swung her duffle over her shoulder, I grabbed the strap.

"I'll take that, baby." I pulled the bag onto my shoulder and gestured toward the pong table. "Go show Drew how you kick ass at pong. I talked a big game, so don't make me look bad."

"Hell yeah! I'll get us the next round." Drew sped over to Nathan. I could throw Drew into a room full of nuns, and he would have everyone laughing at an inappropriate sex joke. He met Nathan a few hours ago, and it looked like they had been friends for years.

Lyla handed me her jacket. "Can you take this too?"

I tucked the jacket under my arm and caught her hand before she could walk away.

Her mouth curved into a mischievous grin, and she studied me carefully. "What?"

"Just making sure you're good, that's all. I wasn't sure if there would be a bag or not." I smiled when she rolled her eyes. I didn't even know who Lyla Brooks was a month and two weeks ago. Now, I couldn't help but smile when she was in front of me.

"I'm good, Deacon. I promise. Now be a good boyfriend and get me a drink from the fridge so I can kick some ass with your brother."

"A *good* boyfriend?" I challenged.

"Good boyfriends get rewarded, and I'm staying here tonight, remember?" Lyla winked and dropped my hand.

My lips parted as I watched her walk away. Maybe Lyla was right a few weeks ago. One of my favorite things about her was that she left me speechless.

Charlie's voice came from behind me. "I'm impressed by the way."

I turned around, and Lyla's performance made sense. She never missed an on-screen moment. I cleared my throat. "What do you mean?"

"I've known Lyla since freshman year, and she's never stayed overnight somewhere."

Since Charlie wasn't offering a reason as to *why* Lyla never stayed anywhere, I moved forward with the conversation. "I told her she could change her mind. I have no problem walking her home if that's what she wants to do."

Charlie shrugged. "I threw some extra clothes in her bag so I can stay here too."

"Andre?" I suggested playfully.

Charlie peered over to where Lyla and Drew stood at the table. "Either him or your brother."

My lips pressed into a hard line.

She shrugged unapologetically. "He's pretty."

The nerves began to settle in my stomach, and I left the party to put Lyla's stuff in my room. I wasn't nervous because Lyla was staying over. I liked that I made her comfortable enough to stay. I was nervous because as much as I missed Cassie, I was excited that the girl laughing with my brother in the living room had *agreed* to stay over.

I wasn't officially breaking our rules, but wanting to spend time with Lyla was probably in the fine print somewhere.

CHAPTER TWENTY-FOUR

Lyla

WITHOUT THE USUAL HELP from Charlie, I scanned the options around me for Mr. October. I usually had two or three individuals I could test drive before completely tossing them out of the running, but tonight, I was struggling. Maybe it was because I was officially on a solo mission. Charlie couldn't know I was looking for Mr. October while I was dating Deacon. It would ruin all of the work we put into our plan.

We ran into Cassie twice during our night out. The first encounter was quick. She was walking out of Brathaus as we were walking in. She offered Deacon a shy smile, and I played the role of the girlfriend who had no idea she was walking by her boyfriend's ex.

The second encounter at The Attic went a little differently. Cassie approached Deacon while he was on the deck with Drew, and I played the role of the girlfriend who was happy to see her boyfriend talking to someone he knew. There were some playful touches between them, but when Drew walked away with a dramatic eye roll that neither Deacon nor Cassie paid attention to, I looked away and laughed. Clearly, Drew wasn't the biggest fan of the girl who broke his brother's heart in front of a coffee shop.

Deacon showed Drew as many bars as we could fit into the evening, and by the time we were ready to walk back to Deacon's apartment, I was riding a good buzz. I had my fair share of drinks and never denied Drew his request for a shot, but for the most part, I stuck to one beer per bar. It was a different way to end the night, but I didn't mind. We would be day drinking tomorrow and going out again tomorrow night. I considered it an exercise to train for a marathon and not a sprint.

By the time we reached the corner of Main, Andre had persuaded Charlie to go back to our place for the night. Deacon grabbed my hand and led Drew and me to Taco Bell where we got a giant bag of soft tacos and a few orders of Cheesy Fiesta Potatoes. It was a quick walk home, and it would've been faster if Deacon hadn't looked back every two minutes to make sure Drew was still behind us.

"He wanders," Deacon explained while he held open his front door.

I stepped into the living room and scanned the mess left behind by the pregaming festivities.

"Lyla, stop hogging all the tacos, girl," Drew teased, plucking the bag from my hands.

Drew resembled Deacon in many ways—smooth brown skin, light brown eyes, and a short, well-kept fade, but their personalities couldn't have been more different. Drew was loud, energetic, and carried a carefree younger brother energy. Deacon took his time warming up to people and stuck to a linear process when doing things.

When I first met Deacon, I thought it was strange that someone so pretty could be so cautious around women. Deacon was a rare jewel on campus. Most guys threw themselves on top of the pile, waiting to be picked up and handled without caring about the consequences. With Deacon, you had to dig a little bit.

A hand slid over my exposed hip, and the familiar scent of cedarwood and lavender accompanied the arm wrapped around my shoulders. I fell into his warm chest and rested my hand on his forearm.

"Did you eat?" Deacon murmured in my ear.

I giggled when his breath trailed along my neck. "Yes. I ate while you and Drew talked about the Michigan and Ohio State game."

"It's a big deal, sweetheart." He released my shoulders, and my back felt bare. "You good out here, man? Nathan might wander back, but I think he went home with that girl from The Attic."

Drew swallowed a mouthful of potatoes and nodded. "I might actually meet up with someone."

"Who?" I asked, incredibly interested in how he found a prospect his first night on campus.

"This girl named Gia. She just texted me and asked if I wanted to hang out."

Deacon patted his brother's shoulder proudly. "Take my key by the door and text me if you stay there."

They smacked hands the way guys do, and Drew crossed the room to me. He placed his hands on my shoulders and lowered himself to my eye level. A giant smile spread across his face as he said, "It was a pleasure, Lyla. Can't wait for the pool party tomorrow."

I laughed at his excited expression before Drew grabbed Deacon's keys and walked out the front door.

"I was going to sleep out here so you can have my bed," Deacon said from the hall. "I put an extra blanket out in case—"

"What are you doing?" I shook my head. "Did we have a fight or something I don't know about?"

His eyes narrowed.

"Why else would you sleep out here? What if Nathan or Drew comes back?"

Deacon looked into his room and then looked back at me. "Are you sure?"

I nodded, feeling more at ease than I expected to. I wasn't sure exactly *what* to expect, but I knew everything would be fine if I was with Deacon. "Very sure."

Deacon's room was spotless, but I wasn't surprised. We usually hung around the living room whenever I came over during the week, but his room looked the same as when I helped him move. It was simple but very Deacon.

I pulled some clothes out of my duffle, planning to change in the bathroom. Deacon stood in the doorway.

"I'm gonna shower real quick, so you're good to change in here." His mouth curved into a boyish grin. "Unless you need to brush your teeth while I'm in there or something."

"Ha ha." I gestured to the bed. "What side do you sleep on?"

"Usually the left. Where you stayed last time was fine." He dipped back into the hall and closed the bathroom door.

Once I heard the water from the shower, I changed into my comfy clothes. I was *dying* to get out of my standing-only pants. They served their purpose, but the tacos I inhaled earlier put me over the edge.

I established a space on the right side of the bed and stared at the empty spot next to me. *Usually,* the left side? What the fuck did that mean? I didn't know anyone who switched sides of the bed. Maybe Deacon did have lingering traces of a serial killer after all.

Sometime between scrolling on Pinterest and deciding what to put on the TV, Deacon came in from the shower wearing a white T-shirt and red basketball shorts. He ran his towel over his head before tossing it in the hamper.

I looked him up and down as he searched for something on his desk. "What do you usually wear to bed?"

He looked at me and smiled. "Honestly? Just boxers."

"Sorry for all the extra layers," I teased, getting under his fluffy blue comforter. I plugged my phone into the charger and adjusted my pillow.

Had Deacon cleaned the sheets because he knew I was staying over? I pulled a dryer sheet from the inside of my pillowcase and hid my smile as I tucked it back in. I expected nothing less.

Deacon slid into the bed next to me, sending a wave of whatever delicious body wash he used directly in my direction. I'm sure he'd still smell that way when he woke up. Why did men's body wash last five years when I couldn't even get a good lotion to last an hour? Society must really want us to know that the men are bathing.

Deacon rested his hands behind his head. "Did you find something to put on?"

I focused on the Netflix options and ignored how the thin material of his shirt hugged his chest. Were there no baggy pieces of clothing in this man's closet? When I turned to ask him what he usually watched, I was equally distracted by how good his arms looked flexed against his pillow.

For all that was holy.

"Do you like *It's Always Sunny in Philadelphia?*" he asked.

I could tell he wanted me to say yes. "I've never seen it," I admitted.

He gasped and took the remote from my hand. I giggled at his obvious excitement and turned so I was facing him.

He clicked on another streaming service and started the first episode.

As the show began to play, I waited for the familiar pull at my chest. I waited for the tingling to shoot down my arms or the nausea to make a home in the lowest pit of my stomach. There were no stars or fogginess. There was no ringing in my ears.

There was nothing. I didn't know what to do with the silence. All I heard was the TV in the background, and I didn't feel pressured to fill the space. It didn't feel uncomfortable. Something about it felt warm, and while that would usually send me packing, I didn't mind it.

Deacon laughed at a line in the episode, and I relaxed into my pillow. The hearty sound repeated after an offensive comment about one of the characters, and soon, I was laughing too.

Deacon reached over and gently squeezed my forearm. It was a small gesture, but I knew the reason I felt at peace had everything to do with the downright delightful man beside me.

Chapter Twenty-Five

Deacon

It was four in the morning when I woke up to Lyla taking deep breaths next to me. She sat against the headboard, staring at the blank TV screen, and holding her knees to her chest.

I slowly lifted my body and reached around her to turn on the lamp. The soft glow gave me a better view of what was happening, and the stoic look on her face told me something was wrong.

"Lyla," I said, my voice just above a whisper. I rested my hand on her forearm and waited for her to speak. She blinked a few times like she was waking herself out of a daydream. I sat up beside her and rubbed her arm. "Breathe, sweetheart."

And there I went with the off-screen pet name.

In my defense, this situation was different. This wasn't a phone call at Kroger or a witty conversation Lyla loved to have when I was on my way to her house. I knew what this was. I had a hunch the first night we went to The Attic—when I felt her heartbeat against my chest and noticed the apprehensive look in her eyes.

Her breathing slowly returned to normal, and she slipped her fingers through mine, giving them a squeeze.

"Lyla—" I hesitated. My next question went against her rules, but I asked it anyway. "Lyla, how long have you had panic attacks?"

Her eyes darted up from my bedspread, and she held my gaze. I squeezed her fingers back, assuring her she could tell me if she wanted to.

She sighed and pinched the bridge of her nose, looking deflated. "They started when I was a freshman."

"A freshman here, at BG?"

Lyla leaned forward and nodded. She dropped my hand and crossed her legs, resting her elbows on her knees.

"Does anyone else know about them?" I prompted gently.

"I never had to say anything to anyone." She let out a nervous laugh and looked at the TV again. "I've always known how to . . . I don't know . . . make them go away? Kind of?"

A month and a half, and this was the second one I witnessed. I had no idea how many others there had been when I wasn't with her. It didn't seem like she was making *anything* go away, but I couldn't say that. It wasn't my place to say that. Right now, my job was to make sure she felt safe where she was.

Lyla looked at me with tired eyes. "How did you know there were others?"

A hard pull on my heartstrings made me fall back against my headboard. "We don't lie?"

The corner of her mouth lifted into a small smile. "We don't lie."

I wasn't sure if I wanted to open the door I tried so hard to keep closed. I didn't have to give her everything right now.

"I had panic attacks a few years ago," I admitted. "They lasted for about a year. What you're experiencing could be something different, but it just feels familiar, that's all."

"What made them go away?"

"Honestly"—I smiled sympathetically—"and you're going to hate this answer. There's no cure-all for this kind of stuff. For the panic attacks, it was time."

"Time," she repeated. "Well, fuck."

I chuckled. "I know that isn't helpful."

"It is, actually." I didn't notice she got closer until we were touching shoulders. "It's kind of wild, isn't it?"

Wild wasn't the word that came to mind. "What is?"

"We might have something in common." Her body shook against mine, and I knew she was laughing. "That's some boyfriend-girlfriend shit."

"If panic attacks are the boyfriend-girlfriend shit we have going for us, I don't think that's promising," I said, smiling at her dark humor.

"We have *plenty* of cute boyfriend-girlfriend shit to balance the real shit out."

"How do you feel now?" I rested my hand on her knee. She was warm, which was unusual for her. Lyla was always cold. "Do you want me to walk you home?"

She shook her head. "No, it's late. Like I said, this happens sometimes. It's not you."

"I know it's not me, sweetheart."

I slid out of bed and grabbed the remote off the floor. One of us must've kicked it off the comforter in our sleep. I turned the TV back on and hit play on the next episode of *It's Always Sunny in Philadelphia*. "Lights off or on?"

"I can turn them off." She clicked off the lamp and settled in next to me. "I have a weird request that I don't want you to take the wrong way."

I rolled on my side to look at her. "What's up?"

"It helped before—when you squeezed my hand. Do you think you could do that for a few minutes?"

I smirked just to mess with her. "If you want me to hold your hand, Brooks, all you have to do is ask."

"Shut up." She smacked me on the chest and extended her hand for me to take.

"It's the pressure, by the way," I explained, lacing my fingers with hers. "It brings your focus to something else when your mind can't slow down. You know, it might be more comfortable if you got a little closer to me."

She scooted closer and leaned up on her elbow. "If you want to lay with me, Scott, all you have to do is ask. You seem like the cuddling type. Is Cassie a cuddler?"

Cassie—the girl I wanted back. The girl I planned my future with. *That* Cassie.

Even in a baggy T-shirt, I could see the curves of Lyla's hips and the dip in her collarbone. It was the first time I thought to skim parts of her skin hidden underneath a material that would lift so easily. Her fingers were warm against mine, and I wondered if the rest of her ran this hot.

Lord almighty, answer the fucking question, Deacon.

"I'm a good cuddler. I wanted to make sure Cassie felt sexy even with her clothes on. It's a sensual feeling, though, being close to someone and not expecting anything. I didn't cuddle with the girls I slept with after Cassie—"

"WAIT!" She shot up, and her eyes went wide.

I bit my bottom lip to keep another obnoxious grin at bay. I knew the questions would pour out of her, and not a single part of me was mad about it. I could talk to Lyla Brooks for as long as she'd let me, and for the next two hours, that's exactly what I did.

Chapter Twenty-Six

Lyla

I lost count of how often I woke up hungover after a night out. However, this was the first time I woke up exhausted from talking and laughing with my fake boyfriend over *It's Always Sunny in Philadelphia*. It was one of those conversations that didn't have a pause button, and I had way too much fun probing him about his bedroom activities.

I woke up in the afternoon around one-thirty and was shocked to see Deacon asleep next to me. He usually started his day with a run and a cup of cheer. I shook him awake when people started showing up across the street for the Bring Your Own Pool Party. Deacon liked to be on time, even if it was just showing up to day drink.

Charlie and I sat comfortably in our inflatable pool, along with everyone else who showed up with a child-size summer toy.

"What do you think their neighbors think of this?" I skimmed my fingers along the water and sank deeper into the pool. It was a piping eighty-five degrees today, and I was starting to feel it. I took another sip of my piña colada, and when Charlie didn't say anything, I lifted my aviators and tried again. "Charlie?"

Her mouth hung open, and she held her giant pink sunglasses on the tip of her nose. She slowly turned to face me and smiled. "What did you say?"

Her poker face had always been terrible. I looked over in the direction of where she was staring.

"A little to the left," she said when I missed the mark.

Andre was standing next to the grill, shirtless, and with a beer in his hand. Tattoos covered his chest, and his shorts were tight around, well, everything.

I pursed my lips and disapproved of Charlie's behavior. "Close your mouth, Charlie. You get to ride that ride, remember?"

"But I've never ridden *that* ride."

Charlie *pointed*—right in the middle of a backyard barbeque—to a few bodies over. My mouth dropped, but for an entirely different reason than Charlie's.

Deacon was laughing with Nathan and Drew about something Drew had just said. The group burst into hysterics, and Drew smacked Deacon's shoulder. The only piece of clothing Deacon had on was his swimsuit, and it was the first time I had *ever* seen him without a shirt on.

Fireworks may have gone off above me. I no longer had to wonder what was under all those tight-ass shirts. It was as if someone took a chisel to his smooth brown skin and left no crumbs. I thought he was pretty before, but I went ahead and tossed that version in the trash.

"See what I mean?" Charlie smiled and pushed her sunglasses back up her face.

"Bitch." I laughed, splashing some water on her perfectly tanned legs. "That's Deacon."

"Oh honey, I know who it is. Anytime you want to ride swap, just let me know."

"He's my *boyfriend*."

Charlie shook her head. "It's still wild to hear you say that. Isn't your one-month anniversary coming up? Don't couples celebrate that shit?"

"We did celebrate last night," I lied. "We took a few pictures, stayed up—"

"Girl, I'm good. I don't need any more details. But feel free to share the photos!"

Maybe the celebration was a lie, but the pictures weren't. Deacon mentioned that we didn't have enough together and that a bi-weekly Instagram post wasn't enough. What the fuck did I know? I didn't know an appropriate posting schedule for couples.

Meanwhile, I was still salty that I didn't have a Mr. October yet. It had been a month since I slept with someone, and I was getting antsy.

Charlie and I laughed when her drink fell into the pool, drawing the attention of everyone around us. I leaned forward to grab a White Claw out of the cooler, and when I looked up, Deacon was staring at me.

The corners of his mouth dug into his cheeks, and he mouthed, "You good?"

"Yeah," I mouthed back with a smile.

These exchanges between us were cute, but they weren't going to cut it. Cassie was never in the audience, and we needed to start taking advantage of when we were in a space together. She'd seen us out at the bar multiple times, but Deacon always focused on the tiny things he thought would fuel her fire.

Deacon knew Cassie, but I knew women. It was time to step up Deacon's game. I agreed to be his girlfriend, but I would also be the best wingman he ever had.

After my third piña colada, I switched to water. I learned early in my drinking career that sunshine and swimming were a dangerous cocktail, but adding in liquor? That was a risky game to play.

We left the party around seven since everyone had to shower and get ready. By the time the guys cycled through Nathan's bathroom, I had just finished a full body shave in Deacon's. Nothing made me feel more prepared to tackle a mission than smooth skin and skimpy panties. Fortunately for Deacon, I was officially armed with both of them.

After my shower, I changed quickly so Deacon wasn't awkwardly hanging out in the hallway.

Cheers erupted in the living room as Deacon backed into his room and kept his eyes forward. "You good?"

"I'm good," I said, smoothing out my top.

Deacon's eyes zeroed in on my chest, and I redirected his gaze with my hand. "Eyes up here, Deac."

Deacon licked the center of his top lip. "You've got a lot of—" He pointed to his chest, and his puzzled expression grew more intense.

"They're boobs, Deacon. I assume Cassie had them? I'm aware that they're extra tonight, but I need them to be because I'm talking to her when we see her."

"*Her* as in *Cassie* her?"

"Who else—" I felt myself growing flustered with the lack of concentration on Deacon's part. "Yes, sweetheart. Cassie. Your ex?"

Deacon walked over to the dresser and pulled out a white shirt. He slipped off his shirt and tossed it into the hamper.

OKAY. So we're doing THAT now.

"Did she reach out to you or something?" Deacon asked with a furrowed brow. "Why are you planning to talk to her?"

"Do you have a black shirt?" I walked over to the dresser and scanned his options. I pulled out a plain black V-neck and shoved it into his chest. "Put this one on."

I was throwing him off with all my demands, but his mouth curved into a slight smile as he pulled his shirt over his head. He was enjoying this.

"What's in your head, Lyla?" he asked calmly. He patted the jeans he was already wearing and waited for my opinion.

"Those are fine," I stated, lowering my voice to make sure no one heard us. "I've been doing some thinking, and these little run-ins you're having with Cassie aren't going to be enough. I need to approach her and say something to pique her interest. Everyone knows the girl doesn't get officially jealous until there is talk about how happy the guy is. It will be even more annoying for her if it comes from me."

"And the black-on-black attire. That's supposed to help our case too?"

"Black is just the elite color option. Everything is better in black."

Deacon processed my game plan. "So you're just going to talk to her? I know it helps when she sees us together, and if you add in that outfit you have going on . . ."

"Yes, the way we look together *helps.*" I placed my hands on his shoulders and smiled. "You can't just rely on looks, Deac. Looks might land you a meeting or get you in the door, but confidence and personality are what sells. *That's* the shit that gets a girl to go home with you at night. There are plenty of guys rolling around in sheets that should just shut the fuck up and do the deed."

"Rolling around in the sheets, huh?" He ran a hand through his hair. "You say the sweetest things to me, Lyla Brooks."

I smirked at his adoring gaze. "As long as I'm your girl-friend, I always will."

CHAPTER TWENTY-SEVEN

Deacon

NO MATTER WHAT TIME of year it was, as long as the sky was clear, I could find the Big Dipper. I wasn't sure if science could back up my optimism, but I could see it whenever I peered at the sky.

A warm breeze rippled through the trees on Court Street. We were running out of nights like this—nights where we didn't dread the walk to the bars. Seasons changed quickly in Ohio, and if you blinked, you might miss the transition. I was ready for the warmer parts of fall to drift to winter. I'd miss the view of the sky, but I'd trade that for a time of the year that wasn't tampered with painful memories.

While Lyla's thumbs danced wildly over my phone screen, I watched Drew put the moves on a girl he met at the Bring Your Own Pool party. It made me happy to see Drew enjoying himself this weekend. I missed my brother, and if this flirty interaction in front of me went anywhere, I would talk about this meet-cute at their wedding.

"She's at Bar 149." Lyla handed me my phone. "Cassie posted to Instagram ten minutes ago."

"Are you going to fill me in on this master plan of yours?" I'd been waiting patiently for four blocks, and the anticipation was killing me. I needed some sort of notice for plans—especially when those plans included my ex-girlfriend and my fake girlfriend engaging in any kind of conversation.

"I read your texts with her after you said I could, and she's doing exactly what I thought she'd be doing. She's reached out to you a few times since she found out about us, right? She's probing you for information without you even realizing it."

When Cassie asked how I had been doing, she was *probing*? This was why the government needed to hire women to find information. They were born with skills in their DNA that men just couldn't fathom.

"You're going to approach Cassie and start talking about, I don't know, anything that makes you both reminisce on the good old days. But you want to make it seem like you're happy."

I stared blankly at her serious expression. "I *am* happy."

"I mean, like over-the-moon obnoxious happy," Lyla stressed and slid her fingers through mine. "And then, as you are talking, I'll come up and slip in a comment. It's simple reinforcement. You show how happy you are, and I reinforce the happiness. If any part of her still wants to be with you or has even *considered* being with you, it'll light up. It's the perfect match."

If I knew I would've had to reminisce on the good old days with Cassie, I would've rifled through my Freshman to Junior Year with C tote for inspiration. We were approaching Main Street, and I was running out of time to decide what memory to bring up in my upcoming conversation.

It was typical that Homecoming Weekend drew large crowds from nearby colleges. On a regular weekend, we'd walk right into Bar 149. Instead, we were tacking onto the end of a long line.

Lyla pulled out her phone, and her thumbs went to work. She smiled at the screen, and I pretended not to notice. It was the first of October, which meant there would be another "Mr." I would soon hear about. I wasn't sure if she saw Jake again after that night at The Attic, but since one of her rules was that we had to hook up with other people in private, I had no way of knowing that information.

Lyla tapped my forearm and nodded toward the window of the bar. "Isn't that Cassie by the tables?"

I recognized her blonde hair and Cassie's roommate, Clara. "Yeah."

The bouncer verified our IDs and let us into the bar. Once inside, Drew broke away with his new friend. Lyla and I ordered beers at the bar and then found a table near the entrance—one that faced Cassie's table but didn't make it obvious that we were there.

Red and blue lights danced across Lyla's face as she studied the scene. I was getting better at guessing what was in her head, but keeping up with how quickly she sifted through her open tabs was hard. Her ability to be upset in one moment and downplay it the next was incredible. I just watched her ponder something that was stressing her out ten seconds ago, and now she was staring at me with bright green eyes—happy and excited to be back on the mission.

I took a sip of my beer and smiled. "So tell me. How do I talk to Cassie about how happy I am?"

"Bring up something that shows you're doing great without her. Then, bring up something that would make her miss you." Lyla pointed dramatically to the dance floor. "Go over there and talk to her about something personal you guys did. Talk about sex!"

I cocked my head. "You want me to go over to my ex-girlfriend and just talk to her about sex?"

"You spent three years doing it with her. How awkward could it be?"

I stole a glance in Cassie's direction. Clara had just left the table to go to the bar, and she was alone.

My lips parted, and I was drawing a blank. Suddenly, I couldn't recall *anything* that Cassie and I did while we were together. "I just—"

Lyla placed her hand on mine. "Do you trust me?" She raised her eyebrows, expecting to have to wait for me to answer, but I didn't hesitate.

"I do trust you." I ran a hand over my mouth. "Probably more than I should, actually."

"Damn!" Lyla exclaimed. "Luckily, no one was around to hear that line."

I chuckled into the neck of my Corona, and soon, she was joining me. Laughing with my fake girlfriend and looking like a real couple was easy, but thinking of something to say to my ex made me anxious.

What the fuck, Deacon?

"You know what? I'll take care of it." Lyla drained the rest of her beer and placed her empty bottle on the table. "Go over there while she's alone. Have that drink finished in five minutes, and I'll pop into your conversation. It's better to have your honest reaction anyway."

"Honest reaction to *what?*" I turned, but Lyla was gone.

Fuck it. If I couldn't talk with a girl I planned on having as my *wife*, my case for being with her wasn't that strong.

Cassie smiled when I approached her table. "Hey, you."

"Hey, Cass." I took the spot next to her and bumped her shoulder. "How are you?"

She nodded once before she answered. "I'm good. Just here with some friends. What about you? Is your girlfriend here?"

The words left her mouth, but I still couldn't believe she was the one who had said them. "Lyla's at the bar getting us some drinks," I said.

Cassie's eyes were bright behind her dark lashes. I always told her she had the bluest eyes I had ever seen, and I had yet to be proven wrong. "What is she getting you?"

I shrugged. "Not sure. She likes to surprise me."

She smiled down at the table, and I knew that look. She was replaying something in her head.

"What?" I asked, stifling a grin.

"Just remembering when *I* tried to surprise you with a drink, and you thought it was foul."

"You brought me pickle juice!" I exclaimed.

"It's a pickleback shot!" She lit up as she spoke. "Part of it is pickle juice."

I shook my head like a disappointed father. "You know I hate pickles."

"I *did* always find that odd." She raised her eyebrows and took a sip of her drink. It was a cranberry vodka, which meant she was a few drinks in already. She only got liquor at the bars if she had a few beers before coming out.

The night she brought me that nasty shot was the night she told me she loved me. It was after her uncle's fiftieth birthday party, and she had snuck downstairs to sleep with me in the living room. We stayed with her parents that weekend, and they had a strict separate bedroom rule. Cassie argued that they couldn't kick her out of the living room, and after she said she loved me, I wouldn't have let her leave anyway.

I opened my mouth to speak when Lyla approached the table. I stared at my drink and noticed I hadn't done the one thing she asked me to. I took two long sips and pushed the empty glass to the center of the table.

"Perfect timing," I lied.

"Look at that!" Lyla beamed. She leaned her elbows on the table and looked at Cassie. "I don't think we've met! I'm Lyla."

"Not officially, no," Cassie said through a fake smile. "I saw your video, and I have to say, I thought it was *amazing*. I'm Cassie."

I hoped to run out of moments when I wanted to disintegrate into the floor, but here I was, just adding to the list.

Lyla let out a hollow laugh, catching Cassie's sarcasm. "One of my best moments. That's it, *Cassie*. You've been friends with Deacon for a while, right?"

Cassie shifted her focus to me. "Friends?"

Was it too late to reminisce on the good old days? I did some mental digging through my Freshman to Junior Year with C tote and begged for something to surface.

"Try your drink." Lyla slid my cup in front of me and took a sip of her own. "It's a little stronger than they normally make it."

I stared down at the dark liquid. "What is it?"

"It's whiskey." Lyla ran her fingers down my arm. "I figured you'd recognize Daddy's drink by now." She never mentioned Aaron Brooks being a drinker, but she sounded surprised.

"Minus the pickle juice." Cassie giggled, directing her attention to Lyla. "My dad's a whiskey guy, too."

I took a long sip of my drink, and when one wasn't enough to teleport me to another table, I took another.

Lyla squeezed my bicep but kept her focus on Cassie. "Your dad?"

Cassie gestured toward my cup. "You mentioned that's your dad's drink. Mine's a whiskey guy, too."

"Ohhh, Daddy." Lyla laughed, moving her hand up to my shoulder. "I was talking about Deacon. He's into all that kinky shit, but I'm not complaining."

I covered my mouth with my free hand to avoid spitting my drink across the table. I couldn't look at Cassie, and Lyla was trying to get my attention by pretending to be concerned with my reaction.

"You okay, baby?" Lyla turned so she was facing me. "I told you they were strong!"

I coughed twice, and before I knew it, I was laughing.

"You know"—Cassie chuckled uncomfortably—"it looks like my roommate is ready to go."

"That was so fucking weird of me to say," Lyla said, her voice taking an apologetic tone.

"No, trust me, you're good." Cassie snuck in one more hollow laugh before she reached across the table and patted my hand. "You guys have a good night."

I coughed one more time to clear my throat. "It was nice to see you, Cass."

Lyla's strained smile pinched her cheeks as she waited for a performance review.

I shook my head and pressed my lips together in a firm line. "So now we have *kinky* boyfriend-girlfriend shit?"

"You can call it whatever you want." She laughed, sipping her drink proudly. "Just know that Cassie is going to spend the rest of her night thinking about everything you like to do now that she's not in your bed."

Chapter Twenty-Eight

Lyla

I peeked over my shoulder and saw Daddy Deacon still fast asleep, lying on his back with his right arm over his head. His left arm draped over his smooth and sculpted chest, and I looked away before my mouth started watering.

Apparently, he wasn't just stripping his shirt off in front of me—he was sleeping shirtless, too.

I slid out of bed, careful not to wake him up. He had gone a little overboard last night, taking shots with Drew and kissing the top of my head as often as he could. I knew they were thank-you gestures. Cassie texted him shortly after we left Bar 149 to say she was happy to see him happy, and I read right through that girl code.

I saw how she looked at him last night, blue eyes practically popping out of her perfect tan complexion and polished fingers that kept inching toward his on the table. Two types of girls wished their exes happiness: girls who were genuinely done with the relationship and had emotionally moved on, *and* the girls who wanted the guy they missed to think they were okay with them moving on. If Cassie made it seem like she was okay, they could both be surprised when Deacon got back with her. It could be their second chance.

I took a quick shower and changed into clothes that didn't smell like Deacon's cologne. It was hard to stay focused when part of me wanted to take some of him back to my place with me. The familiar scent of cedarwood and lavender was beginning to feel like my own personal bottle of calming spray, and that was a fucking red flag in my book.

Not a real relationship, no lying, fuck around in private, and no love.

I repeated the rules in my head. They weren't hard to uphold, and I wasn't in danger of breaking them, but as more time passed, this relationship was getting easier to fake. It showed in the pictures we posted and how we acted around other people. My relationship with Deacon wasn't real, but my friendship? It felt like the most natural thing I'd had in a very long time.

Deacon even encouraged a possible prospect for Mr. October last night. His name was Brady, and he was an accounting major. He had dark blue eyes and made me laugh, so I put him in my phone as Brady Blue Eyes and filed him away.

Since the living room was still empty after my shower, I decided to do a coffee run. Drew paid for a lot last night, and I figured I could thank him with his favorite morning drink—an iced matcha with blueberry and oat milk.

It was a chillier morning, and since all I had for warmth was my leather jacket from last night, I swiped one of Deacon's Champion hoodies. I brought the material that hung over my hands to my nose and took a deep breath. My shoulders relaxed as the scent I just washed off in the shower returned to me at full force.

My phone vibrated in my pocket, and I smiled at my mom's picture.

"Hey, Jean Bean!"

I rolled my eyes. "Mom, could we not? That nickname will never be as cute as you want it to sound."

"Honestly, Lyla, I don't really give a shit what you think of the nickname. It's for me, not you. What are you up to?"

I paused for dramatic effect. "I am *walking* to get coffee."

"And are you walking *alone*?"

I knew what she was really asking me. "Deacon isn't with me. He went a little too hard last night, so I'm surprising him with a pick-me-up. His brother is in this weekend."

"You met one of Deacon's family members before *I* could even meet him?" Mom sighed, and her wheels were turning. "I should plan a trip there. When is Parent's Weekend?"

"Ha!" I exclaimed before I ran across Main Street. "You will do no such thing."

"Your dad gets to come to campus!"

"For Thanksgiving, and campus will practically be empty."

"Well, it's bullshit that he gets to meet Deacon before I do," she spat. "If you won't let me see you . . . you should come home next weekend! We can do lunch and go to the zoo—"

"I am not forcing Deacon to come to our house so he can go to the zoo." I chuckled at the offer, knowing Deacon wouldn't hesitate for a second if I asked him to take a road trip to Cleveland.

"Well, I love the picture you guys posted last night." I could hear Mom's smile return as she spoke. "I think I'm going to hang it on our fridge. You guys really do look cute together."

"I'll think about coming home, okay? But I just got to Grounds, so I'm gonna go."

Mom filled me in on her next book idea before we hung up. There was no line for coffee, so I was in and out of Grounds with my drinks in just a few minutes.

I sipped my iced chai latte and noticed that more people woke up before noon on Sundays than I thought. I'd never admit it to Deacon, but the morning stroll was kind of peaceful. It allowed me to think about asking him to come to Cleveland without getting into my head about it. Perhaps some fresh air did do a girl good.

I tried to be quiet when I entered the apartment, but it didn't matter. The guys were awake, slowly moving around like sloths as they attempted to recuperate after a wild night out. Deacon was sprawled out on the couch while Drew wandered into the kitchen.

"I brought coffee," I offered, placing the drink holder on the counter.

When Deacon's eyes remained closed, I placed his iced black coffee in the fridge for later. Drew dragged his hands down his face, and I handed him his drink.

I smiled, and his eyes narrowed. "Iced matcha with blueberry and oat milk. Deacon mentioned it was your favorite."

Drew nodded reassuringly. "Thanks, Lyla."

The three of us spent the next few hours drifting in and out of sleep. I blamed the shots from last night, not the *Twilight* marathon I forced upon them. Not everyone appreciated a fabulous vampire phenomenon, and I didn't wake Deacon up to ask him his opinion on Bella and Edward's meet-cute.

CHAPTER TWENTY-NINE

Deacon

AROUND FOUR-THIRTY, DREW STARTED to feel human again. He had a five-hour drive back to Penn State and was doing his best to hype himself up for the drive.

"I'm going to head out, too." Lyla patted my leg and hoisted herself off the couch. "Charlie is on her way to come get me."

"I could've dropped you off," I mumbled. Even though I napped for at least three hours today, I was still ready for bed. I wanted to ask Lyla to stay again tonight, but all of her extra on-screen performance time this weekend stopped me. She was probably craving her own space.

"Charlie is dropping off Andre, so she's coming here anyway."

"Do Andre and Charlie chill like that a lot?" Drew asked, placing his duffle by the front door and patting his pockets. He surveyed the area around the couch until he found his phone near the coffee table.

"Chill is one way to put it," Lyla said as she and I exchanged a grin. "She's here now."

"That fast?" Drew asked.

"Her place is like five minutes from here," I explained, forcing myself up before I officially became part of the cushion. I walked Lyla to the front door and opened it for her. "You got everything? Need any help?"

"I'm good, Scott." She smiled and opened her arms for Drew to hug her. "It was so nice to meet you, Drew."

Drew wrapped his arms around her tiny shoulders. "It was nice to meet you, too."

Lyla stood on her toes and planted a small peck on the corner of my mouth. "Bye, Deac."

"I'll text you later tonight." I tried not to look disappointed as she walked out the door, and Andre took her place beside me.

"You leavin', man?" Andre pointed to Drew and looked around the living room. "Where's Nathan?"

I shrugged. "I texted him earlier, and he said he'd be back later."

Andre exchanged a handshake with Drew and told him to have a safe drive home. Once Andre hopped in the shower and it was just Drew and I alone, Drew turned to me and said, "What's going on with Lyla, man?"

My eyes narrowed, and I did my best to sound casual. "What do you mean?"

Drew sighed and ran a hand over his mouth. He was battling something and working out how to say it. "You've been with Lyla for a month and a half and haven't mentioned Dominic?"

It felt like a bullet was burrowing through the center of my chest; like someone had just poured gasoline into the hole in my heart and lit it on fire. I swallowed around the lump in my throat and leaned against the counter. Even though I felt Drew's gaze from a few feet away, I couldn't look at him.

Dominic.

"It's complicated," I admitted softly.

Drew shook his head. "I know you, Deac. You don't *let* things get complicated. Is she just some girl you're seein'?"

There was no reason to lie, so I started from the beginning. I told him about Cassie and the breakup. I told him about meeting Lyla and discovering that she needed help to get her trust fund from her dad. I told him how the whole thing started as a stupid idea, but now Lyla and I had a genuine friendship. I told him everything.

When I finished the recap, Drew blew out an exaggerated breath.

"But you *cannot* tell Mom and Dad," I pleaded. "They've stopped bugging me about Cassie since they found out about Lyla, and it's nice to have a break. I just"—I took a deep breath and sighed—"I just don't want to disappoint them. Not after everything they've lost."

Drew nodded until his mouth lifted into a cocky grin. "Your secret is safe with me. I have to admit, it's a shame, though."

"What is?"

"I actually *like* Lyla. A lot. Somehow, she meshes with you."

I ignored his observation. "What do you mean *actually* like?"

"Cassie was alright. But if I stood them next to each other"—Drew shrugged and threw his hands out in front of him for emphasis—"I don't know. I've always had a thing for green eyes."

I rolled my eyes and pulled him into a hug. "Get on the road. And let me know when you get back."

Drew hoisted his duffle and rested his hand on my shoulder. "Will do."

Instead of working on the two essays I had due tonight, I was doing much more important things on a Wednesday afternoon. I was shopping with Lyla for Halloween costumes.

"What did you have in mind?" Lyla asked, dragging her fingers along a row of costumes.

Since my talk with Drew, I struggled to focus on anything else. Whenever I was with Lyla, I was afraid I'd overflow into our space with word vomit. Drew was right. There was no way Lyla could meet anyone else from my family without knowing about Dominic.

"What about this?" Lyla dragged a sexy Tarzan costume from the rack and held it in front of her. "I bet the bartender from Saturday would love to see you return as Tarzan."

I pressed my lips in a firm line. "What are you talking about?"

"The bartender from Uptown on Saturday. She was totally trying to see if you were down for the cause."

"No, she wasn't," I protested. "And I told her my girlfriend was with me like five times."

"My boyfriend is hot, Deacon, and not to mention a hot *guy*. She handed you her who-ha on a silver platter, and you immediately said no. It was a shocking scene for everyone, honestly."

I rolled my eyes and snatched the costume out of her hand. "Not everyone is just waiting around to see who is *down for the cause*. And she was only persistent because she knew I was there with someone."

"Says the guy who has been in a relationship for his entire college career," she exclaimed playfully. "How do you know what people are looking for? Do you even know who you are in college? Or do you know who you are with *Cassie*?"

I wasn't sure why Lyla brought all of these questions with her shopping, but I was starting to feel the pressure in my chest. The pressure that came with feeling overwhelmed and not in control. I felt the same pressure the day Cassie broke up with me.

"It doesn't matter," I snapped.

Lyla's hands froze in another rack of costumes, and she searched my face to make sure she heard me correctly.

I relaxed my shoulders and softened my tone. "I'm a few months away from my life starting, and now isn't the time to start fucking around."

"A few months away"—her arms dropped to her sides, and she turned to face me—"Deacon, your life is happening *right now*. The next chapter is starting soon, sure, but are you really just going to sit around for months just waiting? What about right now?"

"I thought I'd be in a different place right now," I admitted, swatting a nearby cowboy hat for emphasis. "Literally and figuratively."

She smiled. "You might be the first guy I've ever heard use those terms correctly. There's nothing worse than a guy who had something 'literally blow their mind.' Those guys could *literally* smack me over the head, so I wouldn't have to hear them talking anymore."

I wasn't in the mood to laugh, but I couldn't help it. It was a very Lyla comment and made me feel like my feet were back on the ground. If I didn't say something now, I wasn't sure when I would. "Lyla."

"Costume idea?" She pulled another option from the rack and decided against it.

I took a deep breath and closed my eyes. "Drew knows."

"Knows what?"

Come on, Lyla. Help me out here. "He knows that this is fake."

Lyla's eyes scanned the area around us, and her mouth fell open. "Why don't you just shout that across *the entire* store? How did he find out?"

"Something you said, actually."

She took my hand and led us out of the store.

"Lyla, where are we going?"

We didn't stop walking until we got to my car.

Lyla hopped onto the hood and looked up at me with a small smile. "I can tell there's something else, and I want you to have the space to tell me."

An exasperated laugh escaped my chest, and I leaned against the car to stand beside her. She ran her fingers through my hair, and the innocent gesture made the butterflies go crazy in my stomach.

I forced myself to start with the basics. "Remember when you brought coffee back on Sunday morning?"

"Yes," she stated proudly. "I was impressed I remembered Drew's order."

I dragged my hands down my face and looked up at the sky. "The drink I mentioned that morning we met . . . it wasn't Drew's order. It was Dominic's. Drew knows me, and he knew if you didn't know about Dominic, there was no way we were together."

"You have another brother?" Lyla asked as her nails softly grazed my head.

The relaxing motion made the next line easier. "Dominic is my youngest brother, and he passed away two years ago."

CHAPTER THIRTY

Lyla

THERE WERE A FEW times in my life I considered myself speechless, and I wasn't expecting to add another moment to that list when I invited Deacon to browse Halloween costumes.

I wasn't sure what to say. There was nothing *to* say. Deacon spoke about Dominic in the present tense, and no words could make anything about losing a sibling better. Drew knew about our agreement because the drink I brought him that morning reminded him of a person who was no longer here, and it was clear that Deacon hadn't shared that part of his past with me.

I drew my hand from his hair and wrapped it around his shoulder. I pulled him close and rested my chin on his head. "I am so sorry, Deacon."

Deacon turned and rested his hands on either side of my hips. My heart sank, taking in every ounce of pain I could carry for him. I wished I could take it all and hold onto it for as long as he'd let me. I smoothed the skin under his eyes with my thumbs and waited for him to continue.

"I was with Cassie for almost a year when it happened," Deacon murmured. "Everyone who matters in my life knows about Dominic. When you mentioned that drink, Drew knew. Plus, Drew *hates* matcha." Deacon chuckled, and I wanted to bottle up the sound. "If I were really with you for as long as we've been together, you'd know it was Dominic's."

"I'm sorry," I said, wishing the side of me that knew words would show up already.

"Baby—" Deacon pressed his lips together, trying not to smile. The dreaded B-word sounded adorable as it left Deacon's mouth. "You don't have to be sorry. You had no way of knowing because I never said anything to you."

"That night I stayed at your place," I pondered. "When you mentioned the panic attacks . . ."

Deacon nodded. "I had them for about a year after Dominic passed. I recognized the look on your face at The Attic that night, but we were still so new to each other. It wasn't my place to say anything to you."

I squeezed his shoulders and let my hands fall to my lap. Deacon's sexy half-smile slowly reappeared, and I had to look at the pavement to keep my thoughts at an appropriate level. I hadn't fully processed Deacon's confession, and my mind refusing to leave the gutter reassured me of that.

"You haven't asked the obvious question yet." He sounded surprised, and eventually, he gave up on me guessing. "Now that Drew knows, does that mean our boyfriend-girlfriend shit is over?"

"Honestly, that option hadn't even crossed my mind," I admitted. "Some things are more important than money, Deac."

You mean, Deacon—your fake boyfriend—is more important than the money.

Deacon offered me his hand and slid me off the hood of his car. "Let's go get you those costumes."

I ignored the ringing thoughts in my head. *Now,* my wordy side wanted to show up and have something to say.

Two weeks before Halloween, Deacon had to make another trip to the store to get a sailor hat for his Popeye costume. He had the broad shoulders and arm muscles to pull off the look with a plain navy shirt, but the bag of accessories we picked out had everything but the hat, which was essential to the sailor's beefy appearance.

My costume wasn't hard to throw together, either. I refused to wear the wig but wasn't worried about being Olive Oyl. That bitch had nothing on the skirt and tight red V-neck I had on deck in my closet.

After Deacon told me about Dominic, I could tell he felt a little lighter. It was like he got to put a weight down he had been struggling to hold. I achieved a new level with every piece of information I learned about Deacon Scott. Every advance revealed another side of him, and the more time I spent as his fake girlfriend, the more I wanted to know.

"It's weird not having a costume with you this year," Charlie said from the recliner. We were scrolling aimlessly on our phones while Michelle and Keira were working in the kitchen.

It was Friday, and while we'd usually be getting ready to go out, Mother Nature had a way of spoiling a mood. It was downpouring, and no one felt like walking around in the rain.

"I've officially lost you to a man," Charlie pouted.

"Why don't you go as a can of spinach," I offered. "Deacon won't mind if you tag along."

Charlie chuckled as her thumbs tapped wildly on her phone screen.

I returned to my scrolling, and a picture of Deacon and I came across my Instagram feed. I almost sent the photo to Aaron Brooks and his business account so he could revisit InstaSnap, but I decided against it. He didn't deserve to see the adorable evidence.

In the photo, Deacon had his arm draped lazily across my chest, holding a beer in his free hand. I caught him mid-laugh as I smiled up at the camera. We took it right after our run-in with Cassie at Bar 149—right after Daddy Deacon appeared, and neither of us could stop laughing about it.

"Tacos are done!" Michelle announced.

"Yeeesss," Charlie sang.

It was a quiet evening with tacos and margaritas. Everyone was so busy with school, work, and personal agendas that I hadn't seen much of Michelle and Keira. It was nice to have some time to ourselves in the apartment.

I was serving up a second round of blackberry margaritas when Brady Blue Eyes lit up the center of my phone screen.

I sent him a thumbs-up emoji and placed my phone on the counter. As much as I was itching to get back to a regular sex routine, I wasn't up for it this weekend. I had my period, felt bloated as hell, and the rain was sending me even further into my feels. I was less than a month away from introducing Deacon to my dad, and the anticipation was taking a toll.

Maybe anticipation wasn't the appropriate word. Was damnation better fitting?

Charlie smacked my arm. "Are you seeing Deacon tonight?"

"No. Am I the only one catching the girls' night vibe?" I surveyed the group, and they all nodded in agreement. "It's gross outside, and we've gone out every weekend since we got back."

"We can start a game of Monopoly, just the four of us?" Michelle offered.

"Is that what we've been reduced to?" Keira smiled, popping a chip into her mouth. "A game of Monopoly?"

I sipped my margarita. "Nothing wrong with some Monopoly."

"Okay, bitch." Charlie laughed with Michelle and Keira as they shared a silent exchange.

"Okay, what?" I demanded playfully.

"It's just been entertaining," Keira said slowly. "Watching you completely fall for a guy."

It was stomach-churning to hear a statement about me falling for *anyone*. The only reason I didn't vomit on the spot was my ongoing award-winning performance.

"Cassie even asked me if you were the real deal." Michelle's hand flew to her mouth, and she widened her innocent stare. "I wasn't supposed to say that."

"Who's Cassie?" Charlie demanded.

"Deacon's ex-girlfriend," I answered quickly, turning to Michelle. While I usually blurred Michelle's constant need to speak about nonsense, she officially had my attention. "Wait, are you friends with Cassie?"

"She's in my Tuesday night study group," Michelle said. "We're in the same math section right now, and the professor is pretty brutal with—"

I fanned the last part of her sentence away. "I don't care about the math, Michelle! How long have you known that Cassie was Deacon's ex?"

"Since that video of you dancing at The Attic was flying around campus. It was shared again recently and—"

"Shared *recently*?" I whined. Eventually, I'd let this poor girl finish a statement. I pulled out my phone to scroll through Instagram. I hadn't seen a shred of evidence that the video of me at The Attic was still relevant entertainment. I brought my inner thoughts to the group again. "Have any of you seen it recently?"

The silent sips of margaritas were enough to answer my question.

"Fuuuck," I groaned as I spotted my favorite yellow sundress moving up and down on the famous stripper pole. "My dad is totally going to see this . . . *again*."

Charlie's eyebrow twitched, and her eyes narrowed. She swallowed her mouthful of margarita and patted my hand. "I forgot I need help picking an outfit for tomorrow night." Her accusing stare told a different story. "*Now*."

Keira started around the counter. "I want to help!"

Charlie held out her arm to stop her. "*Bedroom* outfit for tomorrow."

"Oh." Keira frowned, and Michelle giggled nervously. Any mention of the bedroom stopped both of them in their tracks. You couldn't find an apartment more evenly divided when it came to sex.

Charlie grabbed my hand and pulled me off the barstool. Once we were in her room, she slammed the door behind her and crossed her arms.

I opened the top drawer of her dresser. "Are you seeing Andre again tomorrow? Is that why—"

"I don't know why I didn't see it before."

I scanned the room to see if I missed the lingerie displays. "See what?"

"The morning your dad called about the video—the need to convince him you've changed. The knight in shining armor boyfriend . . . and then Deacon just *happens* to date you a few weeks later?"

I swallowed. *Shit.*

Charlie smiled at her accomplishment. "You aren't dating Deacon, are you? It's all for show."

My phone buzzed in my hand, and the light drew Charlie's attention.

She held out her hand. "Let me see your phone?"

I handed it over.

Charlie's mouth fell open, and she chuckled at the evidence. "Brady Blue Eyes. Bitch, you better spill."

I had Brady Blue Eyes on my phone screen and Deacon on my mind. When the fuck did my life sound like a poorly written song lyric?

I spent the next ten minutes telling Charlie everything. Deacon had someone on his side of the line who knew the truth. Now, I just considered us to be even.

CHAPTER THIRTY-ONE

Deacon

AFTER OUR LAST CLASS ended, Lyla and I decided to stop at The Union for some snacks. The basket of sweet potato fries I had in front of me provided a fantastic distraction since Lyla just told me she had officially added Charlie to the list of people who knew about our agreement.

"It's fine!" Lyla assured me through a giant grin. "Now, one person you know knows, and one person I know knows!"

"You know what, now that you say that, having an even playing field makes so much more sense." I popped another fry into my mouth, and she rolled her eyes.

I enjoyed Lyla's sassy side, but since I'd typically get back at my girlfriend by making her roll her eyes in a very *different* way, I settled for how cute she looked in a beanie and one of my hoodies. With the colder Ohio weather came more layers, which meant finding more creative ways to keep warm. Lyla would freeze in her costume next weekend, and I forced away any ideas that involved my bed and Lyla rolling her eyes in any shape or form.

Sheesh. I considered this a reaction to my Petey Pablo withdrawal. I couldn't have sex with Cassie or the fake girlfriend I spent all of my time with. How did Lyla line up guys when she barely saw them? It sounded exhausting.

I needed a change of subject. "What time should I come over tonight?"

"Ten-thirty should be fine." Lyla slid me her iced green tea so I could have a sip. "Charlie's at the light. Did you need anything from the store?"

I shook my head.

"Also, I have an update for you. It's nothing bad, but there's this guy I met last week, and I might see him Saturday night after we go out, that's all."

I ignored the small punch to my gut. "You're good."

She stood up and planted a small kiss in the corner of my mouth. "I'll see you tonight."

I smiled. "Sounds good, Brooks."

I watched her walk across The Union until she left through the double doors. Even though she was gone, the aftermath of the punch still lingered. Maybe that coffee from earlier was fucking with me. I gathered my things and threw the rest of the sweet potato fries in the trash. Suddenly, I wasn't hungry.

"Deacon?"

I knew who it was before I turned around. Cassie stood in front of me in an oversized hoodie and jeans. Moments like these made me feel like Dominic was messing with me. I had a *slight* fantasy about Lyla, so he ensured I ran into Cassie.

I cleared my throat. "Hey, Cass."

She stepped forward, debating whether she should hug me or not. I stuck my hands in the pockets of my shorts to take away the option. I wanted her to want to touch me, and it gave me a tiny bit of satisfaction to know that she wanted to.

Cassie crossed her arms in front of her chest and smiled. "I thought that was you. I saw Lyla walking toward the exit and figured you weren't far behind."

"That's usually how it is with us. Our schedules are pretty similar." That was a lie, but she didn't need to know that.

"I see you guys sometimes." Cassie's smile tapered. "Nice to see you still have a thing for flowers."

"Every Monday. Lyla likes roses, though. You were more of a lilies girl."

She chuckled softly, tucking her hair behind her ear. She was nervous to talk to me. "Never thought I'd miss those flowers."

There was nothing more irritating than a tiptoed conversation. I spent three years of my life with this girl, and now we looked like two strangers trying to play catch-up.

"How are you, Cass? You seem happy."

She nodded. "It's been a hard semester, but the weekends help. Do you know what you're doing for Halloween yet?"

"Depends on the weather. Lyla's costume is"—I laughed and shook my head—"never mind. She wants it to be a secret until next weekend."

Cassie looked off to the side and then back at me. "Well, on Saturday, one of my friends is having a party on Main. You guys should stop by."

"I'll see what Lyla wants to do. Text me the address, okay?"

I couldn't stand there pretending I didn't want to discuss more important things. Cassie and I used to talk about everything, and I was aching to rip off the band-aid. I was happy if she was happy. I just wished I was a factor in that happiness.

Cassie turned to walk away and smiled over her shoulder. "I really hope you come, Deacon."

I wasn't sure if she missed me, but I missed the fuck out of the look she gave me before she left. Cassie texted me five minutes later with the address, and I called Lyla to tell her we officially had a party to go to.

Chapter Thirty-Two

Lyla

When a holiday weekend was on the horizon, sometimes the bar scene just couldn't compete with the anticipation.

Deacon and I decided to call it an early night, and when we stepped outside Brathaus, I did a silent shout-out to climate change as I wrapped my arms around my chest. The only thing worse than the BG wind during the day was the BG *winter* wind at night. I only had a few drinks, so I didn't even have a beer coat to keep me warm.

"Cold?" Deacon started taking off his Champion hoodie, and I held out a hand to stop him.

I smiled at the gesture. "I'll survive."

He raised his arm to let me know I could walk with him, and I leaned into his side to let his body temperature make a mockery of mine. "So, who is this guy you're seeing?"

I loved how casually he asked the question. "His name is Brady. He seems like a decent guy, but we'll see."

"Does it count as Mr. October if only one week is left?"

I chuckled. "You sound like Charlie. I haven't thought about it, honestly. Between you meeting my dad in a few weeks and your whole Cassie situation, my calendar has been put on hold."

"Well, I think it's safe to say that we admire your sacrifices, Lyla Brooks."

Deacon and I were a happy couple talking about the progress we made with other people. It really was 2016.

Deacon was looking up at the sky when I glanced over at him. "What's going on over there?" I prompted gently.

He did a double-take when he noticed me staring at him. His adorable half-smile curved into his cheek, and he shrugged. "It's nothing."

"If it's in your head, it's not nothing. Talk to me, Scott."

He bit the inside of his cheek and looked up again. "The sky looks a little different when you have someone up there. You appreciate it a little more. Pay attention to it."

There was a sharp pang in my chest. "That makes sense. Does it make you think about him?"

"I think about Dominic every day," he admitted. "Even though it happened two years ago, it still doesn't feel real. I'll be in the middle of doing something, and it will hit me out of nowhere."

My heart sank as an intensity I didn't recognize washed over his face. There was heartbreak, but then there was grief. Heartbreak could exist in multiple situations on its own but grief . . . grief fed off of heartbreak, one of the most stubborn emotions we struggled to fight against.

I had seen loss before. I felt it when my grandmother passed away. But the look on Deacon's face was an unimaginable pain that was caused by losing someone who wasn't supposed to be gone yet.

I grabbed his hand. "I always wondered why you look at the sky as often as you do. It all makes sense now."

Deacon seemed amused by that statement. "Do I do that?"

"Yup. What would Dominic say about this whole thing? You having a fake girlfriend to try and get Cassie back."

"He would say it's stupid," Deacon said, laughing. "I do wonder which one of you he'd vote for."

I raised my eyebrows and smiled. "*Vote* for?"

Deacon threw his hands out in front of him. "Well, yeah! I like you, Brooks. Dominic would probably sit there and wonder what I was doing, trying to win my ex back while I'm getting closer to my fake girlfriend."

I stopped walking. "Deacon Scott—"

"Oh, don't hit me with your rules shit," he teased. "Whatever you think you just gathered from that, trust me, I didn't mean it that way."

I narrowed my gaze. "We don't lie."

Deacon laced his fingers with mine. "We don't lie. You've learned more about me in two months than most people learn in six. I like spending time with you, and I'd be lying if I said spending time with you didn't make me like you more."

Was this an example of growth? I heard a guy say he liked getting close to me, and I didn't want to vomit. There was no way I was leaving for Mr. October if Deacon needed the company tonight. I would tackle that red flag in my "Keep Things Casual" novel some other time.

We walked the remainder of the street until we were in front of Deacon's building. It was eerily quiet, but then I remembered it was still early. It was only one-thirty in the morning.

Deacon dropped my hand, and my fingers felt cold. "Do you need anything from inside?"

"No." I exhaled, crossing my arms. "I'm okay. Brady lives a street over, so it isn't far."

"You text me when you get there," Deacon ordered. While I usually hated being told what to do, when those orders came from Deacon, it was incredibly sexy.

I turned to walk away, but Deacon grabbed my hand again.

"And if you feel like walking home, you call me. Understand?" The skin around his eyes went soft, and he squeezed my hand. "I don't care what time it is."

I squeezed his hand back. "I'll be okay."

Deacon's voice echoed down the street as I put a few houses between us. "Call me! I'll be pissed if you walk home by yourself!"

A *pissed* Deacon Scott? For the rest of my walk, I wondered if *that* version said "atta girl" too.

Chapter Thirty-Three

Deacon

When I had my first panic attack, it was right after Dominic passed away. My entire world shattered in a five-minute phone call. I couldn't even remember if it *was* a five-minute phone call. I spent most of it on the floor, begging everything around me—the couch, the floor, the ceiling, every door I tried not to run into—asking something or someone to explain why this was happening. This wasn't supposed to happen to my family.

Certain traumas left scars that stuck with us no matter what we did with them. The reminders faded, but the marks they left would always be there.

When I lost Dominic, it felt like someone ripped a piece of my heart out of my chest. How could I live in a world where part of me was missing? I didn't know how to continue or how to help my parents. There were moments when I caught myself having a good time or laughing too hard. How could I find joy in a world where my younger brother didn't exist?

Every moment I wasn't thinking about him was a moment I allowed myself to forget. Nerves and anxiety always followed the good times and laughter. A physical and mental panic would set in, and the only way to fix it was to find peace in solitude.

When I was alone, I felt closest to Dominic. I looked up to the sky and felt like he was with me. That was hard to do in a room full of people who had the freedom to think of much less complicated things. Everyone had *things*. I never downplayed anyone's personal life or the struggles that they went through, but I lacked sympathy for problems that had easy solutions. My problem didn't have a solution. The person I lost wasn't coming back.

The world continued to spin for everyone outside my family, and sometimes, I wondered if mine was still at a halt.

On nights I couldn't sleep, my mind flooded with the memories I wished would subside. I remembered the phone call, the hospital, the service, and all of the friends and family who couldn't find the words because there were none. An entire week of events was burned into my memory so vividly, and I fucking hated how well I could recall something that still didn't feel real.

After months of rotating heavy sleep medication and melatonin, I enrolled in therapy. My entire life, I had planned out milestones and figured out problems. Losing Dominic was something I couldn't solve on my own. I couldn't figure it out or put a plan in motion to move forward.

As more time passed, I learned it was easy to confuse moving forward with moving on. Moving forward meant bringing the important parts with you, while moving on meant you left it behind. I was still trying to find a way to chisel off the hurt and the heartbreak. It wasn't in my plans to grieve my brother, but I'd never move on from him. I'd move forward and take Dominic with me, living with him instead of without him.

I dragged my hands down my face, irritated that it was three in the morning and I was still awake. Once I parted ways with Lyla, I texted back and forth with her to ensure she was okay. The last thing I wanted was to be the guy in the background, so when she told me she was about to start a movie, I didn't text back. As long as she said she was okay, I'd do my best not to worry about her. Lyla could handle herself. It wasn't her fault I had a habit of overthinking about the people I cared about.

I heard Nathan and Andre stumble in around two. Because I still wanted to try and get some sleep, I stayed in my room instead of engaging in their argument over soft tacos. I laughed every time Nathan's obnoxious cackle rang throughout the apartment, and finally, thirty minutes later, it was quiet again.

It was just me and my thoughts. *Joy.*

It was tempting to take my morning jog now instead of waking up in a few hours. I weighed the pros and cons and finally caved to my burst of energy. After I reunited with my usual running route, maybe I'd finally be able to get some sleep. Plus, my therapist always suggested exercise to work through anxiety. So instead of being the crazy guy running at two-forty five in the morning, I'd be an invested patient following doctor's orders. Yes, that sounded *much* better.

An uneasy feeling settled in my stomach as I slipped on some gray sweatpants and a hoodie. It felt like something was missing, or I overlooked something I was supposed to do. I rifled through the papers on my desk in case I forgot an assignment. I checked my phone for missed calls or texts. Nothing was jumping out, so I shrugged off the feeling as part of the anxiety and shut my bedroom door on the way out.

Since it was still the middle of the night, I took my key so I could lock the front door. I stepped out into the hall, and the uneasy feeling in my stomach grew. When I saw her tear-stained cheeks, I dropped to my knees in front of her, and my heart hit the fucking floor. "Lyla?"

"I'm s-sorry," she managed through a shaky breath. She cleared her throat to steady herself. "I just needed to stop for a minute on my way home. I'm not staying—"

"Your way home." I cupped her chin and examined the same emotionless expression she wore at The Attic. "Lyla, what happened?"

"I just wanted to leave." Her eyes met mine. "But when I started hyperventilating, I ended up here."

My inability to know that Lyla needed me outweighed my instinct to question why she didn't call. I was worried that there was a reason she left in the first place.

"Wanted to leave," I repeated calmly, and then my voice grew louder as images flashed through my head. "As in, that guy wouldn't *let* you leave?"

She shook her head. "No, nothing like that."

I pulled her against my chest and took exaggerated deep breaths. "Breathe, Brooks."

Her shoulders relaxed, and she wrapped her arms around my waist. I stood up and guided her into my apartment. Andre and Nathan returned from the bars about forty-five minutes ago. How long had she been sitting outside in the hall?

Lyla sat on my bed, and as I placed my key back on my dresser, I recognized the look on her face. She was playing back a memory.

"I'm glad you came here," I said, lightly grazing her hand.

"I shouldn't have," she muttered. "This isn't your problem. Whatever *this* is."

I knew what *this* was. Whatever she'd kept bottled up inside was threatening to spill over. It was easy to lash out at people when you were on the verge of exploding. I spent the last two years doing the same thing. Lyla had already walked to one place by herself in the middle of the night. She wasn't doing it a second time.

"Relax here for a moment, and I can walk you home," I offered.

"Didn't you just hear me say this isn't your problem?" she snapped, swinging her legs over the side of the bed.

I reached for her hand before she could get any further. "Then talk to me, Lyla. Please?"

She stared down at my hand, and I released my grip.

"You can tell me as much or as little as you want," I prompted gently. "Whatever you're carrying—it will never be a *problem* to me, Lyla. I want you to know that."

"Nothing even happened, so there's nothing to tell. It's stupid. It's stupid that something like this gets to me when there are people like you who—" She looked away and covered her mouth with her hand. I wouldn't force her to stay and talk to me if she didn't want to, but I felt helpless. There was nothing worse than watching someone you cared about endure pain you couldn't take away.

I pulled her to my chest again, letting her decide where to go from there. If she needed to lean on me, I'd stand. If she needed to cry, I'd hold onto her until she wanted me to let go. If she wanted to talk, I'd listen for as long as she needed me to. I trusted Lyla with a piece of me I was still trying to mend, and I wanted her to know she could do the same.

"I promise you that whatever it is, it's not stupid," I assured her.

"You lost someone." She pulled away, wiping the tears from her cheeks. "You're one of the best people I know, and I *hate* how you and your family had to go through that. It just makes everything else seem so small, you know? I can't get past something that shouldn't even *be* anything while you carry the weight of the world every fucking day."

I felt the familiar sting behind my eyes. It flooded me with questions I often asked to whatever power was in charge of it all. What about me presented so strongly that I seemed equipped to handle losing a sibling? Why did so many others get a second chance when Dominic didn't? Why did it matter if you were good or bad in this world if life took what it wanted anyway?

"Sit down," I suggested softly.

Lyla settled into her usual spot, pulling her knees to her chest. I sat beside her, and it felt good to have the blankets stolen from my side of the bed again.

I took a deep breath and dragged my hands down my face. "I don't know why things happen like they do, Brooks. My entire life, I've figured things out on my own." I shook my head and rested my hand on her knee. "I can't figure out why this happened, but what happened to me doesn't discredit anything you've gone through, whether you think it's nothing or not."

She squeezed my hand, and the corner of her mouth curved into a slight smile. "Time, right?"

"Time." I mimicked her expression. "And having people you trust to listen helps too."

"It really is stupid," she whispered as her green eyes became glossy.

"Nothing you could tell me is stupid. Try me."

Lyla exhaled and rested her head against the headboard. "I told you I had a boyfriend in high school." I nodded, and she continued, "His name was Hunter, and he was one of those guys who was liked by everyone. He was sweet and smart. It was a small town, and people knew Hunter was going places. He'd come out of line and kiss me right before he'd run onto the field before games. The coaches hated it, but he was the starting quarterback. They would never punish him, and he knew that." She let out a laugh that was devoid of any humor. "Everyone loved watching him fall in love with the girlfriend who supported him from the sidelines."

She looked at me, and her eyes narrowed. "Do you ever look back on something and wonder how that was even you in the memory?"

A small snippet of the day Dominic passed away flashed through my head. Sometimes it didn't seem real.

I ran my thumb along her fingers. "All the time."

Tears welled in the corners of her eyes. "It was one night, and every time I think about it, *nothing* happened. He was my boyfriend, and I was his girlfriend, and I didn't tell him no. We'd done it plenty of times before, but this time, I thought I made it obvious I didn't want to. He passed out before anything happened, but if we never had sex, why did it feel so—"

She closed her eyes, and when she opened them, a few tears rolled down her cheeks. She drew in a shaky breath and pulled her hand from mine. "It's like we were two different people. He was drunk, and it didn't matter who I was. I broke up with him two days later, and when I told my best friend Anna about it, she made me feel like an idiot." She shook her head, disgusted at the memory. "She asked me why I was making a big deal about my boyfriend wanting to have sex with me."

The thought of Lyla feeling invalidated by someone she should've been able to trust caused a crack to form down the middle of my chest. I pushed aside my hatred for a girl I didn't know and waited for Lyla to continue.

"Hunter and Anna made me question everything about myself. That night comes back to me every time I try to stay somewhere, and I just can't do it. Suddenly, I'm back in that room, and I have to leave before something happens. You probably think I'm insane—"

"Lyla." I cupped her face, prompting her to look at me. I grazed her cheek with my thumb, and she relaxed into my touch. I knew how painful it could be to relive a memory, and I couldn't imagine hiding that memory because I was nervous to trust someone with it.

"I get so worked up about a night where nothing even happened," she whispered.

It didn't matter how often she said it out loud to try and make sense of it. High school wasn't a stepping stone for a guy to realize he shouldn't make assumptions and for a girl to learn she should say no next time.

"Someone you trusted made you feel like you had no control over a situation, and that can be *scary*," I said, weighing my next words carefully. "Silence doesn't mean consent, and just because he passed out doesn't mean it was *nothing*. It wasn't *nothing*, Lyla."

Lyla leaned into my chest, and I wrapped my arms around her tiny frame.

"It wasn't nothing, sweetheart," I murmured. "And I'm so sorry that happened to you."

Pieces of our conversations floated around in my head, and parts of Lyla's past began to fit together. Her first and only relationship was the reason she moved before her senior year of high school. The first guy she trusted was the reason she didn't get attached.

Lyla peered up at me with tired eyes and a soft expression. "You know what's crazy?"

I leaned back against the headboard, pulling her with me. "What?"

Lyla let out a sniffly laugh, and the emotional shift threw me off. "I'm pretty sure you're my best friend."

I chuckled, and the contagious light behind her eyes returned. "You mean I didn't mention that in my fake boyfriend pitch? I should've warned you that you might actually like me."

"Nope. Totally left that out."

I kissed the top of her head and settled into the mattress. "Thank you for telling me. I know it isn't easy, trusting someone with chapters from your past."

"It's been five years since I tried talking about it with someone," she admitted.

"Anna?"

Lyla sat up. "Yup. She's the only person I've told, and she's dating Hunter now, so it really just adds a layer to the bin of high school memories."

My eyebrows shot to the top of my forehead. "What! Your best frie—" My voice trailed off, and I shook my head. "Fuck, Brooks. I'm sorry." I didn't know what else to say. Her best friend, her boyfriend, her dad—this girl continued to be disappointed by people.

"Believe it or not, I am *trying*," Lyla said with a small smile. "I'm trying to move forward, but it's hard. I changed high schools, left the small town, and went to college. I just want to start over. Keeping people at a distance is an easy way to make sure things happen my way."

"You know I'm always here for you, right?" I eyed her playfully and smirked. "You kind of sort of might be my best friend too."

She winced. "This is getting too rom-com for me."

"I was waiting for you to realize that. Do you want me to walk you home? Or you can stay here if you want. It's totally up to you."

Lyla stretched, letting out an exaggerated yawn. "You don't mind sharing your bed? I know it must be nice to have it to yourself again."

I fell back against my pillow and got under the blankets. "You're always welcome in my bed, Brooks."

She reached behind her to turn off the light. "That's some cute boyfriend-girlfriend shit."

I pulled my shirt over my head and threw it into the closet. Lyla settled in closer and rested her head in the crook of my arm.

When I was with Cassie, I tried my best to seem okay. I could never be tense or guarded or come across as stressed or bothered by something I wasn't telling her. It made her feel awkward. She'd prompt me to talk to her, and then somehow, I'd end up comforting her. Eventually, I just accepted that she was more interested in me accommodating her feelings instead of trying to figure out my own. It was like trying to breathe in a closed-off room. I didn't realize how much I was struggling until Cassie cracked a window and forced me to leave.

Lyla never made me feel like I had to push something away because it would make her feel uncomfortable. I waited until she fell asleep first, and about two minutes later, I was right behind her. The pressure in my chest was gone, and the chaos in my head finally stopped. It felt nice to come up for fresh air again.

Chapter Thirty-Four

Lyla

I thought Charlie was joking when she told me she still didn't have a costume. It was the Friday of Halloween weekend, and this bitch was looking around her room as if the walls were going to hand her a solution.

"If you don't just get in your car and drive us to the store," I muttered angrily. She had dragged me away from a fantasy novel I was four chapters away from finishing for this nonsense.

She laughed at my dramatized response, and fifteen minutes later, we were scouring a pop-up costume store.

"You're lucky this place is still standing," I murmured, dragging my fingers along the rows of costumes. "I think someone just comes and folds the entire store up on November 1st." I smiled at the Tarzan costume hanging on the end of the rack. I was excited to see Deacon tonight, which was another red flag in my "Keep it Casual" series because I spent the entire week with him.

Best friends put in overtime when it came to their fake relationship, right? I came with a lot. As if my daddy drama wasn't enough, I spilled my darkest secret to the man, and he still asked me to stay. I was doing my best not to question it. My next purchase from Grounds for Thought had to be some sort of violent thriller novel. No exceptions.

"I just need something flirty and fun," Charlie said, grabbing a skimpy princess costume from the wall. "Thoughts?"

"Well, since I'm staring at a princess and a *banana* costume, I'm thinking princess is your best bet."

"Fine," Charlie huffed. She bent down to grab the matching crown, and when she stood up, she wore a devilish grin. It was creepy.

"Eww. What is that look for?"

"We're officially alone now, so we can talk about your secret boyfriend. Especially since you haven't been around all week for me to ask you about him."

I heard an eye roll in there and chose to ignore it. "Ask away, I guess."

"I'll start with observations," Charlie declared. "First observation, his presence doesn't bother you. He comes over, you let him stay, and I can tell you like having him around. The second observation is you spend the *entire* night at his place. Don't even get me started on that one. And my final observation that I'll leave you with today is that he surpassed your thirty-day rule."

"Boyfriends are *supposed* to be all of those things." I placed a Dr. Pepper on the checkout counter. The least Charlie could do was buy me a drink for dragging me back to this stupid store. "Everything is going fine. Why are you probing?"

"Because I think you like him," Charlie insisted, handing her debit card to the cashier. He threw our stuff in a bag, and we started toward the car.

I waited until Charlie unlocked the doors to answer. "He's insanely caught up on his ex-girlfriend, Charlie. Don't be insane."

She pursed her lips and slid into the driver's seat. "Interesting."

"*What* is interesting?"

Charlie grinned and started the car. "That your first response wasn't a *no*. Honey, I know the backstory of why Deacon is dating you. I was there when I discovered it, remember?"

I stifled a laugh, and when I turned to look out the window, Charlie's cackling filled the car.

"This entire thing puts me one step closer to my goals," I said. "I told you, once I get this money, I can officially work on opening my bookstore."

"And listen, I think that idea is fucking phenomenal. I'll need to know how much the rent is when I stay in the loft above your bookstore. But"—Charlie sighed—"never mind."

I glared at her. "What?"

"Have you ever thought about pursuing this dream *without* the money from your dad?"

It was a fair question, and the answer was only obvious to me because I rarely shared the whole story.

"If I did this on my own, and I'm not saying I couldn't because I could, I would never leave Cleveland," I admitted. "I can't leave my mom. And if I can help her work toward a dream she couldn't have because she got stuck with me, well, Aaron Brooks owes her that."

Charlie gave me a sympathetic smile. "Jane didn't get *stuck* with you. I just want you to know that I believe in what you want to do, regardless of how you start it."

I smiled. "Thanks, Charlie."

When we arrived at our apartment, Charlie's costume in hand, we were greeted by two people I never thought would be standing in our living room. Michelle and Keira stood side by side in Thing 1 and Thing 2 costumes. They were trying to take a selfie and kept laughing when one of them would mess up a facial expression.

I shared a look with Charlie that asked, "Should we be concerned?"

She cocked her head and answered, "Not at all."

"Hey guys! You look so cute!" I swooned. I lowered my voice so only Charlie could hear me. "Set your slutty princess costume on the counter and help me make the drinks."

We laughed as we threw together a cocktail, not knowing what to call it since we were going off of what we had in the fridge. It was a combination of pink lemonade, Sprite, vodka, Malibu, and half a bottle of white wine.

"Bottoms up." Charlie cringed and clinked her glass with mine. We took a sip, and her eyebrows shot to the top of her forehead. "This isn't bad!"

"No." I laughed, pouring Michelle and Keira a drink. "It's really not."

Charlie surveyed the Dr. Seuss characters and tried her best not to laugh. "So, where are you two headed tonight?"

"Tubby's is having a costume contest," Keira explained. "We didn't want to get too crazy since we're going to a party tomorrow night."

"You're coming tomorrow, right?" Michelle added.

It took me a moment to realize Thing 2 was speaking to me. "Coming where?"

"To Eric and Weston's Halloween party. Cassie mentioned she invited you and Deacon."

I almost spit out my drink onto the counter. I forgot that Michelle knew Cassie.

How long had she known her? Did she meet Cassie at the beginning of the school year? Last year? Did they meet after I met Deacon? After I started *dating* Deacon? Red fish? Blue fish? My questions were beginning to sound like a fucking Dr. Seuss story.

"Deacon did mention a party tomorrow," I lied. "That's why we're getting a late start tonight. Tomorrow is probably going to get a little crazy."

Charlie looked at me like I had just threatened to steal her new tiara.

"Drink up, Char. We have places to be tonight and a party tomorrow." I threw back my drink and made a beeline for my room.

I could play the part of Olive Oyl following Popeye to the bars. But a house party? Two critical components of a Bowling Green house party were tight spaces and lots of people. Cassie would be around every corner tomorrow night, and I just hoped my best friend, Deacon, and I could handle it.

CHAPTER THIRTY-FIVE

Deacon

I NEVER THOUGHT I'D be walking around campus in a tight-ass V-neck shirt, khakis, and a sailor's hat. One time was laughable, but twice? I didn't even recognize myself when I looked back on last year's Halloween. Cassie chose our costumes, and I wanted to stay in instead. She cried and told me that she knew I was mad about something, so I went out with her anyway.

Lyla glanced at me playfully as she fastened her earrings in front of the bathroom mirror. "You didn't tell me Cassie already *invited* you to this party."

I quickly crossed the hall so she could lower her voice. I leaned against the door frame and gestured to our living room full of guests. Nathan and Andre started a game of Flip Cup with Charlie and a few other people we invited to pregame.

Lyla grinned at her reflection. "To be fair, Charlie already knows this is fake. And come on, some bantering before we go out? We sound even more like a real couple."

I didn't argue with her. Cassie loved to pick fights before we went out. They were usually about something I did earlier that week that suddenly became relevant to the present. It was like she reserved all her anger for one pivotal moment during the weekend.

"Fine," I admitted. "Cassie invited me to a party last weekend. But to be fair, you do your best work when it's unscripted!"

Lyla zipped up her make-up bag. "Okay, Daddy Deacon."

Don't go there. I wasn't sure if the dip in my stomach came from the words themselves or because Lyla said them. *Nope, nope, nope.*

"Let's go, Olive." I tugged Lyla out of the bathroom and joined the small crowd in the living room.

Charlie handed each of us a shot glass and winked at me. We cheered for Halloween 2016, and then we were off.

The house party Cassie invited us to was only a ten-minute walk. It was customary for a house party to have an open door. People were good about passing through if they knew someone, but Bowling Green's community atmosphere was always welcoming.

I pulled on Lyla's hand, so she walked in front of me. A few cheers from the stairway greeted us, and multiple guys looked Lyla up and down while we got our bearings.

I slid my fingers over her bare hip and dropped my mouth to her ear. "Let me get your drink. Don't take anything—"

She smiled over her shoulder. "Deacon Scott. Do not give me the spiked drink chat in the middle of a house party. This isn't my first rodeo."

"Charlie!" Michelle ran toward us in a fuzzy creature costume. "I'm glad you guys came! There is pong downstairs. Do you want to play?"

"Go get the drinks," Lyla yelled as Charlie dragged her away, "and meet me downstairs!"

I weaved through the crowd until I found the kitchen, relieved to see coolers with cheap beer instead of giant punch bowls of drinks. I grabbed two Natural Light cans, and when

I turned around, Cassie was in front of me. She stood next to Clara and a girl I didn't recognize. All three of them wore matching black leotards and animal ears. Cassie's left bunny ear folded when she peered over at me.

"What are you supposed to be?" I asked once she got closer. Her eyes grazed my chest, and I forgot how tight my shirt was.

"Regina George from *Mean Girls*." Cassie giggled and gestured to the girls behind her. "Clara is Gretchen, and Sophia is Karen."

In the movie, Cady Heron described them as slutty costumes with some sort of animal ears. Her words, not mine. "Your costume definitely makes more sense with that information."

"Where are your roommates? Did Lyla come in with you? I must've missed her."

"Were you watching me?" I teased. I slipped past her, stopping at the top of the stairs.

Cassie smiled. "Just happy you're happy, Deacon. I'll be down there in a bit."

When someone shared that they wanted you to be happy, the words were supposed to sound endearing. Cassie used the same tone at Shots when she said, "Same old Deacon."

I reminded myself that I had planned my life out with Cassie. She wasn't just the girl who broke my heart in front of a coffee shop. She was the girl who stared up at me through dark lashes with a smile that could tempt me to do anything. It was the look she gave me during our first year of dating—when things were exciting and new. It was the look she used to give me before she watched me lose everything. That look dwindled long before she called to break up with me, and the closer I got to Lyla, the more I realized how far gone those feelings were.

When I got downstairs, Lyla was high-fiving Charlie. There were now *two* fuzzy creature costumes and the four of them were each down to two cups in their pong game. Andre and Nathan cheered from the pool table when Charlie's ball fell into the front cup.

Lyla stood on her toes and peered at the only cup left on the table. She dropped down to her feet again and popped her hip, accentuating how her skirt rested right where her ass met her thigh. Lyla Brooks was a sexy Olive Oyl, and I was happy we couldn't get her hair to stay pulled back in that weird bun. I liked the way her light brown waves sat above her lower back. She was cute with her hair up, but I loved when she wore her hair down.

I sat her beer on the corner of the table and kissed her temple. "Don't slip, Brooks." She giggled when Charlie shoved me away from the table.

"Get out of here!" Charlie laughed. "You'll just distract her."

Lyla closed one eye and dramatically lined up the shot. Her foot popped once the ball left her hand, and I didn't have to look to know she made it.

She threw her arms around my neck, and I placed my drink on the table beside hers. She gave me a quick kiss on the lips and trailed up my jaw. She nipped my ear lobe and whispered, "Go with this, okay? She's behind you."

She didn't need to say anything else. I gripped the backs of her thighs and lifted her off the ground. She tightened her hold around my neck and laughed when I tugged on her bottom lip with my teeth. I wanted to kiss her, but not in a room full of people. Suddenly, a performance kiss wasn't enough.

"Get a room," Charlie said as she reset the cups for the next game.

I gestured to the door behind her. "That one?"

She raised her eyebrows, impressed by my bold statement and the actions that followed it.

I removed my hand from the back of Lyla's thigh to open the door. She tightened her legs around my waist, and I grasped the hair at the base of her neck. I tugged so I had a better angle and pressed my mouth to hers. This kiss was different than the one we had a few moments ago. We were still in view of everyone in the basement, and as soon as my tongue parted her lips, she reached behind me and closed the door.

Chapter Thirty-Six

Lyla

I HAD TO HAND it to myself. I was becoming *scarily* skilled at finding windows of opportunity for Cassie to see Deacon and I wrapped up together. My legs were literally wrapped around his waist. His hand was in my hair as his mouth traveled up my jawline. His lips found their way back to mine, and instead of the quick-paced hunger he demonstrated a few seconds ago, they slowed down and made me realize that I wasn't just kissing Deacon.

I was *kissing* Deacon, and I didn't want it to stop.

I had kissed Deacon more times than I could count. No matter how often we played out the on-screen performance, I always thought back to the first time he kissed me at The Attic, where he asked for permission instead of just laying one on me. I didn't think anything could beat that moment. My skin was on fire, and I was happy to be proven wrong.

My ass hit something hard. Was it a desk? I didn't care. Deacon's tongue was eager against mine, and his hands skimmed the skin under my breasts. What was it about this man and how he took his time that made things so *delightful?* Most guys would've already had my top off. Some of them might not have even bothered to take anything off at all. Everything was rushed and heavy, and when I felt Deacon's erection on my thigh, alarms went off in my head.

I didn't want this to stop, but it needed to. We no longer had an audience. We were off-screen, and neither of us hinted at pausing it.

As if he read my thoughts by pressing his forehead to mine, Deacon pulled away. "Lyla," he whispered.

We made eye contact, and I didn't know what I was waiting for. Was he the one waiting? One of us needed to say *something*. It didn't feel awkward. The only uncomfortable part about this was stopping something that felt completely natural.

Not a real relationship, no lying, fuck around in private, and no love.

I guess this *could be* fucking around in private. It was lacking in climax but offered a nice plot twist.

"Top-tier, Deacon Scott," I whispered back with a smile.

Deacon chuckled, pushing off the desk with his hands. "Come on. Let's get back to your game."

"We can't go out there yet! We've been in here for like five minutes."

"And . . ."

"And do you want Cassie thinking you're suddenly a two-pump chump? Have a seat for a moment."

He narrowed his gaze and glanced around the room. "Cassie would never think that. She's had a front-row seat to—"

"Stop talking." I giggled uncontrollably and covered my eyes. I hoped to help block out the mental images of Deacon bending me over the desk. His chest pressed against my back, and his hand gripping the hair at the base of my neck like he had done a few moments ago before—

"We don't lie, right?"

I moved my hands, and Deacon was lying across the recliner on the other side of the room. His hands were behind his head, and his lips curved into a slight grin.

"We don't lie," I said, leaning back against the desk.

"What was that?" he prompted gently.

"Boyfriend-girlfriend shit." There wasn't a millisecond of hesitation to my answer, and it wasn't a lie. Everyone just witnessed a couple backing into an open bedroom. It wasn't unordinary at all.

"Boyfriend-girlfriend shit," he agreed with the smirk that drove me nuts. "Okay."

I cocked my head. "You don't sound convinced."

"Oh, I'm not." Deacon smiled before he stood up and started walking toward me. "But you're a fantastic performer, Lyla Brooks, and we don't lie. So if you say it's just boyfriend-girlfriend shit"—Deacon leaned forward so his face was inches away from mine—"it's just boyfriend-girlfriend shit."

I pressed my lips together to keep from smiling. There was a playfulness in his eyes I hadn't seen before, and I was getting pretty good at reading this downright delightful human. This version was excited about what just happened, and moments ago, I had the physical evidence against my leg to prove it. When the alarm bells returned, I gripped the desk behind me to keep my hands off his chest.

I smirked back at him. "Let's go Popeye. Olive needs another drink."

Deacon laughed, putting space between us again.

Out in the living room, it was clear the free bedroom routine worked. Charlie, like an asshole, clapped enthusiastically from the pool table. A disappointed Regina George stood by the stairs, and soon, two supportive animal friends followed her up to the kitchen.

I pulled Deacon into the doorway and lifted my phone.

He looked back at the room with a naughty grin. "Again?"

I smacked his bicep and gestured toward the phone in the air. "No, a photo!"

Right on cue, Deacon grinned at the camera and kissed the top of my head for the second shot. I posted the photo and then sent a copy to Aaron Brooks for good measure.

"Good call." Deacon took off his sailor hat and ran a hand through his hair. "I almost forgot about a photo."

"I have to start prepping my dad for Thanksgiving," I explained. "He's meeting you in a few weeks, and I just—"

"I'm not worried, " Deacon said, throwing his arm around my shoulders. "But something tells me you are."

"Can't help it," I admitted, crossing my arms in front of my chest. I hated how my dad wasn't even in the same state and could still make me nervous. "If anything about that goes badly, he'll pull the plug. I'm almost a semester away from graduating, and all I can think about is how much I want to move forward."

"Hey." Deacon nudged me so I would look at him. "This *will* work. Knight in shining armor, remember?"

I rolled my eyes and chuckled at his boyish grin.

"Don't underestimate me," he threatened playfully. "Let me get us another drink, and then I'll teach you how to play pool."

Deacon crossed the room to the stairs, and I yelled, "How do you know I don't know how to play?"

When he turned around, his sexy smirk was back. "I've seen your form, baby girl, and I have no issue showing you how it's done."

Baby girl, huh? The butterflies erupted in my stomach, and heat pooled between my legs. Fuck me.

Chapter Thirty-Seven

Deacon

It had been three weeks since Halloween, and I couldn't stop thinking about how Lyla's hips fit perfectly in my hands. I should've been thrilled when Cassie texted me the morning after the party to say we should meet up more often when we go out. I should've been excited that she hadn't *stopped* texting me.

But only one name lit up my screen and brought a smile to my face—Lyla Brooks.

I was two days away from meeting the famous Aaron Brooks, the man who made Lyla crumble at just the thought of having to see him. I hated how uncertain she looked when she spoke about him. Everything I liked most about Lyla—her smile, laugh, witty responses—couldn't exist in the version she had to be for her dad.

It was my last night in the apartment since I would spend the next two days at Lyla's place. Nathan and Andre were heading home after their classes tomorrow morning, and the thought of the apartment going untouched for an entire week didn't sit well with me.

Andre watched as I sprayed down the kitchen and prepared the mop for the floor. When his staring became obvious, I looked over at him. "What?"

His eyes narrowed, and he laughed. "I've been watching you clean for like two hours. Are you always this way before a break?"

"*Watching*. So you knew you could help, and you just didn't want to?"

"I'm not about to clean everything for it to be dusty in a week when I get back. That doesn't make sense."

I couldn't argue with his logic, but I needed some sort of outlet. I stress cleaned, so what? There were far worse choices out there that people opted for to avoid dealing with emotions.

Technically, if I told Andre what was bugging me, I wouldn't be lying. I paused my mopping and said, "I'm meeting Lyla's dad on Wednesday, and he's apparently a douche. I'm just nervous I'll make things harder for her."

Andre swatted the air in front of him. "You only have to worry about the parents if you're making it official. Until then, does it really matter what they think?"

After I met Cassie's parents for the first time, she told me that they loved me. My parents never offered me a response when they met Cassie. My mom never mentioned Cassie when she talked about me having kids, and my dad always described her as a "nice girl" and dropped the subject. I wanted my parents to root for me and the girl I brought home because what they thought mattered to me. I wanted to check another one of their boxes.

"Are you about to ask this girl to marry you the same night you meet her dad?" Andre's eyebrows shot to the top of his forehead, like that idea was the most appalling thing he'd ever heard.

"Nope," I said through a cocky grin. "I'm all for the happy ending, but I'm not an idiot."

"You're the only person I know who would even consider marriage right out of college."

"You know, lots of people get married their first year out of college," I argued.

Andre had a shit poker face, and his shocked expression grew more intense the longer we lingered on the subject. He shook his head, prepared with another rebuttal. "False. A lot of *women* want to settle down, and that pushes men to pop the question. Marriage is a piece of paper."

"It's not a piece of paper to me. It's an opportunity to build a life with someone. Marriage is a new chapter. I want someone to be my person—to grow old and raise kids with." I looked up, and Andre was smiling. I threw the washrag at him, and he laughed. "Shut up, man."

He raised his hands defensively. "Hey, I get it! I want my person too, just maybe ten years from now."

I chuckled at his response and searched under the sink for garbage bags.

"Question, though," Andre said from the recliner. "I know you're with Lyla, but were you going to ask Cassie to marry you?"

I rested my hands on the trash can. May seemed so long ago, back when I was Googling engagement rings and planning to have Cassie live with me. I always had to stay one step ahead of Cassie, so I knew she was happy.

I changed the trash and tied up the bag. "I was going to after graduation," I admitted. "I had the whole thing planned out in my head."

"Shocking," Andre murmured.

I shook off his comment. "Anything else need to go in here?"

"Nah. You've cleaned every inch of this place like five times."

I left Andre with his Xbox and walked the trash to the dumpster. It was cooler outside, and it was officially sweatshirt season. I stuck my hands in my pockets and leaned against the trunk of my car. My eyes lingered on the stars above me until I found the Big Dipper.

"Every time." I grinned, allowing my gaze to wander.

One of the worst parts about winter was the overcast and cloudy skies. When the sky was clear, I felt closer to Dominic. It was like he had a better view of what was going on below him.

My phone vibrated in my sweatpants.

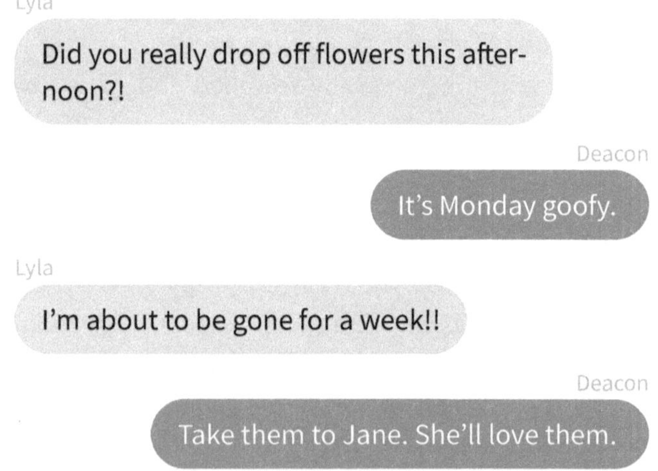

I sighed at the thought of losing more flowers to Lyla's caretaking. It wasn't entirely her fault since it was my request in the first place for her to have them. More dots appeared and then reappeared on my screen. She was in her head about something.

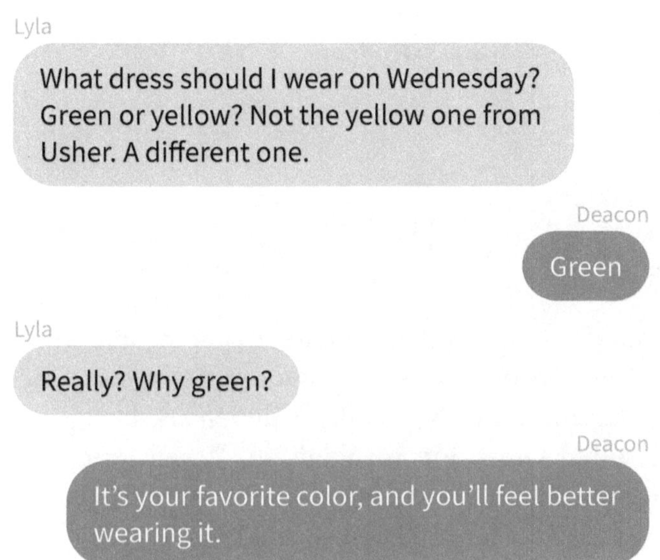

I knew what dress she was referring to. It was a dark green and exposed one of her shoulders.

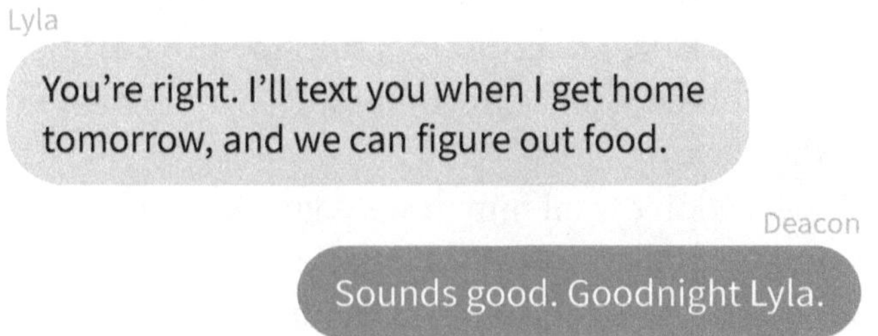

She sent me a heart emoji and her usual "Goodnight, Daddy Deacon" response. It made me smile every time, and when I looked up at the sky, I knew Dominic was rolling his eyes.

Chapter Thirty-Eight

Lyla

It took Deacon twenty minutes to get me into his car.

Because Aaron Brooks required a specific star rating to dine, the small, homey, and perfectly remarkable restaurants in Bowling Green just wouldn't do. When I received directions to a high-rise steakhouse in downtown Toledo, my stomach sank. It felt too familiar, and I wasn't sure if Deacon was prepared for it.

"Park near the back," I instructed when we pulled into the lot. I pointed to an empty spot near the exit and smoothed out my dress. It was starting to wrinkle since I hadn't steamed it. I was a college student who didn't own a fucking steamer, and I knew it would be on the list of insults my dad could throw.

Deacon followed my directions and put the car in park. "Why the back?"

"Because I don't want him to see your car. I *adore* your car, but I don't want to give my dad a reason to comment on something that he has no right to comment on."

Deacon gave my hand a light squeeze. "Relax, sweetheart. It's just dinner. I'll try to do most of the talking so you won't have to."

Deacon slipped his hand through mine as we walked across the parking lot. He held open the door, and I caught myself taking in the full view of Deacon Scott in dress clothes. He looked *deliciously* downright delightful in a crisp white shirt and black dress pants, both tailored to hug every curve of his body. I'd just keep adding Ds to the description of my fake boyfriend since I wasn't getting the D I truly wanted from him.

Cue the alarm bells. *For fuck's sake Lyla.*

We boarded the elevator, and I almost buckled when Deacon rolled up the sleeves of his dress shirt. I pressed my lips together so my mouth didn't fall open, focusing on the task at hand instead of his forearms. In just a few short moments, Deacon would be seated across the table from Aaron Brooks, and all of the strides I'd made toward getting out from under my dad would be in jeopardy.

Deacon squeezed my hand again. "Stop."

"Stop what?"

"Stop getting into your head."

I rolled my eyes as the elevator doors opened, and a friendly hostess greeted us. As I mentioned my father's name, her expression shifted to disapproval. She must have already met the man of the hour.

The hostess led us to a table near the back of the restaurant. It sat in the middle of a floor-to-ceiling window that provided a beautiful view of the city below. It would have been a stunning environment to dine in had it not been tainted by the man already at the table.

Aaron Brooks looked like he always did for one of our reunion dinners—cream suit, black hair slicked back, green eyes surrounded by minimal fine lines, and an expression described as the opposite of welcoming.

He stood up to greet us as we approached the table. I received an awkward side hug, and when I pulled away to sit down, Deacon placed his hand on my shoulder.

"Mr. Brooks." Deacon extended his free hand and smiled. "It's nice to meet you. My name is Deacon Scott. I'm Lyla's boyfriend."

Dad looked him up and down, but he wasn't suspicious. He was too speechless to believe a guy was standing in front of him.

"Deacon Scott," Dad repeated. My god—was that a *grin?* "It's a pleasure."

They shook hands, and Deacon pulled out my chair for me to sit. He placed my bag on the table beside him and rested his arm behind me. It was the most natural setting for Deacon. He had played the boyfriend role for three years with Cassie, and I had no reason to doubt him.

"I ordered some wine," Dad said, leaning back in his chair. He looked relaxed, comfortable even. It was strange, and my look of concern must've shown. "Lyla, I haven't seen your transcript for the semester yet. Any reason you haven't sent it?"

"I—"

Deacon placed his hand on my thigh. "The semester doesn't officially end until December," he interrupted gently. "I don't think you have anything to worry about. Lyla is brilliant."

I smiled shyly, ignoring the delighted tingles that ran up my thigh and into my groin. Deacon's hand was warm through the thin fabric of my dress, and like a pure gentleman, he didn't move it. It was innocent enough to be supportive but tempting enough for me to want him to inch it further toward my pulsing—

"Brilliant, huh?" Dad shook his head condescendingly and chuckled into his wine glass. "Lyla has always had her studies on the back burner. It's a shame, too. I would expect some difficulty with a more challenging program choice, but English?"

"It's just a minor, Dad." I reached for my wine, surprised I waited this long to take a sip.

"Yeah, well, you had to choose something, and we both know you could never thrive in math or science—"

"What did you go to college for, sir?" Deacon prompted.

Deacon knew my dad didn't attend college, so I wasn't sure why he asked. It didn't matter. The only thing I could focus on was Deacon's hand. Nothing was worse than craving skin-to-skin contact but settling for the appropriate option.

Dad studied us for a moment across the table. Then, a sly smile slowly spread across his face, making me take another sip of my red. "Fortunately, my career didn't require a college degree."

Deacon grinned. "So, no late-night papers or anything for you, huh?" He was trying to make a point and did a great job burying his sarcasm.

Dad transitioned the topic of conversation to A. Brooks Financial Firm and highlighted his credentials. If there was one thing that could derail Dad's stream of insults, it was an opportunity to talk about himself and everything he had created.

The waitress came to the table, and I prayed to the goddess of wine that she brought another bottle with her. She took our orders and presented a tray of appetizers to start us off. I picked at the bread basket and rolled my eyes at the plate of oysters on ice in the middle of the table. Dad was guilty of ordering a shit ton of food with no intention of eating it. I didn't even like oysters.

For the next twenty minutes, I heard about the steady rise of Dad's success. Deacon asked engaging questions that required well-thought-out answers and explanations. Dad provided them, and I almost fell out of my chair when he asked Deacon about his choice of major.

"The goal is pediatric surgery. I'd like to start working next fall and begin medical school the following year."

Dad nodded approvingly. "You took your MCAT, I presume?"

I glanced over at Deacon and placed my hand over his. "Deacon took the MCAT his sophomore year. He did great."

"I did have to take it one more time," Deacon admitted, chuckling. "And I'm glad I did. I spent most of sophomore year studying for that damn thing."

"And where will you go to school?" Dad prompted. He cut into his steak, and my stomach twisted as the red juice flooded his plate. I glanced out the window and sipped my wine.

"Not sure yet. Depends on Lyla, too."

I almost choked on my drink. I smiled sweetly at the table and put my glass down to prevent any further damage. I couldn't make eye contact with him, but I knew Dad was staring. I felt the anxiety building in my chest. The belt began to tighten, and I braced for whatever comment was coming next.

"I wouldn't focus too much on that factor," Aaron said. "Lyla doesn't follow through with anything, and once she fails, she'll give up whatever business she plans on starting. You don't want to set aside your potential for a flaky pipe dream."

I wasn't sure what was more upsetting—the fact that I had a father who said shit like that out loud or the way his words felt like daggers every fucking time. I should be used to this, and in a few months, I'd never have to sit through one of these dinners again.

Dad flashed a grin to the left and raised his glass. A woman with a camera snapped a shot and wandered back toward the hostess stand. He usually arranged for a cute father-daughter photo at the beginning of the meal instead of after he insulted me—anything to document him looking like the father of the year.

I waited for the shock to hit Deacon's system, but his face remained relaxed and unbothered. Even when the man was rendered speechless, he was gorgeous. There was another squeeze on my thigh, and I hadn't realized I was holding my breath until I squeezed his hand back.

"With all due respect, sir, my potential doesn't mean anything if Lyla can't have her dream, too. What she does after college is important to me, and I want to help her achieve it. If anyone can see something through, it's her."

I silently reprimanded the tears forming in the corner of my right eye.

To avoid any awkwardness, Dad continued the conversation as if Deacon had said nothing at all. "Will you be spending any time at home for the holidays, Deacon? Where is home, by the way?"

I released Deacon's hand to start on my grilled chicken salad. I usually wasn't a salad type of girl, but it was the only thing on the menu that didn't make me want to vomit at the thought of being stuck at this table.

"Detroit. I'm heading up there tomorrow, and I'll go back for Christmas," Deacon answered, taking a bite of his chicken.

"Will you be going too, Lyla? Have you met Deacon's family yet?"

I took a sip of water to clear my throat. "I haven't—"

"Yeah, actually." Deacon looked at me and smiled. His playful gaze was contagious, and he rested his hand on my forearm. I was running out of body parts for him to catch on fire. "I invited Lyla for Christmas, but she has to clear it with Jane first."

My eyes narrowed, and I forced myself to stay silent. A calm realization came over me that I might have to meet Deacon's parents for the holiday. The thought of meeting the people who raised a man like Deacon didn't startle me in the slightest.

Dad interrupted our intense and somehow flirty stare-down. "Jane?"

"Deacon talks to Mom all the time," I explained, finally breaking eye contact with Deacon to emphasize my next statement. "She really likes him."

In classic Aaron Brooks fashion, he didn't push further into a conversation that didn't include talking about himself or insulting me. "Anyone want their food boxed up?"

After Dad paid for the meal, we took an awkward elevator ride down to the parking lot. Deacon held my hand, and when it was time to part ways, he extended his other toward my dad. "It was nice to meet you, Mr. Brooks."

"Please, call me Aaron."

I smiled weakly and leaned into his pitiful side hug. "Bye, Dad."

The walk to the car was devastatingly cold. The wind picked up as we rounded the corner of the building, and as soon as we were close enough for Deacon to unlock the doors with his fob, he burst into laughter. It was the kind of laughter you were forced to hold in for an hour and a half, and by the time I slid into my seat, I was clutching my stomach.

I wiped the tears from my eyes and let out a final chuckle as Deacon turned on the heat.

He rested his hand on my thigh and gave it a tap. Those damn hands needed to keep to themselves for the rest of the night, or else I was going to implode.

"I'm sorry that dinner sucked," I offered apologetically. "But thank you for sitting through it."

Deacon looked behind us to see if he was clear to reverse. "It wasn't that bad."

What was it about men with their hands on the back of the headrest?

I appreciated the effort to make my toxic father-daughter relationship seem normal. Deacon was the first person other than my mom to meet Aaron Brooks. I felt terrible for introducing him to such a scene that would linger in his mind as an awkward memory.

Mariah Carey's "All I Want for Christmas is You" came through the speakers as heat flooded the car.

"Believe it or not, it was better having you there," I admitted. "I actually smiled during this one because of you."

My eyes lingered on his exposed forearm near the hem of my dress. If this image were Deacon's profile picture on a dating website, I'd swipe right so fucking fast. Those hands could do some things, and it was driving me insane that I couldn't direct their attention to the ache between my thighs. I had to cross my legs just to get my nerve endings to calm down.

"Oh, well, I do that on purpose," Deacon said, leaning closer. His calming scent of cedarwood and lavender mixed with something stronger. It was a cologne I didn't recognize, and I made a mental note to sneak a peek at the bottle on his dresser when we returned from break.

"What do you mean?" I asked softly.

You could kiss him. You could kiss him right now while you're stopped at this red light.

"Your smile is everything," Deacon said. "That's why I'm always trying to make you laugh."

I needed a week away from Deacon. I needed space from the man who made me want to climb over the gearshift and settle onto his lap. I would have that dress shirt unbuttoned and his chest exposed in seconds. I'd finally get to feel his warm skin against mine and run my fingers over the parts of him I wanted to explore. I wanted to feel his hand at the nape of my neck again and the swell of my lips after he nipped them with his teeth.

I wanted to feel *everything*.

When we woke up the next morning, I offered Deacon the friendliest hug I could muster, and we parted ways. It was an exchange between coworkers, an agreement between two parties, because that's what this relationship was. Deacon would get the girl, and I'd start the next chapter of my life.

Chapter Thirty-Nine

Deacon

Snow had officially come to Bowling Green, Ohio. The windchill was fierce, and a miserable blanket of final exams and ice covered the campus. I was ready to check out of the scene for a few weeks.

The base in the living room told me Nathan hadn't left yet. Andre was leaving around six with a buddy of his, and I planned to head out in the next hour. The drive to Detroit wasn't horrible, but the lack of scenery didn't make me want to get going anytime soon. I was also giving Lyla a little bit more time to text me before she headed home to Cleveland. Things had shifted between us since dinner with her dad, and I was nervous I had done something to turn her off.

Aaron Brooks was exactly how Lyla described him. Classic Italian dad appearance, clean-cut business persona, and a clear line of attack pointed at any possible flaw Lyla presented to the crowd. We'd been at dinner for an hour, and he insulted her at least five times. What threw me the most was Lyla's ability to shrug the words off as if they meant nothing. I honestly didn't think she knew how to respond to a man who was supposed to be rooting for her. He set aside a trust fund, for God's sake. Why bet on the winning team if you only wanted them to lose?

My phone buzzed on my end table, and I reached over to tap the screen.

I hope you have a good break. Lunch when
we get back?

I stared at the screen. *Lunch?* That was the last thing I
expected to read today.

You too. Yeah, that sounds good.

With my bags packed and ready, I ventured into the living
room just in time to witness the end of Nathan and Andre's
game of Madden.

"Are you heading out?" Nathan asked. He tossed the con-
troller in Andre's lap and ducked before Andre could smack
him on the back of the head.

There was a knock at the door, and the three of us looked
at each other. Since it was clear none of us were expecting
someone, I peered through the peephole. It was Greg.

I opened the door and stepped aside so Nathan and Andre
could see our guest. Greg walked right past me and set his
bags down in the kitchen.

"Perfect," he exclaimed. "You're still here. Nathan, why the
fuck don't you answer your phone?"

"Madden." Nathan shrugged, falling back into the recliner.
"You good?"

Greg put his hands on his hips and glared at Andre. "You
don't answer either."

Andre threw his hands up in the air. "I put my phone in my
bag!"

Greg looked at me next. "And I didn't have your number, so I couldn't really text you. Even though you're the one I need to talk to the most, I guess."

I eyed him quizzically. "Why?"

He took a deep breath and glanced from Nathan to Andre. Then he turned to face me head-on, and I knew it wasn't good. "Leslie broke up with me last night. When I woke up this morning, she left me a note telling me to leave since I wasn't on the lease. I'm sorry, man, but I need my room back for the semester."

My stomach fell to the floor. I knew this was a risk when I took Andre's offer for his extra room, but halfway through the semester? I hoped that if this bomb dropped, it wouldn't be until we were closer to graduation.

"Sucks, man." Nathan let out an exaggerated sigh. "Deacon can just use the living room. No big deal."

Andre offered me a sympathetic smile. "At least it's just for the semester?"

"You know what, never mind, that's shitty." Greg winced. "I'll just crash in the living room. My shit shouldn't move you out of a room that you're technically paying for."

I recognized the look on his face. The girl he thought was the one broke his heart on a piece of paper. Everything he had planned was going up in flames around him. Another set of Falcon Flames doused because of a girlfriend-initiated breakup. I knew what the right thing to do was. If I had to spend the rest of the semester on a living room couch after Cassie broke up with me, I would've lacked the ambition to do anything productive.

"Nah, man. You take the room. It's yours."

"I would offer a celebratory drink, but we are fresh out of everything," Nathan said through a massive grin.

Greg scoffed. "What is there to celebrate?"

"Your new opportunity!" Nathan hopped up from the recliner and grasped Greg's shoulder. "You just dodged Christmas gifts *and* Valentine's Day. Miracles happen in this apartment! Look at Deac!"

Greg shifted his attention to me. "What kind of miracle happened to you, exactly?"

"This man came here completely devastated over his ex-girlfriend." Nathan grinned. "After two weeks in this apartment, he met Lyla. She's ridiculously hot, and they are like totally in love."

"I wouldn't say *devastated*," I mumbled under my breath. Honestly, all of the content in that sentence and "devastated" was what drew my attention.

Greg adjusted his glasses. "That simple, huh?"

My phone vibrated, and I pulled it from my back pocket.

Lyla

> Hey! Sorry I'm just getting back to you. Much needed girl time with Charlie before break. What time should I come next Saturday?

A pathetic grin stretched across my face. I forgot for a moment that Greg asked me a question. I texted Lyla with a time for Saturday and told her to let me know when she made it home.

"Yeah, man," I said, sounding way too happy for a guy who just lost his privacy for the next few months. "It was that simple."

Chapter Forty

Lyla

There was something nauseating about Christmas. Maybe it was the fact that I never had the classic Christmas card Christmas, where there was a happy two-parent household with a sparkling silver and gold tree in the background. Holiday tunes would play on the radio, and everyone would take turns unwrapping green and red boxes while someone's dad videotaped the event.

It would have to be *someone's* dad because there was no way in hell it was mine. The last time I saw Aaron Brooks for Christmas, I was a junior in high school. It was three months before everything happened with Hunter, and it was the last time I spent Christmas Eve with anyone except my mom.

After being home for two days, I wasn't sure why I looked up Hunter's Instagram account. He looked happy and care-free, playing football for Ohio State, and according to his profile, he was still dating Anna.

Even though I spent most of my childhood with Anna, she looked like someone I had never met. It was wild to think we still existed on the same planet. A person I had known for almost twelve years became a stranger overnight. It made me wonder if our friendship had ever been real.

It still hurt when I thought about how she reacted to my experience with Hunter. She made me feel like I was entirely in the wrong; that I was some sort of prude for not falling even more in love with the guy who gave me a memory I was trying desperately to get rid of. The night of Brady Blue Eyes was the first time I had spoken that story out loud in five years. If my best friend couldn't validate me, how could I be sure someone else wouldn't judge me the same way she had?

My version of the story would still be locked away somewhere if I hadn't told Deacon. It was terrifying to think of another person making me feel embarrassed or ashamed for something that happened to me. He made me see my feelings as *something*. He made me feel seen.

My mom's voice pulled me from the rabbit hole I was nesting in. "Sweetheart?"

I blinked a few times and fell back onto the couch. "What?"

She swiped away at a few tears rolling down her cheeks. "I said thank you for sharing that with me, and I'm sorry you've been—" She drew in a shaky breath, regaining her composure. "Honey, why didn't you say anything?"

That was an easy answer. Seventeen-year-old me had no idea how to process what happened. Shit, I was twenty-two and still didn't know how. In high school, my best friend told me I was overreacting to something that felt like everything. I never told my mom about Hunter because I was embarrassed and confused. But sitting across from her now, she didn't carry any pity in her reaction. She looked proud of me.

Mom sniffed and shook her head. "God, and I just kept asking you about why you would want to change schools your senior year and—"

"Mom," I said, reaching for her hand. "How the hell were you supposed to know? After everything that happened with Anna, I didn't tell *anyone*. I just felt like I couldn't."

She sucked her teeth. "That little bitch. Making you feel that way for *confiding* in her? I let her come to our house for dinner! And you know I only make my homemade vodka sauce for family."

I bit my lip to keep from laughing. It felt good to have this out in the open between us. "Are you angry I didn't tell you?"

"Oh, honey, no. It only breaks my heart that you felt you couldn't tell me sooner."

I shrugged, feeling the dangerous pull behind my eyes. "I don't think I knew how to express it until recently."

Mom sipped her hot chocolate and poured another hefty dose of Baileys into her mug. She let it settle before taking another sip. "I'm so sorry, Jean Bean. There's a lot I wish I could change for you, but that—" She covered her mouth with her hand, and I went and sat beside her on the couch.

I spoke slowly as I tried to process my thoughts. "I think it would do me some good to talk to someone. Like a therapist?"

"Anything you want, we'll figure it out," she assured me. "Have you told anyone else? What made you revisit this after all these years?"

I reached across the table for my hot chocolate. Mom handed me the Baileys, and I helped myself to a small pour. I still had to drive to Detroit to be at Deacon's house by three, and it was already noon.

"Deacon." I grinned unintentionally. "He's easy to talk to. He's—" I struggled to finish the sentence. Deacon was many things, and it was hard to sum him up in a one-word answer.

"He's a special guy," Mom offered with a small smile.

"Yeah." I chuckled at her apparent smitten expression. "He's pretty special."

We rinsed our mugs in the sink, and Mom helped me bring my bags downstairs. I knew she had more questions, but for the first time in my life, she held her tongue.

"Let me know when you get there, okay?" She pulled me in for a hug. "And tell Deacon that he has to visit me before he becomes this big-time doctor."

"He has a lot of school left, Mom. I think we have time."

I didn't have the heart to tell her that I actually only had a few more months and that Dr. Scott would be living in Minnesota with a woman named Cassie.

Since everyone was traveling for the holidays, it took me an extra fifteen minutes to get to Deacon's house. I pulled down his street and rolled slowly, like a creeper from one of those suspenseful kidnapping movies. I scanned the rows of cheerfully lit houses, immediately impressed by how beautiful the street was. My only experience with the city of Detroit came from rap songs and movies, and I was positive that neither of those mediums included a street that looked like this.

I rounded a corner, and when I saw a crisp white house with black shudders in the middle of a cul-de-sac, I knew that was the one I was looking for. I double-checked the address and called the man in charge.

The phone rang twice before Deacon answered. "Hey, baby!"

Cue the on-screen performance.

"Hey!" I mimicked his excitement in case I was on speakerphone. What could I say? At this point, I was a professional. "Where should I park?"

"Just pull in the driveway, sweetheart."

"Well, I'm staring at a car unloading in your driveway. Should I wait for them to move?"

A woman who had to be in her seventies was carrying an oversized canvas tote with bows and tags sticking out the top.

It was hard to miss her light-up "Keep Heaven Crowded" sweater.

"Jesus, Mary, Joseph," I muttered, averting my stare so I wouldn't completely lose myself to hysterics. The last adjective I would use to describe myself was *holy*, and I had a hard time believing that Deacon's family would support my calendar-inspired sex habits.

The car in the driveway reversed and parked a few houses down the street. I slowly lifted my foot off the brake and rolled toward the empty spot. Anxiety crept into my chest at the thought of having to meet a living room full of people. There were at least fifteen cars on this street, and I had a feeling they were all here for the Scott Family Christmas.

"I'm just going to come get you," Deacon said. "That way, you don't have to walk in by yourself."

I parked the car and nodded even though he couldn't see me.

"Relax, Brooks." I heard him smile through the phone. "You're just meeting some family, and they're excited you're here."

I rolled my eyes at his ability to sense my nerves from inside the house. "Whatever you say, Scott."

The front door opened, and I knew right away it was Deacon. He was wearing a black Champion hoodie and—for all that was holy—*gray sweatpants*.

"Keep heaven crowded," I sang and pulled into the driveway. "Merry fucking Christmas to me."

CHAPTER FORTY-ONE

Deacon

"No more," I warned Drew, keeping my voice down so no one else could hear. "Don't bring it up again."

Lyla's headlights crept further into the driveway, and I was running out of time.

"You can't just casually leave out that you have no place to live next semester," Drew argued. "Mom and Dad are going to freak."

I stepped onto the porch, leaning back so I could still see him. "I *do* have a place to live."

"Yeah, a living room in an apartment full of *guys*. Have you seen all the studying you do? There's no way in hell you're going to—"

I shut the door behind me and entered the familiar Detroit winter air. It was fucking cold, and Lyla was in leggings and a thin hoodie.

"That's what you wore?" I teased, squeezing her tiny frame against my chest. She smelled sweet, like apple cinnamon. "You're from the north. You know how cold it is in December!"

She pulled away from me, and seeing her in person again made everything else seem unimportant. Over the last four months, her bright green eyes and loose brown curls became familiar to me, and Facetime could only do so much. I missed her, and I knew by the smile that dug into her right cheek that she missed me, too.

"I *am* from the north, so I know how to deal with it. Your house is beautiful."

I grabbed the strap of her bag before she could hoist it over her shoulder. "Just wait until you see the inside. My mom starts decorating November 1st, and the outside lights go up by Thanksgiving." She handed me another duffle, and I looked down at her book bag. "Jesus, Brooks. Did you bring your whole bedroom with you? It's only for a few days!"

"Speaking of the Lord," she said, following me up the driveway. "On a scale of one to ten, how religious is your family? Like, are you a pray-at-meals type of vibe, or can I not say H-E-double-hockey-sticks in your mother's presence."

I blew a long breath out of my nose. How had I not mentioned this to her before? I stopped in front of the porch.

"My grandfather is a pastor," I said slowly.

"And your name is *Deacon*?" She covered her mouth so people inside couldn't hear her cackling. "Heavenly Father. I just called you daddy like two months ago—"

"I am *begging* you to stop."

We were still laughing when I opened the door, and the look on my mom's face said that it was the perfect way to join the crowd gathering in the living room. Lyla barely got her foot in the door before being ushered into a hug with the woman.

"Lyla!" Mom held out her arms. "Oh my goodness, honey, you are gorgeous!"

Lyla giggled as the woman she just met drew her in for a giant hug.

"Mom," I said, tapping her shoulder. "Let Lyla get in the door."

"I am just about to set the table. Your dad is in the back room." She smiled again at Lyla. "He's very excited to meet you!"

"I'm gonna run Lyla's bags up to the guest room," I added quickly. "Lyla, do you want to see where you're staying?"

"I think Aunt Claire is going to need the guest room." Mom gestured toward the living room. "She's *really* getting into the holiday spirit. Just put Lyla's stuff in your room." She thought she was slick, eyeing me playfully before returning to the kitchen.

Lyla laughed once my bedroom door was closed, and I knew she caught my mom's intention. "I believe you just got permission to get laid, Deacon Scott."

"She's a woman on a mission to be a grandmother." I shrugged, dropping Lyla's bags in front of my bed. "When Cassie and I broke up, it shook my entire timeline of getting married and starting a family. Having you here put the chance on the table again."

Lyla pulled at her solid gray hoodie. "Is what I'm wearing okay?"

I loved how casual she looked. Over-the-top Christmas decorations—yes. Clothing you couldn't have second helpings of food in—absolutely not.

"I'm in sweatpants." I crossed the room and grabbed her hand. "You look perfect. Let's go meet some people."

She followed me back downstairs and let me lead the way to our next stop on the Scott Family tour.

I had her walk in front of me so I could whisper in her ear. "I missed you, by the way."

She smirked over her shoulder. "I missed you too, *Dad*—"

"Grandpa!" I straightened up, ignoring my desire to take her back upstairs. "This is my girlfriend, Lyla. Lyla, this is my grandpa, Reverend Scott."

Lyla offered an innocent grin and shook his hand. "It's a pleasure to meet you."

Grandpa's broad smile reached up to his eyes. "Pleasure is all mine, Lyla. And please, call me Grandpa."

After our first introduction, I pulled Lyla into the hall. "Am I going to have to be there for every conversation you have tonight?"

"That was my last one, promise." She raised her hand honorably and rested it on my chest. "I did miss you, though. It was kind of weird not . . . seeing you?" Watching her stumble over her words was cute, but I knew what she meant.

We toured the rest of the living room, introducing Lyla to aunts, uncles, a few cousins, and some people from Grandpa's congregation who usually spent the holidays with us. She asked questions about pictures and trinkets that were on display. She engaged in small talk and even complimented my aunt's "Keep Heaven Crowded" sweater. I knew the compliment was a tad much, but her laugh with my aunt was genuine.

When it was finally my dad's turn to meet Lyla, I wasn't surprised to find him smoking a cigar on the back porch with my Uncle Henry.

"You must be Lyla!" Dad extended his free hand, holding the cigar away from Lyla. "It's nice to meet you, sweetie. This is my brother, Henry."

"Deacon's been telling us all about you," Uncle Henry said.

"Has he now?" Lyla wrapped her arms around my waist, and I pulled her against me. It felt incredible to be close to her again.

Once Lyla officially met everyone, I brought her into the study so she could have a moment to collect herself. She had just met at least thirty people she didn't know, and I knew how anxious that would make me if I had no way to escape it.

Lyla glanced around the bookshelves. "What room is this?"

"My dad's office. I figured you could use a second before we sit down for dinner."

She nodded, shifting her focus to the family photos on the wall. When she reached the picture of my family at the lake, I studied her face carefully. Her mouth curved slightly into a grin as she placed her finger toward the bottom of the photo. "Is this Dominic?"

I crossed the room and stood beside her. Dominic's cheesy smile sat perfectly between Drew and me. His dark hair was longer in this photo, and his life jacket was snug on his sixteen-year-old body. My mom had just finished saying we needed to purchase new ones for next year.

"Yeah, that's Dom." I smiled, resting my hand against the wall. "He had just turned sixteen a few weeks before this photo. He just started driving on his own. He passed away a month after we took it."

"You and your brothers look so much alike."

I ran a hand through my hair and chuckled. "We always joked that Dominic was the mailman's kid since he had hazel eyes and Drew and I have brown. After he passed, it was like we couldn't get enough photos of him. It's weird relying on pictures and videos of a person when they're no longer here. You just can't get enough of what is left of them."

Lyla opened her mouth to speak, but my mom's dinner announcement stopped her. On the other side of the door, we heard the hustle and bustle of people trying to find a seat at the table.

"Ready for round two?" I said, tucking her hair behind her ear.

She nodded. "Ready for more boyfriend-girlfriend shit."

We rounded the corner of the hall, and before we entered the dining room, she tugged on my hand.

"I'm glad I came," she said. "It's nice seeing where you come from, and it's nice to hear about Dominic."

I swallowed around the lump in my throat and squeezed her hand.

It had been a while since I'd let someone into my world. It was easier to bury the personal items that came with me instead of putting them on display. With Lyla, I didn't feel so exposed. I didn't feel like I had to hide anything from her.

The day I lost my brother, the world went dark. Part of me was missing, like a piece of my soul went searching for Dominic because he left too early. There were holes in my heart I wasn't sure I could mend, but when Lyla smiled at me before she sipped her wine, I felt something different.

A warmth settled into my stomach. It wasn't the food, the family around me, or Dominic's plate at the head of the table. For the first time in a long time, someone turned on the light. For the first time since Dominic passed, I felt hope.

CHAPTER FORTY-TWO

Lyla

I HAD NEVER BEEN around a table with so many family members. It was loud, but it was a good kind of noise, consisting of laughter, excited chatter, and jokes that didn't seem to end. A beautiful energy flowed through the meal, making me feel like I had been here before.

"Now make sure when the apple pie comes around, Lyla, you get a piece before Drew does. He always takes the one with the most caramel sauce," Mrs. Scott said from her seat across from me.

Everything about that description made my mouth water. I wasn't expecting to have room after my two full plates of food, but the dessert offer forced my stomach to expand. Thank God I didn't arrive in standing-only pants.

"Rightfully so!" Drew argued. "If Lyla is part of the family table, she has to fight like everyone else."

Everyone laughed when Deacon threw a roll and hit Drew in the middle of his forehead.

Mrs. Scott's laugh lingered a little longer after the noise dwindled. "Drew must like you. I'd be concerned if he offered you special treatment because you're a guest."

"It was a beautiful dinner, Mrs. Scott. Thank you so much for having me."

She leaned over the table and grabbed my empty plate. The crinkles around her eyes deepened. "Please call me Georgia."

I wondered what his family thought of me being here. I wondered how I compared to Cassie.

I shut that shit down. Why did I care?

I knew the answer I was supposed to give. I cared because I wanted Deacon to be happy. So far, everything I planned had fallen into place. Cassie was texting him again, and they were having lunch when we returned to campus. She was curious about how serious we were, and that was a good thing. It was a *great* thing. Fantastic. Marvelous. Fucking fabulous.

So why did my body toy with me, making me pulse in places I couldn't tend to every time Deacon put his hands on me? They were simple touches—a tap on my arm, his hand resting on the small of my back, a kiss on my temple. Never in my life had I felt so wound up. I was like one of my mother's poorly wrapped Christmas presents sitting under the tree. One wrong pull and I'd fall apart.

This was my punishment for ignoring my calendar routine for two months. The last time I had sex was in October, and that was just appalling.

"I'm going to help my dad bring gifts up from the basement," Deacon whispered in my ear. He shifted so his warm breath was on my neck, sending goosebumps up and down my arms. "Santa comes during dinner, and the kids all open presents while we sit back and have a drink."

He kissed the top of my head, and I took this as an opportunity to fight Drew off for some pie. I approached the counter and purposely reached across him for a plate.

"Don't think I was joking about the pie," he threatened, grabbing the serving spoon from my hand.

"Aren't you needed for gifts? Are you not one of Santa's helpers after dinner?"

"Nah. As the middle child, it isn't my place to have to volunteer for shit. That falls in the older sibling category." Drew bumped his arm against mine and scanned the area behind us. "How are you holding up? You guys do the dating thing well. I'll give you that."

I snatched the spoon back from him. "*Fine.* Believe it or not, I really like your brother. We're friends. He's the only guy friend I have, actually."

"Walk with me." Drew stuck a plastic fork in his mouth and led us to the living room. He waved me closer like he was about to spill a family secret I wasn't supposed to be a part of, and his light brown eyes carried the same playfulness as Deacon's.

I eyed him suspiciously. "What's up?"

"Well, first, I won't take offense that you clearly dismissed me being a friend back there." I opened my mouth to argue, and he held up his hand. "Second, did Deacon tell you about his roommate yet?"

I took a bite of my pie and almost melted into the floor. It was *heavenly.* "Nathan and Andre?"

"Greg," Drew spat as if Greg had come in a few moments ago and stolen the rest of the pie. "The guy who was originally on the lease came back and needs his room."

"What does that have to do with Deacon?"

Drew's shoulders fell. "So he didn't tell you. Deacon only stayed with Nathan and Andre because Greg moved in with his girlfriend."

"First mistake," I mumbled.

"Right," Drew added quickly. "But they broke up, and now Deacon's bedroom is the living room."

I pictured a tidy Deacon Scott trying to study on the couch while Nathan and Andre played Madden for the forty-fifth time that day. Deacon color-coded his closet. There was no way he'd last an entire semester living in the common area with his sloppy roommates.

I knew the answer, but I decided to ask anyway. "He didn't tell me, but is there a reason you are?"

"Deacon doesn't ask for help." Drew's cocky grin dug deeper into his cheek. "So I figured I could ask for him. It will benefit both of you. Cassie will lose her mind when she hears Deacon moved in with you, and you can tell your dad that your boyfriend is your new roommate."

Drew had a point. Aaron Brooks would be beside himself if he found out Deacon was living with me. I never shared my space with anyone, and it would demonstrate a mature relationship shift. But at the same time, what did that mean for our personal lives? Was I signing up for the longest dry spell I'd ever had because I had a fake boyfriend in my bedroom?

I'd have to ask Michelle and Keira if they'd mind having their Monopoly buddy move in down the hall, but I could at least extend the offer to him. Deacon wouldn't hesitate to give me his bed if the roles reversed. After all, what were best friends for?

Thirty minutes later, Drew asked Deacon in front of the entire family how his living situation was going.

I followed the prompt with an innocent, "What happened to your room?"

Deacon glared at his brother from the couch and told everyone about Greg, the original roommate on the lease. His news update paused the gift-giving process as multiple family members muttered comments.

"Well, that doesn't sound practical for studying," his dad noted.

"Or privacy." Georgia shot me a wink from the recliner, and I choked back a laugh. I knew I liked that woman.

"You guys are always together anyways," Drew added sweetly. I read right through his sly grin, but the rest of the family hung on his every word. "Couldn't you just room with Lyla until you figure it out?"

Deacon's hand grazed my thigh, letting me know he would handle his brother's probing. "That's asking a lot—"

I rolled my eyes, playing the role of the annoyed girlfriend who had to repeat herself for the tenth time. "When I found out he wasn't on the lease, I *tried* offering that option to him." I held my composure when Deacon's eyes shot to mine. "Maybe now you'll listen to me?"

Deacon pressed his lips together in a firm line, and I dared him to argue why it wasn't a good idea. A chuckle trickled from his gorgeous mouth as he considered my offer. My futon was one hundred times cleaner than the raggedy couch in their living room.

Deacon draped his arm on the couch behind me as I watched the younger cousins take turns opening gifts, excited about the toys and clothes that followed the ribbons and wrapping paper. Deacon's grandmother did her best to control the chaos, but eventually, she lost to the excitement spiraling up from the living room floor.

My view was interrupted when Drew placed a shiny red present on my lap.

"You got me a gift?" I asked.

He ran a hand through his hair and shrugged. "Well, you know—"

Howard intervened, shoving Drew to the side. "Get out of here," he said through a contagious chuckle. "It's a little something from Georgia and me. I hope it's okay! Georgia has this thing where everyone needs something to open on Christmas Eve."

Suddenly, I couldn't form words. Not a single vowel and consonant combination came to mind. I stared at the silver bow, my throat getting tighter. "Thank you."

Howard patted my shoulder and reunited with Georgia on the loveseat across the room. I was happy he didn't stand over me as I opened it since I was already on the verge of tears.

Deacon nudged me. "Open it, baby."

I shoved the dramatics aside and pulled at the ribbon. Inside the box was a pack of Starburst, a Dunkin Donuts gift card, and a book with gorgeous character art. I sifted through the contents, and when I realized the book had a fake dating trope, I rolled my eyes at Deacon.

He smiled coyly. "Had nothing to do with it."

Georgie passed around the bottles of wine as the gift giving shifted to the adults. I poured myself a glass, and when I offered some to Deacon, he waved the bottle away and got up from the couch.

"I'll be back in a minute. I just need some air."

After fifteen minutes, I decided to look for him. He had turned left out of the living room, which meant he was in the kitchen, the dining room, or his dad's office. After checking all three areas, I had no choice but to peek outside. I opened the stubborn sliding door, throwing my weight into it when it got stuck halfway on the track.

"Does that all the time," Deacon said.

I joined him under the covered deck and stood beside him, leaning against the railing. "What are you doing out here? You're missing a riveting round of gifts."

"I just needed a minute," he murmured.

Snow fell quietly on the undisturbed blanket of white in front of us. There was no wind, and anything louder than a whisper would corrupt the serene sense of solitude the backyard provided. I understood why Deacon was out here. It was peaceful.

"There are times when everyone gets together and laughs, and I feel guilty for being happy because he isn't here."

His words punched me in the gut. The memories scattered around the house showed a family of five. Every photo was a moment captured before his entire world completely shattered.

I stroked my thumb against the back of his hand. "I'm sorry, Deacon."

A small smile curved into his cheek. "There's nothing to be sorry about. It's nice to talk about him. Sometimes, people think hearing his name makes me uncomfortable. It's the opposite, actually. When you talk about people, it reminds you of their existence. It reminds you that they're still here in some way."

"Still here," I echoed. "You know, I've never thought about heaven before."

"Never?"

I shrugged. "I guess I've never had to. I only have a handful of people in my life that I care about losing. I don't really remember when my grandma passed away."

Deacon went quiet for a few seconds, trying to sort through something in his head. I didn't want to push, but I gently squeezed his hand to let him know I would listen if he wanted me to.

"When it first happened, I felt scared for him," he said, his voice barely above a whisper. "Our entire life, I've done everything first. I'm the oldest, so it's my job to go through things so they can see how it's done. I imagined him getting there—" He took a deep breath and shook his head. "I imagined him getting there and being confused. Like he knew he wasn't supposed to be there yet."

More punches came to my gut, and my heart sank. "I don't think it works like that," I admitted, trying to relieve him of his thoughts.

His mouth quirked up again. "How do you know? What do you picture?"

"For heaven, I picture a place where you can come and go as you please. You want for nothing and can do everything this world doesn't allow you to. You can travel, visit people, watch over your loved ones, and be present even if they can't see you. You don't miss out on life; you just view it from another angle and experience it in a place that is more than we could ever imagine."

His eyes had a slight gloss as he processed my opinion. "That's a beautiful way to see it."

"It has to be, right?" I directed my question to the sky instead of Deacon. "What other reason could there be for someone leaving so young?"

"I hated the world when he passed, and sometimes I still do. I don't think I ever truly addressed the anger part. You get so caught up in missing someone and mourning them that you forget to feel anger. It's like I don't know what to do with it."

Deacon dragged his hands down his face and shook his head. Before learning about Dominic, I never saw Deacon as someone who held anger or sadness. He was a master at shielding everything he felt from the rest of the world.

"Nothing else seems worthy of tears," he continued. "Nothing else can compete with the heartache of losing him.

It's like a piece of me is gone, and I'll never be able to fix the hole it left."

I hesitated to ask the next question, but I knew talking like this made him feel better. Deacon didn't have to hide anything from me. He knew my view of him wouldn't change because of his admissions, just like his didn't change about me after hearing mine. "Is it hard having a family so involved with church?"

He stared out into the yard. "I don't know. Maybe sometimes? Some of my family members found peace. I got tired of hearing about how God has a plan. I plan because I know how quickly life can take things from you, and we don't know how much time we have. But it also makes me feel like—"

He turned, averting his gaze to the sky behind me. He wanted to look at me, but he couldn't. He was doing everything he could to keep from falling apart.

"If this was the master plan, then maybe God is just a shitty planner. I don't know. I feel like I'm not supposed to say that. But no one ever knows what to say. No one *really* has any answers for you. Everyone can speculate, but there's no way to tell what happens when we move on from here. It just makes me feel helpless, and I get angry all over again." He blew out an exaggerated sigh and ran a hand through his hair. "I'm sorry for dumping my problems on you. Kind of puts a damper on the Christmas magic, doesn't it?"

I wrapped my arms around his neck. "You know, this amazing person once said something to me that I really needed to hear." I moved my hands down his shoulders and rested them on his chest. "Whatever you're carrying—it will never be a *problem* to me, Deacon. I want you to know that."

He ran his hands up and down my forearms. Even when pouring his heart out, he was trying to keep me warm. "I still can't make sense of it. It's like I woke up one day, and someone told me I couldn't see my brother anymore. There were no warnings. There was no goodbye or knowing that the last time I saw him would actually be *the last time*. I have to wait to see my brother again, and when you have someone you're looking forward to seeing, death doesn't seem so scary." He dropped his hands into the pockets of his sweatpants and shrugged. "But I'm not supposed to say that out loud, either."

"Some people would consider that a concerning statement, but I don't. It's like looking forward to the next chapter with that person, and you know he'll be psyched to see you. Even though he's watching, he'll need a recap in person."

He glanced at the sky and then at me with a slight smile. "You know, for someone who doesn't engage in emotional chit-chat, you're pretty good at it."

"It's not so hard for you," I admitted, taking his hand again. "Just don't forget to mention me in the recap. You can't leave out the best fake relationship you ever had."

"I could never leave you out, Brooks."

"We don't lie, remember?"

"Yeah, I know," he said, leading us back inside. "We don't lie."

Chapter Forty-Three

Deacon

A few hours later, the house was quiet. The only exceptions were the crackling fire in the living room and Drew texting like a madman beside me.

"Who are you texting at this hour?" Mom demanded. My dad, half asleep, sat next to her with a glass of bourbon in his hand.

Drew looked up slowly from his phone. "It's just a friend. I'm calling it a night, though. I'll see everyone in the morning."

A collection of "Merry Christmas" and "Goodnight" filled the room as Drew headed upstairs. I glanced down at Lyla beside me. She sipped her wine and raised her eyebrows, letting me know that she was up for whatever I wanted to do next. Eventually, we'd have to head up to my room, and my mother made it perfectly clear that she was welcome to stay with me. In her defense, my Aunt Claire *did* end up using the guest room. My mom would've escorted Lyla to my room herself if I hadn't dropped her bags in front of my bed.

"I'm going to call my mom to say goodnight." Lyla patted my thigh. "I'll see you up there?"

I nodded, trying not to seem surprised when she kissed me. It was sensual but sweet enough that having my parents sit across from us wasn't awkward. Lyla said goodnight to both of them and once she cleared the top of the stairs, I waited for the questions to come.

When neither of them said anything, I leaned forward and threw my hands out in front of me. "Nothing?"

My mom practically jumped off of the couch. "She's *wonderful*, Deacon."

"She's a pretty girl." Dad tipped his glass to me and quickly added, "Smart, too. A woman who reads is a woman who can change the world. She told me all about how she wants to open a bookstore."

"*So* ambitious," Mom bragged.

"We barely knew anything about the last girl," Dad admitted with an apologetic shrug. "We know you liked her, but you always dimmed yourself to accommodate her. Lyla challenges you, and there is nothing better than a partner who will never let you settle."

The last girl. Cassie had officially claimed a new title in my parents' memory. Cassie and I dated for three years! If I told my parents that Lyla wasn't staying for breakfast tomorrow morning, their disappointment would be more transparent than when I told them about Cassie.

Dad was right about Lyla. She was pretty and smart, and she'd never let me settle. Lyla *would* change the world someday—she sure as hell changed mine.

When I got to my room, Lyla was already in my bed. I loved how it wasn't awkward to have her here. We spent so much time together back at school that a different location didn't matter.

"Did you need anything to sleep in?" I asked, stripping off my shirt. "Anything I can get you?"

She put her phone down to look at me. "Is five-star service always provided at Hotel Scott? Or are you just extra nice to houseguests that you like?"

"Oh, definitely just because I like you."

She glanced around the room. "No TV?"

"It's in the closet." I slipped on a fresh shirt and opened the doors, revealing the TV on my dresser. "My dad has a thing about putting holes in the walls, and I didn't have any other space for it."

"So five-star services *and* fancy closet TVs. I might never leave."

"Then don't." I meant to think it, but I was pretty fucking sure I just said that out loud.

Not a real relationship, no lying, fuck around in private, and no love. The rules weren't that hard to follow. I knew this wasn't real. I never lied to Lyla, the fucking around in private was irrelevant, and there was no *love*. I loved Lyla the way I loved any of my friends. If I had to place them in order, she would be first, but what difference did that make?

Lyla crossed her arms. "Why didn't you tell me about your room?"

"This room?"

"No, goofy. Your room at school."

I sat on the edge of my bed and tossed her the remote. "I don't know. I have a tendency to try and figure things out on my own."

"I know you do, but we're *friends*, Deacon. I would've totally offered to let you stay with me. It was the first thing that crossed my mind when Drew told me."

Maybe I wouldn't give Drew shit for putting me on the spot. "Really?"

Lyla's lips slowly curved into a sexy smile. "We don't lie, remember?"

God, I wanted to kiss her again. The number of times I ached to reach out and do the little on-screen touches was beginning to concern me.

"Yeah." I sighed. "We don't lie."

Lyla's eyes followed the line of trinkets that lined the top of my bookcase. "Can we please discuss the chess ribbons next to your basketball camp trophies?"

"What about them?" I challenged. "Got a thing against chess?"

She bit her lip to keep from laughing. "I didn't know another board game could outshine your Monopoly skills. Were you, like, *cool* in high school?"

I crawled across the bed and slid under the blankets beside her. "I was *very* cool in high school."

She squinted. "And did all of the cool kids have random bear items too?"

I squeezed the sensitive spot above her left hip, and she burst into a round of giggles.

"Bears have been my favorite animal since I was a kid!" I exclaimed. "If I ever go to Jane's house, we are so doing a deep dive into your bedroom."

"She did invite us to the zoo. Maybe we can take a trip there, and you can tell us all about the bears."

The mattress shook as Lyla burst into hysterics over her smart-ass comment. I looked at her and laughed. She held her stomach, rolling onto her side, and I knew she was scanning the room for something else to ask about.

Lyla fired off more questions, and I gave her my best answers. Talking with Lyla about the trophies, gifts, and memories of my childhood made me see them in a different light. It was nice to revisit a time when things were simple—before life became complicated with grief and unwanted experiences.

Sitting in bed with Lyla, I wanted to bottle up this moment as another memory. I didn't have an item to place on a shelf, but it didn't matter. Lyla's presence was enough, and there wasn't a single part about her that I didn't want to keep.

Chapter Forty-Four

Lyla

"Merry Christmas, Lyla."

"Merry Christmas, Deacon," I said, laughing.

It was midnight, and we had spent the last hour talking about places we wanted to go, favorite college memories, and all of the other nauseating nonsense couples talked about in a rom-com. We still hadn't decided on a movie, so Deacon also spent the last hour aimlessly browsing Netflix. I needed a murder movie to reset the tone, but suggesting a Saw marathon on Christmas seemed a bit dark—even for me.

I dragged my hands down my face. "Just turn it off. They never have anything new anyways."

"Ain't that the truth." Deacon leaned over me and placed the remote in the side pocket of the bed frame. He hovered for a second, and I did my best to ignore how incredible he smelled after a day of entertaining the family.

I tried not to stare, but I couldn't help it. Deacon was deep in thought, contemplating something as he looked up at the ceiling. I hated myself for thinking it, but he was so . . . *pretty*. He was one of the most gorgeous guys I had ever seen. It was true the morning I met him, and it was true now.

His light brown eyes always had a glow to them even when he was down about something. He had an amazing set of lips, and the more I stared at them, the more I wondered what else his mouth could do besides drop lines that made me want to drop my panties.

Deacon was smart and funny even when he didn't mean to be. He was gentle and patient and took his time to explain things when I felt differently than he did. I wanted to believe Deacon when he said he'd always be there, but my track record supported me. People were predictable and disappointing, and I didn't want to get my hopes up that Deacon would be any different. This plan would work, and he would get back together with Cassie. They would run off, get married, and buy a massive house in Minnesota with their fancy doctor salaries.

I'd use my trust fund to open my bookstore in Chicago with my mom. Charlie would probably end up staying in the loft above the store, and I'd support all three of us as we tried to navigate life in the city. It would be like a new *Sex and the City* series, only much more realistic.

Deacon and I would get the life we always wanted, and *maybe* we would text randomly about the time we fake-dated in college. *Maybe* I would receive an invitation to their wedding and have to find an excuse not to go. *Maybe* he'd come to visit Chicago for a weekend. No one ever bet on a bunch of maybes.

I sighed, forgetting I was in bed with the man I'd be regretfully declining in a few years because he didn't visit me at Brooks Books.

"What's up, Brooks?"

"What's up with me?" I turned on my side to face him. "You're the one having a stare-off with the ceiling."

"You don't want to know."

"Oh, I *really* do. Please share."

He exhaled through his nose, biting anxiously on his bottom lip. "I'm just horny, sweetheart, that's all," he admitted shamelessly. "There. I said it."

"I hear that. How long has it been for you?"

We didn't talk about sex often, but when we did, it was always an enjoyable topic. I loved hearing Deacon's perspective and seeing what I was wrong and right about. I lost count of how many times I pictured what he would be like. What his hands felt like and if he preferred slow or fast strokes—

"September." He winced, letting out a hollow chuckle. "*Early* September."

I felt his pain. "October."

"Brady Blue Eyes?"

"Yep. Who knew a fake relationship could get in the way of sex?" I said sarcastically. As much as I loved having Deacon around, it did make it harder to take a guy home at the end of the night. Whenever I found a possible prospect, returning to Deacon's place always sounded like a better idea.

"It's just too much."

"What is?"

"It's too much to juggle." He chuckled and turned to face me. "I couldn't imagine talking to Cassie, dating you, *and* finding someone to hook up with. It's too much."

I rolled my eyes. "Add in school too. I barely had time for Mr. October."

"So tell me." His voice dropped, and I knew we were heading in a different direction. "Mr. October—were you satisfied or not?"

I wasn't mad about the lane change. I preferred this lane, actually. "It was okay. Maybe that's why it was just one time."

Deacon looked like he was about to lecture me for the third time today. "I'm telling you, Lyla, anyone can—"

"I know, I know," I whined, running my fingers along his forearm. This man's touch was becoming an addiction I didn't want to quit. I wanted it even when I didn't know I needed it. "How'd you do it?"

"Do what?"

I held his gaze. This was a completely normal conversation between friends. It felt *so* normal that I couldn't stop talking. "How did you make sure Cassie was satisfied? I've tried to picture it. Just tell me so I don't have to guess anymore."

If I had scissors to cut through the tension in the room, I'd toss them out the fucking window. Deacon looked at me with something I hadn't seen before. Sure, there was a shock factor to what I just said, but there was something else.

"You've pictured it?" He flashed a cocky grin and shifted closer to me. He didn't think I'd notice, but I did. I was very aware of how close he was. "Have you tried picturing me having sex, Lyla?"

My ability to string together consonants and vowels failed me again, so I nodded.

His grin was gone, and my stomach sank. "If you were anyone else, this would be weird. But okay."

"Just your *best friend*, remember?" I emphasized through a laugh. "Now tell me."

He licked the center of his top lip, and his voice turned soft again. "I learned quickly that Cassie loved soft touches. There was a spot on the inside of her thigh that worked like a switch. If I snuck a few strokes around that spot, I knew in *seconds* if she wanted to go further."

My eyes narrowed. "The inside of the thigh? That's it?"

I felt his hand on my leg and realized what he was doing. Deacon Scott was giving me a demonstration. I was already dangling by a thread. Where were those fucking scissors?

Deacon's hand was inches away from the heat pooling between my legs, growing stronger the longer his hand remained on my thigh. The touch was gentle; the sensation caused by a feather or a new blanket. He made mindless shapes and lines, and I didn't notice he stopped until he spoke again.

"This spot right here," he teased, his voice a bit raspy. "Is this okay?"

"What else?" I prompted, finding it hard to breathe. My heartbeat pounded against my eardrums. I had *never* wanted someone to touch me as badly as I wanted Deacon to.

"I'd kiss her. Slow at first, but then I'd get a little rougher—remind her what my mouth can do. But I'd make her wait. I wanted to make sure she was ready for me."

His fingers slid further over my thigh, trailing sparks along my skin as he moved closer to my throbbing clit. Just when I thought he would go all the way, he removed his hand and all of my hope with it.

"But that went a long way," he said, his tone returning to normal. "It's all push and pull. Making her wait but knowing how to tease her."

I let out a shaky breath and swallowed. When my mouth refused to close, I stared at Deacon's.

"We don't lie, Lyla."

"Right." *We don't lie, and I want you.* I inhaled sharply, getting lost in my headspace. "Wait, what?"

He stared at me with such intensity that a soft moan vibrated through my chest. "I have a question for you, and remember, we don't lie."

I forced myself to speak. "Shoot."

"When you've pictured me having sex, who is it with?"

"Cassie," I answered quickly. That wasn't a lie. I tried to picture how that girl managed to land this man *dozens* of times.

He sensed my half-assed answer. "And?"

I covered my face with my hands. "Deacon—"

He gently pried my hands away, forcing me to look at him. He was waiting for me to say it, but I needed to hear it from him first. My pulse quickened, and there wasn't an ounce of hesitation in what he admitted next.

"I've pictured it, sweetheart. I know your rules, but—"

"Fine." I giggled but had no idea why. I flipped through the reel in my head of all the things I wanted to do to Deacon, all of the things I craved for him to do to me. Every item on my checklist since he came to my apartment to pick up Andre.

"I've pictured it," I said, only this time there was no humor. "When I imagine you having sex, it's me you're fucking. No one else."

Deacon moved closer, his sexy smirk centimeters away from my mouth. "Damn. You're so sweet, and then you say I'm *fucking* you."

I stifled a grin to keep my nerves at bay. Why the fuck was I nervous to have him so close? "Gotta keep it interesting."

"Yeah." He returned his hand to my thigh and pulled my hips to his. He was hard under his shorts, and I cursed myself for wearing so many layers to bed. "Can I kiss you?"

I dropped my hand between us and felt him through the thick fabric. I've wanted this man's dick in my hand since Halloween. I pumped him slowly, and when a hoarse groan drifted from his chest, I stopped so he would look at me. "We don't . . . *have* to kiss."

He cupped my chin, tracing my cheek with his thumb. "Oh, I'm gonna kiss you, Lyla, and I'll do more if you let me. But if I'm crossing the line, just—"

I kissed him so words couldn't get in the way. I *wanted* Deacon. I *needed* Deacon, and now that I knew we were both in the same lane, there was no turning back.

Chapter Forty-Five

Deacon

Lyla had her hand wrapped around my cock, and there was no way in hell I was going to question it. I couldn't pretend like I hadn't imagined her hands stroking me the way they were now. The only thing that would make it even more incredible would be her mouth at the end of it.

I slid my hands over her hips and pulled her against me. She shivered as I made my way up her stomach, arching her back and pressing harder against me.

I scoffed. "Why the fuck do you have this tight-ass bra on?"

"Because I wasn't expecting a hand up my shirt tonight."

I kissed her again, and she giggled when the band snapped lightly against her skin. I loved that sound, but there was something else I wanted to hear more.

"Take your shirt off," I murmured as my hands traveled under the waistband of her—*fuck*. How many times had she slept beside me with no panties on?

Lyla tugged at the hem of my shirt. "I don't need to take it off. I'm ready now."

My fingers slipped through the slit of her pussy, warm and wet, allowing me to glide effortlessly in and out, her hips riding my hand, trying to coax me to go faster. A soft moan fell from her mouth, and she pulled me in for another kiss. I was doing everything I could to keep it together, but I was dangerously close to crumbling. This woman's touch was intoxicating.

She tightened her grip under my shorts. "I'm ready *now*."

Fuck it. I grabbed a condom from the end table, and Lyla licked her lips as she watched me roll it on. *Christ.* I wanted that mouth, but I wanted to be inside her more.

I leaned over her and brushed the hair from her face. "You're sure?"

"Yes," she whined. "And we don't have to—"

I captured her mouth with mine and slowly slid myself inside her. She inhaled sharply, and I tried to control my inflating ego, allowing her to adjust. When her eyes locked on mine, I rocked my hips, sinking deeper between her legs.

There was no way a woman could feel this good. I raised her hands above her head, pinning her against the mattress with slow, deep strokes. She groaned, and as if it were possible, my dick grew even harder inside her.

"My parents are across the hall, baby. You have to be quiet."

"I can't help it," she whispered, her voice growing louder again. She wrapped her ankles around my lower back and pulled me deeper. "You feel . . . *fuck*, Deacon."

Butterflies rose into my chest. I kissed her harder, hungry to hear my name on her lips again. I wanted to do everything for her, *be* everything for her. If this were the only chance I'd get to sleep with her, I'd be damned if she didn't come twice.

"Faster," she whimpered.

"You want faster, Brooks?" I drew away from her, using the mattress to steady myself. Lyla could beg me all night to go faster, and I fucking hoped she would, but I wasn't letting this end anytime soon.

"Yes," she pleaded through a strained laugh. "Please."

I licked my thumb, making slow circles around her swollen clit. Her head fell back into the pillow, and she gripped the rods of my headboard. I slid inside her again, using her body's reaction to gauge my pace—the rise and fall of her stomach and the sweet circles she made with her hips. She arched her back, and I pressed harder against her clit, quickening the movements with my thumb as her mouth parted again, only this time I knew what was coming.

Her teeth sank into her bottom lip as she tried to control her breathing. I gently pushed under her navel and watched her lose control below me. With each sharp inhale, she grew louder until I felt her body shaking against my hand.

I had pictured this in my head before, Lyla coming undone with me on top of her. She closed her eyes, and before she could cry out, I kissed her. She moaned into my mouth while her walls tightened around me. She felt fucking incredible, and I didn't want it to stop. There was no way I could come back from this. Lyla coming on my cock was an image I wanted to brand into my brain.

I smiled against her lips. "I'm trying to make this last, baby, but you feel so fucking good." I slowed my strokes, and her hips eagerly met mine.

"Deacon, please. I want you to go harder."

I kissed down her neck, sucking softly on her collarbone. When I made my way back up, she held me against her, and I slammed my hips until I couldn't hold out any longer. Her breathing climbed again, and before I could catch her next moan, my name slipped from her perfectly parted mouth. I gripped the pillow above her head and stifled my groan into the base of her throat.

I knew I was getting heavy on top of her, but she didn't seem to care. Lyla wrapped her arms around my neck and cradled my head against her chest. Her heartbeat slowly came back to normal, bringing mine with it. I propped my weight onto my forearms and kissed the sensitive skin behind her ear. We stared at each other, waiting to see who would cave first.

She leaned her forehead into my shoulder, and a soft laugh danced across my skin. I kissed the top of her head and rolled onto my side, leaving my arm out in case she wanted to come closer. I didn't know what to expect from her next. I had no expectations of *sleeping* with her. I just wanted her close, and when she shifted so she was in the crook of my arm, I pulled her in.

"Can I have your shorts?" she asked, her voice laced with exhaustion.

"Why? Can't you just stay like this for a little longer?"

"I don't know where mine are," she murmured through a sleepy laugh. "And I have to pee."

I watched her leave my bedroom in her shirt and my shorts. I just had her a few moments ago and already wanted her again.

A few minutes later, Lyla climbed back into bed and snuggled into my chest. I wrapped my arms around her, running my hands down her back and pulling at her stupid sports bra.

She settled deeper into the crook of my arm. "I think that was top-tier boyfriend-girlfriend shit."

I exhaled slowly, planting a soft kiss on her temple. "Yeah, that's definitely up there. Do you always hold your breath like that?"

"What?"

I smirked as the pull in her forehead grew deeper. There was no way I knew something about her body that she didn't. It was too much of a tease of what I could really do to her. "Do you hold your breath when you're coming?"

She pondered my question. "I guess I never noticed. Maybe?"

I gave her body a tight squeeze and closed my eyes. The thought of asking her if she wanted to find out threatened to make me hard again. I trailed my fingers across her lower back, lifting her shirt. She was warm and soft and perfectly pressed against me. I wanted her to feel safe. I wanted her to fall asleep, knowing that I would never do anything to hurt her. I'd knock the lights out of *anyone* who hurt this girl.

"You'll just have to use your imagination, Scott," she said, drawing me out of my headspace. "This isn't happening again. It was a horny hall pass."

I did my best to keep my voice free from disappointment. "Whatever you say, Brooks. Is that rule number six?"

"Yes," she deadpanned, and my chest vibrated with laughter. She sounded so serious that it was funny and agonizing at the same time.

Once again, Lyla left me speechless. She was beautiful and made me laugh. She was strong-willed and ambitious. She was my best friend, and I wasn't sure how I made it this far in my life without knowing her sooner.

CHAPTER FORTY-SIX

Lyla

WHEN I WOKE UP, I was still in Deacon's bed. However, when I rolled over to face him, he wasn't there.

I sat up slowly and put my hand to my forehead. Last night had happened, correct? I let the man I had been wanting inside me actually *come* inside me. We used protection, so at least we had that going for us. I had never *not* used protection, but as my hand slid over the empty side of the bed, one thing was clear. Last night definitely happened because I still felt where he had been.

Deacon left me sore but wanting more. He also left me sounding like Dr. Seuss for the second time this year. I replayed the reel of last night's performance, and my core tightened at the memory of his mouth on mine and the slow, delicious pace of his dick as he—

"Morning, Brooks." Deacon closed the bedroom door behind him and pulled a towel over his head. He was shirtless, and a few lucky water droplets ran down his chest.

Good morning to me.

"Good morning." I crossed my legs and ran my fingers through my tangled mess of bedhead. "How long have you been up?"

"Not long." Deacon rummaged through his closet and pulled out a T-shirt. His black boxer briefs hugged his ass, and it was a shame he had to cover it with a pair of sweatpants.

"Maybe fifteen minutes? I haven't gone downstairs yet. I wanted to wait for you."

The new rule I presented last night left a horrendous taste in my mouth. A man couldn't look like Deacon while also being well-spoken and thoughtful. He was the holy grail of men, and I could sip on him all fucking day.

Deacon finally faced me, and when his eyes met mine, I lost all control of my effort not to smile. I waited for the alarm bells to go off in my head, but there was nothing but silence. I needed the crew to buck up and get back on their shit.

Not a real relationship, no lying, fuck around in private, and no love.

We continued staring, both of us trying to read the other. This was a crucial moment in our friendship, and everything we had worked for hung on how we handled the morning after.

He leaned over the mattress and rested his hands on either side of me. "Are we good?"

I kissed him softly, keeping my mouth closed because I was terrified of morning breath. "We're good. Can I shower before we head down?"

"There are towels in the closet outside the bathroom. I'm actually gonna go downstairs to see if I need to brew more coffee." He stopped halfway out the door and looked over his shoulder. "Wear one of my hoodies when you come down."

"Why?"

He smiled. "Because it's cute."

I was glad he left because even when I hopped in the shower, I still felt the heat in my cheeks and the pull in my groin. I closed my eyes as the warm water ran over me, and I was thankful for the distraction. I washed away the feelings that seeped over from last night's decision, and when

I emerged from the bathroom, I felt replenished and ready to face the Scott family.

I slipped on one of Deacon's hoodies and spritzed myself with some perfume. I might be wearing his clothes, but I still needed to make sure I was bringing some of the Original Lyla with me. This version of myself couldn't be trusted to make sound decisions, especially since I was reliving the feeling of Deacon's hands on my clit for the twelfth time this morning.

What was that song called? "The Twelve Days of Christmas"? The twelve *orgasms* of Christmas sounded much better. If anyone showed up with that many birds and expected me to be happy about it, I'd be fucking livid.

As soon as my feet left the bottom step of the stairs, I smelled the cinnamon rolls and coffee coming from the kitchen. I rounded the corner and found Drew standing in front of the coffee maker. It had been a while since I had coffee from a pot instead of a pod, but I was looking forward to the incoming caffeine high.

Drew handed me a mug and moved aside. I eyed him suspiciously as I poured, trying not to lose it at his innocent stare and boyish grin.

"Sleep okay?" he asked, lowering his voice to a whisper. "Feeling well rested?"

"Yes, actually." I placed the pot back on the burner and sipped my coffee. Drew pulled out a few creamers from the fridge for me to choose from. I picked up the caramel and gave the bottle a shake. "How about you?"

"I slept good. It was a quiet night before Christmas before something woke me up. I think it was a 'Fuck, Deacon,' maybe? I'm not entirely sure."

The bottle slipped from my hand, and Drew caught it before it hit the floor.

"Relax," he said, amused by my clumsy reaction. "Your secret is safe with me. I support this. Love this for the both of you."

"Now it's *your* turn to relax." I brushed past him on my way to the living room, and he caught my elbow.

"Was last night the first time?"

"Drew, *please* drop it," I practically begged. I was trying my damndest to forget it even happened, and my own body was turning against me. I didn't need the lovable younger brother egging me on too.

Drew shook his head, unimpressed with my answer. "I just assumed it happened a while ago, that's all."

I rolled my eyes, putting on my best smile before I entered the cheerful scene in front of me. "Good morning, everyone."

Deacon opened his arm as I sat next to him on the couch. His fingers grazed the side of my neck, and I swallowed.

These hands, these hands, these hands.

"Good morning, Lyla." Georgia smiled, handing me a stocking.

I almost chucked it at Drew when he appeared in the background, mouthing, "Love this for you."

"The glitter glue is a tradition," Howard added. "So please excuse my sloppy handwriting."

My heart swelled, and I wasn't sure how much more I could take from this precious family. I knew Deacon helped them with their gift ideas, but it showed how much he paid attention and how his parents wanted me to feel included.

I ran my hand over the shiny green writing. "It's perfect. I love it."

Georgia insisted that Deacon and I open our stocking stuffers first, and it wasn't long before an impatient Drew went next. Howard brought out a small gift box for Georgia, and they exchanged an adorable glance when she unwrapped a gorgeous pair of earrings. It was completely different than the Christmas morning I was used to, and when my phone buzzed in my pocket, I knew it was my Christmas text from Aaron Brooks.

Dad

> Merry Christmas, Lyla. I booked Miami for our spring break lunch. I'll have Tonya send you the flight information. Let her know if Deacon has TSA so she can add it to his ticket.

Leave it to Dad to burst the Christmas bubble of cheer. Fuck. I completely forgot about spring break.

Lyla

> Merry Christmas. I'll let Tonya know.

Good ol' Tonya. I had no idea how that woman did anything for my dad. I imagined him as a no-nonsense boss who didn't allow time off or paid maternity leave.

Deacon's breath was hot on my neck. "Everything okay?"

"Spring break plans. I *completely* forgot about spring break."

"Busy thinking about other things?" His raspy voice reignited the fire I was desperately trying to put out.

I drained the rest of my coffee. "Did you want more coffee?"

He smirked at the change in subject. "I'm good."

I took our empty mugs to the kitchen and stopped when I saw Georgia leaning over the sink. She held a stocking to her chest and stared out the window. Her eyes were glossy, and like Deacon's did so often, they focused on the cloudy sky.

I placed the mugs on the counter to announce my presence. Georgia looked over her shoulder and swiped at her eyes.

"I'm sorry," I whispered. "I didn't mean to intrude."

"It's okay!" She assured me, glancing down at the memory she was holding. "It happens sometimes, and I just need a moment."

She squeezed my shoulder as she passed, and I held it together until she rounded the corner. I didn't have to guess the name on the stocking she was holding, and I didn't know how to stop the tears from gathering in the corners of my eyes. I imagined Georgia pulling out the stockings, only for her to remember that there was one she wouldn't be filling.

As cheerful as the holidays were, they didn't pause for grief. They served as a yearly reminder that a loved one should be here and that the world didn't care what kind of person you were. Life took what it wanted, and we were left to figure out the aftermath.

Howard and Georgia Scott would do anything to get one more day, fuck, one more *hour* with Dominic.

Meanwhile, I had a dad who didn't care what I was doing as long as I wasn't disrupting his image. The only reason I played into his toxic ways was because I needed something from him. The money he set aside for me would provide a life for me and my mom; the default parent who wasted away her twenties because she got stuck with me. I was a lot, and I kept adding layers to the life my mom didn't ask for. If I couldn't give her the chance to chase her dreams, then she had no reason to stick around. I'd have two parents who saw me as a burden. I'd never be enough on my own.

I borrowed Georgia's spot by the window and looked up. I understood why Deacon felt angry because it didn't make any sense. I gave myself two minutes to feel, then returned to the living room.

Drew and Deacon's parents were nowhere to be found, and the afterglow of gift giving had faded. Deacon sat on the couch with a pained expression. Tears were in his eyes, and he didn't have to say anything. I knew by the scattered present wrappings and the empty room plastered with memories from the past.

The corner of his mouth lifted into a small smile when he saw me, and I climbed onto his lap. All I wanted was to take his pain away—help him carry a handful if the world allowed it. I settled naturally into him and kissed him on his cheek. Before I could pull back, he cupped my chin and brought my mouth to his. The hunger and excitement of last night was no longer there, and the slow and sweet tempo of whatever this was assured me that one thing was clear.

It didn't matter if it was Cassie, me, or any other woman on this planet. No one deserved a guy as downright delightful as Deacon Scott.

CHAPTER FORTY-SEVEN

Deacon

WHEN CASSIE ASKED IF I wanted to go to lunch when we returned for the spring semester, I didn't think she meant the first day back on campus. My last class ended at two, so I told Cassie we could meet for a quick lunch somewhere on campus. I wanted to be at Lyla's by four so I could have some time alone with her before we started a game of Monopoly with her roommates. I hadn't seen Lyla since Christmas, and it was pathetic how much I missed her.

I took a deep breath as I entered Mr. Spots, once again making shit complicated when it didn't need to be. So what if I missed Lyla? In technical terms, Lyla *was* my girlfriend, and sleeping with your girlfriend didn't warrant itself as a red flag. The only red flag in my current line of vision was that I was having lunch with my *ex*-girlfriend while missing my fake girlfriend—who I promised not to fall in love with.

"Don't say that," I groaned.

Who the fuck are you talking to, Deacon?

I liked to think Dominic was weighing in with his opinions when I thought out loud. He would tell me to stop over-thinking and do something more exciting with my time. I imagined it had to be painful, watching the people you loved act like idiotic characters from *The Sims* that you had no control over.

I knew that analogy would've made Dominic laugh. "See, now that's a good one."

"Did you say something?"

I felt a hand on my elbow and saw Cassie standing beside me. Her blonde hair was down around her shoulders, and a green fluffy beanie sat on her head.

She smiled. "Hi, there."

"Hey, Cass," I said, gesturing for her to walk in front of me.

She led us to a table in the back and took the seat against the wall. I sat across from her and removed my hat.

"Haircut?" she asked.

"Yeah," I said with a chuckle, running my hand over my head. "I had to get it cut by Barry one more time before I came back."

Cassie's eyes lingered on my mouth, and I pretended not to notice. "I always loved your hair short. Especially when you trimmed your facial hair to match it."

I leaned forward on my elbows. "Are you saying I had a scraggly beard at one point?"

"No!" she exclaimed with a giggle, and the sound of it made me smile. I was always a sucker for Cassie's laugh. "I always thought you looked good."

"Well, your hair is *long*. It was never this long when we were together."

Cassie shrugged. "You always liked it shorter, so I tried to get it cut every now and then."

"You got it cut back in April. So, what, it's been—"

"Nine months," she answered quickly. "Nine because May was eight."

I knew time had gone by, but eight months? I attempted to change the subject. "Do you wanna order some food?"

"I'm sorry, Deacon," Cassie whispered. Her voice was so low I almost had to ask her to repeat herself, but the look on her face told me that I had heard her correctly. "I'm sorry about the way it happened. You deserved better than that, and I'm—" Her lip began to tremble, and I instinctively reached across the table for her hand.

"Hey." I prompted her to look at me, offering her a sympathetic grin. "It's okay."

"I was s-so afraid that you hated me," she stammered through a nervous breath. She wiped a tear from her cheek and shrugged. "And then I saw you with Lyla, and I wasn't sure if you were dating her just to make me mad or—"

"Why would I date Lyla to make you mad?"

Cassie rolled her eyes. "Come on, Deacon. When we were together, you *never* wanted to go out. You never wanted to do anything outside our usual routine, and I always felt like the bad guy for asking you to. Then you go and date the girl I saw riding up and down on a stripper pole in some video?"

I covered my mouth so she couldn't see my smile. It was my first memory of Lyla; the morning I called her Stripper Pole Girl and the moment she found out she was on the internet. I wondered if she still had that yellow dress—

"It's not funny!" Cassie exclaimed.

"It kind of is funny, Cass. First, let me say that I don't hate you. If I hated you, I wouldn't be sitting across from you right now. But Cassie—*you* broke up with *me*. What was I supposed to do? Wait around for you to decide if there was someone else who was better than me?"

Cassie closed her eyes, and I recognized the tired look on her face. "After Dominic passed, Deacon—"

"Please stop." I pushed my chair back and stood up.

"Deacon, hold on—"

"I don't *want* to hold on, Cassie," I said, trying to stay calm. "I don't want to hear about how I wasn't the same person I was when you met me. You met me when I was a freshman. *Of course,* I wanted to party and have fun and study when it was convenient instead of making it a priority. I wanted to go out and close down the bars with you and wake up the next morning just to do it all over again."

When I returned to my seat, Cassie's blue eyes were glossy. I wasn't prepared to have the conversation we should've had back in May. I showed up for that conversation, and instead, she picked up the phone.

"My entire world fell apart," I whispered angrily, my voice growing louder. "It fucking fell apart, and when I came back to school, yeah, I was different. I didn't want to party, and I didn't want to be around people. I focused on school and on making you happy. I did everything I could in the only ways I knew how. That might not have included parties and late nights, but I *tried* Cassie."

She shook her head and wiped more tears from her cheeks. "I never knew how to help you."

My shoulders relaxed, and I felt the heat simmering in my chest. I focused on my breathing, ensuring I was calm before speaking again. "You never asked. I felt like you kept waiting for me to snap out of it. Like it was a phase I'd eventually grow out of, and I'd suddenly just get back to normal."

Cassie stared at the table, and I knew this conversation was over. I didn't feel like staying for food, and I didn't mean to snap at her. It wasn't my intention to make her upset.

"What was the point of this today, Cass?" I prompted gently. "Is this what you wanted to talk about?"

She shook her head. "I just wanted to see you. I wanted to see if you were still happy." She tucked her hair behind her ears, hesitating to say what else was on her mind. "And I wanted to see if you were still with Lyla. I was surprised to see she went home with you for Christmas."

Still with Lyla.

"I am happy, Cassie, and I am still with Lyla."

Her blank stare made it obvious she didn't want to hear that. I couldn't sort through my thoughts with Cassie in front of me. I needed time to clear my head and figure out how to move forward. I still had a few months left with Lyla, and I wouldn't lead Cassie on if I no longer had plans to get back together with her.

"Can we do this some other time?" I suggested.

She didn't look upset when I proposed a raincheck. We needed a clean slate, and too many items from our past marked up the conversation.

When we left Mr. Spots, we went in separate directions. I had no idea where she was going, but I knew exactly where I wanted to be.

Chapter Forty-Eight

Lyla

I had watched Michelle and Keira clean our apartment at least one hundred times since Charlie and I signed our lease. They took cleaning to a whole new level. They vacuumed the outside of the vacuum cleaner and cleaned the inside of the dishwasher. I was grateful for their attention to detail, but no one would ever catch me wiping the outside of a Pledge can—which was exactly what Michelle was doing.

Charlie rolled her eyes and flipped through her playlist on YouTube. "It's just Deacon coming over. Why do you guys care if the apartment is clean?"

"Especially since I *don't* care," I added. I sat beside Charlie on the couch, reading my new book and enjoying a White Claw.

"I always clean when we get back from a break," Keira said. "I just want things to look nice."

Michelle sighed when Keira opened the vacuum's canister too early, allowing debris to settle along the side of the trash can.

"I'll help," I offered, stealing a chip from Charlie's bag of Doritos.

There was a knock on the door, and I immediately shifted my focus to that task instead. The debris would have to wait. I knew who was at the door, and I'd be lying if I said I wasn't excited to see him.

Deacon stood in the hall with a smile and a—*backward hat?* He'd never worn one before and chose moving day to try out the new style.

Fuck me. Why did I tell Deacon we couldn't sleep together again? I couldn't renege on rule number six, not with the guy trying to get his ex-girlfriend back. He had his entire future mapped out, and this friendship was just a stepping stone to his life with Cassie.

Deacon stepped inside and pulled me in for a kiss. His lips lingered on mine a little longer than I anticipated, but I wasn't mad about it. He smelled like his usual cedarwood and lavender, and a warmth settled in my chest. It was like wrapping myself in my favorite blanket. It had been three weeks since I'd seen Deacon Scott, and I missed the hell out of him.

"I missed you, Brooks." His tone was so casual that it might as well have been a statement about the weather. I had to hand it to Deacon. He was moving past our Christmas Bone much better than I thought he would.

I tightened my grip around his waist and smiled. "I missed you too, Scott."

The right side of his mouth had a slight curve, and I tugged on his hand when he tried to walk to the living room. "Where's your stuff?"

"Right." His shoulders slumped, and his smile vanished. "It's in my car."

"I'll come with you."

I followed him down to the car, and before he opened his trunk, I forced him to look at me. "What's the matter?"

"Nothing's the matter." He guided me out of the way so he could get his bags.

His tongue grazed the center of his top lip, and I knew there was more. "Deacon."

He smiled. "Just because we're top-tier boyfriend-girlfriend now doesn't mean you know me."

"*Uhm*, we were always top-tier, and I know you pretty well. Now, what's up? What happened?"

He dropped his bag and took a seat on the curb. "I met with Cassie before coming here."

I followed his lead and sat beside him, ignoring the dip in my gut. "And?"

"And I just . . . honestly, I don't fucking know. She wanted to meet for lunch, so we did, and then she apologized for how we broke up. But then she brought up Dominic and how everything—*I* changed, and I just couldn't hear it. It's like I looked back on our relationship and couldn't remember being happy."

I touched his shoulder and slid my fingers across his upper back. "That's a lot, Deac. I'm sorry." Another moment of silence passed between us, and I realized there was a question I needed to hear the answer to. "Do you still love her?"

"I think part of me always will. I just . . . I don't know." His tired expression told me he had been thinking about it since he saw her this afternoon.

It was time to channel the best friend who knew him better than either of us wanted to admit. I sat up and cleared my throat. "Can I say something, maybe a little out of line? I feel like I've earned that level with you, you know, since you've been inside me and all."

"*Jesus*, Brooks." He chuckled, and it was nice to see a smile back on his pretty face.

"Sorry. Okay, so you're dating for a year, and at twenty-one years old, your boyfriend's world completely shatters overnight. I don't know—" I struggled to find the words because the last thing I wanted to do was invalidate feelings I couldn't imagine having to bear. "I can't say there was right and wrong because I don't know everything that happened between you guys, but does anyone really know how to help someone after they have gone through the unimaginable? I'm not making excuses for anything she *did* or *didn't* do. But there isn't a manual that tells us how to help someone, Deacon, and I've known you for . . ."

I began counting on my fingers. For someone who usually ran their sex life as a calendar, I certainly sucked at—

"Five months," Deacon said.

I smiled at his quick answer. "Five months. And in those five months, you've never asked me for help. You've offered me a proposition that benefits us both, but that doesn't count."

He covered his mouth with his hand so I couldn't see the sexy smirk he was hiding underneath it. "It's never been easy for me to ask for help."

"I know," I prompted gently. "But sometimes we need to ask for it, and that's okay. Because of you, I've actually thought about therapy. I mentioned it to my mom over break, and a few months ago, I *never* would've done that. None of what you went through . . . what you're continuing to go through, is easy."

Deacon's features relaxed, and I knew he was fighting against whatever dark thoughts surfaced. I pulled him closer so my head rested against his shoulder.

"I guess Cassie didn't have it easy either, huh?" he mumbled.

I exhaled slowly, leaving a light kiss on his temple. "No. I couldn't imagine watching you go through what you went through when it first happened. It's hard watching you going through it now."

"I'm sorry."

"There's *nothing* to be sorry about," I emphasized, leaning back to get some air. I wanted to kiss him, pull him from every dark moment he had to relive. "You don't ever have to be sorry for being *real*, Deacon. Not with me. We don't lie."

"We don't lie," he echoed in a raspy voice.

Deacon stood up and offered me his hand. I grabbed his book bag off the ground and led us back upstairs where Deacon officially unpacked into part of my closet, two dresser drawers, and half of my desk. It was a small space, but I wasn't worried. I was more concerned about the fact that I *wasn't* worried. In just five short months, I went from Lyla Brooks, the girl who got physically ill over the thought of getting close to anyone, to whoever *this* version of me was. I couldn't even label this version because I was still trying to understand her.

Deacon had the trust factor—something I had given out a handful of times only to have it thrown back in my face. I'd known for a while that Deacon was *different*. I kept searching my reader's brain for a better word to describe him, but every time I tried, it was like I had never picked up a book.

The first night Deacon slept in my room as an official roommate, his duffle sat unpacked on my futon, and his fully clothed body took up the right side of my bed. He hugged me against him, and we fell asleep quickly, both tired from returning to a new semester on campus.

The next morning, Deacon woke up around eight and was out the door in twenty minutes to get to his first class. He did his best not to wake me, but after spending so many nights with him next to me, it was hard not to feel the empty spot on the mattress when he left.

I rolled out of bed, ready to tackle the admission I had been putting off since Christmas. I had to tell Charlie what happened over break before I talked myself out of it. Right before she started her morning scroll through Instagram at the breakfast counter, I dragged her by the elbow into my bedroom.

"What the actual—" Charlie protested, stumbling in behind me. "Good morning to you, too?"

I closed the door behind me and blurted, "I slept with him."

Charlie furrowed her brow. "Last night you did?"

"No, on Christmas Eve." I rolled my eyes. "Christmas *Day* if you want to get technical."

She flashed me a flirtatious grin. "Oh, Lyla. How *Hallmark* of you! I love that detail."

I dragged my hands down my face and groaned. I wanted to laugh at her comment and punch her at the same time. She didn't think I was serious. She thought I was giving her a story update.

I felt the bed shift next to me, and she pried my hands from my face. "You know, fake relationship or not, it's a little unconvincing that you would wait this long—"

"*No, Charlie,*" I emphasized, making direct eye contact with her. "I *slept* with him. I slept with Deacon."

"Like you, actually . . ."

I nodded.

"*Yes,* bitch!" Charlie cheered, jumping up from the bed. "This is what I've been waiting for! I honestly thought you slept together when he started staying over, so color me surprised. Well done, both of you."

I winced at her satisfied grin. "What?"

Her face fell, but a sad smile still lingered against her soft features. "I just wasn't expecting to lose you to that team while we were still in school."

"What are you talking about?"

"You *like* him."

I couldn't argue with her statement. I did like Deacon. He was one of my favorite people. I noticed the pep in Charlie's step as she approached my bedroom door, and the alarm bells sounded.

"Charlie," I warned.

"You know, you really don't help your case whenever I ask about him, and you're speechless. It's not as convincing as your fake relationship." She grabbed the doorknob and spun on her heel to face me. "It is still *fake*, right?"

"Yes," I practically growled, throwing a pillow at her head.

"I was interested in this whole charade when I discovered it, but now I'm completely invested in how this will end." She picked up the pillow and threw it back at me. "Lyla Brooks likes a boy."

"I do like Deacon, but it's not like that."

Charlie rolled her eyes and opened the door. She glanced down the hall to make sure we were home alone, and her upbeat tone confirmed we were. "You can tell yourself whatever you need to make sense of it. But if it helps, I know he likes you too."

More alarm bells. The entire squad was alerted as my heart rate skyrocketed to a dangerous speed. Deacon couldn't like me. I mean, I knew he *liked* me, but it was the same way I liked him. That comparison wasn't entirely reassuring either. How the hell did this happen?

Not a real relationship, no lying, fuck around in private, and no love. Don't ask about the past, and only fuck one time.

"He's in love with Cassie," I said, trying my best to look unbothered.

Charlie's smirk told me I had failed. "Like I said, tell yourself whatever you need to."

This weekend, I had to nail down a Mr. January. Deacon wouldn't have been upset last night if he wasn't considering getting back together with Cassie. As his fake girlfriend, I was thrilled our plan was working. As his best friend, I was still working through the idea of Deacon getting back together with the girl who broke his heart.

Chapter Forty-Nine
Deacon

For the second time this school year, I was the unofficial roommate. It had been a month of sharing Lyla's bed and fighting the urge to touch her in all ways I didn't the first and *only* time I ever would. She told me it was a one-time thing, and since I respected her too much to tempt that boundary, I continued to play the night we slept together on repeat like any other best guy friend who couldn't get his fake girlfriend out of his head.

Yes. Totally normal shit.

We were inching closer and closer to spring break with Lyla's dad, and even with hefty class schedules and study sessions, we still managed to go out every weekend since the semester started. I expected Lyla to have another prospect by now, and I even encouraged her to look for a potential Mr. February at the bar. It killed me to do it, and I hated how guys stared at her like she wasn't with me.

I knew it was *fake* with me, but it all felt the same. Weekends passed, and Lyla always insisted on heading back to her place. The part of me that craved her wasn't entirely convinced that Christmas never crossed her mind.

It was Valentine's Day, and I knew I was taking a risk with a small bouquet of red roses and a Christmas gift I should have given her two months ago. In my defense, I had to do *something* since I was under the watchful eyes of Michelle,

Cassie's newly found study buddy. I planned for Lyla to see it as a cute gesture, and then she'd thank me with one of her adorable hug squeezes. If it tanked, well, I hadn't thought of that outcome.

There was a set of keys at work on the other side of the front door, and I knew it was Lyla. She walked in and didn't notice me at first. Her hair was still curly from yesterday, and she had it in one of those buns on the top of her head. She chose my biggest hoodie to wear to class today, and she looked fucking adorable.

I smiled at the sight of her in my clothes. I pushed the small red bag across the counter, grabbing her attention.

She tucked a stray curl behind her ear and rolled her eyes. "Deacon Scott, we are *not* doing Valentine's Day!"

I pointed to her gift. "*This* is a late Christmas present."

"And the flowers? Are those late, too?"

"Technically, yes, they are. I usually buy you flowers on Mondays."

She continued her playful prompting. "And did you delay them so you could buy me flowers on Valentine's Day?"

"It's okay to buy a girl flowers on Valentine's Day," I argued. "Even if that girl is just a friend."

She pulled the gift bag in front of her, lifting a piece of tissue paper. "Is this really a late Christmas gift?"

"It's honestly just a little something." I stifled the urge to smile adoringly at her ability to make opening a gift bag take five years. "I couldn't give it to you Christmas morning after everything happened. You would've had some smart-ass comment."

"Would've felt very *Pretty Woman*," she agreed, pulling out the final piece of tissue. She stared at the metal object for a moment, and I knew with some investigating, she'd figure out what it was.

A soft gasp fell from her lips. She examined it closely, turning it over repeatedly in her hand.

"It's a book embosser," I said, admiring the scene in front of me.

Lyla giggled, looking in the drawer beside her for a piece of paper. She stamped the paper between the press, and it read, "From the Library of Lyla Brooks." Underneath the script was an open book with a rose in the middle.

She smiled down at the design and then up at me. "*I* know what it is, but how did *you* know this existed?"

I shrugged as if I hadn't spent days browsing pages of gift ideas for new bookstore owners. "Google. Lots of '*book girlies*' have them."

My air quotes made her laugh. "You're pretty fantastic, you know that?"

"Don't you mean downright delightful?"

"Well, that too," she said, running her hand over the print. "Thank you, Deacon."

"You're welcome. And I expect you to use it when I come to Chicago and buy a book from you."

"You realize I'll be marking it as my property instead of yours, right?"

I followed her back to her bedroom and leaned against her door frame. I didn't want to talk about her gift anymore. I wanted to bring up my plan for us this afternoon. "Are you doing anything today? Any prospects in the running for Mr. February?"

"No." She removed her moccasins, tossing them in the closet. "I'm starting to lose hope in my system. Either that, or I'm maturing out of the calendar method. I'm not sure."

I tried to hide my excitement. "Let's do something then."

She eyed me in the doorway, and her teeth grazed her bottom lip. I'd seen that look once before, and it was right before she came on my cock.

"Lyla?" I smiled, pulling her out of whatever daze she was in. I was totally fucked. "Did you want to do some boyfriend-girlfriend shit outside of this apartment?"

"You mean there isn't a riveting game of Monopoly or chess planned?" she teased.

"Tempting, but no. I can kick your ass some other time."

I could do *a lot* to Lyla right now. This was new territory for me. When I was with Lyla, I tried to suppress how much I wanted her—keep a clear boundary drawn between our fake relationship and my feelings for her. No matter what I was doing, I always thought about her in the background.

If I pushed an idea onto Lyla, she'd shove it right back. She was too stubborn. She would completely retreat if I told her I had feelings for her. I knew she cared about me, and more importantly, she trusted me. She trusted me to see our agreement through, and I wouldn't do anything to jeopardize that.

If we stayed in tonight, her roommates would eventually interrupt us. I loved a good game night, but I didn't feel like sharing. I had three months until graduation, and I planned to squeeze as much boyfriend-girlfriend shit into that timeframe as possible.

Chapter Fifty

Lyla

When a gorgeous man in a backward hat stood in your doorway, leaned up against the frame with captivating brown eyes, it didn't matter what that man asked. You said yes.

I had missed his question the first time, but when Deacon dropped the boyfriend-girlfriend-shit line on me, I did my best to look past the flowers and amazing gift. I stared at him from the safety of my bed, shrugging off everything I'd rather do if we stayed *in* the apartment. It was Valentine's Day, for Christ's sake. Didn't couples thrive off of this shit?

Of course they did, and that was probably the reason Deacon asked me to do something in the first place. Mr. Relationship was probably going insane at the idea of being in this apartment while couples all over the city were falling deeper in love.

I swallowed my desire and returned his playful gaze. "What did you have in mind?"

About forty-five minutes later, I stood in the lobby of a place I hadn't visited since high school.

"Are you sure you want to spend your evening *here*?" I watched a couple drag their two children out to the parking lot. The toddlers kicked and screamed while Mom and Dad looked *fed up*. It was clear that neither of them would be getting laid tonight.

It was incredible how growing up sounded fun one moment and looked miserable the next.

Deacon handed me a pair of bright orange socks. "What were you expecting, Brooks? Fine dining and a rose petal bath?"

I considered the thought as he pulled me to a small hallway. He wore his cheesy ass smile the entire time we took off our shoes, putting on socks that I'd be tossing in the trash immediately after we left.

"Maybe not a rose petal bath, but we could've done pizza and a movie?"

"We always do pizza and movies." He rested his elbows on his knees, eyeing me impatiently. "Ready?"

I sighed and accepted my fate. "Let's do this."

Deacon grabbed my hand, and we walked to the end of the facility where there were fewer kids and an open floor of trampolines. As soon as his foot hit the tarp lining, Deacon took off. He jumped forward, landing on his hands and prompting his body into a flip. My mouth dropped, and I cackled at his expectations for this trip. While Deacon was a closet gymnast, I only hoped I didn't fall on my face in front of the father-daughter duo in the corner.

"Jump to me!" Deacon yelled from four trampolines away. He kept a steady hop as he waited, and I adored the boyish grin plastered on his face. I leaped forward and followed the momentum, gaining more speed the closer I got to Deacon.

"Stop me, stop me, stop me!" I crashed into his chest, and when we fell onto the trampoline, we burst into hysterics.

"Damn, Lyla!" He held his hand to his chest, catching his breath. "Have you *never* been on a trampoline?"

"I'm sorry," I said between breaths. "Did I not disclose that information before you told me we were going to a *trampoline park?*"

"Well, stand up." He swatted my thigh and hopped back on his feet. I was exhausted just watching him. He bounced over to a basketball hoop and waved me over.

"Is this the kind of Valentine's Day celebration you'd spring on Cassie?" Her name left an unwanted taste in my mouth, but judging from movies and TV shows, she probably didn't like my name either. "What kinds of things did you guys do for special occasions?"

"I could never bring Cass here," Deacon said, recalling a giddy memory. He tossed me a ball, and when I took a shot to distract myself, he shook his head like a disappointed coach. "The one place you can do a dunk, and you toss a crappy free throw?"

"What!" I exclaimed. "So I'm not good at basketball or balancing on a trampoline. Any other things you want to rub in my face?"

Deacon bit his bottom lip as a flicker of temptation ignited in his brown eyes. Blood rushed to my cheeks.

"Deacon Scott," I reprimanded him proudly. "You've got a dirtier mind than people think."

He shrugged. "Maybe."

"So why wouldn't you bring her here?" I prompted, keeping us out of dangerous territory. "Orange socks aren't her thing?"

"Just not her scene. She loved to go out to dinner and do the Instagram-worthy desserts." He fidgeted with the ball in his hand. "I never realized how much effort she put into making us *look* like an amazing couple to other people. It's like if she could keep that image going, she could pretend she still wanted to be with me."

"What do you think you'll do differently?" I snatched the ball from his hand, and when he tried to swat it back, I spun around and launched it toward the hoop.

The ball bounced off the rim, and Deacon caught it. "I spent so much time making sure our future was okay. I think I lost sight of what was happening in front of me. I was missing out because I was protecting time I thought we had together."

I offered him a sympathetic grin. "You could still have that time, Deacon."

"I know." He returned the gesture right before he took three giant leaps and performed an award-winning dunk.

I cheered like a proud girlfriend and tried not to act completely surprised at the heavily supported shot. I could do the same thing with the right amount of bounce, and when Deacon offered me the ball, I mimicked his footwork.

When Deacon lept for a dunk shot, he flew effortlessly through the air and did a spin trick on his way down. I was on my fourth attempt and could only conquer two ways of jumping—too soon or too late.

"Fuck it." I laughed as I came down from my fifth shot. I was breathless and sweaty and growing more pissed off by the second. "I give up."

"I'll help you." Deacon stood under the hoop and laced his hands in front of the impressive bulge in his shorts. "Run up and use my hand as a boost."

The thought of running toward Deacon again and falling on my face terrified me. I might not have a hot Valentine's Day date to attend, but I didn't feel like having a tarp burn on my forehead.

His shoulders pulled against his T-shirt, and I remembered what it was like to have him hovered over me. Why the fuck didn't I buy him looser T-shirts for Christmas? What a missed opportunity.

I checked to ensure I wasn't drooling over how good his arms looked. "I don't want you to drop me," I protested lamely.

"I'm not going to drop you. Come on." When I shook my head, Deacon narrowed his gaze and straightened up. "I promise I've got you."

I took a deep breath, and before I could talk myself out of it, I ran at him. I felt my foot land on his hands, and he pushed up, giving me the perfect lift for my dunk.

He spun me around in a hug, his cheers bouncing off the walls of the open area. We were officially the last two people left among the trampolines.

His hands slid down my sides as heat radiated through my shirt. His thumbs grazed under my breasts, and for a glimmer of a second, I didn't want him to stop. A woman gets a handful of horny hall passes, and when I slept with Deacon, I robbed myself of half the show. I was so eager to have him inside me I didn't even take my shirt off.

I ran my hands down his back and ignored the slight part of his lips. We were off-screen, and everything I wanted to do with him on this trampoline involved behind-the-scenes footage. I loved being close to him. The innocent touches drove me crazy, but the idea that I'd never be wrapped up in Deacon again filled me with regret.

Sex had never been a doorway to developing feelings for someone. I disassociated from that a long time ago. It was never something I dragged out when I just wanted the end result. With Deacon, I wanted . . . *more*. I wasn't sure what that was yet, and I was afraid I lost my only chance to try and figure it out. This had to be some Valentine's Day bullshit. I didn't habitually spend the red-hearted holiday doing a deep dive into my emotions.

I swallowed all of the questions I wanted to ask him because I wasn't sure if I wanted to hear his answers. "Ready to get going?"

His hands fell to his sides, and he let out a slow breath. "Yeah."

It was cold on the walk back to Deacon's car. February in Ohio wasn't the friendliest, and the layer of sweat I was wearing wasn't helping the cause. I slid into the passenger seat, and Deacon cranked the heat. I held my hands in front of the fan, and an aching laugh escaped me as my body shook against the cold.

"Has it always been hard?" Deacon asked through chattering teeth. "Letting someone take care of you?"

"Take care of me? There's no reason to." His question surprised me, but my answer surprised him more. I rubbed my hands together and smiled. "Why, as my fake boyfriend, do you want to?"

He stared at me, wearing the same electrified expression from the night I couldn't get out of my head. "I do want to, Brooks," he admitted softly. "But there's nothing fake about that."

Chapter Fifty-One

Deacon

Our flight to Miami left Cleveland on Tuesday morning. It took some convincing to get Lyla to drive to her mom's house, which was twenty minutes from the airport. She finally caved when I told her we'd have to leave Bowling Green at 5 a.m. to make the flight.

It bummed me out that I didn't get to meet Jane in person. We arrived late Monday night, and when I asked Lyla if she wanted to wake her up to let her know we were leaving, she insisted we let her sleep. Jane was much more personable than Aaron Brooks, so I couldn't understand why Lyla rushed us out of the house so quickly.

Maybe she didn't want me to meet her mom since our relationship deadline was approaching. Or perhaps I freaked her the fuck out when I told her I wanted to take care of her. Because that was exactly what a fake boyfriend would say, right?

Fuck no.

Three weeks had passed since our Valentine's Day outing, and while I was overthinking my comment, she acted like she hadn't heard it. Nothing had changed between us, and I envied her ability to separate everything. Lyla didn't do relationships, so it didn't matter what was said or not said. We had off-screen moments that slipped in sometimes, but my emotions blurred the line between real and fake.

My plan no longer included Cassie. How could it?

Before Lyla, there were moments when the world felt heavy. I had been through pain and heartache that I wasn't sure I could recover from. No matter what I did, my thoughts wouldn't slow down. I couldn't sleep, I couldn't focus, and I couldn't recognize who I was in the dark. Lyla Brooks became a light in my life, and she was my favorite thing I never planned.

It didn't matter if I wasn't supposed to fall—it was happening. Lyla didn't need someone to take care of her, but she sure as hell deserved it. The more time I spent with her, the more I wanted to be that person. Regardless of how this ended, she'd always have me looking out for her from a distance. Love didn't have to be a contract, and Lyla didn't owe me anything for it.

The turbulence shook me back to the present, and a cheerful voice came over the loudspeaker. We'd touch down in Miami in twenty minutes, where the weather was a piping seventy-eight degrees.

"What did the guy say?" Lyla asked, leaning her head against my shoulder. She continued scrolling through one of her playlists, and I chuckled when another song by Nick Jonas belted against my eardrum.

"This guy again, huh? We just listened to the other brother."

"The Jonas Brothers are no laughing matter," Lyla said. "I was beside myself when they announced their breakup."

"Along with all of the other women in America," I mumbled, feeling a tiny slap against my chest.

Lyla turned down the music, and I knew one of her nosey questions was on deck. "Are you a jealous person?"

"I'm jealous of time," I admitted. "I love it when my girl gets attention, as long as she isn't disrespected. If you're giving someone else your time when I wish it were me, then yeah, I get a little jealous."

"Have *I* ever made you jealous?"

I thought of Brady Blue Eyes and the nights she didn't sleep in my bed after we went out. I hesitated to answer, but there was no reason to hide it. "Maybe a little."

A silent exchange flowed between us. I couldn't tell if she was shocked or reassured to hear my response. If the second option was even a possibility, maybe I wasn't being as crazy as I thought.

"We don't lie, Deacon Scott," she reminded me with a playful grin.

"We don't lie," I echoed softly.

I rested my hand just above her knee, dragging my thumb across the warm fabric of her leggings. There was a slight pull in my groin, and I wasn't sure if I should stop. I didn't feel like arriving in Miami with a hard-on.

It was painfully refreshing, wanting someone this way. I always wanted Cassie when we were together, but the draw I felt to Lyla was different. There was a primal desire to fuck her the way she imagined me doing. I wanted to know what she pictured when she thought about it. I wanted to feel her coming undone beneath me with my chest against her back, her hands on a countertop or—

I pulled my hand away from her leg, pretending to have an itch on the back of my neck. I had an itch all right, but there was nothing I could do about it now.

"You haven't mentioned Cassie since you met for lunch," Lyla added. "Has she reached out to you?"

I swore this girl had an alarm system for when I was thinking about her. Whenever I was close to exploding, she'd drop a bomb first and mention Cassie.

"We talk here and there, but not about anything important. I think she just wants to make sure her name stays at the top of my inbox. She used to say that to me as a joke, but even when Cassie and I were just hooking up, I never talked to anyone else. I'm just not programmed that way."

"That's good," Lyla said and then quickly added, "about wanting your attention, I mean. But why does it sound like you don't want hers?"

Hearing the words out loud felt like a shot to my chest.

"It's because of what you talked about, isn't it?" Her voice was barely above a whisper. "About Dominic?"

I cleared my throat and waited for the stinging in my chest to subside. "Let's not talk about that now. What's going on in that pretty head of yours?"

Her lips curved into a grin at my compliment, but they fell just as fast as the wheels turned behind her green eyes. Her hands danced nervously in her lap. "I told my mom about Hunter. I'm not sure why I did it, but I looked him up on Instagram over break."

"Did you want to talk about it?" I prompted gently.

As the wheels touched down on the runway, Lyla's hand shot to my knee. She giggled at her reaction and hit pause on her playlist.

The captain's voice echoed through the plane. "Welcome to Miami, folks. The temperature is seventy-eight degrees, and there's no rainfall expected for the rest of the day."

Lyla pulled the earbud from my ear and responded to my question. "One thing at a time. Let's focus on Aaron Brooks first."

It didn't take long to get off the plane since we flew first class. We followed the signs to the arrivals platform and caught a cab outside. I pulled the handle of Lyla's suitcase from her hand and hoisted it into the trunk.

"Do you do things like that to take care of me?" she asked, eyeing me playfully as she rounded the car.

I slid into the backseat beside her and rested my arm above her head. "If putting your bags in the car is considered taking care of you, I'll have to give you a checklist to take to Chicago for your next prospect."

She laughed, leaning into my side. I was already creating a column of red flags for her in my head. Lyla had zero expectations of men, and why shouldn't she? From everything she had told me, they either disappointed her or she predicted their true colors.

The hotel we arrived at was a gorgeous building that overlooked the ocean. It was hot, and my shirt clung to my chest when I stepped out of the car. The driver brought our bags to the side, and I tipped him.

Lyla glanced up at the building, putting on her sunglasses. "Tonya never disappoints."

The hotel employees held open the double doors, and I tried not to look like a complete tourist as I marveled at the lobby. The chilly temperature contrasted with the muggy air outside, and I was glad Lyla wore my hoodie. She would have frozen in her tank top.

"Reservation for Lyla Brooks. It should be under Tonya," Lyla said, and the concierge nodded.

"Who is Tonya?" I asked.

She glanced back at me with her lips pressed in a straight line. "Tonya is my dad's secretary. I've never actually met the woman, but she basically runs his life behind the scenes."

She handed me the room keys, and there was a tiny flutter in my stomach as we entered the elevator. I was holding a *room key*, and while Lyla and I had spent more nights together than I could count, something about a hotel room felt dangerous. For the first time, we could hide away from the rest of the world and everyone we knew.

Our room was on the second-highest floor. I tried to have realistic expectations, but as the elevator kept rising, I knew that was out of the question. We stepped into the suite, and the room was bigger than my apartment in BG. There were floor-to-ceiling windows along the back wall. We had a beautiful view of the ocean from the private balcony, and it was hard to ignore the rose petals that trailed from the hot tub to the bed.

Fucking rose petals. I should've got on my knees right there and begged for a lifeline. It was times like these when I knew Dominic was snickering above me.

Lyla's hand grazed my shoulder as she slipped past me. She dropped her luggage near the bed, stripped off my hoodie, and padded across the living room.

"See?" She smiled before taking in the view of the ocean below us. "I told you Tonya never disappoints."

I admired how her tank top hugged her curves and mentally punched myself in the face. I wanted to test that bed. I wanted to lay her down and kiss up her neck, hear her soft moans as my hand slipped under her leggings.

"What?" She noticed me staring at the bed. "You better clean that mind up, Deacon Scott."

I smirked. "I don't know what you're talking about. I was trying to decide what shirt to wear to dinner tonight."

"Fuck I almost forgot why we were here." She dragged her hands down her face and groaned. "I'm gonna hop in the shower now. He said we have to be there by six."

"It's only three, sweetheart." I crossed the room, closing the space between us. I pulled her in for a hug, and she buried her face in my chest. It was one of those moments I knew she needed but wouldn't ask for. "Everything's going to be fine. We'll go to dinner, remind him how amazing you are, and then we'll go to the beach or something."

She pulled away to look at me. "I'm still getting in the shower now." On her way to the bathroom, she glanced over her shoulder and smiled. "And don't follow me in there. I've seen that look on your face before."

I was still biting my bottom lip when she closed the door. I ran my hands through my hair and walked onto the balcony. I needed some separation between me and the girl I wanted to explore every inch of in all the ways I didn't do the first time.

The waves crashed in the distance, and the warm Florida air flooded my senses. Dominic always loved the ocean, and the smell of salt and sand took me back to our last family vacation at Myrtle Beach. I craved the memories I had when everyone was just *present*. There was a happiness we didn't have to work for because we didn't know what the future held.

The familiar sound of the Jonas Brothers came from the bathroom, and I gripped the railing. I smiled like an idiot as Lyla sang along and reminded myself, once again, how fucked I was. There was nothing clean about the thoughts I'd have over the next few days.

Chapter Fifty-Two

Lyla

As much as I hated getting ready to face Aaron Brooks only a few hours after arriving, part of me looked forward to the rest of our time here. After all of the experience I had with the quarterly dinners and lunches, I liked the idea of getting it over with instead of the slow dread that came with waiting it out.

Something about having to travel to be insulted made everything feel ten times worse than it was. I was glad Deacon was getting some excitement out of it. He'd never say anything, but I knew he was happy to get away for a little while. It had been nothing but school and grades and preparing for graduation these last few weeks. Deacon deserved some time to himself.

After some curling cream and a quick blow-dry, I pulled my hair back into a loose bun to run through my casual makeup routine. My dad would comment how natural I looked if I wore too little. If I wore too much, he'd ask if I had plans to go clubbing after dinner. I decided to play it safe with a pink lip, some mascara, and a thin line of eyeliner. It was too hot for foundation, so I opted for a tinted moisturizer.

No matter what I wore, Aaron Brooks would have a comment to make. It was pointless to stress about, but I couldn't help it. There was always a sliver of me that thought this time could be different.

"Damn, girl." Deacon leaned against the doorway of the bathroom, crossing his arms. He smiled, his shoulders pulling at his white dress shirt as he rolled the sleeves to expose his forearms. "You look beautiful."

I smiled back. "Thank you."

"You know I've got you, right?"

"I know that," I said, a breathless laugh escaping my chest as I pulled out my hair tie to fluff my curls.

Deacon rested his forearms against the top of the doorway and leaned forward. If this man made one more move in that fucking doorway, I was going to combust.

I knew that as long as Deacon was with me, he had me. There wasn't a part of me that doubted his words. Deacon made everything easier, and that's when I realized the part of the trip that was eating at me. My dad's decision about my trust fund didn't scare me, but running out of time with Deacon did.

My phone buzzed on the counter, letting me know our car was outside. I sprayed one more round of perfume and gestured toward the front door. "Ready?"

Deacon rested his hand on mine the entire ride to the restaurant. With every stroke of his thumb, my heart rate returned to normal. I was afraid if he pulled away, I would have a full-blown panic attack before we even stepped into the restaurant.

I was a little confused when we pulled up to a hotel downtown. I knew most hotels in the area had five-star restaurants, and some even provided a gorgeous view of the ocean and the city skyline. We rode the elevator to the top floor and were greeted immediately by a hostess, who made it very clear that if we weren't there with a reservation already, we might as well not even step onto the floor.

Since I was running out of time to formulate words, Deacon told her my dad's name, and she led us to a table near the windows. In about an hour or so, the bright lights of Miami would illuminate from across the bay, and I secretly hoped we weren't still at dinner to see it.

Dad stood up when he saw us crossing the room. Deacon laced his fingers with mine and extended his free hand toward my dad.

"Nice to see you again, sir." Deacon flashed his sexy grin and brought our clasped hands to his chest. "Lyla hasn't stopped talking about coming here since we landed."

The squeeze of my hand dragged my brain back to the dining room and out of whatever cloud it was hanging in. I cleared my throat and delivered my most convincing smile. "It's nice to see you, Dad."

"I'm happy you both could come." The corners of Dad's mouth reached his eyes, and I did my best not to recoil against Deacon. What was it about this man's happiness that was so sketchy?

I knew the answer to that question but hated admitting it. No daughter wanted to admit that her dad was smiling because some guy with a camera was probably hiding out among the other patrons.

My shoulders fell, and the familiar dip settled in my stomach. Deacon noticed the shift in my demeanor and pulled out my chair so I could sit. He lowered his mouth to my ear and whispered, "I've got you."

I nodded, taking a long sip of water. Deacon's arm rested on the back of my chair, and I was grateful when he asked my dad about the business. I didn't want to talk, so when the waiter brought a bottle of wine to the table, I practically jumped him. I cupped the bottom of my glass as he poured the red and impatiently wiggled my toes. I should've pregamed for this shit.

"Oh, perfect!" Dad exclaimed, pausing his business conversation with Deacon. He stood up and adjusted his black suit jacket. A *genuine* smile appeared on his face, and his green eyes grew as bright as mine did when the wine arrived at the table.

Dad and I just happened to get excited by different reds.

A woman who couldn't have been much younger than my dad approached the table. Her dark hair flowed in perfect waves down her back, and her lips matched the burgundy color of her dress. The fabric hugged her body, and the strapless style accentuated her petite shoulders. The way my dad's eyes glazed over her figure made me want to toss up my wine. As the shock of another dinner guest started to resonate, a girl who could've passed as the woman's younger sister walked up to my dad and hugged him.

I decided I didn't want to be introduced to these people with my mouth hanging open, so I placed my glass on the table and kept my composure behind a closed-mouth grin. The corners of my mouth dug into my cheeks, and when Aaron Brooks fanned his hand over the table toward Deacon and me, I prepared for his next line.

"Tonya, Lily, this is my daughter Lyla and her boyfriend Deacon," Dad said proudly, tightening his grip around Tonya's waist. A small flash went off in the back left corner of the room, and he continued to display his pearly whites. "Tonya and I are getting married this summer, and I wanted everyone to finally meet in person."

I wasn't sure how many times a person could shock me in a sentence, but so far, the total was three. The first shock was Aaron Brooks officially declaring Deacon as my boyfriend and acknowledging that I was his daughter. The second shock was my horrible assumption of making Tonya out to be this wispy-haired woman who sat behind a desk in comfortable walking shoes. The third and final shock was that my dad was getting married to his assistant and that she came with a daughter who could model for Vanity Fair.

This was the Tonya who emailed me about reservations and travel arrangements? There was no fucking way this was happening.

"It's very nice to meet you both," Deacon answered since I was once again rendered speechless. He stood up and extended his hand to both of them.

Tonya eyed me suspiciously as she lowered herself into the seat across from me. Lily practically drooled at the sight of Deacon and took the chair at the head of the table.

"It's so nice to meet both of you!" I exclaimed breathlessly and cleared my throat. I extended my hand toward Tonya and added, "All of the times we spoke through email, I never imagined you were . . . *with* my dad."

Tonya pursed her lips in a way that pinched her cheeks.

"It took them a year to tell me they were finally dating." Lily rolled her eyes, laughing into her water. "Anyone who saw them together could see they were completely crazy about each other."

"How often did you see them together?" I prompted, reuniting with my wine. I sensed Dad's nervous shift but refused to give him my attention.

"We try to go away once a month for at least a weekend, but my schedule at Yale is so crazy," Lily said innocently. It was a genuine answer, and I saw the wheels spinning in her head. She had known about me, but she was under the impression that I also knew about her. "I was always so bummed when you couldn't come with us, but Aaron said you're pretty busy too with school?"

I wanted to disappear under the floorboards and take the elevator back down to the street. I desperately wanted to fast-forward the next hour of my life and spare Deacon the front-row seat to a reality show he didn't sign up for.

"Yeah, super busy," I offered, ignoring the stinging behind my eyes. Once dinner was over, I'd allow myself two minutes to react like I usually did after seeing my dad. Until then, the waterworks would have to subside.

Deacon's arm returned to the back of my chair. "Lyla's schedule is pretty hard. I don't know how she does it all."

"Does *what*, exactly?" Tonya asked, sending shivers down my spine.

Deacon's eyebrows pulled slightly, and he cocked his head.

"What are you studying?" Lily asked before Deacon could say something. It was probably best since he was shooting daggers across the table at the happy couple.

"Business with an English minor," I answered sweetly. Every time I said those words out loud, I plunged a knife into my dad's perfect painting.

Lily's eyes lit up at my response, but before she could ask her next question, we were interrupted again by the Wicked Witch of the West end of the table.

"How is the room at your hotel? I wanted to book the penthouse suite for you guys, but the last time I did that, Lyla decided to throw a frat party and sleep with the pool boy."

I choked back my wine and placed my glass on the table to prevent it from spilling.

My dad laughed at his fiancée's comment and raised his glass of whiskey. "Deacon seems to have a good head on his shoulders. This is probably the one trip you could've done that, sweetie, and we would've gotten our deposit back."

Tonya joined him in laughing, and the two toasted to something no one else at the table understood. I was positive it was something fucking annoying, just like this horrendous dinner that hadn't even started. "And what are you studying, Deacon? You *are* in college, right?"

"Medical," Deacon said politely. "I'm studying to be a pediatric surgeon."

"Money, then." Tonya shrugged disapprovingly, locking eyes with me across the table. "That isn't shocking at all."

"Lyla is no Lily," Dad explained. It sounded like an apology for the daughter he never wanted. "Numbers and logic were never really her strong suits."

Deacon's grip on my chair tightened, and he was seconds away from lunging across the table. I placed my hand on his knee and did the one thing I knew would put his attention on something else. I trailed my fingers up his thigh until I was dangerously close to his—

His hand stopped my attempt, and his eyes met mine. His shoulders relaxed, and the pressure on my chair shifted under the weight of his arm.

"I'm going to the restroom," Lily announced. I was glad to see I wasn't the only one trying to escape this conversation. "Lyla, do you want to come with me?"

"S-sure," I stammered, removing my napkin from my lap. As soon as I placed it on the table, Tonya stood across from me.

"I'll join you, girls." She smiled condescendingly as I caught the last second of Lily's eye roll.

Deacon squeezed my hand one last time, and before I left him to face Aaron Brooks alone, I gave him a small kiss on his temple. At this point, I didn't care if Lily planned on dragging me through a hallway of flames on the way to the restroom. She got me a few moments away from my dad.

Chapter Fifty-Three

Deacon

Growing up, I always knew my parents were proud of me. They may not have always liked my choices, but they never made me feel like they loved me any less because of them. My parents always jumped at the opportunity to talk about their sons, and they lit up whenever they relived our accomplishments or shared our dreams.

As I sat across from a man who had an amazing and accomplished daughter, I couldn't understand why he was such a jackass. His smug grin and extended whiskey glass over the table made me want to take a swing at him.

He was everything Lyla said he would be—predictable and disappointing.

When I didn't clink my glass against his, he raised his hand to the right. A photographer ducked into the corner table and continued with his meal.

"Another photo op, huh?" I said, sounding much angrier than I intended to.

"I'm not sure what you're implying," Aaron stated. "My brand manager hires content creators to capture moments of my life I want recorded."

"Like introducing your daughter to the fiancée you've had for over a year? Those kinds of moments?" I raised my glass to my mouth, watching his lips curl into a disapproving smirk. "Or comparing her to a girl she just met a few minutes ago, only to learn that your soon-to-be stepdaughter has spent more time with you than she has?"

"Lyla isn't someone I can just introduce to people. She's difficult and can be a lot. You *have* to know this by now. She's never been someone I can have by my side for long periods of time before she draws the attention of a negative storyline."

"Lyla is a lot of things—"

"See?" He clapped his hands, resting them on his lap. "She's impulsive, unorganized, and completely lacks the common sense that's needed to do anything productive with her life—"

"With all due respect, sir," I interrupted, placing my glass on the table. His mouth went slack, and it was clear that people didn't usually speak to him in my choice of tone. Now that I had his attention, I took a deep breath to steady myself. "You're not going to talk about my girlfriend like that."

His face relaxed as he took the floor again. "Lyla was my daughter before she became your girlfriend."

I leaned on my elbows and tightly clasped my hands. "You think you get to call yourself a father because you set some money aside?"

His lips formed a hard line, and his green eyes met mine in a cold gaze. There was nothing paternal about this man. Driven by money and power, he would never put anyone else before himself, no matter how hard they tried to impress them.

"If you continue to disrespect her, I will take Lyla home tomorrow," I threatened calmly. "You don't get to drag her to any location you want when you decide to pop up every few months. Any promos or other bullshit you plan to use her for while she's here stops now."

"I don't know what Lyla has told you, Deacon," he said cooly, "but when she gets bored of you in a few months, remember this moment."

"And you remember this," I mimicked his tone. "As long as I'm with Lyla, you're no longer going to treat her as someone who is disposable to you. You have a brilliant and beautiful daughter with a passion for a dream that she just wants your help to build. Do you know how many parents would do anything to give their kids the opportunity you're holding against her? And why? Because she doesn't fit the mold you've tried to push her into?"

He didn't respond, but I knew he was listening.

"Time is a precious thing, Mr. Brooks. We don't always have as much as we think we do with the people we love. I don't doubt that you love your daughter, but you have a shitty way of showing it. She'd do anything to get some kind of approval from you, and as long as I'm in her life, she isn't going to do it anymore."

Lyla and Lily returned to the table, laughing at something right before they sat down. They continued the conversation as Tonya took her seat, rubbing Aaron's forearm and trying to steal his attention away from me.

Aaron and I exchanged no other words for the remainder of dinner. Still, the heat simmered in my gut when Tonya asked Lyla about her plans for Chicago, and Aaron commented about visiting for Christmas. Lily asked Lyla more about how she and I met, and when Lyla brought up the Stripper Pole Video, I stole glances at Aaron to gauge his response. He sipped his whiskey as the girls chatted, and when a photographer came around the table again, we all threw on a smile to wrap up the night.

"You're going to have to let me know when you're moving after graduation," Lily exclaimed on our walk out of the elevator. "I'm taking summer classes, but I should have a little bit of a break so we can plan a time to get together!"

Tonya hid her disapproving smirk behind Aaron as the engaged couple watched their daughters hug goodbye. They lingered by the concierge desk to check on the cars while we stood near the entrance.

Lily extended her hand, and I shook it gently. "It was nice to meet you, Lily."

"I'll be seeing you again soon, I hope? I never got to ask if you were moving to Chicago, too."

I felt Aaron's stare from across the lobby.

"We're still figuring out the details," I said, kissing Lyla's temple. "We want to make sure she's got everything in order before she makes room for me."

Lyla rolled her eyes. "He's just being modest. He has to decide which school he wants to go to since he has so many options to choose from."

"Impressive." Lily crossed her arms. "I'm glad we got to meet in person, Lyla. Our parents can be, well, you know."

"I know." Lyla leaned into my chest. "I'm glad we met before my dad mentioned you. He has a way of ruining things before they can even start."

Lyla and Lily shared one final round of laughter before Aaron and Tonya approached us.

"Lyla," Tonya said with a soft smile. "Always a pleasure."

"It's nice to finally put a face to the name," Lyla offered.

"When is your flight home?" Aaron asked once it was just the three of us.

Lyla nervously tucked a curl behind her ear. "Thursday. Tonya booked a short trip."

"She knows you're pretty busy."

"She made that part pretty clear," I said before he could drag this out any longer. "It was nice to see you again, Mr. Brooks."

I held out my hand, and we parted ways after a firm handshake. I stepped outside so Lyla could have one last moment with her dad before their next quarterly meeting. We both knew his chances of visiting in December were slim, but since it was only March, he had plenty of time to find another reason to meet up.

I leaned against our taxi and watched Lyla exchange a stiff hug with her dad. When she made a beeline toward me, I opened the door for her and allowed her to slide in first. She stared out the window, and I knew she was trying to hide from whatever was happening in her head.

I reached for her hand, lacing my fingers with hers. "Hey."

She looked over as a single tear rolled down her cheek. I reached to brush it away with my thumb, and she grabbed my wrist. "Don't," she warned. "I'm okay. I just need two minutes."

My heart sank as she rested her head against the seat and closed her eyes. "Two minutes?" I repeated.

"Two minutes is the usual time I give myself to recover. My dad doesn't deserve anything more than that."

Her dad didn't deserve any of her time, but I kept that comment to myself. I scooted closer so she could rest her head against my shoulder.

A few months ago, I remembered thinking that I would knock the lights out of anyone who hurt this girl. As I witnessed Lyla's reaction to a person who was supposed to love her unconditionally, I realized I didn't want to just bring pain to the person who hurt her—I wanted to be the one to protect her from it all in the first place.

Chapter Fifty-Four

Lyla

I never thought a hotel room could feel like home until I was forced out of it for three hours. It was the only place that secluded us from the rest of Miami and the one place I knew my dad would never show up to.

After two minutes of my emotional breaking point, Deacon and I filled the silence with effortless conversation like usual. He took every chance he could to have his hands on me, and I pretended like my skin wasn't on fire. He'd sometimes take too long to answer one of my questions, and his tongue would graze the center of his top lip. I'd pretend like I didn't notice and continue going down the list of things in my head that I wanted to do to him in the backseat.

It was a torturous game I invented called, We Said We'd Only Fuck Deacon Scott One Time. It was a lonely one-player mission, and I always failed the first level.

I *wanted* Deacon to touch me again. I needed more than the little touches he gave me throughout the day. I craved them as soon as I woke up and right before I fell asleep. I wanted him to touch me in a way that made me his, and I wanted him without limitations. Deacon seemed like a stamina kind of man, and I desperately wanted to know how long that engine ran for.

Deacon closed the door behind us and tossed his jacket on the couch. I went straight for the minibar and cracked open the fridge. My new Mother Dearest would find a new appreciation for a bar bill instead of a security deposit. I was half-tempted to toss one of the lounge chairs at the window just to kiss that chapter of my life goodbye. I could leave her with one final send-off before I left for Chicago.

I scanned the drink selection, pulling out all eight bottles of wine. I held one over my shoulder and waved it at Deacon. "Nightcap?"

He rolled up his shirt sleeves and let out a tired breath. "Yeah."

Fuck me, and fuck that shirt.

I took off my shoes and padded across the room. We both unscrewed the tiny caps, and I held up my drink. "Cheers?"

We tapped them together, taking a long sip. I was mildly impressed when Deacon downed his in one gulp. I decided to take the rest of the bottle to the bathroom, eager to wash my face and clean my headspace of this evening.

Deacon appeared in the doorway, watching me take out my earrings as I placed them on the counter. My earlobes throbbed after holding my studs for a few hours. I never wore earrings, and they loved to remind me how much we hated them.

"Can I kiss you?" Deacon asked in a low and husky voice, sending a ripple effect of sparks throughout my chest.

I wanted to make sure I heard him correctly. "What?"

"Can I kiss you?"

Deacon walked toward me, looking completely edible—cleaned up in a dress shirt that hugged his chest and accentuated his broad shoulders. The scent of his cologne made my mouth go dry.

I eyed him playfully as he closed the space between us. "There isn't anyone around."

"I know that," he said in a cute yet cocky way, his lip curving into the sexy smirk I loved.

Heat pooled between my legs, and the need grew incredibly hard to ignore. My response was barely above a whisper. "Yeah."

Deacon cupped the back of my head and met me with a soft kiss. His tongue grazed my bottom lip, and I wrapped my arms around his neck, pulling him closer. I drew his tongue into my mouth, and a soft moan resonated in the back of his throat. He tried to keep our pace slow, but I fought against it. I tugged his bottom lip with my teeth and trailed kisses down his jaw.

"Fuck it," he murmured.

His hands slid under my dress, hoisting me onto the counter. I pressed my hips into his erection and began to move. He spread my thighs, trailing his hand until he was teasing my panty line and rubbing his thumb over my clit. My breath hitched as the hands I had wanted on me since Christmas reignited the fire under my skin.

I threw my head back as Deacon slid a finger inside me. Soft circles continued with his thumb while his mouth traveled up my neck, rounding the corner of my jaw and nipping my earlobe.

I let out a shaky breath and stared into his brown eyes. They were eager, yet they still carried the familiar warmth that made me feel completely at ease.

His lips barely brushed mine as he slid another finger past my panties. "Do you want me to stop?"

My body ached for more of him. He sucked softly on my bottom lip before leaning away. When a frustrated whine fumbled out of me, he chuckled, keeping himself within reach but not budging when I pulled at his shoulders.

"No," I pleaded.

As soon as the word left my mouth, he kissed me again. He cupped my face with his free hand as his fingers curled inside me. I inhaled sharply, staring at him as the pressure began to build. He knew exactly what he was doing, and he was driving me insane.

"I know this isn't real," he murmured. "But I've been trying all night to ignore how incredible your ass looks in this dress, and your smile . . . your smile gets me every time."

"We'd just be using each other, Deacon," I said through a staggered breath. I wasn't sure who I was trying to convince—Deacon or myself.

He removed his hand, leaving my body begging for a release. "Then use me, Lyla. Use me for as long as you want to. Let me show you how beautiful you are. Let me make you feel good. Let me show you how all of those guys on your calendar should've been fucking you."

I completely plummeted into new territory. As soon as the words *fucking you* left his sexy smile, I was a goner.

I ran my hands through his hair, bringing his forehead to mine. "Do you have to plan to talk this way, or is this a hidden side of you?"

"I've never had to worry about planning when it comes to sex." He blew out an aggravated sigh and closed his eyes. "I'll be right back."

He kissed my temple and ran out into the living room.

I slid off the counter and followed him. "Wait, where are you going?"

"I have to run down to the lobby."

I watched him step into his dress shoes. "What for?"

"Condoms."

"You didn't bring any condoms?" I exclaimed.

"Did *you* bring any condoms?" he teased. "You told me this wouldn't happen again."

It sounded like a challenge, and I was willing to bet I could make him cave first. The longer we stared at each other, the more the tension built between us.

"Don't look at me like that," he warned, averting his gaze to the floor.

I took a few steps forward, giving an innocent shrug. "Like what?"

His tongue grazed the center of his top lip as he watched me move closer to him. "Like I don't need to go and get something."

"I've never had sex without one."

Deacon's eyebrows drew to the middle of his forehead.

"Okay, you can wipe *that* confused look off your face," I demanded playfully.

"I didn't mean to look that way!" He laughed. "I was trying to remember if I've ever seen you take the pill."

"I get the shot. A lot less to remember."

"I'm hanging by a thread here, Lyla," he said with a pained expression. He ran his hands through his hair before they fell back to his sides.

I backed away from him until my legs hit the mattress. "Then just come here."

Deacon stepped out of his shoes and began unbuttoning his shirt. I pressed my lips together to make sure I wasn't drooling by the time he was in front of me. My heart was racing, and my pulse was going wild behind my ears. I ran my hands down his chiseled chest as he leaned me back on the bed. He hovered over me as I traced the V-line of his hips, gently teasing the waistband of his boxers.

"The only person I didn't use one with was Cassie," he said. "I had a physical two weeks before I came back to school."

I swallowed. "We don't lie, remember?"

"We don't lie."

His mouth crashed into mine, his tongue pushing past my lips as he shifted us back on the bed. His hands couldn't decide where to rest, and neither could mine. He slid them up and down my thighs and over my stomach, igniting bursts of heat where his fingers met my skin. I cupped his ass through his dress pants to pull him against me, grinding my hips into the erection I so desperately wanted more of.

He kissed across my chest and slid the straps of my dress over my shoulders. "Tell me what you want."

"You," I panted. "I want you."

He lifted slightly to look down at me. "You have me. I'm right here. Now tell me what you want me *to do*. I know you have ideas."

The wicked grin on his face made it hard to concentrate, and it grew when he lifted my hips to pull up my dress.

"I know you like to be teased at first," he prompted, slowly sliding my panties down my thighs. He pushed two fingers inside me and massaged the muscle that was on the brink of exploding. "You like some chase."

My mouth dropped as the pressure picked up right where he had left off in the bathroom. A small moan slipped from my lips, and he slowed his pace.

"What do you want, baby girl?"

"Use your mouth," I panted.

"Where?" He kissed my inner thighs, his warm breath sending goosebumps up and down my legs. "Here?"

Even with my eyes closed, I knew he was smiling. I sat up on my elbows and stared down at him. I was tired of waiting. "Get on your knees, Deacon."

His cocky smirk resurfaced as he stripped off his shirt. "Atta girl."

Chapter Fifty-Five

Deacon

I DROPPED TO MY knees and pulled Lyla to the edge of the bed by her thighs. I loved how ready she was, and I had barely touched her. If I had this much of an effect on her with a few kisses and strokes of my thumb, I couldn't wait to be inside her again. My cock ached against my thigh, but he'd have to wait. Lyla told me what she wanted, and I'd stay on my knees all goddamn night if that meant I got to taste her.

I brushed my lips softly up the delicate skin of her thighs, chuckling when I felt her hips grinding impatiently into the mattress. I teased her with gentle kisses, taking my time as I made my way between her legs. When she wouldn't stop moving, I steadied her hips with my hands.

"You didn't let me do this last time," I murmured, running my hands up her thighs and draping her legs over my shoulders. "You wanted me on my knees, Brooks. So watch me."

Her gorgeous mouth curved into a wicked smile. When she grabbed her bottom lip with her teeth, I smothered a groan. My head was between this beautiful woman's legs, and there was nowhere else on this fucking planet I wanted to be.

Keeping eye contact, I circled her clit with my tongue. I cupped her ass with my hands, pulling her closer, delivering soft, slow strokes while she threw her head back. I felt her eyes on me again, and I moaned, sending warm vibrations against her most sensitive spot. I loved how she watched me, her jaw slack and pleading eyes begging me to go faster. She whimpered as I moved two fingers inside her in a slow glide. I wanted this image branded right next to how glorious she looked coming on my cock.

The rise and fall of her stomach quickened as her hands tugged on my hair, her pussy grinding against my mouth until I finally caved. I sucked hard on her clit, licking in quick, deliberate strokes I knew would push her over the edge. Her breathing told me she was close, and when her nails dug into my scalp, I tightened my grip on her thighs.

"Keep doing that," she whimpered through another groan.

Lyla's legs began to shake, and I worked her with my tongue until she cried out. Last time, we were mindful of the noise. I hoped every room on this floor heard what she sounded like after she fucked my mouth.

I released my grip on her legs so she could ride out her orgasm, keeping my tongue steady as I slid out of my pants. Her body stilled, and when I wrapped my lips around her and sucked again, she pushed her palm against my forehead.

Lyla's green eyes met mine; she didn't need to tell me what she wanted. I climbed onto the bed and crawled over top of her. My hand traveled up her stomach, my thumb grazing the soft skin under her breasts. She shuddered at my touch and kissed me harder.

"Let's take this off, baby," I whispered. I leaned back, pulling her with me as I sat against the headboard. She straddled me, raising her arms so I could pull her dress over her head.

A breathless sound left my mouth as I stared at the woman on top of me. I had pictured her like this for months, but none of my daydreams did this justice. She was beautiful and sexy, and when she leaned down to kiss me, I thought my heart was going to pound out of my chest.

She grabbed my cock and teased it against her entrance. "This is one way I pictured it." She tightened her grip, and I moaned into her mouth. "I want you, Deac."

I forced my other head to take a moment. She was so wet, and the temptation to push inside her was killing me. "You're sure this is okay?"

Her gaze never left mine as Lyla lifted her hips and sank herself onto me.

A low growling noise escaped the back of my throat. "*Fuck.*"

Lyla kissed up my neck, adjusting herself so she could take me in all the way. She was slick and tight, and the tiny moans she was breathing into my mouth were driving me crazy. I cupped the back of her head and used my other hand to guide her hip. She didn't need the help, but if she kept this pace, I was going to come. Just when I thought there was no way she could feel any better than the first time we slept together, she tightened around me with nothing between us.

I released a long, ragged breath. "You better slow the fuck down, Lyla."

Her mouth curved into a naughty grin as she ground her hips against me. "What? You told me to tell you what I want."

"And what is that?"

She stopped moving and dragged her hands down my chest. "I want to ride you, Deacon Scott. And I want you to tease me while I take my time doing it."

She pulled my hand to her clit and wrapped her arms around my neck. She pressed her body against me, slowly moving up and down on my cock. With every thrust, I felt the pressure building at the base of my spine. I nipped her shoulder, kissing across her chest and pulling her nipple into my mouth. I sucked softly, making her arch harder into my chest while her hands raked down my neck. Her ass fit perfectly in my hands as I quickened her pace, bringing her body up and down against me in a way that made us both gasp for air.

Sex wasn't supposed to feel this incredible. This was the shit people got addicted to. Her eyes locked on mine, and when she inhaled sharply, I knew she was coming. Right before she threw her head back, I drew her to me and kissed her. Her walls pulsed against my cock, sending shudders down my back and butterflies into my stomach. A low groan settled in the base of my throat as I poured into her.

After we both recovered, the eager movements of our mouths turned to soft kisses. Lyla traced up and down my jawline with her fingers, and I opened my eyes. I could've fallen asleep against the headboard with her touching me, but then I would've missed the way she looked at me. It was a gentle expression full of longing and comfort and everything neither of us wanted to say because words would ruin the moment.

I leaned my face into her hand, and she rested her lips against my forehead.

"Come shower with me," she whispered.

I chuckled, bending down to kiss her shoulder. "Are you sure? You might have to watch out for me in there."

Lyla slid off the bed, looking over her shoulder as she walked to the bathroom. I tried not to stare like an idiot as the incredible view of her backside grew further away from me, but I couldn't help it.

She shrugged like my protest to join her didn't bother her in the slightest. "I mean, I planned on it. You should see the other ways I pictured you fu—"

I closed the space between us and cupped her face, kissing her until I had her pressed against the wall of the shower and the hot water cascading over us.

They say when a loved one comes to us in a dream, we're seeking something we can't figure out. It might be a thirty-second guest appearance or a glimmer of them in the background, but when we opened our eyes, we remembered they were there.

Just as my brothers and I all clinked our bottles of Corona, I woke up. Images of last night played through my head as I scanned the quiet hotel room.

I slept with Lyla last night—*twice*. And it was fucking incredible.

My heart melted when I saw her snuggled into my side. She draped her arm across my chest, and tiny breaths trickled across my stomach. I nuzzled my face in her hair and kissed her forehead. She smelled like the warm vanilla body wash I coated her with last night, and when I remembered how nervous she was to shower with me, it brought a sleepy smile to my face.

Lyla talked a big game, but she was on her guard whenever she was out of her element. Inviting me into the shower was one thing, but once she got me there, I had to show her she was safe with me, that I was still the same Deacon who took care of her back on the bed.

I didn't need words to read Lyla, and I knew whatever was buzzing around in her pretty head was driving her insane. She swore off getting involved with men, and even though I knew she cared about me, the last thing I wanted to do was scare her with questions. She required statements without the bullshit, and right now, I wasn't ready to hear her tell me that last night could never happen again.

When all of this was over, and Aaron Brooks approved her trust, the process of Lyla moving to Chicago would begin. Her plans wouldn't include me, and I'd have to pretend it didn't hurt like hell. There was no way I could even consider getting back together with Cassie after being with Lyla—not after I saw my future written in a bookstore.

My mind began to spiral with the possibilities. Northwestern Memorial Hospital was in Chicago, and they had a great medical program that would provide me with the opportunities I needed to be successful. For the first time since I entered college, I didn't care where my plans took me as long as I had Lyla in my life. I spent the last six months falling for the girl who brought me back to a version of myself that I recognized, and the thought of losing her left me with an empty pit in my stomach.

Lyla tightened her grip on my side, and when I looked down, her green eyes stared back at me. She smiled, pulling the blankets further up her body. "Good morning."

"Good morning," I murmured. "How did you sleep?"

Lyla shifted so she was on top of me. I tucked her hair behind her ears and grazed her cheeks with my thumb. She was beautiful on an average day, but she was pretty damn spectacular when she was on top of me in my shirt.

"Good." She rested her chin over my heart. "Nervous?"

"About what?"

"No." She giggled. "Are *you* nervous? Your heart is beating really fast."

I shook my head, but she wasn't convinced. "It's just wild, that's all," I admitted, resting my hands above my head. Lyla needed honesty, and I was prepared to give it to her. "I've been touching you for weeks. *Kissing* you for weeks. But last night was—"

Her lips curved into a cocky grin.

"You know what? *Never mind,*" I teased, moving her to the other side of the bed. Her fingers trailed off my arm as I got up and walked to my suitcase.

"We don't lie, Deacon. Tell me."

"It felt like I was touching you for the first time," I confessed, throwing my arms out to my sides. "There. I said it. Write me off."

"I won't write you off," she said with a reassuring smile. She rolled out of bed to grab her purse from the couch, my shirt resting right on the curve of her ass. "I get it, I do."

I instinctively licked my lips. "How?"

"I've had my fair share of fun—" Her eyes narrowed, and she pointed at me with her chapstick. "Now don't go and take this next line to your pro-relationship friends and dissect it or some shit, but with you, it's different. I crave something about you, and I don't know what it is yet."

My stomach flipped. "Can I be honest?"

"Always."

"I kind of wondered if it would feel different for you. Believe it or not, Lyla Brooks, you care about me."

She crossed her arms, daring me to continue.

I slid my hands under her shirt, grazing the soft lines of her hips. "Now, don't go dissecting that shit either, but emotions can add a whole new layer to *fun*—even if it's just two best *friends* who care about each other."

She scrunched her nose. "Why did that all sound like a textbook excerpt?"

"Shut up." I laughed, cupping the back of her head to kiss her.

She smiled against my lips. "Professor Scott, I am so impressed."

I needed to get us out of this hotel room. I could spend the next thirty-six hours showing Lyla how different it could be with me. I'd never leave her guessing. I'd never make her feel scared or embarrassed to be exactly who she was—the girl I was falling in love with.

I gripped the backs of her thighs and pulled her into my arms. "I'm going to need you to stop talking. There are a few more things I want to do with you before I take you out today."

Chapter Fifty-Six

Lyla

My only instruction for Deacon's agenda was to wear the red dress I packed as a backup dinner outfit. When I asked him why, he answered with a simple, "It's cute, and I love that color on you."

We arrived at a small Italian restaurant around five o'clock. The host walked us out to the patio and seated us at a table by the water. There was a clear ocean view over the small stone wall that circled the outdoor dining area. String lights wove in and out of the giant wood pergola overhead, and massive drums of red roses scattered along the perimeter.

While Deacon focused on his menu, I admired him across the table. He was wearing a plain white V-neck that hugged his shoulders and chest. It drove me insane to know what was waiting underneath the light fabric. He was right to get us out of that hotel room. While I was a little sore, I wanted more of him. I could still feel where he had been, and I had to cross my legs to ease the ache.

A place as nice as this didn't just have open tables during spring break season, and Deacon was too much of a planner. Everything about the setting was beautiful, and I decided to wait until we were halfway through our first basket of bread before I popped the question.

"When did you make this reservation?" I prompted sweet-ly.

Deacon's brown eyes shot up from the menu. At the realization of getting caught, his mouth fell into a faint smile. "I called the restaurant on Sunday. I wanted to make sure we had something to offer your dad if he asked to join our plans."

"I suppose I'll accept that."

He clinked his wine glass to mine and walked me through the two options he debated for food. His voice blurred into the background as he stressed the importance of ordering a side of sweet potato fries, and my common sense took over.

I accepted Deacon's answer because I didn't—no—*couldn't* accept anything else. I didn't want to fall for Deacon even more than I already was. In a few weeks, he wouldn't be mine anymore, and he'd belong to Cassie—the girl we started all of this for in the first place.

Once Deacon settled on a seafood pasta, we placed our order and spent the rest of the bottle of wine talking about vacations we took as kids and summer memories we had from growing up. I sat back and listened to him talk about the beach trips he took with his family before Dominic passed. I loved how he spoke about his brother, allowing his smile to deepen into the sides of his cheeks, laughing at the moments he was thankful to relive.

"My parents always said he should've been born on a beach," he said, his grin falling slightly. He shook his head and looked out at the water.

I followed his gaze until the sound of his husky voice brought my attention back to him.

"Sometimes I wonder if I took advantage of all my time with him. I get caught up in memories where we fought, or I thought badly of him for some stupid shit that didn't matter." He chuckled and rested his elbows on the table. "He was my younger brother, you know? We weren't supposed to get along all the time."

"You were always there for him, right? If he ever needed anything, he knew he could come to you?"

Deacon nodded, running his thumb across my fingers.

"I see how you and Drew get along. I see how you both look out for each other," I offered, prompting a small smile from his relaxed expression. "Dominic couldn't have had better brothers."

"What about you, Brooks?" he asked, his voice growing louder as we shifted to a different topic. "We haven't talked about dinner."

I rolled my eyes. "Deacon, I cannot listen to one more five-star review about their sweet potato fries."

"Not this dinner, goofy. Last night with your dad."

I finished the rest of my wine, eyeing Deacon over the glass. He chuckled at my obvious reaction to the catastrophe of a dinner with my father and his newfound family.

"While the news was shocking, the delivery and scattered comments throughout the meal were not." The words I wanted to say were trying to escape the tightly wound ball I forced them into. "How are things going with Cassie?" I asked, eager to change the subject.

Deacon stopped mid-pour of refilling my wine glass, and a hollow laugh fell from his lips. "I don't want to talk about Cassie."

"Why not?"

"Because I'm here with *you*, Lyla," he stressed gently. "Right now, I just want to be here with you."

I swallowed around the lump in my throat. I was becoming a cocktail of nerves, and my stomach took an unexpected dip. What the hell was happening to me?

Deacon reached across the table and squeezed my hand, causing everything that had me on edge to slip away. "Stop getting in your head, Brooks. Stop thinking about what happens next."

I giggled. "Deacon Scott, are you telling me *not* to plan something?"

"I guess I am." He flashed me a smug grin. "Can I ask you a question?"

"Shoot."

"Have you thought more about what you mentioned to your mom? About talking to someone?"

"I have." I lowered my glass back onto the table. "I was actually going to ask you for help getting started if that's okay?"

"Of course that's okay. We'll make time for it as soon as we get back."

We'll make time for it.

The wine started to kick in, and I followed Deacon's warning and shut my mind off for the next hour. Dinner was delicious, and after we topped off with a cannoli and an espresso martini, we decided to walk back to the hotel.

"Are you cold?" Deacon slipped his hand into mine, pulling me away from the curb.

He shifted so he was closest to the street and smoothly switched my hand to his left. It reminded me of an old black and white movie when the guy offered the girl his coat, saving her from a car about to drive through a nearby puddle. Deacon's white shirt would get soaked, giving me a reason to strip it off when we got back to the hotel.

"No," I lied, smiling shyly at the gesture.

He tugged gently on my arm. "Let's cut through here."

Deacon pulled me into an ally that connected the two main roads. It was wide enough for one car to drive down, and lights hung above us between the buildings. We rounded the corner, and the sound of a violin made me slow my pace.

A woman with beautiful braids stood outside a small boutique, and soon, a man playing the saxophone joined her. As they played, I couldn't look away. The way the instruments blended was mesmerizing. Other people around us noticed, and soon, a small audience gathered around the duet.

"I haven't heard this song since Dominic's service," Deacon murmured. His eyes locked on the performance, and when the corner of his mouth lifted slightly, I knew he was thinking of a memory.

As the chorus picked up, I recognized the tune. Lee Ann Womack's "I Hope You Dance" poured gracefully down the street. An older couple sitting outside at a nearby bakery got up, making their way to the middle of the pavement. When the man held out his hand, the woman blushed before she took it.

Deacon took a step forward, pulling me with him. "Dance with me."

I glanced nervously at the people around us. The crowd had doubled in size, and as I pondered my decision, a few more couples took to the concrete dance floor.

"Do you trust me?" he asked softly.

"Yeah, but—" I ignored how quickly I answered him. "Did you *plan* this?"

"No, I did not plan this," he answered with a soft laugh. "Come here."

I let him pull me toward the other dancing couples, and he spun me to face him.

"This is very rom-com of you," I teased, resting my other hand on his shoulder. "It's up there with your meet-cute obsession."

"I love our meet-cute"—he smiled, sliding his hand around my waist—"and nothing was planned about that."

The music continued, and we swayed along as the lyrics played in my head. For the next few minutes, I allowed myself to forget it was fake. I let myself pretend that Deacon Scott was someone I was worthy of keeping.

When the song ended, Deacon cupped my chin and kissed me. It was soft and slow, like we had nowhere else in the world to be. Right in the middle of the street, surrounded by people we'd never see again, everything felt real.

By the time we returned to the hotel room, I couldn't take it anymore. Between the dinner and the dancing, the wine and the martini, my body was on fire. Heat pooled between my legs, and there was only one person I wanted there. I needed Deacon again. It was like a bottle of champagne was about to go off in my body, and my nerves had no idea how to handle the pressure.

I fisted my hands in Deacon's shirt and pulled his mouth to mine. His lips moved roughly against me, hungry like we hadn't just returned from a four-course meal. His shirt was gone, and my hands started on his belt buckle.

"Doing this again, huh?" he whispered.

"Please," I begged.

He guided us backward until I felt something hard against my hip.

"That's very rom-com of you, Brooks." Deacon spun me around so I was facing the dresser. We hadn't made it ten steps into the room and were already gasping for air. "Hold onto that," he instructed.

I did as he asked, gripping the polished wood in front of me.

"That's my girl," he muttered, adjusting my hips so I could lean forward.

Anticipation flowed through me at his choice of words. Everything sounded different coming from Deacon's mouth. His lips grazed my earlobe, and I thought I was going to implode. It was intoxicating being this close to him. I would never get enough.

Deacon pulled my panties to the side and slid into me slowly, giving my body the time it needed to adjust to the angle. I groaned as I reunited with the feeling of having him inside me. He rested his chest against my back and laced his fingers with mine. I used his hands for balance as he started to speed up, only to slow down again.

"Breathe, baby," he whispered, his breath hot against my neck.

My body trembled underneath him as he trailed soft kisses from my ear to my jawline, filling me over and over again in a way that no one else had. A low groan vibrated against my back, and I was confident no sound would compare. Hearing Deacon this way sent sparks into my stomach, igniting a build-up I wasn't sure I could handle in this position. I loved how he felt behind me, heavy and needy yet warm and all-consuming. With every thrust of his hips, the pressure climbed. My chest felt tight, and air entered my lungs at an unsteady pace. I was close, and when I leaned my head against our hands and my sighs turned to whimpers, he knew it.

Deacon pulled out, and I immediately looked over my shoulder. He spun me around so I faced him and pulled my dress over my head, his eyes working their way up my body. "I wanna see you, sweetheart."

Deacon grasped the backs of my thighs and carried me to the bed, placing me gently on the mattress before he crawled over me. The change took me by surprise, but when I stared into his brown eyes, I knew I didn't want to be anywhere but here. It was like reuniting with familiar territory, and I knew exactly how Deacon liked to play.

I exhaled into his mouth as he slid himself back inside me. It was effortless, being with him. My body welcomed every thrust and every kiss. He took his time until there wasn't an inch of me left that he hadn't taken over.

He leaned his forehead against mine, forcing me to look at him. "Do you trust me?"

I nodded. I trusted Deacon with everything I had.

His lips brushed my temple while his hand settled on the base of my throat. "If you want me to stop, you tap my shoulder, understand?"

"Yes," I breathed.

Deacon rocked his hips and pressed down with his hand. My fingers trailed up the back of his neck and through his hair. He quickened his thrusts, slamming against me as I felt the pressure building in my core. I opened my mouth to cry out, but no noise came. The limited airflow made it feel like my chest was going to explode, and the throbbing between my legs grew more intense.

Deacon groaned as he trembled above me. My nails dug into his shoulder blades as I arched my back, unable to control the sensation coursing through my body. I had never experienced something so incredible. It was what people meant when they saw stars. It was being at the mercy of the person who made you feel everything all at once.

Deacon released his grip, skimming his nose down my face until his lips found mine. "Are you okay?" he asked in a husky voice. His heart hammered against my chest, and he kissed me again before I could answer.

I blinked a few times and swallowed. When I opened my mouth, a sound that resembled a laugh came with my next breath.

"Lyla Brooks." Deacon chuckled softly. "Where have you *been*, baby?"

I skimmed my thumb over his cheekbone and smiled sleepily back at him. Where had I been? The answer was simple yet painful. I had been wasting my time on calendar options.

Deacon rolled on his side, pulling me close to him. He kissed the sensitive spot behind my ear, and I closed my eyes, relaxing into his touch as I came down from what had just happened. He traced imaginary lines on my stomach, trailing over my hips and down my thighs. I nestled into my pillow, pushing away thoughts that threatened to fly into my head and ruin this feeling.

A few moments ago, Deacon had the same hands he was using to lull me to sleep pressed against the base of my throat. Yet somehow, being wrapped in Deacon Scott's arms, I never felt safer.

Chapter Fifty-Seven

Deacon

THERE WERE MANY THINGS I wanted to do with Lyla during our last day in Miami, but listening to "Closer" by the Chainsmokers on repeat wasn't one of them. I threw my arm over my face and sunk deeper into my pillow.

Instead of waking up peacefully to the sunrise, going for a run on the beach, and then grabbing Lyla for breakfast like I planned to, I opened my eyes to Lyla poking me in the chest and shoving my side.

"It's ten-thirty, Deacon. We have to be out of this room in thirty minutes!" Lyla exclaimed through a round of giggles.

"I'll do whatever you want," I murmured. "Just turn off that song."

Lyla scoffed. "Don't blame the song for *your* poor planning. You told me yesterday you were setting an alarm."

I smirked at her cute little jab and slipped my arm around her waist.

"*My* poor planning." I rolled so I was on top of her and dipped down to kiss her neck. My erection rested between her legs, and I moved my hips against hers. "I got a little side-tracked last night."

Her hand slipped under the waistband of my shorts. "How much is a late checkout fee?"

"Does it matter?" I challenged, sliding her panties to the side. "It's gotta be better than a security deposit, right? Who was it, a pool boy?"

"Shut up." Her laughter faded into a satisfied groan as I eased myself inside her. "Think you can finish in ten minutes?"

"You say the sweetest things to me, Lyla Brooks." I nipped her bottom lip and bucked my hips a little harder. "It just depends."

She wrapped her legs around my waist and pulled me deeper. "On what?"

I laced my fingers with hers and bent down to kiss her again. "On how long it takes you to come."

Lyla cried out as I slammed into her, her moans echoing off the walls around us and prompting me to go harder. She arched her back and pushed against our hands, her breathing climbing higher and higher as the pleasure began to build. I pulled away to admire how she looked pinned underneath me before I trailed kisses down her chest and stomach.

Her mouth went slack as my tongue grazed her clit, her head falling back against the pillow. "Four minutes, Deac."

"That's all I need, sweetheart." I kissed her inner thigh and returned to her pussy, paying attention to the rise and fall of her stomach and the movements of her hips. Her fingers clenched the sheets, and I knew she was close. I swept my tongue across her, moving back and forth until her nails dug into my shoulder.

"Fuck, Deacon," she whimpered, her body shaking as she rode out her orgasm against my tongue. My stomach dipped as my name left her mouth. There was no way in hell I'd ever get tired of hearing her say it when I was between her legs.

She sat up, taking me by surprise. "Your turn. Lay down."

"No, no, no," I protested through a hollow laugh. "Four minutes, remember? Three now, actually."

Her green eyes examined me playfully, looking brighter than usual as the sun peeked through the curtains. "That sounds like a challenge."

Lyla pushed against my chest, and I fell back so she could climb on top of me. She took me in her mouth, and I watched her lips glide further down my cock. I was prepared to hold out if I was inside her, but when her tongue swirled around my shaft and her hand cupped my balls, I was teetering on the verge of combustion.

"Fuck me, baby," I murmured as her eyes locked on mine.

I grazed the corner of her lip with my thumb, and she sucked harder. Just as I had teased her last night, she knew what she was doing, and the low moan that vibrated in the back of her throat threatened to put me over the edge.

I threaded my hand in her hair, guiding her up and down. I watched her take me again and again, each stroke pulling me further until I was grazing the back of her throat. She started to move faster, her mouth meeting her firm grip as she pumped me with her hand.

"I'm gonna come, Lyla," I breathed as the pleasure rippled through my body. I rested my hands above my head so she could move if she wanted to, but she stayed put, taking me deeper. I groaned when she continued to suck, stroking my release with her hand, and letting me thrust into her mouth.

"Holy shit." I exhaled slowly, trying to catch my breath. "I might have a new favorite thing you do with that mouth."

She flashed me a satisfied grin, sending me into another dimension when she licked me off her bottom lip. "And what's that?"

I sat up to cup her chin. "The gentleman in me is supposed to say your smile."

She giggled right before she kissed me. "Pack up, Scott. We're a few minutes past checkout."

Our flight touched down in Cleveland around five in the evening. Lyla and I were exhausted, and neither of us felt like making the drive back to BG. Her mom knew she was picking us up from the airport, but she couldn't control her excitement when she found out we were staying the night.

Jane pulled me in for a hug before I could even put our bags into the car, and I hugged her back like I had known her for years. She was still smiling when she pulled away. "You must be Deacon. I am so excited to meet you in person."

"Mom, please don't smother him." Lyla rolled her eyes, and I flashed Jane an apologetic grin. "Even though I'm pretty sure you're more excited to see Deacon than me."

Jane waved off Lyla's comment and pulled her in for a hug. "I missed you, Jean Bean. And I'm happy you guys are here."

When Jane slid into the driver's seat, I snatched Lyla's luggage out of her hand and insisted she get in the car while I loaded the bags. Unlike Lyla, I savored the cool Ohio breeze as it rippled against my hoodie, grateful to be back in weather that didn't make me immediately sweat through my shirt.

It was nice to get away to some sun, but the purpose of the trip would catch up to Lyla eventually. Regardless of whether she admitted it, I knew the shock of finding out her dad was getting married still hadn't settled. It was painful how we tried to numb ourselves from the people who hurt us the most, only to feel everything ten times more when they knocked down the last defense in their path. I wanted to be a wall in Lyla's life, one that wouldn't threaten to crumble if she felt she wasn't good enough.

About fifteen minutes later, we approached a bright red bungalow with white shutters. Jane's street was quiet, lined with houses that represented a similar style only in different color palettes. Lyla gave me a quick tour of the first floor and explained that the second floor was her bedroom. She shot me a playful smirk when I looked upstairs before she led me into the kitchen.

The kitchen and dining area were small, but I enjoyed the intimate space. Once Dominic passed away, I learned quickly that the size of the room didn't matter if the people you missed weren't in it. I sat comfortably next to Lyla with my hands on the table, keeping them in plain sight if Jane decided to turn around while she prepared the tacos.

What could I say? It didn't matter what my hands did in the hotel room twenty-four hours ago. When it came to leaving a good first impression, Relationship Deacon appeared front and center.

Lyla sighed, and I sensed an admission coming forward. "Mom, Aaron is engaged."

Jane scoffed over her shoulder, scanning Lyla's face to make sure she was being serious. "That asshole. He flew you all the way to Miami to tell you that!"

Lyla nodded. "But the good news is, that should be my last trip."

"Jesus," Jane muttered under her breath. She placed frothy red and yellow drinks with a pineapple garnish on the table. "I tried to tell Lyla you should meet me first, Deacon. I'm much more fun and way less of an asshole."

I chuckled at her blunt admission, and Lyla palmed her face. As embarrassed as her mom could make her sometimes, I loved seeing Lyla in this element. I could see why Lyla wanted to help her mom chase her dream, and it melted my heart to see the small, happy exchanges between them.

I sipped my drink, savoring the sweet taste as it flooded my mouth. "Holy shit. This is amazing. What is this?"

"Pineapple upside down cake *drink*." Jane smiled adoringly at Lyla. "Usually, you order them as a shot, but Lyla and I got it as a drink on one of our trips to Florida. We haven't been able to let go of them since."

"Okay, *Mom*." Lyla sucked her teeth. "Don't distract me with the drinks. I love how you casually left it there on top of the microwave."

Jane shrugged, returning to her chopping at the counter. "I don't know what you're talking about."

It felt awkward to look over at the microwave, so I took another sip of my drink while they sorted out the silent conversation happening between them.

Lyla rolled her eyes and stood up. "Let me at least take a shower first." Her hand grazed my shoulder as she leaned down to kiss me on the cheek. "If you think you're good at chess, I can't wait to see your skills at Uno."

Jane cheered, placing a saucepan on the stove and reaching behind her for the game. She took the chair across from me, bringing along a notepad and pen.

"The woman is a *fiend*," Lyla whispered, sending goose-bumps down my neck. "And you better not pull some sort of travel Monopoly out of your bag while I'm gone."

I watched Lyla leave as she ran up the stairs to her bedroom. When I turned my attention back to Jane and her decks of Uno cards, she was beaming at me. The way the corner of her mouth pinched into her cheek told me she had a comment brewing. Lyla wore the same expression when she wanted to tell me something.

I decided to start the conversation. "Thank you for having me, Jane. I'm glad Lyla decided to stay here tonight."

Jane shuffled the cards and dealt to all three chairs. "You know you're only the second guy Lyla has brought home?"

I tried not to look surprised. I knew the first guy she was referring to, and the thought of him made my blood boil. I wasn't sure if Lyla told her mom I knew about Hunter, and it wasn't my place to say anything.

"It's okay." Jane smiled reassuringly. "She told me she talked to you about her high school boyfriend. It says a lot about how she feels about you. She trusts you, and I think you're really good for her."

"She's really good for me, too," I admitted, deciding to roll with the rest of the thoughts coming into my head. "I care a lot about your daughter, and I'd never do anything to hurt her. She's my best friend."

"I appreciate that." Jane placed the deck in the middle of the table and flipped over the first card. "And the fact that you've met Aaron twice and still haven't gone running tells me you're something special."

We clinked our glasses together and laughed.

I winced. "Has he always been—"

"A dick?" Jane smirked. "Yes. I knew he was a piece of work when I met him. But"—she sighed—"he's just one of those people that sprinkles hope like it's fucking glitter. You find pieces of it when you shake out all the shit he put you through, and you believe this could be the last time. He makes you feel like there's a chance he can change."

"Do you think you'll go to Chicago?" I asked.

Jane smiled faintly. "I know she wants me to, and I might once she gets settled, but not for why she wants me there. Aaron has it shoved so far into Lyla's head that she owes everyone something. I know she wants to fit my dreams into hers, and she deserves every goddamn penny for having to deal with that man. But to answer your question, I'll go because she wants me to go, not because of what she's offering."

"I'm sorry," I said quickly. "I wasn't implying that you would go for any other reason."

She fanned the air in front of her. "Oh, sweetie, I know you weren't. Now, do I need to explain the rules of the game to you, or do I need to show you how to keep score?"

I gestured for her to hand me the pen, and she laughed as she refilled our glasses.

When Lyla came downstairs, she shook her head, smiling at the scene. She sat beside me, and I rested my arm on the back of her chair. The familiar flowery scent of her body wash drifted into the room, and I fought the urge to pull her in for a kiss.

She scooted closer to me and started picking up her cards, quickly shoving them into her chest. "Back off, Deac!"

"I'm not looking!" I exclaimed, shifting my body so I could hide my cards.

We spent the next hour and a half playing Uno with Jane before we called it a night. I was looking forward to crawling into bed and getting some sleep before we left for BG tomorrow morning. Since Lyla's mom would be at work by the time we woke up, we said our goodbyes before we headed upstairs.

The second floor of the house was cozy, with only one bedroom and a bathroom across the hall. Lyla's bedroom was much more personable than it was in Bowling Green. The space had been lived in for a few years, and it was nice to see a bright green color on the walls instead of the cream plaster that covered all of the BG rental properties.

Lyla took the spot closest to the wall and gestured for me to lay beside her. She draped her arm over my chest and snuggled into me. "Thank you for playing Uno tonight with my mom," she mumbled. "I know she was excited to meet you."

"No problem. It was nice to meet her in person." I relaxed into the mattress and let my hand drag lazily across her back, making her jump when I hit the sensitive spot on her shoulder blade.

"I'm sorry, but I'm so tired," she groaned. "I'd reward you for another on-screen performance, but I can barely keep my eyes open."

I closed my eyes and pulled her closer. "You have nothing to be sorry about. I'm tired too."

"I wasn't sure if you expected to have sex tonight. I'm sorry if you're disappointed."

I was glad the work of her blackout curtains made it dark enough to hide my confused expression. "Being here with you is more than enough. I don't need anything else."

Lyla rolled on top of me and rested her head on my chest. I wrapped my arms around her, savoring the way her body felt against mine. We were both completely clothed, but somehow, I never felt more exposed. My feelings for Lyla were beginning to show, and there was no way I was letting this girl go.

Chapter Fifty-Eight

Lyla

"I'm sorry." I laughed sarcastically into my phone and stared at my computer screen. "The next appointment you have is in *June?*"

"That's right, ma'am, yes." The healthcare worker on the other line was already annoying me with her obnoxious availability offers, but now Sylvia insulted my age by throwing in a "ma'am."

My mouth hung open as I processed my options, although it didn't seem like I had any. I guess I could book the appointment in June and just take notes on all of the shit that happened in my life? Provide a bulleted list of emotions and situations where I felt like my heart was going to hammer out of my chest.

I didn't know what to say, so I sighed and admitted defeat. "I guess I'll take the appointment in June then."

"Great! Your appointment should appear on your account in two minutes. Please make sure you complete the intake paperwork at least two weeks before your appointment." Sylvia sounded like she had just helped me solve an outstanding case, but her excitement made me feel like I had taken ten steps backward.

I was trying to move forward, to get on track to take care of things that were happening in my head that I couldn't explain. Our entire healthcare system preached about mental health, yet when I tried to make an appointment with a therapist, I had to wait three months before I could see one. I understood why some people never followed through with therapy. It took a lot of energy to make the phone call and figure out who to talk to. Then, when I finally spoke to someone, they told me my problems could hold off for two months.

It was Sunday afternoon, and classes would resume bright and early tomorrow morning. Charlie was on her way back to campus, and Michelle and Keira were doing some sort of volunteer event in downtown Bowling Green. The apartment was quiet, and it was wild to think it would no longer be home after graduation. All of the parties and pregaming would be a memory. The nights around the breakfast counter with margaritas and tacos would be a thing of the past as we all followed our paths. I spent so much time wishing for my next chapter, but I never considered that I might miss being in this one.

Just as I was getting a little too sentimental for my taste, Deacon walked through the front door. He wore a compression shirt, gray sweatpants, and a backward hat. It was a *delicious* combination, and I wanted to devour every inch of him.

"Hey, baby." He smiled, plopping down on the couch next to me. His eyes narrowed as he searched my face. "What's the matter?"

I closed my computer. "Nothing. How was the gym?"

"Good, but what's the matter? You look like Keira just asked you to clean the apartment before everyone gets back."

I must've looked pretty pathetic. "Remember how I said I wanted to look into therapy?"

"Let me shower real quick, and I can help you." He sat up, and I reached for his hand, pulling him back onto the couch before he could get away.

"I *tried*," I whined. "They weren't able to get me in until June. I just don't understand. In the movies, people get into therapy the next day—"

Deacon sucked his teeth. "Nah, that's bullshit."

I sank further into the couch, defeated by Deacon's blunt response. "Oh."

"No, baby." Deacon chuckled softly and prompted me to look at him. "That's bullshit that they couldn't get you in until June. Can you call the number again for me, please?"

I followed his instructions and handed him the phone. It was attractive watching him take charge like this. He usually saved his assertive tone for the bedroom.

"Yes, hi, my girlfriend, Lyla Brooks, called earlier today and tried to schedule a therapy appointment—" Deacon rested his arm above me on the couch. "No, she's sitting next to me, but I had a question regarding her appointment . . . yes, I'll hold." Deacon raised his eyebrows eagerly, digging his finger into my side. I smothered my laugh when he started talking again. "Yes, that's correct. Her birthday is August 7th."

There was a soft pang in my chest as my birthday left his mouth. It saddened me to think about a date when Deacon wouldn't be next to me. His birthday was a month before mine, and I wouldn't be there to celebrate his either. I wondered what he and Cassie would do to—

"Yes, I understand that," Deacon offered in a charming tone. "However, I wanted to ask what third-party companies you'd recommend or even contract through for someone who wants to get an appointment this month."

He leaned in closer and turned on the speakerphone. It was Sylvia again, only this time she sang like a canary, eager to answer Deacon's question. She listed three companies with offices around Ohio, providing virtual and in-person options to accommodate different needs. I jotted down the information in a Google Document while Deacon said goodbye to his new phone-a-friend bestie.

After he hung up with Sylvia, I stared at the three options on the screen. "How did you know to ask that?"

"Dominic," Deacon answered proudly. "After he passed away, I called my doctor and requested more information about therapy services. He explained that the general offices might take a while, and when I told him why I was calling, he gave me more information. Doctors aren't *technically* supposed to mention third-party clinics unless they're asked."

I leaned into his chest and sighed. "Do you still go to therapy?"

"Sometimes," Deacon said softly. "I reach out to her when I think I need a session. She's in Michigan, so it's nice that she has virtual appointments. I find myself needing to go around milestones or certain dates."

"That makes sense."

"I thought about scheduling one in a few weeks," he admitted. "No matter how much time goes by, the twenty-fourth of every month—" He lifted his hat and ran a hand through his hair. "It's just hard."

I couldn't imagine having monthly reminders of a date you couldn't escape. I had been with Deacon for six of those days, and I never noticed anything different. He did an amazing job masking the emotions he didn't want to explain to anyone else.

"Do you ever do anything on those days? Is there anything I can do?" I looked up, and he met me with a soft smile.

"I usually take a half hour out of that day to talk to him. It helps just having that time—just me and him. I tell him about things that happened and ask him questions."

I nodded as tears pricked the corners of my eyes. I knew if I spoke, they'd come loose.

Deacon's smile dug deeper into his cheek. "You already do it."

I cleared my throat to adjust my tone. "Do what?"

"You asked if there was anything you could do, and you already do it. You have since the moment you became my best friend."

I nodded again, faster this time because I was on the verge of a full-blown breakdown. Deacon pulled me into his chest, and I wrapped my arms around his waist.

A few silent tears melted into the fabric of Deacon's shirt, and a warmth settled into my stomach. He was like having a cup of my favorite green tea the morning after a night out or going in blind with a book and falling in love with the plot. Deacon helped me in ways I didn't even know I needed, and I hadn't realized how much until he put it into words a few moments ago.

Chapter Fifty-Nine

Deacon

St. Patrick's Day fell on a Friday this year, and with about a month and a half left of school, even the professors were antsy. The holiday weekend resulted in many classes getting canceled, and I was grateful mine was one of them.

It was quiet when I got back to Falcon's Pointe. Lyla texted me to let me know that she and Charlie were making a liquor run for our afternoon pregame. I put her keys on her nightstand and plugged in my phone. When the screen lit up, I noticed a missed call. It was from Cassie.

My mouth went dry. I would have done anything to have her name littered in my notifications a few months ago. Now, her contact photo made me feel like I was cheating on my fake girlfriend.

Fake. Fuck, what about this was still fake?

Not a real relationship, no lying, fuck around in private, and no love. There were two other rules, but I already forgot the phrasing. The only rule we hadn't broken was rule number two—no lying. But as things grew more intense between us, I started to wonder if that was true. We never *spoke* lies to one another, but I was lying to myself if I said I didn't want more.

I played it safe and sent Cassie a text instead of a phone call. I asked her why she called, and before I could put my phone down, her name lit up my screen again.

Cassie

Going out today? I wanted to see if we could meet up.

I started to respond, but my thumbs froze over the keyboard. I didn't know what to say back. I just wanted to be in the same room together without feeling like we still had closure to take care of.

Deacon

Yup. I'm not sure where we're heading yet. I'll know more when Lyla gets back to our place.

I hit send before I realized the word that slipped in there—*our* place. When I got out of the shower, I checked my phone, and my inbox was empty.

"Deac, you here?" Lyla yelled, her voice growing louder as she came down the hall. She popped her head into her room and looked me up and down, smiling when she saw my towel. "Hey."

"Don't look at me like that," I warned her playfully and stepped into some shorts. She watched me closely from the doorframe but didn't approach me until there was some material between us.

Lyla was already dressed in green attire, wearing black jeans and a top that showed her stomach. Shiny green necklaces draped her neck, and her hair rested on the collar of her black leather jacket.

"I have news," she squealed, keeping her voice down so only I could hear her. She threw her arms around my neck and leaned into my chest.

"Yeah?" I said right before she planted a soft kiss on my lips. I grabbed her hips and drew her closer to me. "What's that?"

"My dad called. He just pushed the paperwork through for my trust."

A pang vibrated through my chest, and the lump in my throat made it clear. I needed to tell Lyla how I felt, and I needed to do it now.

"That's amazing, sweetheart," I said through a massive grin. "I—"

She grabbed the back of my head and kissed me again. This one was much more eager than the first, and when I had to turn us toward the wall so I could steady myself, I knew the words weren't coming out before we left. She tugged gently on my bottom lip with her teeth and smiled.

"If you keep doing that, you're gonna have to stay in tonight," I murmured, putting some space between us. "Pick me out a shirt, Brooks."

Lyla spun around and pulled my plain black V-neck from the hanger. When I scanned her choice of color, she removed one of her necklaces and placed it around my neck.

"There," she stated proudly. "Now you've got a little bit of green and a little bit of me."

I wanted all of her, but I filed that cheesy admission away for tomorrow. Today was about celebrating and enjoying our last holiday at BG. My eager inner thoughts would have to wait until a more sober occasion.

When Michelle and Keira confirmed that Tiki Bar was open, we headed out twenty minutes later. It was an outdoor bar near the end of the strip and a crowd favorite when the weather was nice. It was a comfortable sixty-eight degrees, and in Bowling Green, Ohio, that meant the shorts and T-shirts were out to stay until October.

The bar was packed with groups of people dressed in various shades of green. I lost count of the number of shamrock headbands and shiny strings of beads I saw throughout the dance floor. Lyla's outfit choices fit right into the scene, and when giant cups of green beer were served to us from across the bar, it finally felt like a holiday.

"Cheers!" Lyla shouted over a song that featured a fiddle and a man singing about whiskey.

I grinned, tapping my plastic cup to hers. "Cheers, baby."

She scanned the bar as she took her sip and pointed to a table in the corner. "There they are."

I turned to see Nathan and Andre approaching the table with a few other guys I recognized from our pregaming sessions. Charlie lit up at the sight of Andre, and I pressed my lips together so I wouldn't smile at their interaction.

"I think I want to get another round of Fireball for everyone. Can you take these over to Charlie?" Lyla pushed two cups of green beer to the edge of the counter for me to grab.

"I can wait with you," I offered as Lyla delivered her order to the bartender. I watched her slide her card back across the counter. "You aren't going to be able to carry them all by yourself."

"Have you seen this place?" She gestured to the crowd around us. "They aren't going to have these ready right away. I'm going to go to the bathroom while you get Charlie and Andre their drinks, and when I get back, you can help me."

Before I could respond, the corners of her mouth fell, and she focused on something over my shoulder. "Come here," she said quickly through a shy smile.

Lyla cupped my chin and pulled me in for a kiss. She tasted like cinnamon whiskey, and my heart thumped loudly against my chest. If my hands weren't occupied with the green beer, I would've leaned her against the counter.

She pulled away and squeezed my shoulder. "Cassie just walked in." I narrowed my gaze, and she shrugged. "I'll be right back."

Cassie. Lyla hadn't asked for an update since Valentine's Day, and I never offered one since there was nothing to report.

I tried to dodge the cheering frenzy I received when I dropped the beer off at the table for Charlie and Andre. The guys were so drunk I was positive anyone could've shown up at the table and received the same greeting.

There was a tap on my shoulder, and when I turned around, Cassie was all smiles with shamrock stickers on her dimples. Her blue eyes had enough gloss to tell me she was well into her St. Patrick's Day celebration, and her white tank top popped against her tan skin. She must've gone to Georgia with her family over spring break.

"Hey you!" she beamed, throwing her arms around my neck and hugging me.

"Hey," I said awkwardly, taking a step back. I could feel Michelle's eyes drilling into my back. "It's loud over here. Let's move away from the speaker."

We walked to a much less crowded corner of the bar. Once we had some space, Cassie's tipsy gaze flooded with a different expression. I recognized the redness in her cheeks and how she looked at the ground.

"What's up, Cass?" I prompted softly.

Tears welled up in the corners of her eyes, and she blinked them away. "I miss you."

She reached for my hand, but I pulled it away. "Cassie—"

"Just let me finish," she pleaded. "I feel like we've both had our chance to have some fun and see what's out there. I watch you with Lyla, and I think you really like her, but there isn't a single part of you that misses what we had?"

I shook my head. "I spent all of last summer and the first month of school missing you, Cass. But then I met Lyla and—"

"Why her?" she snapped, crossing her arms in front of her chest. "I know what kind of girl she is, Deacon. She sleeps around and parties and does whatever she wants, and nothing about her makes sense for you. You never came to Georgia with my family for spring break because you said traveling gave you anxiety, but you'll go with her to *Miami*?"

It wasn't uncommon for Cassie to use things I shared with her as ammunition when I did or said something she disagreed with. I hadn't realized how often she did it until I noticed that Lyla never did.

I took a deep breath to keep my composure. "You don't know what makes sense for me," I stated. "And you don't know Lyla."

"We should at least talk about *us*, though—"

"I'm done with this, Cassie," I said calmly. "I wish you the best, I really do. I hope we can keep in touch after graduation—as friends."

She flinched as the word "friends" left my mouth. I might as well have invited her into a vat of snakes. "Do you love her?"

I pressed my lips in a firm line. There was no way I'd admit how I felt about Lyla to anyone else before I said it to her.

"Yeah, friends." She nodded and looked out into the crowd on the dance floor. "Bye, Deacon."

I watched the girl I had planned my entire life with cross the dance floor, and a weight shifted in my chest. Seeing someone you thought would be in your life forever settle as a piece of your past was an odd feeling. They became part of the foundation instead of the structure you built your life with. Their impact would be permanent, but you knew you'd never see them again unless you needed to repair the damage from which you started.

When I passed our table to help Lyla with drinks, Charlie waved me over to her. I hesitated, but when I saw Lyla bent over the counter laughing with the bartender, I knew I had some time. The way her ass poked out in those jeans reminded me of our hotel room in Miami. My chest was against her back as she bent over the—

"Did you do it?" Charlie asked, sipping her green beer.

My mind officially left the gutter. "Do what?"

"Did you get back together with Cassie? You were over there for a while."

I glanced around our table to check for any familiar faces. Charlie might as well have yelled the question to Cassie before she left the bar.

"Relaaax," Charlie sang through a naughty grin. "It's just us. Lyla told me her dad pushed the paperwork forward for her trust, so that means you got back with Cassie, right?"

I laughed at how casual and judgemental she could sound simultaneously. "Cassie told me she missed me and that she wanted to talk about us, but I told her no. I told her I was done."

The straw fell from Charlie's lips. She looked across the bar at Lyla and then back at me before flashing a sweet, closed-mouth smile. "You broke rule number one."

"You know about the rules?" I exclaimed, bumping my shoulder against hers. "I thought those were our thing."

"Oh, sweetie." Charlie patted my shoulder. "I helped verify the rules once I found out! Lyla might have written them, but every important document needs a second set of eyes."

"I think it's the first rule I've broken since I got to BG," I admitted.

"Oh my god." Charlie swooned, putting her hand over her heart. "Lyla is going to freak."

I chuckled at her reaction. "About what?"

She shook her head in disbelief. "When she discovers that she fell into a fucking rom-com."

Chapter Sixty

Lyla

If I had a dollar for every time a man spoke to me without me wanting them to, I would no longer need my trust fund to buy my bookstore in Chicago.

The man with meaty hands and a horrific bro tank featuring a giant leprechaun was still going on about something I really didn't give a shit about. All I wanted was to get the shots I ordered and return to the table to check in with Deacon. There was a reason Cassie stumbled into this bar, and I had a hunch that Deacon was the one who brought her here. But what could be unreasonable about that epiphany? Cassie was Deacon's endgame, and I was a stop on the way to his happy ending.

I hated how much it hurt to say the words on repeat in my head. I was afraid if I stopped the track, there would be a piece of me that thought this could end differently.

"Anyway, did you want to head over to The Attic?" Bro Tank prompted. "A few of my friends and I are making one last stop before we call it a night." His hand rested on my thigh, and I immediately slapped it away. The only thing worse than a man with unwanted words was a man with entitled hands.

"Well, that's disgusting," I said, brushing his attempt off with a laugh. "Don't touch me again."

My stomach churned when I still felt where his hand gripped me through my jeans. Even though the sun was beating down on my leather jacket, a chill ran through my chest. The belt began to tighten, and I felt my breath hitch in my throat.

No. No. No. All because an asshat decided to make a move? This couldn't be happening, not on the holiday weekend.

Bro Tank's eyebrows pinched together, and the same set of eyes that glazed over my bare stomach looked at me like I was wearing a trash bag. "Why you gotta say it like that?"

"Because I don't want to have to say it twice," I snapped.

He went to rest his hand on my elbow, and I shifted so it hit the counter. He stood a little taller and shook his head. "You don't have to be a bitch about it."

I stepped back, ready to take the loss of the round of shots I ordered. I'd have another comment on deck if the panic weren't setting in. Another step to the left, and I felt him—the lavender and cedarwood loosened the grip around my ribcage, and my shoulders relaxed.

Deacon stepped between me and Bro Tank. "What the fuck did you just say?"

Bro Tank held up his hand for a high five. "It's all good, man."

A condescending smile spread across Deacon's face. "It's not. I don't know what she already had to tell you, but her voice should've been enough for you to stop the first time." Deacon took another step forward. "That never seems to be enough for assholes like you. So this is me telling you again."

Bro Tank muttered something under his breath as he merged into an incoming group of people.

Deacon searched my face for the answers I wasn't giving him as the bartender returned with our shots and my card.

When she noticed my hand was shaking, the corners of her mouth fell to a concerned frown. I plastered on my best fake smile and slipped my wallet into my bag. The familiar thumping started behind my ears, and my mouth went dry. If I took this shot, I'd throw up.

Deacon put his arm around my shoulders and picked up the tray. "Let's drop these off, and we can head out, okay?"

The crowd around us was becoming more intense. As the afternoon slowly melted into the evening scene, people became rowdier after day drinking, adding new energies to the mix. Heavy bass and upbeat tempos replaced the casual country and festive Irish music. I wanted to sink into my bed and pull the blankets over my head.

Deacon placed the tray on the table, and everyone grabbed their shots.

Charlie moved so she could whisper in my ear. "Is it happening? Do you need to leave?"

"I just need a second," I said through a broken smile, "but take this for me."

I handed her my shot as everyone else took theirs. Cheers erupted from the table as one last country song came over the speakers. Who knew "Wagon Wheel" by Darius Rucker would be such a college bar hit?

When I sensed Deacon following me, I peered over my shoulder. "You don't have to leave. It's St. Patrick's Day. You should stay."

Deacon grabbed my hand and led us through the crowded bar until we were on the street. It was like every student in Bowling Green was out to celebrate.

"Sheesh," Deacon said, peering over the incoming swarms of people. He tugged on my hand, and I looked up at him, his warm gaze reminding me that we were on flat ground. "Do you wanna head home for a little bit? Get some space?"

Home. Hearing that slip so effortlessly from his lips brought butterflies to my stomach.

I nodded, and as we weaved our way to the side streets to avoid traffic, I focused on getting air in my lungs and keeping the nausea at bay. Now and then, Deacon would glance over to make sure I was okay, but he didn't force me to talk about it. This wasn't the first time he witnessed me losing my mind.

The living room was littered with White Claw cans, solo cups, and empty juice cartons. A bottle of vodka sat unbothered next to the sink, and pieces to the blender sat in a puddle of cloudy pink water. The place looked like a disgusting episode of *Kitchen Nightmares.*

Deacon cracked open the back windows before turning on the TV for background noise. I felt him watching me as I took a bottle of water from the fridge, taking slow sips as I tried to realign my senses. The last thing I wanted to do was draw attention to something that would pass in an hour.

"I'm sorry for all the walks we seem to take together," I offered casually. "I really could've walked back by myself. "

His mouth lifted into a slight smile. "I wouldn't have let you leave by yourself. You know that."

A lump formed in my throat. "I just feel bad."

He crinkled his brow and leaned his elbows on the counter. "Why?"

"Because it seems like I always need you." I looked up to meet his gaze, and his expression softened.

"You don't *need* me, Lyla. You have me, and there's a difference."

I created space between us by going into the living room. I was already struggling to keep my heart rate down, and being near the first man who made me feel like it was okay to crumble wasn't helping.

I cleared my throat. "I'm sorry. I just need a second, and then we can head back out." The knots in my stomach tightened, and suddenly, the words were leaving my mouth before I could think through them. "I know it's dramatic—"

"It's *not* dramatic," Deacon interrupted gently, crossing the room so he was in front of me. "Stop downplaying something that happened to you because you're afraid other people won't think it's heavy enough. Pushing away how you feel about something doesn't make it go away, Lyla. Until you let yourself feel it, it will follow you no matter where you go."

Everything was adding up. The shit I tried to ignore but couldn't. Trying to move past things like they weren't always coming back. Hunter. Anna. My mom and the bookstore. My dad and the trust fund. Deacon provided the perfect description—*heavy*. I was tired, and I didn't want to carry it anymore.

"It took almost a year of therapy for me to learn that after Dominic passed away," he said as his thumb grazed my chin. "Sweetheart, I'm just trying to help you. If I'm overstepping, please tell me, but I care about you too much not to try to help you."

"It's like every time I don't have control, I'm suffocating," I admitted as another staggered breath left my chest. "There was something about the way that guy touched me. It wasn't you, and I didn't like it."

A pained expression came over him, and he turned so he could rest his hands behind his head. He pressed his lips together and exhaled slowly, closing his eyes as he waited for the wave of anger crashing through him to pass.

I had seen Deacon work through emotion before. Anger, sadness, confusion—everything he tried to process whenever he talked about Dominic. Something about this was different. His warm brown eyes met my gaze before he took my face in his hands and leaned his forehead against mine.

"I didn't know that he touched you. If I would've known that—" He took a deep breath, exhaling slowly. "If anyone ever touches you like that again, you need to tell me, understand? I don't care how little something might seem to you. I want to know about it. You'll never be too much for me, Lyla."

The more he spoke, the more I felt at ease, wanting to be pressed against him—wrapped in his arms where I was safe, and the weight would be gone for a moment.

"Why do you care so much?" I said, my voice barely above a whisper. I couldn't fathom why someone who walked into my life six months ago would care as much as Deacon did.

His mouth parted slightly, and the electricity in the room was intimidating. I couldn't focus on anything but the sound of his soft breaths and the look in his eyes as they searched for a reason not to say what he was thinking. He was going to say something to me that would answer all of the questions floating around in my head. He was going to tell me how he felt, and while half of my heart begged me to listen, the other half of me was scared to hear it.

"Lyla, I—"

I shook my head. "Don't answer that."

"We don't lie, Brooks."

My knees threatened to buckle when his sexy smirk accompanied his reminder. I kissed him before he could say anything else. "We don't lie."

There might not have been words, but I didn't need them. I knew in the way his body spoke to mine and how he took his time. I knew when his hand cupped my face while his other rested on the small of my back, hugging me to his chest as he rocked his hips. It was sweet, slow, and all other forms I wasn't used to. The thought of someone else's eyes staring down at me felt foreign. I didn't want it if it wasn't Deacon who smiled right before he kissed me.

I wanted this. I wanted him.

I fell in love with Deacon Scott, and no part of me would hesitate to do it all over again.

Deacon

THE NEXT MORNING, I let my arm slowly lose blood flow as Lyla's head dug into the inside of my elbow. I was happy I woke up before her. I needed her to hear the words I was working on in my head and needed more time to finalize them.

I wasn't going to lose Lyla over a miscommunication. Yesterday, I had every intention of telling her how I felt, and in strategic Lyla fashion, she cut me off before I could say it. I knew what I wanted, and I understood that Lyla might not. It didn't matter to me that she might need some time to figure it out. She was worth it.

The sun caught my eyes through the curtains, and I peeked up at the sky. A feeling of relaxation washed over me as the warmth hit my face. I didn't need to overthink what I wanted to say. We didn't lie.

Lyla's desk clock read nine-thirty, and I knew her headache from the lack of caffeine would kick in soon. As if her internal wake-up call read my mind, she stirred against my arm and peered up at me through thick lashes. She still had some makeup on from yesterday, and tiny black specks rested under her eyes. It didn't matter if she woke up looking like Pennywise—I'd still find her beautiful.

"Good morning." I kissed her forehead, running my fingers along the sensitive spot on her shoulder blade. She laughed into my chest and tried to move away from me.

"Hold on." I sat up and pulled her into my lap. "I'm going to say something to you, and I don't want you to run from me." If I let the L-word slip into the open, Lyla would leave for Chicago tonight. "Do this with me."

She traced a lazy finger down my chest as her teeth grazed her bottom lip. I focused on the different tones of green in her eyes to ignore the erection that was resting against my leg.

"No," I said, laughing. "No more pretending like this is fake. *Be* with me. I want to be with you."

She wrapped her legs around my waist and kissed me. I moved my hands under her shirt and up her back. Eventually, this girl would have to get out of answering me with her mouth instead of words.

"Lyla," I pleaded against her lips. "Baby, I need you to say something."

She stared at me and bit the inside of her bottom lip. The corners of her mouth pinched together in an adorable grin. "I want to be with you, too."

I moved to kiss her again, and she pushed down on my chest.

"Maybe just, like, a little bit," she teased. "Boyfriend-girl-friend shi—"

I tightened my grip on her waist and flipped us so I was on top of her. My tongue slid past her lips, and her legs opened wider for me. I pulled my shirt over her head and kissed down her neck, nipping lightly at her skin. Her hand slipped under the waistband of my boxers, wrapping around my cock, prompting a low groan from the back of my throat as I rocked into her grip.

Her lips brushed my jawline. "I like you a lot, Deacon Scott."

"Mhm," I murmured, pulling her panties to the side. I could settle on the third base L-word for now. "I like you a lot, too."

I sank into her in one smooth motion, and she sighed into my collarbone. Her breaths came warm and quick against my skin, igniting a fire inside my chest. All the soft touches from last night were replaced with a hunger I didn't think was possible. The way her hips fit into my hands and how her fingers dragged down my back. Sweat began to slick between us, and I steadied my hand on the wall behind her.

She tugged on my wrist, and I let her guide me to the base of her throat.

I stared down at her with a cocky grin and slowed my strokes. "All you have to do is ask, sweetheart. Tell me what you want."

She dragged her thumb across my lip. "Choke me, and don't stop until you feel me coming."

"Atta girl." I grinned, giving her one more kiss before I slammed into her. "I know you're close. Breathe, baby."

Lyla nodded as she bit her bottom lip to keep from crying out. I admired the sight of her underneath me, staring down at a pair of green eyes that made my heart feel like it was going to burst.

"I love how beautiful you look when I'm fucking you," I murmured against her lips. "And I love that you're mine."

Her sighs turned to whimpers as she placed her hands on my shoulders, remembering what I told her the last time I pressed against her throat. Her breaths grew sharper as she arched her back, my hips meeting hers in a rhythm that almost pushed me over the edge. I knew when her legs shook around my waist, she was almost there.

"Deacon," she groaned, throwing her head back into the pillow.

I pushed against the base of her throat as her walls pulsed around my cock. I moaned into her neck, keeping my voice down as best as I could since I wasn't sure who else was in the apartment. Lyla squeezed my shoulder, and I immediately shifted my hand to her ribcage, peppering her jawline with soft kisses. It turned me on even more that she trusted me to take care of her, trusted me to learn her body so I could do things to her to make her feel like she was mine.

Her heart hammered against my hand as I lowered my mouth to graze the soft skin under her belly button. "Can I call you that?" I murmured, kissing slowly up her stomach.

She sighed, flashing me a satisfied grin. "What?"

I rested my weight on my elbows so I could look at her. "Mine." I couldn't say it without smiling. "Can I call you mine?"

Her eyes softened, and she pressed her lips into a hard line. "I kind of hoped you would," she whispered, her voice breaking toward the end.

With six soft words, my entire world shifted. I'd be Lyla's as long as she wanted me. I'd never belong to anyone else. For the first time in a long time, I was happy. And for the first time since Dominic passed away, I didn't feel guilty about it.

On the twenty-fourth of every month, I'd find time to sit and talk to Dominic. Drew and I would always check in with each other in the morning, and sometimes, we'd video chat later that afternoon. After a while, we both realized it was harder to try and act like the twenty-fourth wasn't a reminder. Numbers began to matter when you associated them with people and dates you'd never forget.

I sat outside the library, sipping my iced black coffee with caramel and vanilla, and stared at the green drink across from me. I wasn't sure why I ordered it since I wasn't going to drink it, but the choices we made after losing someone didn't always make sense. Dominic's iced matcha with blueberry and oat milk created a puddle on the table, but I'd let it sit until I was done with our conversation.

"What day is your thing again?" Drew asked.

"You mean my *graduation*?" I snapped. "It's the first Saturday in May."

"And it's just your graduation, right? Like you're not about to pop out a ring or some shit, are you?"

I rolled my eyes. "No."

Drew's annoying cackle vibrated against my ear. "That's a fair question, man."

"I told Lyla I wanted to be with her, and she told me she wanted to be with me too."

"Yes, and it was very seventh-grade of you," he murmured, and I pressed my lips together to keep from laughing. "So, is your fake relationship real now, or is that tailored for a more eighth-grade conversation?"

"Yes, asshole. Lyla hasn't had a relationship since high school, and with us both being so close to graduating—"

"Has she mentioned Chicago to you?"

I leaned my elbows on the table. The pit in my stomach opened up even wider, and I felt my anxiety creeping in. "No, she hasn't."

"You'll figure it out, Deac. Not everyone needs four layers to their plans like you do."

"I'm hanging up now," I said through a groan. "I love you, and I'll talk to you later."

Drew laughed. "Love you too, man. Later."

I sat silently for the next few minutes, embracing the first few ribbons of summer air as it weaved through campus. The trees were dressed in leaves, and the grass was turning from brown to green. It was nice to see life bounce back to Bowling Green.

I peered up at the sky and sighed. I always pictured us having these conversations in beach chairs by the lake, the sun shining with drinks in our hands. I'd sit here all day if I didn't start talking, so I started with the first thing that came to mind.

"I miss you, Dom. I'm sorry I haven't been around that much, and I don't have an excuse for it. It's just been crazy, you know? Well, I guess I don't know if you know since I have no idea what kind of news you get up there. Anytime you want to give me a hint, please feel free."

I shifted my focus to the drink in front of me.

"I keep thinking about how I'm turning twenty-four in June. Before I came back to school this year, it really hit me—just another milestone you're not here to see in person. I keep getting older, and you'll forever be sixteen. When I see you again, will you look any older? Do you age up there, or do you just get to be the good-looking younger guy while the rest of our family is wrinkled and old?"

I smiled at the thought of Dominic laughing and shaking his head. My throat tightened as tears pricked the corners of my eyes. I took advantage of the cloud coverage and peered up to the sky again.

"This is never going to get easier, is it? I thought I could try and figure it out if I just focused on making it to the next step in my life. I'm stuck between feeling bad when I'm happy because you aren't here and feeling like I should be doing everything possible because I know you'd want to see me live. It's just a shitty feeling, to be honest with you—knowing no matter what I do, I can't bring you back.

"Sometimes I think Mom and Dad try too hard." A tear escaped down my cheek, and I swiped it away. "Everyone tries too hard to act okay when we aren't. I feel like, as the oldest, I should know how to fix . . . *something*, anything to help, but I don't know how. I don't know if I'm supposed to bring you up as much as possible to them so they can talk about you or if I'm just digging a deeper wound because it reminds them you're gone. It's like when you first passed. Once I had a moment to just *be*, I'd get a text or a call from someone just to say they were thinking about me. Everything would come rushing back as if I found out five minutes ago that you were gone."

My phone vibrated on the table, and I looked at my alarm.

"I purposefully did that," I explained, chuckling. "I didn't want to ramble to you about all my issues for an hour. I have class in about ten minutes, and it's across campus." I closed my eyes and took a deep breath, momentarily allowing myself to feel it all before I said goodbye. "Fly high, Dom. And I'm sure I'll talk to you soon."

Chapter Sixty-Two

Lyla

It was officially day fourteen of being Deacon Scott's girlfriend for the *second* time this year. Graduation was only a month away, and while Deacon and I were still blissfully in the stage of labeling our new relationship, we also faced what would come after we both crossed the stage. I had Chicago, and Deacon had medical school. He was willing to shove everything aside for one girl already, and I didn't want him to see me as someone who required him to do the same.

I wasn't sure what I did in a past life that caused me to overthink every hand I was dealt. It didn't matter if things were good or bad. I was always looking for the one thing that could go wrong.

My first therapy session was Thursday, and I was starting to get nervous. I practically had "Help Me" plastered on my forehead. Childhood trauma, a memory I couldn't escape, *and* self-doubt? Add in the possible panic attacks and anxiety, and I was a case waiting to be solved. If that wasn't a golden tagline introduction to the doctor who picked me up, I wasn't sure what was.

"Stop!" I groaned loudly to the empty apartment. I had the entire place to myself, and I was tired of hearing myself dig deeper into an unnecessary hole.

Deacon went out with Nathan and Andre to celebrate something that involved beer and pool at City Tap. Charlie went home this weekend while Michelle and Keira were on a bike tour of downtown Toledo. Their activity didn't make my top ten choices of what to do with the dwindling weekends left in our college career but to each their own.

I had overworked my already tired brain long enough. It was time to channel my last bit of academic motivation to knock out my unfinished business assignment. As part of our final, we had to create a presentation to walk the class through our proposals. Since I already had a business in mind, the task was simple. I had to make a riveting slideshow about the bookstore I planned to open.

However, my laptop had other plans when it decided to perform a three-hour update as soon as I signed into my account. I rolled my eyes as the estimated time to completion went up. This thing had all day to do this shit. I even had it plugged into the charger this morning and most of this afternoon. Technology was so ungrateful.

As if he could hear my thoughts across town, Deacon's name appeared on my phone screen. I placed my computer on the coffee table and leaned against the cushion. "Hello?"

"Hey, baby," Deacon said. No matter how many times I heard him say it, *baby* hit differently when I knew it was real. "I'm probably going to be another hour or so. Andre just signed me up to play some guys who have been running the table."

"Enjoy your night out. Isn't it normal to want some time away from your girlfriend?" I pointed to my blank computer screen even though he couldn't see it. "I'm living it up right now with my homework."

"I keep waiting to want the space, Brooks. But ever since you called me downright delightful, I always want to be around you."

"Don't lie. We'd only known each other for a few hours when I called you that."

He chuckled. "We don't lie, remember?"

My smile dug into my cheeks. It was a Friday night, and I had a cheesy grin plastered on my face while staring at my laptop screen. At this rate, I could handwrite the damn presentation faster.

"What paper are you working on?" he asked.

"No paper at the moment. My computer is taking forever to update."

"Just use mine." I heard Andre's voice in the background. "I'm about to start this game, but yeah, sweetheart, just use mine."

Once we hung up, I padded down the hallway to my room and pulled Deacon's Macbook from his book bag. I hated how personal it seemed, like I was getting a peek into a hidden side of him that I didn't know about.

Annnd restart the overthinking process. From the top, please.

I couldn't wait to read my presentation notes and ignore the depressing tone shift on the second page. I'd always been guilty of allowing whatever emotions were in my head to flood my writing. After a weekend with my dad in eighth grade, I completely annihilated my Shrek vs. Donkey argument. I didn't think a charming fairytale could sound so sad until thirteen-year-old me took the podium.

A notification announced itself on the screen with a soft chime. Cassie's name appeared next to the messages icon, and a lengthy text showed underneath.

Cassie

I can't stop thinking about our conversation at Tiki. I miss you, Deac. Can we please talk at our spot? If you still don't want to try again, I promise you won't hear from me.

And there it was—the one thing that could go wrong. Fuck me, and fuck my laptop for having a long-ass update.

Conversation at Tiki? How did I get so swept up that I forgot to ask about Deacon's conversation with Cassie?

I desperately tried to escape my survival way of thinking, but my mind was racing, and my anxiety had officially kicked in. What the hell was I doing? Deacon had a plan with Cassie, and that plan was inviting itself back into his life. I couldn't offer Deacon anything more than a trail of shit I needed to work on and examples of people who were better off without me.

Even after a double dose of melatonin, I was still wide-eyed and in my thoughts when Deacon strolled in at twelve-thirty. Even though he had just spent the night with the guys, he looked like he hadn't had a drop to drink. He was a walking triple threat with a fresh haircut, a backward hat that covered it, and a shirt that hugged his chest and shoulders.

"You're still up?" Deacon placed my spare key on the counter and crossed the living room. He cupped the back of my head and kissed my forehead. His lips on my skin made my next breath an agonizing exhale.

As I stood up, I hid it through a forced yawn and a dramatic stretch. "How was your night?"

"It was fun." He smiled, retreating to the fridge for a bottle of water. "How was yours? Did you finish what you were working on?"

I stared at him from across the room and hugged my chest to keep my hands from giving me away. "Yeah," I said a little too enthusiastically. "I'm actually going to go to the library to print."

He slowly lowered his drink to the counter. "You're shaking, baby."

"I'm fine," I insisted, reaching for the keys. "I just need a second."

He grabbed my hand as I rounded the corner. His warm expression forced me to pull in another stream of staggered air. If he kept staring at me like that, there was no way I could go through with the conversation that needed to happen. It *had* to happen for us to get out before the mess began.

"Lyla, I know when you need a second, there's something you're not telling me," he prompted gently. "And the library closed a half hour ago."

I swallowed. "Are you sure this is what you want?"

My question caught him off guard. "What?"

I pulled my hand from his and gestured to the space I created between us. "This. After graduation, I'll be in Chicago trying to start my business while what? You—"

"Please don't do this right now." He shook his head, his calm exterior close to breaking. "We can figure out what that looks like, but don't make it a problem."

"I'm not *making* a problem, Deacon. I'm only stating what will cause this to be over. We haven't talked about *anything*, and I think we both know why we're avoiding it."

"Who says anything has to be over?" He grabbed my hand again. "Look at me. Where is this coming from?"

I shook my head. "You had someone you were going to build a *life* with. That kind of stuff doesn't just go away."

"But things change, Lyla, come on." He took a step back, throwing his hands in the air. "I lost one of the most important people in my life because of an accident. I had to find a way to move forward and find out who the hell I was without him. Cassie was—" His mouth went slack, and he eyed me pensively. "You saw, didn't you? Cassie's text. Is that what this is about?"

"She texted you saying she missed you. That's a *good thing*." Deacon ran his hand over his mouth. He smacked the counter next to him, and his hand recoiled into a fist. I knew he wanted to touch me, to do anything to navigate this conversation in another direction. I hated seeing him like this, and the panic began to make its familiar sweep across my body. This was the part where he lost his shit before walking out. He'd never make this decision on his own, and if I needed to be the bad guy for him to move forward, then I could do that.

"Why are you doing this?" he said with a pained expression. "What do you need from me right now? Do you need me to leave? Because if that's what you need, that's okay, but I promise I'm coming back."

The belt tightened around my chest as the tingling returned to my hands. The nausea boiled in my stomach, and my heart beat rapidly against the back of my ears. I swallowed again to keep my voice steady, but I lost the battle when tears pricked the corners of my eyes. "I don't know what I need. I think I just need a break."

He closed his eyes and exhaled slowly. He was trying hard to focus on me when he opened them again. "A break from what?"

I couldn't say it, and he knew I wouldn't say it. Silence passed between us, and the apartment grew uncomfortably quiet.

"We weren't in your plans," I said. "Cassie wants you back, and my dad signed my trust over to me—"

"I told you I wanted to be with *you*," Deacon snapped, moving so he was only a few inches from me. "I don't give a shit about *anything* else. You just wanna settle for what we said would happen back in August?"

"You planned your entire life around a girl who wants to get back together with you, Deacon," I stated unapologetically. "That's why we're here in the first place."

"No. I'm here because your dad—" He pressed his lips together in a firm line and looked away.

I watched him ponder whatever thoughts were scrambling around in his head. He was probably scrolling through every insult my dad had said in front of him, replaying every time he went back and forth on whether I was worth keeping around because of how many stumbles I caused. There were dozens of reasons Deacon could throw at me to end this conversation. We didn't have to watch each other become strangers for this ending to make sense.

I couldn't wait in silence any longer. "Just say it," I whispered.

Deacon shook his head and placed his hands on his hips. "I'll go stay with Andre for a few days," he said without looking at me. He took a deep breath, and I wondered how long part of me would feel like his even after this conversation.

"But I want you to hear me," he demanded softly as he walked toward me. "You can pick fights with me all day, and it won't matter. I can give you some space, but you'll get the same guy who followed you home that first night you stayed with me. I'm not *going* anywhere, Lyla."

But *why?* I wanted to scream it from the rooftop so I didn't have to look at him when he answered.

Deacon kissed my forehead and went down the hall, returning with a duffle bag and his book bag. I felt like I was going to be sick. I couldn't move, and I couldn't speak. For the first time in my life, I watched a man leave, and all I wanted to do was pull him back.

Chapter Sixty-Three

Deacon

One day. It had been one day, and I was going fucking insane.

Ever since I left Lyla's apartment, our last conversation played on repeat in my head. I hated how close I was to saying something I'd regret. I winced every time the cut-off sentence emerged in the flashback.

No. I'm here because your dad—

The look on her face practically finished the sentence for me. Who knew what kinds of phrases she replaced my silence with? I couldn't finish the sentence I had in my head about her dad. It would've just been hurtful shit I said out of anger and confusion. Those words would've cut right through Lyla. It would've been like spitting fire. You didn't spit fire at the people you loved, even when it felt like you were the only one burning.

"What are we looking for?" Nathan winced at the floral arrangements as if he had never been to this part of the store. It was near the entrance of Kroger, so I wasn't sure why he looked so confused.

"Roses." I rifled through the options and chose a small bouquet of six red roses. I grabbed a complimentary card and stuck it in the rubberband around the stems. "Do you need beer?"

"Of course. It's Sunday Funday. But why are you buying flowers when Lyla kicked you out last night?"

"She didn't kick me out. I left."

"So you left, yet you're the one shopping for flowers?" I could see the confusion on Nathan's face as we walked to the beer and wine section of the store. "This year has shown me why I don't fuck with girlfriends."

"I buy Lyla flowers every Monday," I said, smiling as Nathan's mouth fell open.

"Doesn't that shit add up!"

"Sometimes," I admitted. "But it isn't always a large amount. Sometimes, it's just a single stemmed rose I snag on the way home from class." We stopped in front of the Bud Light, and I placed a hand on Nathan's shoulder. "Effort doesn't have to cost a lot, my man."

Nathan rolled his eyes before grabbing a case. "Neither does beer, and I know exactly what I'm getting with that."

Back at the apartment, Andre and Greg were in the living room. Both were on their phones, but Andre jumped into action when Nathan showed off the beer purchase. Greg stayed seated, his thumbs hard at work with whatever message he was composing.

I took the seat next to him on the couch. "What's up, man?"

"Sorry to see you back," Greg murmured. "And I mean that respectfully."

I didn't know what to say. I pulled out my phone and checked my notifications, hoping to see Lyla's name. It didn't even matter what kind of notification it was. I just wanted to hear from her.

I knew I needed to travel at a different speed when it came to Lyla. The physical stuff was easy for her. If I had touched her the way I wanted to last night, we would've ended up in her bed, waking up to the same conversation this morning. Every time I made it over one of her emotional walls, she was already building more for me to climb.

Last night, Lyla gave me an out. She tested me to see if I would end things and break it off because it would be easier than working through whatever thoughts were inside her head. She fought with me because she was scared I'd leave when things got hard. When I wanted something, I worked for it. I was a fucking climber, and I'd keep at it until she got tired of carrying everything by herself.

Andre's voice boomed from the kitchen. "Beer, Deac?"

"Nah, man. I'm good." If I had a few drinks now, it would only heighten my anxiety. Being numb was fine for a while, but when it wore off, the emotions came back ten times worse.

I also didn't feel like sitting in my temporary bedroom all day. Once I gathered enough energy to get off the couch, I'd head to the gym for a workout. I needed some sort of stimulation other than the sports report on TV.

"You left a box in the closet, by the way," Greg said. "Andre said to leave it where it was and that he'd hit you up at the end of the semester to see if you still wanted it."

"What box?"

"It's a tote, actually. Red?"

Freshman to Junior Year with C. "Do you care if I get it from the room?"

Greg sunk deeper into the couch. "Go for it."

It felt weird reuniting with a space I lived in for a few months. Seeing Greg's stuff on the floor and the unfortunate way he organized his closet almost made me forget why I returned to the scene in the first place. I reached into the back of the closet, dragging the tote across the carpet. I didn't remember it being this heavy when I packed it, but I realized I hadn't opened it since I moved back to Bowling Green. My parents loaded it onto the truck, and Lyla was the one who brought it into the apartment.

I sat down next to the tote and removed the lid, chuckling softly at the collage of photos, ticket stubs, and trinkets that littered the top layer of memories. Photo albums Cassie made me during our first year of dating came next, along with a Detroit Lions blanket she bought me for Christmas and a used Lemon Sugar Cookie candle.

I unscrewed the top of the candle, and the overpowering smell of sweet lemon immediately triggered every conversation of me giving Cassie shit for such an odd scent. She always kept one lit when it was just her and I at her place, and even though I hated the way it smelled, I bought one for my room back home because it reminded me of her.

I thought back to moments when I thought everything was perfect. I was barely holding myself together, trying to convince myself that if Cassie and I could graduate, get engaged, become Falcon Flames, and have the Prout Chapel wedding, everything would fall into place. The more stepping stones I walked across, the further I could get from everything that happened on July 24th, 2014.

My hand grazed one of my favorite photos in the bin, and my heart sank. I held it so many times the corners of the picture were bending, but that didn't stop how the image made me feel whenever I saw it. Cassie stood between Drew and Dominic in our living room, her arms wrapped around their shoulders as they lifted her into the air. She kicked her foot out, and their smiles made it clear they were laughing when I took the photo. It was the only picture I had of Cassie with Dominic.

I touched Dominic's face with my thumb. Resting my arms on my knees, I stared out the window, overlooking how Greg hadn't cleaned that part of the room either.

On the floor of my old bedroom, I felt Dominic give me a sign that everything would be okay. Nothing moved, and nothing spoke, but it was always the signs I couldn't hear that seemed to be the loudest. I knew he was there—he was always there. But the tote's memories dragged me back to when my world was dark. I held onto plans and outcomes I could control because I couldn't prepare for something else to happen that would completely shift my world. I couldn't do it again—not a second time.

Through the streaks on the glass, the sun still peeked through. In the moments we couldn't see clearly in front of us, a light would always be on the other side. We just had to adjust to let it in.

Later that day, I removed a few items from the tote I wanted to keep and tossed the rest away. There was no reason to keep parts of the past, not when I knew what I wanted for my future. Tomorrow, I'd drop the flowers off at Lyla's apartment and hope, with everything I had, that she wasn't ready to give up on me.

Chapter Sixty-Four

Lyla

THE WORST DAYS ARE those you wanted to end before they even began. Mondays already sucked, but this one exceptionally sucked since I woke up tired after a third night of not sleeping. I barely made it to Literary Theory, only to discover the barista at Dunkin made my order wrong. All an emotionally spent woman wanted was an iced matcha with blueberry and oat milk, and the man behind the counter forgot the syrup. To add to my misfortune, I found out the hard way that he also used regular milk in my drink.

I entered a shitshow before noon, so when Charlie offered to order Campus Pollyeyes, I almost cried on the spot. She knew the basics about my conversation with Deacon and why he hadn't been around the past two days. Since Charlie always had an opinion about everything, her silence was a loud enough answer. I knew it was only a matter of time before she grew tired of my stoic reactions. All I did was bask in the results of my own decision by moping around my bedroom. Charlie would slip me tea and food like I was some troll living under a bridge, communicating only through eye contact.

Charlie gave me a ride home from campus, and while I was trying my best to engage with her story about running into No Style Kyle at The Union, the savory aroma of cheese and chicken breadsticks was causing my nausea to spike. The box was warm on my legs, and I fought the nerves brewing in my stomach. Ever since Deacon left on Saturday, my anxiety had been all over the place, making it hard to eat. I was a bundle of nerves, ready to snap at the next altercation, and I was staying away from the one person I knew could calm me down.

"Does he still have his New Balance shoes?" I asked as we pulled into the parking lot.

Charlie looked at me, shocked that I had any comment at all. "Yes, bitch. He still has his shoes."

I laughed, focusing on the shimmer of positivity and hoping it would be enough to push the negative thoughts aside. Once I got the ball rolling, my mindset was easier to shift.

Charlie snatched the food from my lap once the car was in park. "And he can still pull off the '90s dad look, in case you were wondering."

"I wasn't. There's a reason social media wasn't invented until after the dawn of the matching windbreaker suits. The world wasn't ready for anything in that era to go viral."

"Okay, Usher. *You* would know about going viral!" She took off up the stairs, and I followed close behind her.

"In my defense, I haven't seen anything about that—"

Charlie shifted so I could walk in front of her, her eyes begging me for an explanation. In front of the door was a small bouquet of red roses. They had a card tied around the stems, but it wasn't necessary. I already knew who they were from.

Don't think I forgot just because I'm not there.
I like you a lot,
Deacon

"Jesus, Lyla," Charlie practically growled over my shoulder. She unlocked the door and placed the food on the counter. Her tone was gentle, but it didn't lack the urgency. "He's pretty amazing, you know that? What are you *doing*?"

The ball might've started rolling, but the flowers brought it to a dramatic halt. Deacon had given me flowers every Monday since our first conversation on campus. My heart hammered in my chest, and I felt the tingling in my fingertips. It ran up my arms as my mouth went dry, the nausea settling in my stomach as I tried to figure out what to say next.

Charlie threw her hands up in the air, her voice growing louder at the time it was taking me to answer. "You haven't said *anything* other than you guys were taking a break, and he left. Why are you doing this? Is there something you're not telling me? Did he do something? Should I hate him? Put a hit out on him? Why else would you sabotage this—"

"Because I'll never be *enough* for him, Charlie!" I snapped, the pressure behind my eyes allowing a few tears to slip. I placed the flowers on the counter to steady myself. The crumbling had started, and there was no stopping it. "I've never been enough on my own. I'm either never enough or too much—there's no in-between."

My exhales turned to heaves. Becoming too lightheaded to stand, I shifted to sit with my back against the wall, slowly sliding down until I was on the floor. I brought my hands to my forehead and closed my eyes. I was spinning, and I was afraid if I opened my eyes, I would pass out.

"I'm sorry this is happening," I cried. "I always try to push this away so you don't have to deal with it—"

Charlie gently pried my hands away from my face, and when I opened my eyes, she was sitting cross-legged on the floor. I focused on the blue gemstone in her necklace. It was easier to zone in on an object while the thoughts filtered through my head. The more my eyes fluttered around my surroundings, the harder it was to relax. I needed something that required no attention, and Charlie's necklace was the perfect distraction.

I wasn't sure how long we both sat on the floor, but Charlie waited until I made eye contact with her to speak. The corners of her mouth dipped into a slight frown, and she squeezed my hands. "I'm just going to start from the beginning of my thoughts, and you tell me if I should stop, okay?"

I nodded.

"This—" She gestured to the small space between us. "When this first happened, you told me it was no big deal and then disappeared into your dorm room for a weekend. You never brought it up again, and I didn't want to ask because we had just met at the beginning of the year. I know you keep parts of your life from me, and over the years of being your friend, I've accepted that. You choose to avoid relationships and anything that would bring you closer to people—especially men." Her mouth lifted into a small smile. "We've been friends since freshman year, Lyla. What just happened a few moments ago . . . the *episodes* as you like to call them"—she sighed—"I know they happen more than you admit."

Charlie reached above her, pulling the box of Campus Pollyeyes from the counter. She opened the lid and offered me a cup of my favorite ranch dipping sauce. "Can you tell me a little more about them?"

A small, tired laugh forced me out of my stoic gaze. Relief washed over Charlie's face as I reached into the box for a breadstick.

"I don't know what's wrong with me, Charlie," I admitted in a raspy voice. "I have my first therapy appointment on Thursday—" I paused to gauge Charlie's reaction. I felt okay to continue when she nodded reassuringly and bit into a breadstick. "You know, since you started from the beginning, maybe I should do the same."

"I'd like that," Charlie said. "Tell me as much as you want. And Lyla?"

I raised my eyebrows as the throbbing behind my ears started to subside.

"I've never once felt like I had to *deal* with anything. I just want to make sure you know that."

As Charlie listened to the first chapter of my saga, I could see the desire to gather the torches and pitchforks behind her bright blue eyes. I left nothing out. I admitted to thinking that everything that happened with Hunter was my fault; that I fed into the incident because I was too young to understand it. I told her how I confided in my best friend Anna, only for her to make me feel like I was making a big deal over nothing. I topped off the introduction to my first round of trust issues with the fact that they were still dating.

Once I started sharing, everything else came effortlessly. Hearing my thoughts put into words offered a feeling I wasn't expecting to experience—relief.

Charlie knew about my parents and how my dad had no interest in my life until he found out he could control me with the one thing my mom never had—money. She tried not to look disappointed when I said my mom was forced to be the default parent, and I appreciated her objective response.

Eventually, the natural energy flowed between us again, and when a pathetic chuckle escaped my chest, the two of us burst into hysterics.

"I needed to throw in a fake boyfriend so my dad could have someone else to approve of!" I wiped the tears from my eyes and took another bite of my breadstick. "Me on my own . . . it's not enough for him to give me something I'm not even sure he planned to give me in the first place. But as soon as I showed up with Deacon, suddenly it's *okay*? And now that we're"—I squinted at the ceiling—"is this considered a break? Do people still do that?"

"Babe, you can call it whatever you want," Charlie stated confidently. "I personally don't do breaks, but to each their own. As long as Deacon is at least in the running, I don't think he cares what you call it."

The pressure behind my eyes returned. "I'm sorry, Charlie."

She scoffed. "For what?"

"For not trusting you with this part of me sooner. Maybe things would've been different for me if someone else had known about it."

Charlie reached for my hand and squeezed. "You got screwed over by your best friend and had a dickhead high school boyfriend. You don't owe me any apologies for having boundaries."

CHAPTER SIXTY-FIVE

Deacon

IN MY FRESHMAN YEAR of college, if I wasn't in class and I wasn't sleeping, I was planning the next time I could get drunk. It was due to the sheer realization that a lifestyle outside my parent's house existed. Even though I grew up in a church-oriented family, my immediate family couldn't have been further from the religious normal. My parents had me four months after they got married. To this day, my grandfather never said out loud that he was disappointed in my dad, but I imagined being a reverend in a small town made it difficult to process the situation.

I wouldn't say that my brothers and I had a sheltered childhood. We got into trouble just like any other kids would, but our parents kept a pretty vanilla household. We didn't openly talk about sex or anything else that was deemed explicit. My parents never really drank in front of us unless it was a glass of wine after dinner or a beer when we went out to eat. I wasn't one of those college freshmen that had a crazy ass household to blame my bad choices on. It was almost the opposite; like I hadn't tried enough ridiculous shit in high school and had to get it all out in my early twenties.

Everything changed after Dominic passed. I returned to campus a completely different person. I no longer wanted to spend my time absent in a world that took people too quickly. I didn't see the point of being numb, feeling dizzy, and floating above the ground while people around the world would do *anything* to have a person they knew walk beside them again.

When I drank, I made sure it was because I wanted to—not because I was hiding anger, sadness, or shame. Eventually, I didn't want to deal with the party scene, and it didn't take long for Cassie to notice.

I put my recap of the past on hold and slowed my jog, recognizing the house that made me think of Cassie back in August. About eight months ago, the front porch was covered in mums and pumpkins. Now, white and light pink flowers littered the stairs.

I couldn't listen to music the morning Cassie broke up with me. I was afraid all the lyrics and melodies would make me think of the girl who left me broken on a sidewalk. The truth was, I was scared that I had nothing else holding me together without Cassie. My relationship with her took over my entire headspace. It allowed me to plan for my future and push away the person I used to be. That person didn't know how to live a life without Dominic in it, and while I'd never move on from losing my younger brother, I was slowly finding a way to move *forward*.

I knew in my heart that moving forward was what Dominic would want. He would want me to achieve and be happy, to love and be myself in a world lacking his light. He'd remind me that it still needed mine.

I returned to my running playlist and continued my jog. The first song that came up was "Hey Daddy" by Usher. Not only did the singer remind me of Lyla and her iconic dance moves on the pole at The Attic, but the title brought me back to the night she almost made me spit my drink out.

As I turned down North Enterprise, "Closer" by the Chainsmokers came on next. I pictured Lyla singing in the backseat of my car as we drove to my apartment the morning she helped move my stuff and discovered Dominic's favorite drink. I remembered her alarm going off in Miami and sleeping together one last time before we hopped on a plane back to Cleveland.

"Closer" by Ne-Yo bumped through my headphones as I reached the stop sign. It was the night I kissed Lyla for the first time. The entire scene was for Cassie, but I remembered *everything* about that kiss.

More songs continued to play, and more memories around them surfaced. I included Lyla in my day without realizing it because I *wanted* her there. I wanted the reminders, and I wanted to create more of them.

I slowed my pace and walked across the lawn of the apartment building. I was met with the stale smell of alcohol and bacon grease when I entered the front door.

Nathan scanned the inside of the fridge. "You didn't happen to grab creamer, did you?"

"I'm afraid not," I said, letting myself fall onto the couch.

Andre started cracking eggs into a bowl. "Why are you here? Did you skip class?"

"No," I mumbled. "Professor is sick."

"Why do you sound miserable about that?" Nathan winced. "Did the flowers not work?"

Andre looked over his shoulder. "You bought your professor flowers?"

"Why would I buy my professor flowers?"

"He bought Lyla flowers," Nathan explained.

Andre turned to face me. "Charlie told me you guys were on a break."

"We are *not* on a break," I exclaimed, sitting up on the couch.

Andre scoffed. "Okay, Ross and Rachel."

"Don't *Friends* reference me," I said, laughing. "Make me some of that, will you? I'm gonna hop in the shower really quick."

A few hours later, Nathan and Andre were deep into a game of Madden. I was trying to study through the fake cheers of the crowd when my phone buzzed on the coffee table.

Lyla

Can you come over on Thursday after my session?

An exasperated laugh escaped me before I realized I knocked my computer onto the floor.

"You good, man?" Andre said without breaking eye contact with the screen.

Nathan beat me to a response. "He's good." He threw a touchdown and looked at me. "Flowers work, I take it?"

Chapter Sixty-Six

Lyla

Dr. Riley Arden's office was comfortable. There were two oversized couches to choose from, and she even had the fluffy pillows I always admired at TJ Maxx. She provided good lighting by pairing her giant window with sheer curtains, and a cute lamp sat next to the couches. It was a much better setup than I expected.

"Was there a specific topic you wanted to discuss today, Lyla?" Riley asked, leaning against the back of the couch.

I crossed my legs. All I had done so far was confirm that the information from my intake survey was accurate and provide her with some reasons why I wanted to see her in the first place.

She smiled reassuringly. "It can feel overwhelming sometimes trying to pick something to start with. Would it help if I asked a question?"

I nodded.

"You mentioned feeling overwhelmed last time you went out with friends. Can you describe this feeling?"

I played nervously with my hands and swallowed. Whenever I tried to put my feelings into words, I struggled. The only way they made sense was when I was in the middle of experiencing them.

"My chest gets tight," I explained. "It's almost like there's all this energy that I don't know what to do with, but all I want to do is find a place to make everything slow down and stand still. I shake, and sometimes I get dizzy. I feel like I'm going to throw up, but since I can't, the feeling just *sits* in my stomach. I can't get a deep breath; like no matter how much air gets into my body, my heart just doesn't slow down. I feel cold and hot at the same time." I realized I was rambling and looked up.

Riley met me with a soft expression. "Would you describe that as a panic attack?"

"Panic attack?" I echoed, thinking back to my conversation with Deacon. "I'm not sure."

Riley leaned forward and laced her fingers. "They can be triggered by something happening around you *or* nothing at all. What you described sounds like a very real experience with a panic attack."

"Lovely," I groaned.

She offered me another award-winning grin. "Whenever that happens, do you feel like you have things that calm you down? Are there certain things that do or don't work for you?"

I thought of how I bumped into Deacon's chest that night at The Attic, and the admission rolled off my tongue. "My boyfriend Deacon was there. Being near him helps."

"And how did Deacon make you feel?"

A lump formed in my throat. "Safe."

Jesus, Mary, Joseph, what was Riley pumping into this room?

"Are there other people you feel comfortable going to when this happens?"

I nodded again. "My mom and my friend Charlie both know about the . . . *panic* attacks. Talking about them helps, and trying to explain why I feel them coming on in the first place. Deacon was the first person I talked to about them."

"Let's talk about when they first started happening." Riley picked up her notebook without breaking eye contact. "You mentioned in your intake survey that something happened in high school with a boyfriend. Is it okay if we talk about that event?"

I rubbed my face with my hand and peered out the window. I wasn't expecting therapy to be so exhausting. I just talked through a layer, and already, Riley was peeling up the next one.

We spent the next twenty minutes talking about Hunter. Riley didn't interrupt with questions or ask me to go into more detail about the parts I skimmed through. It felt good to talk through it to someone outside my circle, and when I finished, she didn't look at me like I was someone to feel sorry for.

"I'm sorry you went through that, Lyla." She placed her notebook on the table and picked up her mug. "Much of what you just shared with me is common for people who have been in a similar situation to feel."

My eyes narrowed. "Really?"

"Absolutely. When things happen to us or we experience something triggering, it's easy to feel alone. These events we go through . . . they place us into clubs we don't want to be a part of. No one wants to be included, but for some people, it's comforting to know they aren't alone. There are a few support groups I can get more information about for you if you'd like. You can request it from my office online anytime."

"That's good to know," I murmured.

"It sounds like you've built a good support system," Riley offered. "You also mentioned in your survey that your boyfriend gave you the idea to look into therapy?"

"Yeah." I nodded again. I was starting to feel like a god-damn bobblehead. "He still goes sometimes. He actually helped me make the appointment."

An overwhelming sense of emotion washed over me as I looked around the room. Did Deacon sit on a couch like this one when he went to his first session? Had the therapist probed him with questions about Dominic? Did they ask him why he was there in the first place when the survey provided all the information? Did he even fill out a survey?

The questions flooded my headspace, and before I knew it, I was blinking back tears.

"Tissues are behind the plant," Riley said, pointing to the end table beside me.

We fell into a moment of silence as I formulated my next sentence. The layers I had waiting for Riley could wait. The only thing I had on my mind sat right on the surface, a surface I didn't know how to clean since I spent so much time staining it with reasons why things couldn't work. "I have a topic I'd like to talk about if we have more time?"

"We have twenty minutes," she said. "Let's go for it."

I relaxed into my seat, and a weight shifted in my chest. In about an hour, I was going to see Deacon. I knew what I wanted, and I needed help figuring out what I was going to say.

CHAPTER SIXTY-SEVEN

Deacon

WHEN I STARTED PACING around the living room, I decided to walk to Falcon's Pointe. I couldn't sit still, and every time I tried, I'd check the time on my phone and start over again. I needed something to do with all of my energy, and the anticipation of seeing Lyla again was driving me insane.

I wanted to see her. I wanted to ask how her appointment went. I wanted to order food and suggest we watch *It's Always Sunny in Philadelphia*, only to hear her argue that we should watch a movie instead. She'd scroll through a list of movies for ten minutes, and before I could snag another piece of pizza, she'd settle on the next episode of the show. I wanted her to fall asleep in my arms on the couch after she insisted she wasn't tired for the fifth time. I wanted my best friend every day—from the tiniest moments to the biggest milestones, I wanted Lyla Brooks.

When my phone read six, I knocked on the door of Lyla's apartment. The door swung open almost immediately, and I smiled.

Lyla's light brown curls were in a bun on her head, and she wore one of my Champion shirts with a pair of leggings. I was a sucker for the beautiful girl standing in the doorway, but I was a goner when she wore my clothes.

"Hey," she said shyly, her green eyes peering at me through dark lashes.

I stopped myself from reaching out and touching her. "Hey, Brooks."

She stepped aside so I could come in, and I was relieved to see we were alone in the living room. Her bedroom didn't provide much space, and I could tell by the way she kept playing with her hands that she was nervous. I'd let her give me signs that she wanted me close to her.

I placed my book bag on the couch. "How was your first sess—"

"Wait." Lyla crossed her arms in front of her chest. "I want to tell you something."

"Okay," I said softly, lowering myself onto the couch. I studied the lines that ran through her soft features. Her brow crinkled when she was deep in thought, and the corners of her mouth turned into a slight frown when she was uncertain about what she wanted to say.

She drew in a staggered breath and sat next to me. "Did you know everyone has anxiety?"

Her opening sentence threw me off, but I kept my voice as casual as possible. "Uhm, yeah, yeah, I did."

"It keeps us safe and helps make us scared of things we should be scared of in our everyday lives. Until about an hour ago, I didn't know that. I knew everyone got nervous, but I didn't know everyone had anxiety." She relaxed her shoulders and brought her legs to her chest. "Because of some things I've experienced, mine can be harder to manage. But I also learned that it makes me creative and a good problem solver. And sometimes, my mind moves so fast that while I'm actually pretty good with words, it doesn't always seem that way. I know what I want to say, but because I'm balancing ten open tabs at one time, I either say the wrong thing or nothing at all."

I nodded to let her know I was listening.

"My challenge today was to tell you all my fears without a filter. I'm supposed to go with everything I'm thinking and just . . . *speak*." She pursed her lips, waiting for my reaction to the look of disgust that covered her face.

I smiled. "Lay it on me, Brooks. It's been almost five days since I've heard your voice, and I wanna know everything."

"When I asked you for a break—" Her voice trembled, and she looked away. "I don't think it was you I needed a break from. It was me. You're the first person I've shown everything to . . . I mean, literally, I guess." She rolled her eyes, and I chuckled softly.

A warm sensation flooded my chest, and I grabbed her hand before I could stop myself. She let me, nervously stroking her thumb over my fingers.

"Meeting you." She smiled down at our hands. "*Being* with you has made me realize that I do need help. I've always told you it's okay to ask for that, but I never took the steps I needed to help myself. Keeping people at a distance was easier. Making sure I was always in control was *safer*. Whenever those things shift, I don't know how to handle it. I have a lot of shit to work through," she said, blinking away a few tears. "No matter what I seem to show you, for whatever reason, you're still here, and I'm waiting for the time I become too much. I'm afraid you'll resent me when I don't meet the expectations you have for your life."

Squeezing her hand, I reached up to cup her face with my other. I stroked her cheek with my thumb, swiping away tears before they could roll any further. She was crying now, and I wasn't sure how many more heartstrings I had left for her to pull. She wrapped her arms around my neck, and I hugged her, holding her against my chest. I closed my eyes, breathing in her scent and the traces of my cologne that lingered in her shirt.

A year ago, I had a plan—an agenda of events that would inch me closer to what I thought would make me happy. Like the list a child left out for Santa Claus or the wish you made before throwing a quarter in a fountain. They were desires you tossed out into the universe, hoping for whatever magic was left in the world to pick it up. We put the weight of the want on something else so we could go about our lives, not knowing that change and misdirection could disguise as pathways leading us to where we were meant to go.

If the past few years had taught me anything, it was that we didn't control time the way we thought we did. Time was many things; it sped up, slowed down, dragged on, and could fly by if you ignored it. Time was a precious thing, and I wasn't going to waste another second of it.

Lyla ran her hands down my chest as she pulled away. "I'm sorry I let you leave," she whispered. "I know we haven't talked about what happens after we graduate, and I don't know if I've already fucked this up—"

"Sweetheart, can I just have a *second*?"

She opened her mouth to speak and giggled when I challenged her next move.

"I'm going to say something to you, and I don't want you to run from me," I started, repeating the line from a few weeks ago. It got her attention, and when her green eyes met mine, there was no going back.

I smiled and shook my head. "I wish you could catch a sliver of what I see when I look at you. Before you read me all your rules on campus, I was operating in survival mode. You brought back parts of me I thought were lost when Dominic passed away and when Cassie broke up with me . . . it's a place

I don't want to go back to. I know there will be times when things get hard, but I have a lot of shit to work through too, baby,"—I grinned—"and you're still here."

Lyla chuckled softly and tucked a loose curl behind her ear. I thought my heart was going to fumble into my lap. It had been too long since I had her in front of me.

"I've meant every word I've ever said to you. You're my best friend, and you'll never be too much for me. If you think going through something means you've fucked this up," I said through a breathy laugh. "There's nothing you could do to fuck this up, because I'm in love with you, Lyla."

Her shoulders relaxed, and I listened for the shaky exhale she made when she was nervous. "We don't lie, remember?" she murmured, her voice barely above a whisper.

"We don't lie," I echoed.

"You love me," she stated, shaking her head in disbelief as tears welled in the corners of her eyes.

"Yeah, baby, I do." My voice was raspy, and seeing her so against someone caring about her broke my heart. "I'm sorry if that scares you, but I'll love you every day if you let me." A nervous laugh slipped through my admission. "I promise you with everything I have that I'm not going to be predictable and disappointing. I want you just the way you are with nothing in return."

Lyla nodded, taking a deep breath to regain her composure.

I recognized the tiny smile that crept into the corners of her mouth. "Can I kiss you?"

As soon as her lips touched mine, everything fell into place. I had experienced loss and heartbreak. I was damaged in ways I had no idea how to fix. There were days when grief snuck in and decided to stay, threatening to pull me from all of the progress I'd made in trying to move forward. With everything I had been through in the last few years, it was rare when time stood still.

Lyla pulled away and met me with a pondering gaze. "I think I love you too."

"You say the sweetest things to me, baby girl."

"No!" she exclaimed, covering her face with her hands. "God, I'm horrible at this." She dropped her hands in her lap and looked at me. "I know I love you because I'm about to ask you to come with me."

A cocky ass grin formed on my face, but I couldn't help it. "And where am I going?"

"I want you to come to Chicago with me," she whispered like she'd scare me away if she said it any louder. "I don't know what you're plan is after graduation, but—"

"Lyla, *you* are my plan after graduation. Going with you to Chicago or wherever you wanted to go . . . it would be the first time in a long time I'm choosing to do something because I want to and not because I feel like I should."

She stared at me for a moment until, finally, an exaggerated sigh slipped through the faint smile on her face. "Fuck."

I leaned her back on the couch as I crawled over her, trailing kisses up her neck and keeping my body off of hers until she admitted defeat. Her hands ignited sparks along my skin as she found her way under my hoodie, gripping my hips and prompting me toward her.

"Not until you say it, baby," I teased, my erection hard against her stomach. I planted a gentle kiss on her lips and murmured, "I can show you how much I love you right now on this couch—"

"I love you," she said, her green eyes staring up at me. I could've melted onto the floor. The words left her mouth so effortlessly that they almost caught me by surprise.

We moved to her bedroom in case one of her roommates came home. She let me take my time as if five days had been five years without seeing each other. We were a song of soft moans and kisses, playing softly in the background while our bodies spoke whatever words were left.

Lyla Brooks was mine, and she loved me. I knew there would be times when the world felt heavy, but as long as I had the girl in my arms, I trusted myself to carry it.

Chapter Sixty-Eight

Lyla

THE WEATHER IN OHIO liked to fuck with people. It was the first weekend in May, and while it was almost seventy-five degrees yesterday, it was in the low-sixties today. It wasn't the kind of weather you wanted to wear a cute graduation dress in, even if you just graduated with your bachelor's degree.

Since there were so many colleges within Bowling Green State University, Deacon's graduation was in the morning, while mine took place that afternoon. When they called his name, and he walked across the stage, my chest swelled with pride. His parents clapped beside me, Georgia tearing up at the sight of her oldest son holding a diploma. Drew whooped and hollered even though the announcer asked us not to, but the charming smile that followed made it hard to reprimand his behavior.

It was bittersweet knowing that as Deacon completed a milestone he had worked so hard on, Dominic wasn't here to see it. Even though I never got the chance to meet Dominic, I had a hunch that he was just as bold and persistent as Deacon was. Once we stepped outside, the skies cleared, and the wind picked up, making it challenging to manage the long graduation robes and tasseled hats. If Dominic were missing a photo opportunity, he'd make damn sure that his family felt him present in other ways.

My ceremony didn't take as long as Deacon's. He sat with my mom up in the stands, and when the announcer called my name to walk across the stage, it sounded like there was a party of ten there to support me. I shook the hand of a professor I didn't recognize and focused on keeping one foot in front of the other. The last thing I wanted to do was leave Bowling Green with a video of me falling down the stairs. I already had one video floating around campus. I wasn't trying for a second.

Back at my chair, I stared at the brown leather-bound diploma cover. Even though my dad wasn't there to watch me walk, I never felt closer to him. He gave me the greatest gift he could've given me by not attending. I received an email that my trust was finalized this morning, and I *liked* to think that Aaron Brooks waved his magic wand to make it happen. I was free of him.

After we said goodbye to my mom, Deacon and I finished packing the apartment. Call me a typical rom-com girl, but after Deacon told me he loved me, I asked him to move back in for the remainder of the semester. I couldn't help it. Michael Myers would just have to continue waiting in the background.

I placed the last box of kitchen supplies on the counter and glanced around the empty space. Charlie, Michelle, and Keira left right after graduation, and since we threw an impromptu "I Liked Living With You" party last night, there was no need to stick around for sappy farewells.

"It's quiet without your crew," Deacon said, taking my hand and pulling me onto his lap on the couch. "How does it feel to spend your last night in a BG apartment?"

"I just don't know what I'm going to do without over-priced student living."

Deacon chuckled, leaning forward to grab his laptop from the coffee table. "You still haven't looked at the apartments I showed you, have you?"

"No, because it will ruin my optimism. We will have a perfect-sized apartment close enough to the perfect space I'll rent for Brooks Books."

"Brooks Books?" Deacon beamed. "Wait, are you serious?"

I downplayed my cheesy grin. "For now. We'll see how it looks on all of the marketing materials I have in mind."

His hand moved under my shirt as he shifted closer. I knew where this was going, and my body agreed before I could think through the next step.

"Wait, wait, wait," I protested, pushing against his chest. "We said we'd have three options nailed down so we could make appointments to look at them next weekend. I want to make sure we have a place before you figure out your school schedule. Not to mention Lily wants to visit this summer, and my mom is all ready to come—"

"I sent you apartments," he countered, his mouth moving to the sensitive skin behind my ear.

"I don't know if the options you sent me are good. We haven't *looked* at them."

He chuckled, groaning in defeat at my incoming stream of questions. "Why would I send you bad apartments? Don't you trust me?"

"I do trust you, probably more than I should, actually," I said, repeating the phrase he used a few months ago at City Tap.

His eyes narrowed. "Clever, sweetheart."

I kissed up his jawline, brushing my lips playfully against his. "And we don't lie, Deacon Scott."

The sexy smirk I loved crept into the corner of his mouth. He kissed me, and we spent the next hour saying goodbye to my Bowling Green apartment in a much more exciting way than looking at apartments. Deacon probably already had the appointments set up anyway since I knew he'd never let us go that long without a plan.

I wasn't sure how I ended up here, but I thanked whatever stars needed to align to make it happen. I had no idea that the guy who showed up on my doorstep that morning, who agreed to be my fake boyfriend, would end up the person I was missing. There was something incredible about someone who could make you believe that love could be unconditional, but there was something irreplaceable about a best friend who made you believe in yourself.

Epilogue

Deacon
June 25th, 2019

The weather in Chicago reminded me of the weather in Bowling Green. There was always a breeze, and the winters were brutal, but the atmosphere outweighed any chill the colder months brought.

We moved the summer after graduation, and city life was busier than what Lyla and I were used to. Once Lyla walked through the two-bedroom apartment two blocks away from the space she wanted for Brooks Books, I couldn't tell her no. It was small, affordable, and needed some renovations we could do on a medical student and new business owner's budget. There was also enough room for whenever Jane, Lily, Drew, or anyone else in the family wanted to stay for a weekend. It was perfect.

Brooks Books was sandwiched between two other businesses that recently opened up. Darling's was a new and trendy restaurant serving only appetizers and themed cocktails, while Green River was a print shop and apothecary whose sales skyrocketed around St. Patrick's Day. It was a great location, and it made me smile every time I passed the curvy black letters of Lyla's last name.

Part of me hoped Aaron Brooks would stop by one day to see it, but the man kept his distance ever since Miami. We were polite in passing, but there was a mutual understanding about the protection I felt toward Lyla. When she declined the invitation to Aaron and Tonya's wedding, I was so fucking proud of her. Lyla wasn't his to toy with anymore, and he finally accepted that.

Every Tuesday after work, I swung by Brooks Books with our usual mid-afternoon coffee order—a large iced coffee with vanilla and caramel and a medium iced matcha with blueberry and oat milk. The bell on the door chimed when I entered, and the cozy smell of coffee and fresh balsam greeted me. I smiled at the sight of Lyla behind her desk, working on paperwork and squinting at her open MacBook. She had her loose curls in a bun on top of her head, and I unintentionally bit my bottom lip when I saw her in thick black-framed glasses.

Just when I thought Lyla couldn't turn me on more than she already did, the woman went and got glasses because of how much reading and screen time her job required. She didn't make it far the first time she came home in them. The second time I saw her in them, I flipped the WE'RE CLOSED sign on the shop door and had to buy her a new desk chair the next day.

"Hey, baby. Still going with the holiday scents, huh?"

Lyla looked up from her screen, smiling when she saw me. She sunk into her chair and threw her head back. "There's nothing better than reading a good book around the holidays. It lets people escape the madness of them. Is it four-thirty *already?*"

"Yes." I leaned over her computer to kiss her, and she cupped my chin so I couldn't pull away. She always lingered a little longer when we went an entire day without seeing each other.

"You look exhausted." She stuck out her bottom lip and stroked her thumb against my cheek. I could've fallen asleep standing up if she hadn't stopped. "I picked up the balloons, and they're in the back. Let me grab them really quick."

Lyla ran across the store and dipped into a small room off the hallway. She emerged with a bouquet of balloons, and I chuckled at her choices. There were solid colors of gray, white, and gold, but then there were bigger balloons that looked like a basketball, a beer mug, and a red rose.

I was still laughing when she handed them to me. "I love you."

"And I love you. I tried to pick things that were relevant to you and the occasion. Twenty-one is a big number!"

I admired the shimmering silver of the beer mug. "These are perfect."

I walked the balloons out to the car while Lyla locked up the store and adjusted the timer for the lights. She double-checked that the script lettering was off as she crossed the parking lot, and my heart swelled with pride as I admired the image of Lyla Brooks—the love of my life—with her dream in the background.

I opened the passenger door for her and leaned against it. "How many times I gotta tell you that my last name would look good on that sign?"

Lyla scoffed playfully and rolled her eyes. "Scott Books? It doesn't have the same ring to it. And how many times are you going to say that line and wait for me to laugh?"

"You laughed the first time," I countered, sipping my coffee.

Lyla was still grinning when we pulled into traffic. "Well, it was so downright *adorable* I just had to," she teased. "It was very clever. But I would say by the thirty-third time, it started to lose its charm."

I placed my hand on her thigh and gave her a light squeeze. My shoulders tensed as we pulled into the parking lot for Oakwood Beach, and when Lyla offered me the Sharpie from her purse, my mouth went dry.

"Hey," she prompted softly so I would look at her. "Do you want me to come with you, or do you want some space? What do you need from me?"

"I think you should come," I said with a weak smile. "And then maybe I'll keep one and take a moment to myself before I let that one go."

The balloons batted against each other in the breeze as Lyla and I walked hand in hand on the beach. Lyla squeezed my hand, and we both looked out into the water. More weight settled into my chest, and I could feel the pressure building behind my eyes. Something about the sound of the water and the wind on my face made it all come flowing back. It really did come in waves, and once the dam broke, there was no stopping it. Grief was a raw emotion. It was the only time in my life when I couldn't put my feelings into words. Tears fell willingly as I locked onto the nearest subject. Without warning, I was that same open wound I was the morning I got the phone call. I felt everything and nothing simultaneously, and it didn't matter how much time passed. It never got easier.

Lyla offered me her balloons. "Do you want to do them all?"

"No, you keep your half." I took a deep breath and looked down at her. "I think he'd like that."

We stood for a few minutes as I focused on deep breaths and the pressure of Lyla's hand. My shoulders relaxed, and I closed my eyes. I was here with Lyla, and I was here with Dominic. I slowly pulled my hand from Lyla's to separate the balloons, keeping the one that looked like a rose apart from the rest.

"Happy birthday, Dominic," I said hoarsely. "I love you."

"Happy birthday, Dominic," Lyla echoed as a few tears rolled down her cheeks.

We let go of the balloons and watched as they drifted away from the city. Lyla wrapped her arms around my waist and rested her head against my side. I pulled her close and kissed the top of her head. I was able to catch a few more glimmers of the beer mug before it rose past the clouds and into a place we could no longer see.

Lyla kissed my chest through my shirt and gave me one last squeeze. "Take your time."

Once Lyla made it to the car, I secured the rose balloon around my wrist and reached into my back pocket. I pulled out the envelope addressed to Dominic and read the letter I wrote him out loud.

Happy Birthday, Dom! You're finally twenty-one, so the Corona you're sneaking is finally legal! I remember when we used to sneak them out of Uncle Henry's fridge. We were pretty bad-ass back then, huh?

Are birthdays any different up there? Do you get to party with celebrities and stumble back home after a long night of celebrating? Knowing you, you're taking today to travel the world and seeing things I couldn't even imagine. You were never meant to stay put in one place. Up there, you're finally free.

Let me get the family updates out of the way. Drew is still an asshole (even though we love him for it), and apparently, a girl named Iris does too. Drew has been dating her since last February, and it's kind of been wild to see. But you would be proud of everything he's accomplished. I know I am.

Mom and Dad are doing okay. They started going on vacations again, and they find joy in things like they did before. For a while there, I wasn't sure if they would ever venture out of Michigan. I wasn't sure if they would keep our house or try to start fresh in a new place. But our home in Detroit will always be our home. It will always be your home, and I know that's why they will never give it up.

I miss you, Dom. I miss you every day. Since you left, I've been chasing cardinals, believing in butterflies, and just trying to find peace knowing you're still here. It still hits me sometimes, and I'm reminded that the day I found out you were gone actually happened. It feels like a bad dream, and then I wake up and realize that I will never move on from losing you, but I'll find ways to move forward, because I know you would want me to.

I don't know if you've seen her from up there, but I met a girl. I like to think you have since we've been dating for over two years. Her name is Lyla, and you're probably sick of me talking about her. In my defense, I never know if you get my messages! It's not like I get read receipts, so give me a break.

Here's the deal—I need nice weather on Saturday, so put in a good word for me with whoever runs that shit. I want you front and center on Saturday, June 29th. I'm asking Lyla to marry me, and I want you to be there for it.

Chicago is where our dreams started, and it's where I want our future to begin. We have an incredible life. Lyla has Brooks Books, and I'm at Northwestern Memorial Hospital. I'm almost halfway done with medical school, and Lyla is a natural at running her business. Every morning, I have to remind myself that this is my life and that I'm allowed to be happy with where it is going.

It's a good life, Dominic, and since yours was cut short, I promise to make the most of mine.

It's weird, isn't it? No matter how much you prepare for something, things happen, and everything changes. Time is precious, and the people you spend it with are important. Losing you taught me that.

I miss you, Dom. I know I already said that, but I'll say it every day for the rest of my life. I wish you were here. I wish you could meet Lyla. I like to think you had something to do with me meeting her that morning. How else would it explain that I found exactly who I needed when I didn't think my world could get any darker?

People say death is hard, but I'd argue that living with grief is harder. You were the best son and younger brother. You were such a light in this world, and you had the best smile.

Keep the skies clear and your dreams big. Fly high, and I'll do my best to remember everything happening here. We have a hell of a lot to catch up on when I see you.

Until we meet again, I love you.
Deacon

"Fly high, buddy." I smiled proudly and watched the rose float past the clouds, where I knew Dominic was watching from the other side.

Author's Note

WHEN MY BROTHER PASSED away unexpectedly in June of 2023, my world completely changed. I became a different person—a version of myself that I'm learning to live with as I continue to process grief and navigate a path I didn't know I would be placed on.

I remember the first time I flew after Cody passed away. Gliding right along the lower thread of clouds in the sky, I wondered how much further up I had to go. Where does heaven start? It was like he was resting in the line of pink sky that glows as the sun rises. Even when I was thousands of feet in the air, it still wasn't close enough. I was seated on something that could take me anywhere in the world—anywhere except the place I thought about visiting most.

It had to be incredible, right? A place that was so exclusive we had to wait to get up there.

When I started writing *The Trust Factor* in May of 2023, I knew the basic plot line of the story. I wanted a fake dating college romance with a woman who needed her trust fund to start over and a man who wanted his ex back. I wanted Lyla to be outspoken and blunt about sex, and I wanted Deacon to be a green-flag guy who was aware of his emotions. I had the building blocks, but I knew something was missing.

Then a month later, I couldn't think about reading or writing. Nothing else mattered except the fact that I lost one of the most important people in my life.

With time, I began to process different emotions and recognize differences in myself. I started having panic attacks and heightened anxiety. I noticed appearances of my anxiety in high school, and it only worsened in college, but now it was at a point where I couldn't manage it on my own anymore. I started therapy that October, and it has been an incredible addition to my mental health. There is peace that comes with learning more about yourself, and I'm slowly learning how to play the hand I've been dealt.

Then August came around, and two days before Cody would've been twenty-five, I started writing again. I knew the words would come eventually. I've always made sense of the world through words, music, or some sort of creative outlet. I wrote *The Trust Factor* in four months, and with it came two characters who helped me put all of my vulnerabilities on paper.

Deacon Scott and I have the most obvious things in common. He lost his youngest brother unexpectedly. He is the oldest sibling. He hates change. He is a planner. He has anxiety and has gone to therapy. He has experienced panic attacks. He talks to Dominic the way I talk to Cody. Deacon expresses words and thoughts that I haven't been able to say out loud.

I knew there would be some readers who wanted to know how Dominic passed away, and some would be bothered that I didn't include it. The truth is, no matter how I tried to word it, nothing seemed right. I wanted Dominic to represent anyone who has left too soon and Deacon to be someone that other people relate to when it comes to grief and loss.

Lyla Brooks took many directions when it came to finding her character. I wanted an outlet to talk about my panic attacks and anxiety, and she provided that. She shows how easily they can be triggered and how sometimes our thoughts don't seem like our own. She is someone who holds onto events she tried to move past. She's afraid to create emotional ties that can be severed. She's afraid to depend on people. She feels like she's "too much or not enough," which is something I know a lot of women have been told at one point in their lives. I wanted Lyla to be someone who was trying to make something for herself and move forward.

Lyla also represents anyone who didn't or couldn't say no, but shouldn't have had to. She represents the "no big deals" that happened to someone—the "no big deal" that caused a ripple effect in who they are and how they think about themselves.

I'm thirty years old, and I'm just now unpacking things that I experienced ten years ago. For anyone who couldn't react to something because they felt like they couldn't or shouldn't, I see you, and your feelings deserve to be validated. There are going to be people who think Lyla overreacts, overthinks, and is dramatic. But honestly, Lyla embodies so much of the anxiety and thoughts I had when I was her age, and I hope she can help other people who can relate to the things she's going through.

Everyone at one point in their lives will carry something, and as Deacon says to Lyla, "Stop downplaying something that happened to you because you're afraid other people won't think it's heavy enough."

I read once in an interview with Daniel Levy that he wrote and produced a movie as a love letter to his grandmother, who passed away that previous year. I already adore him as a human (Hello! *Schitt's Creek*?!), but when I heard that comparison I knew that's what this book was. *The Trust Factor* is a love letter to Cody, and I can only hope that he is proud of it. It contains so many reminders of him, including a drawing of a rose he left behind. A few days after he passed, my dad found a small notebook of tattoos that Cody drew. Deacon is holding Cody's rose on the cover of the book, and Cody's signature can be found next to the drawing on the dedication page.

The Trust Factor is a stepping stone in my healing process. It is a story about two characters who go through traumas and experiences that aren't always easily put into words. They were stories I felt were too important not to tell, and I cannot thank you enough, as a reader, for getting this far and giving Lyla and Deacon a chance.

Thank you to everyone who read, reviewed, and supported *The Trust Factor*.

Thank you to my husband, Noel, who embodies so much of Deacon's supportive nature. Thank you for loving me during the hardest year of my life and supporting these wild dreams of mine.

Thank you to my family. I have so many amazing family members who provide so much love and support, and I appreciate each and every one of you.

Thank you to the incredible Booktok community. I have found a place with the most inspiring people who share my creative dreams, and I appreciate all of the help and support you've given me.

Thank you to Lin-Manual Miranda for writing *Hamilton*. Even though you'll never see this, your soundtrack was the only music I could listen to for months after Cody passed away. So many of those songs hold a new meaning, and I fell in love with your work even more.

And finally, thank you to you, reader, for giving *The Trust Factor* a chance. I know I thanked you above, but you deserve to be mentioned twice!

Here's to chasing cardinals and believing in butterflies. Here's to remembering that time is precious and that the people you spend it with matter.

Here's to writing the next story and moving forward. Here's to remembering that even after our loved ones pass over, they are always with us. Remember, you have a hell of a lot to catch up on when you see them again.

With love,

Brittany

About the Author

Brittany Wilson is an author who writes romantic comedies and contemporary romance. She graduated from Bowling Green State University with a degree in education and the college serves as the setting for many of her books! Brittany has always had a love for writing and a passion for telling stories. She is currently living in Ohio with her husband and their son. Her books are available on all platforms! Make sure to follow Brittany on social media to stay updated on her author journey!

TikTok and Instagram – @brittanywilsonauthor
www.brittanywilsonauthor.com

9 7989 88 2 2 1630